STRANGER
IN TWO WORLDS

STRANGER
IN TWO WORLDS

by

HUGH CLEVELY

 APPLETON-CENTURY-CROFTS, INC.
NEW YORK

FOR SARAH
WITH LOVE

STRANGER
IN TWO WORLDS

Chapter 1

EVERY MAN comes into the world with the active connivance of two other people of whose activities he is, at the time, completely unaware. His first yell is uttered in complete unconsciousness of what he is complaining about. He does not know if he has been born a little prince or a little garbage collector.

Today I am an ordinary, rather prosperous American citizen, but I can, if I wish, claim descent from one of the aristocratic families of Ireland. My grandfather was Major General Sir Horace Lurgan, K.C.B. To balance this, I can also claim descent from peasant stock. My other grandfather, whom I never met, was the owner of a small and dingy saloon bar in the obscure village of Glenaly, halfway between Wicklow and Dublin.

This publican had three sons named Timothy, James, and Michael. The eldest, Timothy, inherited the bar; the second, James, emigrated to America and became an actor; and the third son, Michael, took the Queen's shilling and went away soldiering in the British Army. After some years service he held the rank of Colour Sergeant in the Company of the Leinster Fusiliers commanded by Major Rupert FitzStephen, who was a nephew of the Earl of Bracca.

In 1848 Lord Bracca and his son both died of the cholera while on a visit to Madrid, and young Major FitzStephen succeeded to the title.

The FitzStephen family was among the noblest and wealthiest, not only in Ireland, but in the whole of the United Kingdom. They lived, when in Ireland, in a massive Norman castle, set in wide spreading parklands, and approached by a winding, four-mile-long avenue of limes. Their scale of living was lavish; their horses and equipages were magnificent; the number of their servants and tenants ran into hundreds. Young Lord Bracca was, among other things, on the Board of Governors of the Honourable East India Company; the rent roll from his Irish estates was reputed to bring in £65,000 a year. In those days the wage of a full-time laborer in County Wicklow was around ten shillings a week.

Two other families of some local note, though ranking far below Lord Bracca in wealth and importance, lived within easy riding distance of Bracca Castle. These were the Lurgans of Springhill, and the Corfields of Woodlawn. Both these families were descended from settlers who had come to Ireland during the reign of Elizabeth, when an attempt was being made to keep Ireland quiet by establishing a ruling class of "landed gentry." The Lurgans and Corfields, though neither very rich nor influential, lived in largish houses, hunted, dressed for dinner every evening, sent their sons into the Army or the Protestant church, and affected a correct aristocratic disdain for all people who engaged in commerce.

In addition to these three families there were, of course, some hundreds of other families in the district, but these were merely peasant Irish, inhabiting small, leaky whitewashed cottages, with clay floors, and existing mostly on potatoes, when there wasn't a famine. The God-given function of these people was to serve as laborers, navvies, grooms, small shopkeepers, domestic servants, and recruits for the British Army. Nobody paid a great deal of attention to them except when, as sometimes happened, they began making nuisances of themselves by dying in large numbers of starvation, or by shooting at landlords and their agents from behind walls and hedges.

During the summer of 1849, Queen Victoria and the Prince Consort visited Ireland, and large numbers of the native population who had managed to survive the great famine of 1846-49, lined the roadways and cheered her enthusiastically all the way from Cork to Dublin. Great festivities were organized in her honor.

One of the greatest celebrations was at Bracca, where a double event was to take place. The Queen was to stay for two nights, and was also to be present at the marriage of young Lord Bracca to Mary Lurgan, the daughter of Major General Sir Horace Lurgan, K.C.B.

Preparations for the royal visit and the wedding went on for weeks. The whole interior of the Castle was redecorated, the village cottages received new coats of whitewash, triumphal arches were erected, and rows of white tents sprang up in the park surrounding the Castle, where a battalion of the Leinster Fusiliers, the regiment in which Lord Bracca had once served, was encamped to provide a guard of honor.

The royal visit and the wedding were the talk of the whole countryside, and everybody was agreed that, in marrying Lord Bracca, Mary Lurgan was landing the catch of the century. There were also suggestions that marriage to a resolute girl with high principles and a strong sense of duty might steady the young man down a little. It was known that so far, during his twenty-nine years, Lord Bracca had shown no evidence of high principles or a sense of duty.

A few days before the royal visit and wedding, vast numbers of guests began to arrive. Not only Bracca Castle itself, but all the surrounding houses of any consequence were filled with them. The whole of the countryside was overrun with Dukes, Earls, Countesses, and other people of quality. In the words of a contemporary account, taken from a report in the London "Times": *This simple Irish village has now become the centre of the world of wit and fashion, and begins to wear somewhat of the aspect of a Royal garden party.*

On a fine afternoon in August, the royal coach, with its outriders and escort of cavalry, jingled through the streets of the village and up the long drive to the Castle. That evening a big reception was held, and Mary Lurgan had her first and only meeting with Queen Victoria. The Queen was gracious. As a mark of her special favor, she presented Miss Lurgan with a small diamond brooch, made in the shape of a heart.

That night bonfires were burning on the hilltops to celebrate the coming of the Queen, and the wedding on the morrow. From her bedroom window in Springhill House, Mary Lurgan could see them. What was she thinking of, alone in her room, on the night before her wedding? What violent and desperate tides of emotion were surging under her calm exterior, to make her act as she did? Had she been meditating on what she was going to do all day, or did she make up her mind suddenly, in a moment? I don't know the answer to these questions.

In the morning her maid, entering the room, found the bed empty. Miss Lurgan could not be found anywhere. Her favorite horse, also, was missing from the stables. She had ridden away during the night.

At the same time a certain Colour Sergeant Michael Kelly was missing from the lines of the Leinster Fusiliers. For some hours nobody thought of connecting these two disappearances.

Search parties were organized, and still she was not found. The wedding did not take place. Instead all the guests stood round talking in hushed voices. What was to have been the biggest wedding of the year had turned into the biggest scandal of the year.

Three days later a telegram arrived for Sir Horace Lurgan, telling him that Mary had married Michael Kelly, in London. She made no apology; perhaps she felt that her offense was too great to merit

[3]

any forgiveness. That was how Sir Horace felt. He tore up the telegram and gave instructions that his daughter's name should never be mentioned in his presence again.

But other people mentioned her name; for some days society conversation was full of it. Queen Victoria expressed her displeasure. In a letter to her friend Baron Stockmar, she wrote: "I am bound to conclude that Miss Lurgan's behavior, so lacking in *right feeling* and *consideration for others,* can only be due to some defect of character caused by a lack of firmness in her early training." Lord Palmerston, the most important political personage in the country at that time, expressed views which, as was usual with him, were not quite in accord with those of the Queen. "A Colour Sergeant, by God," he was reported as having said. "And he ran away with the girl from right under Bracca's nose. And then people try to tell you there's something wrong with the Army." His words were repeated widely from dinner table to dinner table.

Talk was so loud and widespread that it was plain that something would have to be done to still it. The mere existence of Colour Sergeant Michael Kelly and his young wife was a source of embarrassment to quite a number of people. Nominally Colour Sergeant Kelly was absent without leave from his regiment. He should have been brought back to Ireland and tried by court-martial. But the Colonel of the Regiment did not want to try him, and he certainly did not want to have him back. It would have been most unsuitable for any regiment to have on its strength, as the wife of a non-commissioned officer, a young girl who, in addition to being the daughter of a Major General, had also distinguished herself by insulting the Queen and jilting Lord Bracca.

A compromise was quickly found. Colour Sergeant Kelly was quietly discharged from the Queen's Army, and at once appointed to the rank of Ensign in the Honourable East India Company's Native Infantry, and shipped off to India by the next troopship.

I was born in Calcutta on May 27, 1850, and christened Justin Kelly. This is my story; but I will not pretend that it is entirely the result of my own unaided recollections. I am indebted to other people for memories of various times and places, and particularly to my friend the late Mrs. Elsie McLeod, whose detailed day-to-day journal of events came into my possession some time after her death.

[4]

Chapter 2

IT IS, I suppose, impossible for any man to pinpoint his earliest recollections to definite times and places. One retains images of childhood, which are blurred at first, but gradually clear, like a landscape revealing itself in brief pictures through gaps in a dispersing mist.

Naturally my earliest memory is of my mother, and it consists only of a sound—the slight click of her heels tapping on the stone floor of the passage as she came towards the nursery. The only people in our bungalow who wore shoes or boots were my father and mother; the native servants, so far as I can recall, all went barefooted. So my first recollection is of a light tread, which I could recognize, and then of a tall presence, smelling sweetly of lavender water, bending over and lifting me gently and easily.

She was a tall, quiet woman, blue-eyed, fair-haired, and fair-skinned; and she was beautiful. A crayon sketch, drawn by a woman friend of hers in India, which I still have, shows her rather tightly buttoned into a kind of tunic, with a long full skirt falling below it, and wearing a straw hat tilted forward on her head. The clothes are ridiculous to modern eyes, but do not hide the erect pride of the figure nor the calmness and kindness of the lovely, regular features. Calm, and kind, and rather silent is how I remember her, and always gentle. Though she could be firm when she had to, even her reproofs were gentle.

My memories of my father are much more vivid. He was tall, and dark, and handsome in a rather dashing military way, with dark hair, which was inclined to curl, dark side whiskers, and dark eyes which flashed engagingly in his hawklike face when he smiled, which he did frequently. He was very strong physically, and delighted in his strength. Nothing pleased him more than lifting enormous weights, or jumping long distances, or displaying his skill as a marksman. He was, perhaps, childishly proud of his strength, but nobody minded this because he was also gay and good-natured. And he was no fool. He had a good memory, a quick mind, and a genuine enthusiasm for learning. He read constantly and eagerly,

[5]

and was always prepared to discuss any subject, whether he knew anything about it or not. His fellow officers called him "Meehawl," and sometimes laughed at him a little, and liked him a lot. I think almost everybody liked him, and my mother adored him.

Digging down into my remote past, it seems to me that my first clear pictures are of the bungalow in the cantonments at Lucknow, where we moved in '55, when my father was a Lieutenant. I remember the wide verandah, supported by arches, the high, rather dark rooms, the white turbaned servants, who seemed to be everywhere, so that no European ever had to do anything except give orders.

As I concentrate, disconnected memories come crowding back, flickering through my mind like lantern slides. The sound of bugles, and the tramp of marching feet. The elephants, with their painted tusks, coming for their early morning bath in the sluggish Gumti River. The huge sprawling city of 700,000 people, with its gaudy painted palaces, its hovels, and its bustling, jostling, shouting population, and its queer, meaty, spicy smell. The wailing sound of Indian singing at night, the wild barking of dogs, and the huge birds which used to wheel among the trees. The Residency, standing in its gardens on a rise overlooking the city and the river, with the Union Jack flying from the flagstaff on the tower flanking the main building.

I remember the Residency very well.

Early in the morning, my father, very smart and impressive in his uniform, would leave the bungalow, and my mother always waited at the edge of the verandah till he was out of her sight. A little later Mrs. McLeod and her two children would arrive, and two or three other young children would be brought by their Ayahs from neighboring bungalows, and for an hour and a half or so there would be "lessons."

Mrs. McLeod was a plump, energetic, brown-haired, birdlike little woman, who had once been employed as a teacher of music and drawing in a girls' school somewhere in London. She had come to India as governess to the children of a British Colonel, and had afterwards married a sandy-haired civilian clerk with a good tenor voice. The McLeods were an earnest couple; they liked discussing serious subjects, and held strong views on what was good and what was bad in art, music, education, literature, and politics. They were also poor, as so many earnest people are, and Mrs. McLeod was very glad to earn a few rupees giving lessons to the children of the officers in the garrison.

They had two freckled, sandy-haired children of their own—Jeannie, who was the same age as I was, and Ian, who was two years older. But already I was nearly half an inch taller than Ian.

In the beginning I rebelled against these lessons, and disliked Mrs. McLeod and her children almost equally. I resented receiving orders from a woman who, as my Ayah had told me, was the wife of a mere civilian, and I made my resentment very plain. I was an unruly little brute, and must have tried Mrs. McLeod's patience severely, especially when I fought with Ian and gave him a bloody lip. My father was called in to deal with me.

"We'll have no more of this fighting, and you'll do what Mrs. McLeod tells you," he told me. "She's a good woman, though argumentative, and it's a thankless enough job she has, trying to instill the elementary principles of education into the thick skulls of young hooligans the likes of you."

Smiling, half sternly and half humorously, he held me, his big strong hands on my shoulders, looking down on me from his great height.

"Do you know what education is?" he went on. "Then I'll tell you, and you must believe what I say. Education is the one thing you'll need most if you're going to get anywhere. It's the man that knows things who can do things, if he has any sense at all, and is not just a mass of undigested information with little power of reasoning. So from now on you'll oblige me by learning all that Mrs. McLeod can teach you; and you'll obey her orders, because while you're in class with her she's your commanding officer, and no man is ever fit to give orders until he's learned how to take them."

"Men don't take orders from women," I objected.

"I take orders from a woman: I'm here because the Queen sent me here. So you be sensible, and learn your lessons and take your orders like a man, and spare me the trouble of giving you the beating you'll be getting if I hear of any more insubordination."

After that I attended to my lessons, and because I had a retentive memory I learned fairly quickly, and Mrs. McLeod commended me. But I still resented having to obey her.

In the evenings, when I went to bed, my father and mother would come and sit with me for a while, and I would demand a story. It was always my father who told me stories, and they were tales of the legendary saints and heroes of ancient Ireland which he had heard in his childhood—of the Kings who had reigned in Tara, of Cuchulain, the small dark champion of Ulster, of Conn of the hundred fights, of Fin McCool the Chief of the Fian, and of Maeve, the great queen of Connacht. He told his stories graphically, acting the parts of the characters himself, thoroughly enjoying the telling of them. After all these years I can still picture him, eager and vivid, his eyes shining: I can still hear his voice.

My mother and I would listen, enthralled, she with a little smile on her lips, watching him all the while. There was great harmony between the three of us on those warm Indian evenings.

So the days and the months passed, and I grew bigger and more informed about what was happening, and learned to read and do simple arithmetic. And a new Chief Commissioner came to Lucknow—his name was Sir Henry Lawrence.

That was in the year 1857.

Chapter 3

A LOT has been written about the great mutiny of the Sepoy Army in Bengal, and most of it has been deliberately biased. That is the way with histories, which are usually written by thoughtful gentlemen whose chief object is to manipulate events to coincide with their own political and religious prejudices. Some writers have even referred to the mutiny as "The Indian War of Independence," hoping perhaps, by thus miscalling it, to show that it was a spontaneous rising of the oppressed masses against the booted imperial tyrant. This theory hardly fits the facts.

The mutiny, which began on May 10, 1857, in the garrison town of Meerut, and spread like a flame in dry grass over a third of the country, was not a "national" rising in any sense of the word at all. It was a rebellion of the Native Army of Bengal, which numbered about 150,000 well-armed and well-equipped men, and its leaders were mostly ambitious Moslem and Hindu priests and a few native princes who objected to losing despotic powers which they had misused. The forces which finally quelled the mutiny were mostly Indians themselves; two-thirds of them were native troops. In the Punjab, where Sir Henry Lawrence had spent the greater part of his career, thousands of men came flocking to fight under the British flag.

My own memories of those early days in May, 1857, are a child's memories, but they are fairly clear. A child's mind is sensitive. Like a barometer, it registers changes of atmospheric pressure; and during those weeks of May I could not help becoming aware of undercurrents of tension among the grownups surrounding me. Chiefly, I think, I noticed the way my mother and father and their friends talked a little loudly about ordinary things when the servants were listening, and how they talked quietly, in serious voices, when the servants could not hear. I recall roughly a conversation one evening between my father, at ease in a green silk smoking jacket, with a drink beside him, my mother, Mr. and Mrs. McLeod, and two other friends, Captain Moorhouse and Lieutenant Aitken, who had come in for drinks. I was playing with a picture book in a corner of the room.

[9]

"Sir Henry takes a grave view," Captain Moorhouse said. He added impatiently, "General Hewitt seems to have made a complete bungle at Meerut. If only he'd struck quickly, and hanged a round dozen of them, instead of doing nothing . . ." His voice faded into a sigh; he shook his head sadly. "Delhi gone. It seems unbelievable."

"Is hanging the remedy for everything?" asked Mrs. McLeod in her clear, cultured, schoolteacher's voice. "Wouldn't it be even better to ascertain the grievances which led these men to mutiny, and to remedy them?"

Captain Moorhouse looked disapproving, as most Army men did when Mrs. McLeod made one of her utterances. Lieutenant Aitken took up the argument.

"What grievances?" he demanded. "The men haven't any grievances. They're as happy as sandboys."

"Well . . . I wouldn't say that entirely. They have grievances," my father said slowly. His eyes were shining, and he was smiling slightly, as he always did when he got into an argument. "There's lack of promotion, for one thing. Of late years, and especially under Lord Dalhousie, all the best positions have gone to Englishmen. I know that was part of Lord Dalhousie's plan for introducing Western reforms, but it hasn't pleased some of the native officers and officials: it couldn't be expected to. But the cause of the trouble goes much deeper than that. It has its basis in the religious beliefs of the population."

They all looked at him. Mrs. McLeod said, "I think Mr. Kelly has something to say. I'd be interested to hear your views, Mr. Kelly, especially your opinions about the religious basis of the mutiny."

She and my father were old antagonists in argument.

"Well now . . ." my father said. He stretched out his long legs comfortably, and went on, "Well, this is how I see it. The people of this country are greatly addicted to religion—Brahmins and Muslims alike. That is well known. They obey the orders of their priests. You tell me that Lord Dalhousie introduced reforms. He built schools, did he not? Do you think the priests, Brahmin or Muslim, wanted those schools? Have you ever heard of any priests, of any sect, being in favor of education which is not taught by themselves? Lord Dalhousie encouraged the building of railroads. You may remember what happened when the Missionary Societies issued a pamphlet explaining that the railroad was one of God's chosen instruments for uniting the people of India in the one true faith."

"I remember the fuss about that pamphlet," Aitken said. "The Government had to issue a statement denying that the railroads were being constructed with the idea of forcibly converting the Hindus and Muslims to Christianity."

"But that was ridiculous," protested McLeod.

"It was not ridiculous. It was one of a chain of causes which have led to the present situation. This business of the cartridges is merely the fuse which has fired a keg of powder which was ready, waiting."

"What business of the cartridges?" I asked.

My words caused a sudden silence. I think that the grownups had forgotten for the moment that I was there. My mother turned to me.

"This doesn't concern you, Justin," she said.

"Ah, why not?" my father asked. "It'll be all over the town within the next three days." He looked at me. "Some of the native troops at Meerut have mutinied and marched away to Delhi. They will be caught and punished."

"Everybody knows there's been a mutiny," I said. "But what happened about the cartridges?"

"The cartridges—that's just one of those silly things. Somebody spread a story among the troops that the grease for the cartridges had hog's fat and cow's fat in it, and you know the hog is unclean to the Muslim and the cow is sacred to the Hindu. So the native troops refused to use the cartridges."

"Why did they put hog's fat and cow's fat in the grease if they knew the soldiers wouldn't want to use it?" I asked.

My father laughed briefly.

"I don't know what they put into the grease; I doubt whether anybody does except the contractors. Anyway, the cartridges are being withdrawn now, so the trouble will be over very soon."

He spoke reassuringly, and all over Bengal, except in Meerut and Delhi, people were still speaking reassuringly. Sometimes there seems to be a peculiar blindness about the Anglo-Saxon race which makes them refuse to acknowledge the real facts about any ugly situation till something gets up and smacks them between the eyes. Even after the mutiny had begun a lot of officers and officials refused to believe that *their* troops could mutiny—till they were shot down on their own parade grounds, their bungalows looted and burned, and their wives and children raped, tortured, and finally hacked into small pieces. That evening, while my father and his friends were talking, women and children, made captive by the mutineers in Delhi, were being roasted alive over slow fires. Their husbands and fathers had mostly been luckier. They had been killed fighting.

During the following weeks the mutiny spread. In station after station the Sepoy troops rose and massacred their British officers, and in big towns, like Delhi, the townspeople, anxious to be on the winning side, joined them. And it was not only the British who were murdered. With the suspension of law, feuds sprang up everywhere. Villages raided and looted other villages, Hindus fought against Moslems, and bands of men went about murdering everybody they didn't like, or to whom they owed money. Village shopkeepers and moneylenders had a very bad time.

But so far we, in Lucknow, were not involved; we went on living painstakingly normal lives. The customary social activities—dinner parties, card parties, dances—continued. To a child those days were monotonous. My mother watched me continually; I was never allowed to be alone. Mrs. McLeod still gave me my morning lessons, but her interest in teaching seemed to have waned. Her husband had been sent on a mission to Cawnpore, and she was worried about him.

The feeling of tension increased. One morning when we children were having our lessons, we heard my father's voice calling my mother. A few minutes later he and my mother came into the room. My father wore an expression of brisk, rather grim cheerfulness. My mother looked perplexed and worried.

"Good morning, Mrs. McLeod. I'm sorry to interrupt the lesson." My father paused, and then added, as if it were of no great importance, "I'm afraid this is the end of lessons for today; we'll all have some packing up to do. Sir Henry has issued an order that all women and children are to move into the Residency without delay."

"Into the Residency," Mrs. McLeod echoed in a stunned voice. "But . . . there'll be no one in the bungalow. Harry's still in Cawnpore. What will happen to all our things?"

"I expect some kind of arrangement will be made." My father spread out his hands slightly, as if to indicate that he quite understood her feelings, but there was nothing he could do for her. "It's an official order," he added.

"But if Harry . . ." Mrs. McLeod began. She too raised her hands, as if in protest, and then let them fall to her side. "I understand," she said slowly, and then, looking at my father, she asked, "Has there been any news . . . from Cawnpore?"

"Oh no. Nothing unusual, I can assure you. This . . . this order is merely a measure that Sir Henry considers it advisable to take. Merely a . . . a precaution."

"Are we all going to live in the Residency with Sir Henry—all the women and all the children?" I asked. "Will there be room?"

"There'll be room," my father answered.

"And you'll be remaining here," my mother said in a calm voice.

"With my men," my father agreed.

My mother and I, with all the other women and children, moved into the Residency. Remembering the big dignified building, set in its picturesque gardens, I had looked forward to some kind of childish treat. I was soon disillusioned. Everything was in a state of wild turmoil. In the gardens coolies were busy with picks and shovels, digging entrenchments and putting up earthworks. A long trail of bullock carts carrying stores was winding in procession through the main gate. Harassed officials, with papers and pencils, were trying to allocate quarters. We waited, and we waited, and we waited, sitting on our bundles of luggage; we had only been allowed to bring the barest necessities.

After a long time we were shown our quarters. Mrs. McLeod and her two children, and my mother and I, were to share a small basement room, formerly a clerks' office.

"Have we all got to live in here?" I demanded.

"Yes, Justin. For the time being." My mother, sitting on the edge of a charpoy, a low Indian bed, looked hot and tired. The room was in a state of confusion, with our belongings strewn all over the place. We were all tired and thirsty.

"We mustn't grumble," my mother said. She rose wearily, and spoke to Mrs. McLeod. "I'm going to try to find the children something to drink."

"I'll see if I can get the place a bit straight," Mrs. McLeod said.

Life for the five hundred women and children in the Residency became very uncomfortable. Arrangements for sanitation and feeding were necessarily haphazard, and there was a lot of grumbling. The voices of some of the women, accustomed to moderately luxurious quarters and plenty of servants, were raised shrilly and continuously.

"It's perfectly scandalous; it creates the worst kind of impression on the natives to see us living like this."

"I agree entirely. There's no reason to suppose that any of the troops here are likely to be disaffected—certainly not the men of my husband's regiment. His men almost worship him."

"I wonder how much longer we shall be expected to endure this squalor. We might as well be living in the bazaar. Somebody should write to the Governor General about it."

"Mildewed old hags," said my father. "Going about screeching

[13]

like a lot of wet peahens in a thunderstorm. Some of these women make me want to puke."

"Michael!" My mother spoke in soft-voiced reproof, coloring slightly, as she sometimes did when my father used a coarse expression.

"Sorry, m'dear." My father smiled at her, and then addressed me with elaborate politeness. "Some of these ladies cause a severe contraction of my abdominal muscles, accompanied by symptoms of nausea, which can only be relieved by vomiting. There, boy; that shows you what education can do for a man—how it enables him to express himself in refined and elegant language."

"Don't take any notice of him, Justin. He's talking a great deal of nonsense," my mother said placidly.

The days passed, and the weather grew steadily hotter and hotter. Our lives became increasingly miserable. At night, in our small room, the heat was stifling.

Sir Henry Lawrence, the Chief Commissioner, went on his daily rounds, a sick man with an intense flame of determination burning in him. Everything depended on him, and he knew it. To look into that haggard, bearded face with its deep-set glowing eyes was to realize that he was a man who had set himself on a course from which nothing would swerve him. A mere glance from him could quell arguments and silence criticism. He moved among us constantly, supervising, giving orders, visiting the troops in their cantonments, visiting the townspeople, visiting the women and children. His stern presence commanded awe and even fear; and yet, for a crying child or a sick soldier he never failed to have a word of comfort or consolation.

On an evening at the end of May we were all in our stuffy room. We children were in bed; our mothers were sitting sewing, mending our clothes by the light of a tallow candle. Our door opened, and a Mrs. Barker, a neighbor, came in quickly. She spoke in a hushed, excited voice.

"There's something going on. There's trouble somewhere. Have you heard anything?"

"No. What kind of trouble?" My mother put down her sewing.

As if to answer her, a sharp sound of firing came to our ears from somewhere in the distance. Almost immediately we could hear sharp shouts of command in the Residency grounds, and a clatter of horses' hoofs as men rode away from the Residency. Mrs. McLeod rose and went to the window. She had to stand on a charpoy to see out clearly.

"There are fires somewhere," she said. "I think . . . yes, they seem to be in the cantonments." She sprang down from the charpoy. "I'm going to try to find out what's happening," she said grimly.

She left the room. We children began to ask questions.

"What is it, Mama? Is it a fire? Do let me look out of the window."

"Lie down, children. We'll know what it is, all in good time."

In less than a minute Mrs. McLeod came back, accompanied by Mr. Harris, the chaplain.

"There's a big fire in the cantonments," Mrs. McLeod announced. "I don't know what the shooting is. Nobody would tell me anything." She glared rather defiantly at the chaplain.

"It's nothing to be alarmed about," Mr. Harris said. "There is a fire, and men have been sent to deal with it. Colonel Inglis wants all the women and children to stay quietly in their quarters."

"If it's only a fire, what's all the shooting for?" Mrs. Barker demanded. "You don't put a fire out by shooting at it."

"I can only repeat Colonel Inglis's assurance that there's no cause for alarm. And his order that all women and children should remain in their quarters." Mr. Harris slightly emphasized the word "order." "Sir Henry has gone to the cantonments himself to see to things," Mr. Harris added.

"We must do what we're told," my mother said. "Lie down, children, and try to go to sleep. We shall hear all about it in the morning."

The sound of firing gradually died away. We lay down, and we did sleep fitfully. But later in the night I woke up and saw my mother sitting in a canvas chair, her chin on her hands, waiting. I don't think she slept at all that night.

We were up with the dawn. In the morning light we could see, through our window, a black pall of smoke hanging over the cantonments. Everything was quiet then, but about an hour after dawn a sound of heavy firing broke out again; the heavy thud of gunfire mingled with the drumming of rifle fire.

In the Residency grounds there was a brisk coming and going of men on horseback. For us, women and children, there was only the suspense of waiting; nobody seemed to be willing to tell us anything. The women still talked, but their voices were a subdued murmur; the shrillness had gone out of them. And the word "mutiny" was being whispered. The huge city, stretching away below the Residency walls, was quiet. It was very quiet. Looking down from the Residency verandah on to the town, it could be seen that few people were moving about in the streets.

Early in the morning my mother went to the hospital to work. She returned soon after midday. And in the middle of the afternoon my father suddenly came in to see us. I remember my mother's face, the utter relief in it as, with a little cry of joy, she rose and went to him. She seemed to be half crying, half laughing.

"Michael!" She leaned on him, and he put an arm round her and kissed her. She drew away from him.

"I've been a little worried about you," she said in a prim, half apologetic voice. "I heard things in the hospital . . ." Her voice broke off.

"You didn't tell me you heard anything," Mrs. McLeod said in a jealous voice. She turned to face my father. "Was there a mutiny?" she demanded flatly.

"There was," my father answered. He sat down abruptly, a tired man, his scabbard clattering on the hard floor. He looked profoundly unhappy.

"Was it bad?" I asked.

"It was bad. It was very bad. But it's over now." He paused. "We must hope it's all over now."

"What happened?" Mrs. McLeod demanded. She was bursting with curiosity. We all were.

"I suppose there's no harm in telling. It will be known by everybody soon enough." My father paused briefly again, as if wondering what he might tell.

"It began with the 71st," he continued. "They broke out of their lines and began setting fire to the quarters. General Anscombe rode down to them and ordered them back to their lines, and they shot him."

"They . . . killed him?" said Mrs. McLeod.

"Yes." My father's voice was deep. "And Grant. And young Jimmy Marlow; they found him lying down in his quarters. Sixteen years old, and he'd only been in the country nine weeks."

My father sighed; his face looked sad and sick. He went on. "When the uproar began I was in the old bungalow sorting through some things. I grabbed my sword and ran to the lines. My men were half fallen in, their muskets in their hands. I shouted to them to fall in, and they all stopped, and looked at me. Then one of them raised his musket . . . and the man next to him struck him down with the butt. I shouted to them again to fall in, and they didn't move. They only looked at me. The man who had meant to shoot me was lying on

[16]

the ground. I shouted to them again, not to be fools—not to be fools—and began to draw my sword. The Subahdar-Major gripped my wrist; and I saw that half a dozen of the men were covering me with their muskets. The Subahdar-Major was crying—the old man had tears running down his cheeks. He said, 'You can do nothing, Sahib. We like you, but if we see you again, we shall kill you.' Then they all went off into the darkness. Not quite all. When the others had gone, five men came out of the darkness. Jemadur Narayan—you remember him—seemed to be their leader. I drew my sword. I thought they wanted to murder me and I didn't care much if they did. I asked them what the devil they wanted, and Narayan answered, 'We are staying.'"

My father paused. I saw that sweat was running down his face. He was looking at my mother, and she was looking back at him sympathetically. It was as if he was talking to her alone.

"Five of them," he said. "And two of them have paid for their loyalty with their lives."

He raised a hand, passing it through his hair in a perplexed way. He was very tired. Mrs. McLeod said: "How . . . ?" and then broke off abruptly as if she had been going to ask something and had thought better of it. My father glanced at her.

"Eh," he said, and then, "Oh yes." He looked back at my mother.

"Five of them," he repeated. "There was a kind of wavering half light coming from burning buildings, and a hellish yelling coming from the officers' quarters. I shouted to my men to follow me, and ran towards the flames. There was some fighting going on. Near a mess tent I found Slingsby and half a dozen men of the 13th engaged with about twenty of the devils. We joined in and drove them back a little way, and then another twenty or thirty attacked us, yelling and snarling like wild animals. All men of the 71st. For a few moments we were surrounded. Slingsby was down, and we were fighting over his body. Two of my men were down. I thought we were done for . . . but, by God, we'd done for a few of them too. Then there was a burst of firing and a sudden almighty cheer, and a Company of the 32nd came in at the double . . . and, by God, the way they went into those fellows; there was no stopping them. They went past us like a wave, taking everything in front of them. Narayan and I picked Slingsby up and carried him out of the melee. He was still breathing. Two of Slingsby's chaps and two of my fellows were dead."

"Did all the regiments mutiny?" Mrs. McLeod asked.

"No. Oh no. And it was only the 71st who ran amok. But a lot of men simply marched away—men of the 13th, the 48th, and the 2nd Cavalry. And about half the Native Artillery went, taking their guns with them. This morning we heard they'd all assembled on the race-course and were waiting for us. We found them there, drawn up in battle order, about a thousand strong, with guns posted in the center and on their flanks. Our guns opened on them with grape, and then the 32nd went in with the bayonet. In ten minutes it was all over; they dispersed in front of our bayonets like chaff in a wind."

"Will there be any more mutiny?" I asked.

"I don't know. I don't know anything. My own men . . ." My father paused. "The whole thing was carefully planned; they must have been got at by influences from outside. This may be the end of it. I heard Colonel Inglis say that it may turn out to be a blessing in disguise. We know now who's for us and who's against us. Men who didn't join the mutiny last night aren't likely to mutiny tomorrow. We know where we are now."

His prediction was being proved wrong while he was speaking. At that moment the 7th Native Cavalry, who had taken no part in the previous night's mutiny, and had been sent to pursue the fleeing mutineers, were joining forces with them outside Lucknow.

The days which followed were days of acute tension. A kind of deathly peace brooded over Lucknow. News which reached us from outside was scanty, and nearly all of it was bad. Native garrisons were rising in outlying stations and murdering their white officers and their families. A few fugitives who escaped these massacres came straggling into Lucknow. Delhi was still in the hands of the mutineers. And, worst of all for us, Cawnpore, only forty-five miles away, with its small white garrison and its 250 women and children, was being besieged by a well-armed rebel army several thousands strong.

For another whole month the peace continued—a peace that was maintained solely by the personality of one worn-out husk of a man, Henry Lawrence. The days grew steadily hotter. Conditions became more and more uncomfortable as greater numbers of people crowded into the Residency. Cholera broke out, and there were several deaths. But now there was no more grumbling. Women went about their work quietly, knowing what had happened to their sisters and friends at out stations, and what might be happening to them very soon.

Children grew older quickly in such conditions. We heard talk, and we talked among ourselves, repeating what we had overheard. We had classes—Mrs. McLeod's class had swelled to twelve children between the ages of seven and about thirteen; we had restricted opportunities for play in the Residency grounds, where preparations for defense were now going on without any attempt to hide them. We acquired a surface sophistication that was rather horribly grown-up. When one of our number vanished and did not return, we knew what had happened, but we did not talk about it. In fact, three of the class died of cholera during that month. They simply went, and we were tight-lipped about them. But we talked a lot about soldiers and fighting.

"My father says that whatever we do the position will still be militarily indefensible."

"What does *he* know about it. My father says that two companies of the 32nd could take on the whole rebel army. And he's a Major. Your father's only a Captain."

"My father fought at Gujirat. He knows more than any old Calcutta Major."

"My father's not a Calcutta Major. If you say that again . . ."

"Oh, do stop bickering, children," Mrs. McLeod would admonish us. "This is not a time to be quarreling among ourselves."

My own father, ironically, had received his Captain's brevet, with no troops of his own to command. He was drilling a scratch lot of civilian clerks and pensioners. My mother worked in the hospital for five hours a day.

There came a day when a rumor spread, and was presently confirmed, and a cold blanket of stupefaction seemed to settle on the garrison. Cawnpore had fallen—Cawnpore, with its British garrison, and 250 women and children. We had known it might happen, but had never believed that it would. Now it had happened.

In our little room Mrs. McLeod went about her duties silently, calm and dry-eyed. When she wasn't doing anything she sat still, looking at nothing. Her two children, Ian and Jeannie, were silent. I wanted to say something sympathetic to them, but felt shy and awkward, and could think of nothing to say. My mother came in from the hospital, looking distressed.

"Elsie . . . I've just heard. It may be only a rumor. It may not be true."

"It is true. I went to see Sir Henry, and he confirmed it," Mrs. McLeod answered. Small and birdlike, but with a kind of hard composure, she added, "I have to look after my children now, and perhaps other people's children." She took a deep breath which seemed to hurt her, and was instantly composed again. "It was kind of you to come," she said.

There were fires burning in the streets of Lucknow that night, and the town was noisy; a fierce hubbub, like the buzzing of huge bees, rose from it continually. During the night many of the coolies working in the Residency grounds deserted. Those who remained had to be given double pay. The next day began quietly; the morning dragged by lethargically, but during the afternoon a stir of sudden activity began. Officers could be seen hurrying to and fro, eager and alert, with smiles on their faces. Soon after five, Bob Earnshaw, a boy in our class, the son of a Captain in the 32nd, burst unceremoniously into our room.

"I say, have you heard. There's going to be a battle."

"A battle?" Mrs. McLeod said. "Who told you that story, Robert?"

"It's not a story. It's true. My daddy said so. They're going to give those murdering devils what for."

A few minutes later my father came in and confirmed the story.

"Yes, it's quite true. We've had intelligence that a body of the Cawnpore mutineers is marching on Lucknow. Four or five thousand of them I believe: they've reached Nawabganji, about twenty miles away and some of their advanced units have been reported in Chinhat."

"Chinhat. But that's only a few miles outside the town," my mother said.

"Eight or nine miles. They seem to have halted there for the time being. We're sending a force out at dawn to meet them and stop them from reaching the town. If we can give them a really sharp lesson, and drive them back running the way they came, it might make a lot of difference to the situation here. It might make all the difference."

"Are you going with this force?" my mother asked.

"No such luck. I shall be drilling my clerks and pensioners." He sounded very disgusted. But my mother looked relieved.

At dawn the troops, in their long red lines, began to fall in in the Residency grounds. They looked cheerful and animated—men who were looking forward with eagerness to a pleasurable prospect. From one of the verandahs my mother and I and the McLeods watched them. Owing to the desertion of native clerks and storekeepers, there had been some hitch in the distribution of supplies, and we had none of us had any breakfast. Nor had the troops had any breakfast.

Time passed, and the sun came up in its full summer strength, blazing down on the dry ground. The men stood there, waiting; some of their animation seemed to die away. I began to feel bored, and tired of waiting, and I was hungry.

"When are they going?" I asked.

"Hush," my mother said.

An officer named Colonel Case came out of the Residency and shouted angrily to a Major, "Why are all these men standing in the sun? Give the order to fall out at once, and wait in the shade."

At the same time I saw my father thrusting his way urgently through the crowd on the verandah. He came up to my mother and me; his eyes were shining with a light of joy and excitement.

"I can't stay, Mary. I only came to tell you that I'm going with them. Yardley of the 13th has gone down with fever, and I'm taking his place."

"I understand, Michael," my mother said.

He put an arm round her and kissed her; I saw her hand gripping his arm hard. He put his hand on my shoulder and bent and kissed me briefly. Then he hurried away.

"Is he going to be in the battle?" I asked. I felt awed, and rather frightened.

"Yes," my mother said. She took my hand in hers and held it.

It was just after ten when the men fell in again, in the pitiless sunshine. Do I seem to be emphasizing the sunshine? It needed no emphasis at the time. Had the men marched at dawn, as planned, they would have marched in the cool of the morning. The temperature when they finally marched out was about 115 degrees.

But they made a brave show as, red-coated, with a band playing, they marched out through the Bailey Gate. The force was about 750 strong, consisting of 300 British Infantry, 230 Native Infantry, 36 British Cavalry, 120 Native Cavalry, and ten guns, six of which were manned by Sepoys. Seven hundred and fifty men, marching out confidently in the sunshine to meet five thousand mutineers, and looking forward with eagerness to the encounter. They had no doubt about the result.

The sounds of the band and the marching feet died away. A silence settled over the Residency. It seemed curiously empty. Men and women stood about in groups for a while talking, and then dispersed. My mother went to her duties in the hospital; there would be preparations needed for receiving wounded men. Mrs. McLeod assembled her class, but the lesson was listless; nobody paid much attention. Soon after midday we had a meal, and then, as was customary, the children were sent to their beds, to rest during the intensest heat.

In the afternoon a noise made itself heard, and became quickly louder—the harsh, heavy sound of constant firing. Wisps of smoke were rising not far away. People came crowding on to the Residency verandahs, leaning over, peering, their faces blank with incredulity. With a deep booming sound the guns of the Machi Bhawan joined in the firing. In the distance we could hear a thin, savage, exultant yelling, growing steadily louder.

In through the Bailey Gate galloped an officer, hatless, blood streaming unchecked from a cut in his forehead. His uniform was ragged, his face contorted with pain and rage. He reined in his horse, and stood in his stirrups and yelled in a hoarse, strained voice, "Get to your posts. Every man to his post. For God's sake. . . ." His voice broke off. He crumpled in the saddle and fell sideways from his horse. A man ran forward to pick him up and began to drag him towards the Residency.

Near me a woman gave a gasp and collapsed, clutching her right shoulder. Chips of stone flew as bullets spattered the walls of the building. Coolies, working on the unfinished defenses, flung away their tools and scrambled madly to climb over the earthworks and make their escape. All round the Residency the firing was now a continuous roar, and in the Residency grounds the men manning the walls and earthworks were also firing. There was a continuous yelling, mingled with a screaming of horses; the whole building and its grounds were ringed by flame and smoke.

Through the Bailey Gate came staggering the shattered remnants of our small, defeated army. Wounded men were clinging to gun limbers, and to the tails and stirrups of horses. Wrecked and spent, in the last stages of exhaustion, they came staggering in through the gate and, once inside the Residency grounds, many of them fell to the ground and stayed where they lay.

Horses, guns, men were mixed in a dreadful confusion, in an atmosphere thick with smoke and acrid with the fumes of burnt powder. Women were looking for their husbands, others were trying to help the wounded, men were shouting hoarse orders, terrified children were running around aimlessly. I had broken away from Mrs. McLeod's control, and with stark terror in my heart I was looking for my father.

A man right in front of me, staggering blindly, fell to his hands and knees. I stopped, and he glanced up at me sideways, and reached out a hand and grabbed my ankle. His uniform was in rags, his eyes red-rimmed; the wrinkles in his face were red with dust. I knew him; he was a Sergeant in the 32nd.

"Hey, get me a drink, sonny. For God's sake, boy, get me a drink," he gasped. He released my ankle and slumped forward onto his face.

"All right," I said.

Immediately it became extremely important to me to fetch this man a drink. This so occupied my mind that I forgot my terror; I forgot even my fear for my father. Dodging through the confusion, I found water, and a tin cup, and holding it carefully in my two hands returned to the Sergeant. There were two women by him, helping him to rise. One of them was my mother. She looked at me, startled and horrified.

"Justin! What are you doing here?"

"I brought Sergeant Mellish a drink." I thrust the tin cup towards the soldier and he grasped it eagerly in hands that trembled. "Thanks, sonny." He raised the cup, and swallowed the contents, and gasped with obvious relief. "My God, I needed that."

"Go back inside at once, Justin," my mother said sternly. "And don't come out again without permission."

All my resolution vanished abruptly, and I began to snivel like a miserable child. "I'm looking for father," I said tearfully. "I want to find father."

"I know, Justin. But you must do what you're told. Now go back to Mrs. McLeod at once, and stay with her. I'll come to you as soon as I can." The sternness had left my mother's voice. She sounded sad and helpless.

"I think the Captain's all right. He was six or seven minutes ago," Sergeant Mellish said. My mother turned to him eagerly.

"You saw him . . . six or seven minutes ago."

"Yes. With one of the officers and some men from the Residency, down by the Iron Bridge. They were putting up a covering fire as we came across." Sergeant Mellish drew himself up erect, but still swaying slightly. "You look after the boy, Ma'am; take him back to his quarters." He smiled at me, the dirt crinkling on his face. "Thanks for the drink, sonny."

"If you're sure you'll be all right . . ."

"Bless you, yes. Got to go and see if I can find my section—what's left of them."

The tall sergeant staggered away. My mother hurried me into the Residency and down to our semi-basement room. The other two children were there. Mrs. McLeod wasn't there.

"Mama's looking for you: where have you been?" Jeannie said accusingly, and Ian said, "What happened?"

"I don't know. I think we lost the battle," I answered.

Yes, we had lost the battle, and the day was the last day of June in the year 1857. On that day the siege of Lucknow began.

Chapter 4

WE DID NOT take our clothes off that night. We three children lay on our charpoys, occasionally dozing a little, but not much. Mrs. McLeod sat in the canvas chair. We hardly talked; it would have been difficult to make ourselves heard. The candle burned dimly in the stuffy room. Outside was a clangor as if giants were beating iron trays, and mingled with this noise was a sound of nearby shouting and, from the distance, a continuous high-pitched yelling coming from the city.

Soon after dark we had a visitor. Mr. Harris, the chaplain, came in to see us. He looked hot and bedraggled, his clothes covered with filth and blood.

"I called to see how you were faring," he said to Mrs. McLeod, and then, looking at me, "And I have a message for Master Justin. Good news, my boy. Your father is safe—slightly wounded, but nothing very serious. In fact, he has resumed command of his men. Your mother requested me to deliver this message."

He leaned against the wall, smiling, trying to look comforting and reassuring, but he was plainly almost dropping with fatigue. Mrs. McLeod rose quickly from her chair.

"Mr. Harris, you're wounded. Your hand . . ."

There was a streak of blood across the back of his hand. He looked down at it wonderingly.

"No. I'm not wounded. That must be the blood of one of the poor fellows of the 32nd," he said sadly. "Poor fellows," he repeated in a whisper.

"Do sit down, Mr. Harris. You look worn out." Mrs. McLeod took the chaplain's arm and urged him towards the canvas chair. He sat down heavily.

"Thank you. But only for a moment. I mustn't stay. There is so much to be done."

"Why did we lose the battle?" I asked.

He shook his head, as if dazed.

"Our information appears to have been wrong," he said. "The enemy was in overwhelming force, and well provided with artillery.

[24]

And there was treachery. When the order Action Front was given, the native gunners first turned their guns on our troops and then deserted in a body to the enemy. The Native Cavalry all deserted. Our infantry, almost unsupported, and under constant heavy attack from the rebel infantry and horse artillery, had to fight their way back into Lucknow along that narrow road. The losses have been fearful—fearful. The wonder is that any of them returned."

"And what . . . in your opinion . . . is the position now?" asked Mrs. McLeod in a quiet voice. "Can the Residency be defended?"

"I don't know. I don't know. We are in the hands of God; we must put our trust in him. I think we might all offer up a brief prayer. Shall we kneel."

We all knelt.

"Oh God, in thy great mercy, look down upon the members of this garrison . . ."

It was not a long prayer, but I don't think I heard any of it beyond the opening words. My father was safe, and I could think of nothing else. Soon, perhaps, I should see him, and he would tell me about the battle.

The long night went on. Sometime in the early morning, possibly at two or three o'clock, my mother and father entered the room together. My mother looked fairly clean, with a white apron over a dark blue dress; my father looked like a gigantic scarecrow. His face and hands were black with grime, his clothes were in tatters, and a grimy bandage circled his head. Beneath it, mingling with the dirt on his face, were trickles of dried blood.

I rose from my charpoy with a yelp of joy and sprang to meet them.

"Father! Mama! Father, you're wounded. Does it hurt?"

"What's that? Why aren't you asleep?" My father picked me up under the armpits, and swung me upwards, and put me down again. "No, it doesn't hurt. A bullet nicked the top of my ear and the side of my scalp. Made me dizzy for a few moments, and I bled like a pig, but it's only a scratch. Lucky for me it wasn't an inch more to the right."

"Father, you have a funny smell."

"I smell like a midden," he agreed cheerfully. "And I'll probably smell worse presently." He glanced over my head at Mrs. McLeod and Ian and Jeannie. "I expect you're all finding it rather noisy, eh? You mustn't let it worry you. There's nothing to worry about so long as we all keep cheerful and obey orders, and that includes all of you children. No naughtiness and playing the fool—no running away on your own so that people have to look for you." His hand tightened slightly on my shoulder as he spoke this sentence.

"I was looking for you," I protested.

"I know you were, and you mustn't. Where d'you think we'd be if everybody began looking for everybody else? What you have to do is to obey orders, and no argument. That's a soldier's duty, and we're all soldiers now."

"Do you think the position can be defended?" Mrs. McLeod asked for the second time that night. Possibly she was thinking of her husband, murdered in Cawnpore by these same mutineers, and of her children. And doubtless many of the other women in the garrison had similar thoughts in their minds.

My father looked greatly astonished.

"Defended?" he repeated. "Bless me, Madam, what else d'you think we're doing? We're defending it, ain't we?" He laughed a hearty, rather insincere laugh. "We can defend it; have no fear about that. So long as everyone does their duty."

"Do you really believe that?" persisted Mrs. McLeod.

He put his hands on his hips and stood looking at her, his legs apart, smiling slightly.

"Yes, I believe that. What else is there to believe?"

Mrs. McLeod did not answer. My father turned to my mother.

"Try to get some sleep—all of you. I must go back to my post. I'll come again when I can."

He left us. My mother said, "We must at least try to get some sleep. Come, Justin." She put an arm round me, and drew me gently down beside her on one of the charpoys, her arm still round me. Mrs. McLeod extinguished the candle.

I lay there in the darkness, close to my mother; I could feel her heart beating strongly, and once I heard her sigh deeply, and then her lips touched my face softly. The noise of gunfire became a rhythm in my mind, and, after a while I did fall into a kind of half sleep, in which the noise of the guns continued as a background. At dawn the gunfire died down a little and my sleep became deeper.

When I awakened my mother had already gone to her work in the hospital. The sound of firing still continued, though it was not so heavy as it had been the previous night.

All day long we hardly left our room. There were no lessons. For a while Mrs. McLeod tried to read to us, but it was difficult to hear her, and she gave it up. As the heat of the day grew fiercer, a horrible smell began to drift in through our window from a dead horse, lying just outside, in the grounds. The hours passed with a slowness that was almost unendurable.

"Shall we always have to stay in just one room?" Jeannie wailed in sudden despairing irritation. "And can't somebody make them stop that horrible noise."

"We must try to be patient," Mrs. McLeod answered in a flat, dull voice.

During the afternoon my mother joined us, and stayed with us for several hours. She was very hot and tired, with dark smudges under her eyes; her smile was pitiful. She sank into the canvas chair as if her limbs were weighted.

Mrs. McLeod anxiously demanded information.

"Have you heard anything? Is there any news—anything fresh?"

"I don't think so. I heard Major Banks say he doesn't think there'll be an attack today. There are a lot of fires in the town—shops and houses being looted. But their batteries keep firing. Sir Henry had a very narrow escape; an enemy shell burst in his office in the tower."

"No news about the reinforcements that are supposed to be on their way from Calcutta?"

"No."

"I wonder if they've started yet," Mrs. McLeod said grimly. She gave a despondent sigh. "We must keep hoping, mustn't we," she went on. "And be cheerful . . . when we know our defenses are unfinished, and our men are too few, and half of them are sick or wounded, and the enemy are out there in their thousands with the blood of the Cawnpore garrison hardly dry on their bayonets. Can we fight them by being cheerful? Are you cheerful?"

"I'm too tired to be very cheerful," my mother answered. "But so long as we're still here and the enemy are outside the walls, I shall go on hoping."

"Spoken like a soldier's wife," Mrs. McLeod said. She gave a rather brittle laugh. "You're quite right, my dear; I'm being foolish. Now you must lie down and have some rest."

"Yes, I must. I have to return to the hospital at seven."

"Is father coming today?" I asked.

"I don't know, darling. I expect he's very busy. He'll come when he can." My mother rose wearily, and stretched out on one of the charpoys. We all slept for a while during the heat of the afternoon. Sheer tiredness made us sleep.

At seven my mother left for the hospital, and the second dreary night of the siege began. The sound of firing had died down to an occasional crackle of musketry, but the light of flames from burning buildings in the town flickered redly in the window of our room. Shortly before midnight there was a stir in the Residency grounds; we could hear men moving, and shouted orders. Mrs. McLeod's charpoy creaked as she sat up and lit the candle. She went to the window and peered outwards and upwards, trying to find out what was going on. The sounds in the Residency grounds died away, and she returned to her charpoy. But she left the candle burning.

A gigantic explosion seemed to crack the sky wide open right over our heads. It cracked and re-echoed in an avalanche of stupendous sound; the Residency shook violently in the shock of a great blast wave, and a glare of light shone briefly in through our window. The explosion was followed by a hush, and then by the patter and plop of innumerable objects falling.

We children sat awed, open-mouthed. Somewhere, in a room near us, a woman was screaming shrilly. Mrs. McLeod leapt from her charpoy in desperate haste and rummaged in a carpetbag beneath it. Kneeling, she turned to us; her right hand was holding a long kitchen knife, sharpened to a fine point.

"Keep still, children. Stay where you are," she said.

Her features contracted in a horrible wry grimace, as if she had something unbearably bitter in her mouth. She rose from her knees, and with slow, almost stealthy paces, she made for the door. She opened it slightly, and peered out, bending, her shoulders hunched, the knife held at her side. We children did not stay still where we were. We all rose quickly, and Jeannie called in an urgent, frightened voice. "What is it, Mama? What are you doing?"

Another sound penetrated the room—a sound of men cheering. It was right outside our window, swelling louder and louder. Mrs. McLeod opened the door wider and put her head outside. The sound of cheering went on, and with it was mingled women's voices, and even laughter.

Mrs. McLeod stepped back from the doorway as my father suddenly appeared. He was even dirtier than he had been the previous day, but happy as a schoolboy—grinning broadly with delight.

"I can't stay; I've only slipped in for a moment. How are you all? Did the bang wake you up?"

"What was it, father?"

"Oh, about three or four hundred barrels of powder and a million cartridges. Made quite a good bang, didn't it? We've got all our men in from the Machi Bhawan—every man jack of 'em, and not a casualty. Two hundred of 'em, and all good men—mostly Sikhs

[28]

and the 32nd. Spiked all the guns and blew the place up when they left. By Jove, they caught the enemy right on the hop."

He turned, grinning on Mrs. McLeod.

"Why, Mrs. McLeod, what are you brandishing that thing for?"

Mrs. McLeod began to laugh. Her laughter doubled her up; she sank on to her charpoy, clutching her stomach, screeching with laughter. But in a few moments her laughter turned into hysterical tears. My father looked very alarmed, and said, "Hey, hey, don't take on like that," and then to me, "Is there any water in this place?"

We had some in an enamel jug; I poured a cupful and handed it to my father. He took a small silver flask from his pocket and up-ended it over the cup.

"Strictly for emergencies," he said. "Here now, drink some of this." He held the cup to Mrs. McLeod's lips. "Come along now, drink it down, and you'll feel better."

Mrs. McLeod drank, and spluttered; some of the drink ran down her chin. "Now the rest," said my father.

She made a great effort, and drank, and seemed to master herself.

"I'm all right now. I'm sorry I was silly."

"You're all right," agreed my father heartily. "You thought it was the enemy, eh, and you had that long knife all ready to defend the position to the last. It's a fine spirit we have in this garrison; it should take us far."

Mrs. McLeod did not answer. Not till long afterwards did she tell me that the knife had not been intended for use against the enemy. She had meant to use it, at the last moment, to kill both us and herself to prevent us from falling alive into the hands of the mutineers.

Apart from providing badly needed reinforcements, the successful withdrawal of the troops from the Machi Bhawan did something to dispel the gloom caused by the failure at Chinhat. As if to revenge themselves, the mutineers kept up an incessant and furious fire on our positions all the next day and night. And they had their revenge. Another of their shells exploded in Sir Henry Lawrence's office, shattering his thigh and hip. He was carried to the garrison doctor's quarters, where he died the following morning.

He spent his last painful hours dictating detailed instructions for the defense of the position. He took the last sacrament, and expressed a wish that his grave should be marked by the epitaph: "Here lies Henry Lawrence, who tried to do his duty. May the Lord have mercy on his soul." His last words were, "Never surrender."

There was no funeral procession or other ceremonial parade; no men could be spared for it. At night four private soldiers and one officer carried the body to its shallow grave. Before they lowered the body, one of the soldiers raised a corner of the blanket which covered it, and bent and kissed the cold forehead. The others followed suit.

Colonel Inglis succeeded Sir Henry Lawrence as the commander of the garrison.

Chapter 5

THE RESIDENCY was no fortress. It was exactly what it was called—a Residency—a large house for the Chief Commissioner and his staff, and smaller houses for other officials, all standing in a partly walled garden of about thirty acres. In its original state the position would have been quite indefensible, but Lawrence had had earthworks and entrenchments constructed all round the mile-long perimeter and a system of interlacing trenches dug connecting different parts of the grounds with each other. When the siege began, these defenses had not been completed.

In many places the streets of Lucknow came right up to the defenses; the mutineers and the garrison were only a few yards apart. All the time the grounds were under fire from enemy riflemen posted in the housetops. It was courting death to show yourself out of a trench. In the early days of the siege many of the defenders were killed simply because they did not keep their heads down.

When the siege began, the garrison consisted of about 1,750 fighting men, including 750 loyal Indians, some civilian retainers, and between five and six hundred women and children. As the siege progressed these numbers lessened, as violent death and disease carried off men, women, and children without discrimination.

Most of the troops were distributed among seventeen strong points, each commanded by an officer, whose responsibility it was to defend his own allotted area. At these strong points the troops lived, and fed, and slept; they had no "off duty" periods. At night they buried their dead, and drew their rations, and worked on strengthening the defenses.

The rebel army, their numbers enormously swollen by fresh troops coming in from outlying garrisons, had about forty thousand men under arms surrounding the Residency. There was nothing wrong with the quality of their troops; it was leadership which they lacked. Ignoring the claims of experienced native officers, the Princes and priests and other high-caste nobles had taken over all the higher posts in the rebel army.

Day after day the siege went on. Always, all the time, there was the crackle of musketry, the deeper booming of gunfire, the thudding of balls against the walls of the Residency, the savage yells and shouts from the city at our gates. The Residency began to wear a battered look, its windows broken, its verandahs crumbling, its walls pitted by gunfire.

The sun shone pitilessly by day; smoke drifted; a horrible stench of death, disease, and decay permeated the air. And, of all the discomforts I remember, one of the greatest was the flies. They crawled over our food, over our faces when we slept; they clustered in great swarms on the walls and ceilings. There was no escaping them.

Day after day . . . sickness and death. The fever and cholera which were more deadly than enemy bullets. The sick and wounded moaning and twisting through the long hot hours in the overcrowded hospitals. The gangrene, the operations without anesthetics, the cries of men in delirium. The women, no longer complaining, who tended the sick and dying, administering what consolation they could. And after dark the sound of spades, digging the nightly quota of graves.

But a pretense of normal life, of a kind, still went on. Children, thin and hollow-cheeked from bad food and lack of exercise, collected for lessons and games. Something had to be done to keep them occupied. But what I chiefly remember is the hours lying on my charpoy in a kind of languid torpor in the everlasting heat of the afternoons.

One morning when we had just come in from a lesson, my mother appeared suddenly, standing outside the open doorway of our room. She made no move to enter; she stood there, one hand against the wall, supporting herself. Her face was deathly; her eyes were on me with a look of utter agony in them. I stared, and began to go towards her, but she motioned me back sharply.

"No. Keep away. Don't come near me."

I stopped; and my mother smiled very sweetly and said in a gentle voice, "I only came for a moment to look at you, Justin. I want you always to be a good boy."

She turned, stumbling slightly, and went away down the passage outside the room. Mrs. McLeod followed her quickly, closing the door after her.

We children stayed silent, uneasily not looking at each other. There was no need for us to talk, or ask questions. We all knew.

When Mrs. McLeod returned in ten minutes, her face was rigidly composed, but her eyes were red. She said in a strained voice, which she tried to make sound natural, "Your mother's not very well, Justin; she's gone to lie down. I expect she'll be better presently."

I turned away and flung myself down on the charpoy, my face in the pillow. I didn't believe her. Later I learned that my mother had collapsed halfway down the passage outside the room, and been carried away to the hospital. I never saw her again.

The following afternoon my father came in to see me. As he entered, Mrs. McLeod took her two children by the hand and led them out, leaving my father and me together. He was quite composed, but he had a haggard appearance, as if his cheeks and eyes had sunk deeper into his face. He sat down in the canvas chair. He said, slowly and gravely, as if considering every word, "Justin, I have to talk to you about your mother."

"She's dead, isn't she," I answered.

"Yes." He leaned forward, putting his elbows on his knees, and looking at me, and at something beyond me. Outside, the sound of firing was continuous, but it seemed remote from us, like something happening in another world. My father and I were in our own world, alone in that small room.

I said, "Perhaps we shall all be dead soon."

He looked at me in surprise, with a kind of poignant sorrow in his eyes and said, "Eh! Oh, you know that. Yes, of course you would."

He held out an arm, and I went to him, and he put his arm round me. We stayed there like that, him holding me close to him, for some seconds, without speaking. Then he gave a deep sigh, and said slowly, almost in a whisper, "She was the noblest woman that ever drew breath. She was the kindest friend and comrade that ever a man could have. She was my queen and my treasure."

When he said that I felt an unbearable heartache, and I began to weep, and my father wept too. It did not last long. My father rose abruptly.

"This will not do," he said sternly. "This is no time for private sorrow. There are other people to think of. I have to return to my post."

He put his hands on my shoulders, looking down at me.

"We all have to be men now, even the children—though God knows that's a hard enough thing to ask of any child."

"Has Mama gone to Heaven?" I asked.

"I don't know, Justin. I don't know where we go when we die. We'll find out in good time when we get there." He sighed again. "Your mother lived her life well and met her death bravely. Nobody can hope to do better than that. She may be somewhere now, watching the two of us. I don't know. I can only hope that sometime, some-where, I shall meet her again."

He raised me in his arms, till my face was on a level with his, and held me to him, and kissed me with unusual tenderness.

"I must leave you now. I'll be in and see you whenever I can."

He left. I sat on the edge of the charpoy, a miserable little boy. Mrs. McLeod and her children came back into the room, and Jeannie, crying, ran to me and put her thin arms round me. I began to cry again too, and Mrs. McLeod came and sat by me and held me close to her comfortingly. Lanky Ian shuffled about awkwardly, and then came to me shyly and pressed his favorite clasp knife into my hand. They were all very kind, and this, I think, was the real beginning of my friendship with them, which was to last a great many years.

That night, surprisingly, the enemy gunfire died suddenly away. All night long hardly a shot was fired. The silence seemed unnatural; our ears had become accustomed to the constant din. Unfamiliar sounds became clearly audible—the clack of voices in the passage outside our room, the tap of feet on stone floors. There was a lot of talk and whispering among the women in the Residency that night. It was known that the enemy was massing in great force all round the walls and parapets. The big attack was coming.

Shortly before dawn the chaplain came and spoke to Mrs. McLeod, and we all followed her to one of the upper rooms in the Residency. A lot of other women and children had collected there; a small gun had been mounted outside the door, commanding the staircase. Major Banks, one of the staff officers, came in and spoke to us briefly.

"I think you all know why you're here. It will be everybody's duty to remain calm, and stay under cover. There may be some hard fighting, but our defenses are now complete and our men are in good heart. With God's help we may be confident of the result."

Mrs. Barker, our neighbor, came to Mrs. McLeod and sat down on the floor by her.

"I'd give everything I have to be with my husband at his post," she said. "It's the women who have the heavy load to carry—the sitting and waiting."

"Yes," Mrs. McLeod said. "And our children with us."

The silence outside continued. The usual swarms of flies were buzzing about the room. Outside the building, all round the mile-long perimeter, men were lining the parapets. Among them were some of the wounded, who had left their hospital beds to swell the numbers of defenders. We waited, some of the women silent and motionless, others moving about restlessly. The children were agitated and uneasy; they kept asking questions.

A woman opened a Bible and, in a loud, clear voice, began to read. Other women gathered round her, some on their knees. When the first woman tired, another took up the reading.

Then came the attack. It began with the explosion of an enormous mine outside the defenses—a mine which, luckily, had not been tunneled deeply enough, and failed to breach the outer wall. Following the mine explosion, all the enemy artillery opened fire simultaneously; the air was full of crashing and banging. Then, yelling like madmen, and advancing to the music of a military band which was playing, of all things, "God save the Queen," the enemy closed in.

We could hear what was happening, but we could not see it. The noise was nightmarish, a hellish pandemonium that went on and on. Smoke drifted in over the bags of earth which half blocked the shattered windows. A faint haze spread through the room. The air was very hot. Women, sweaty and pale, sat, some with their eyes tightly shut; lips were bitten and fists were clenched. Jeannie thrust her fingers into her ears, and hid her face in her mother's lap. The woman who had first begun reading the Bible raised her voice and began singing "Jesus lover of my soul" and other women joined in. Soon every woman was singing. One hymn tune followed another.

After a while the noise of firing lessened and we could hear distant cheering. The hymn-singing stopped; the women looked at each other hopefully. A woman, standing on a chair, tried to look over the top of the sacks of earth which blocked most of the window.

"I can't see anything," she complained. "It's all smoky."

Major Banks entered the room, and the women all began crowding round him, asking questions. It was a few seconds before he could make himself heard.

"We've beaten them back. That's all I can tell you at the moment. All our posts are intact and our casualties seem to be slight. Theirs must have been enormous."

"Are they likely to attack again?" "Is my husband safe?" "How long shall we have to stay in here?" Questions were showered on him from every side.

"I can tell you no more. Yes, you must remain here for the present. We shall have to see what happens now."

Even while he was speaking the roar of firing was mounting again; it was to continue, with brief intervals of quiet, during the next four hours. Bloodily repulsed, the mutineers re-formed and came on again. And were repulsed again, and again.

At about four in the afternoon a blanket of exhaustion fell over the garrison and mutineers alike. Firing became rare and spasmodic, a mere occasional flurry of shots. The cries of the wounded, lying in heaps outside the defenses, were piteous.

At dusk, drained and exhausted ourselves, we returned to our little room, and an hour or so after dark my father came in to see us. He looked gaunt as a greyhound, black with grime, and stinking of sweat and burnt powder.

"What a day!" he said. He kissed me and grinned at the other children; his eyes were shining with a light of almost drunken exultation. "God of battles, what a day!" he repeated.

"Were our losses very heavy?" Mrs. McLeod asked.

"No. Very slight. Barely a round dozen, though by the end of it all half the men were fit to die of weariness." He sat down and went on, speaking in short, jerky sentences.

"The luck was with us. If that mine had done its work properly . . . but it didn't. Our defenses were not breached. But the enemy came on . . . by God, you should have seen them come . . . and our men were steady as rocks . . . magnificent . . . magnificent!" He broke off, laughing apologetically.

"I'm getting a bit carried away by my enthusiasm," he added. "All the same it was a great day, a truly wonderful day. We held them, and that may make a big difference to our futures—to the future of the whole country. For that we have to thank Sir Henry Lawrence."

"Will there be another battle tomorrow?" I asked.

"No. I wouldn't think so. Not tomorrow, nor for some days to come. If they have any military sense at all they'll not venture another major assault till they can find some way of breaching the defenses. And by that time, with any luck at all, we may be relieved."

"You think that probable?" Mrs. McLeod asked.

"I think it probable." My father turned back to me. "And what have you been doing with yourself all day?"

"We were in a room. A woman read the Bible till the noise stopped her. It was dull. I wish I'd been with you."

"I've no doubt you do. But fighting is not for women and children."

"Fighting, I take it, is a strictly grown-up male privilege," put in Mrs. McLeod a little acidly. "I hate it. What did all those men die for today? What good has it done to anybody?"

My father considered her, smiling, his eyes half closed.

"They died because the priests and leaders assured them that

[36]

God was on their side, and that if they were killed they would go straight to paradise," he answered. "I fought to defend this position, and to safeguard my child and the wives and children of other men. I am a simple soldier: I go where I am sent and fight when I must. But where would we be today without soldiers?"

"I should be in my own country, with my husband and children," Mrs. McLeod answered. "If we hadn't sent armies to this country in the first place, we shouldn't have to defend this position, and there'd be no need of fighting."

"True enough," agreed my father good-humoredly. "If we had no armies we should make no conquests, and anybody who wished could conquer us. And that is precisely why I am a soldier."

He paused for a moment. His smile broadened, and he added, "But that's a big lie, too. If you want the truth, I took the Queen's shilling because I wanted to get out of the village and see the world. For the same reason my brother James went away to the United States of America, and became an actor."

The day following the big assault was quiet. Both sides were tired. During the night the mutineers had removed most of their dead; the garrison lookouts had watched great cartloads of them being taken away.

The members of the garrison were elated by their victory, but it was a subdued elation. The general feeling, once the flare of triumph had died down, was expressed by Mrs. Barker, when she came in to visit us during the evening.

"Yes, we've beaten them off once," she said to Mrs. McLeod. "But what about the next time? They may have learned one or two lessons from yesterday."

"It's foolishness to attack a fortified position without first breaching the defenses," I observed with the parrot-like wisdom of seven. "My father said so."

"Thank you, Justin," Mrs. Barker said. "I'm glad to know that."

The next night, between midnight and dawn, a clever native spy, who had been sent out some days previously, slipped through the enemy lines and entered the Residency at a prearranged point. He was carrying a letter hidden inside a stick. At once, as soon as Colonel Inglis had read the letter, a ripple of excited talk began, which rose to a clamor as it widened, spreading outwards through all the rooms of the dark building. Candles were lit, and people clustered outside the rooms, in the passages, jabbering shrilly.

"What is it? Are they expecting another attack?"

"No, nothing like that. It's good news. Colonel Inglis has had a letter. We're going to be relieved."

"What! Is that true? It can't be. Has anybody seen the letter?"

"It is true. I had it from Dr. Fayrer himself; Colonel Inglis has sent him to give the news to the men in hospital. Listen . . . you can hear them cheering."

Mr. Harris, the chaplain, came along the passage, and women and half-asleep children thronged round him.

"Is it true, Mr. Harris? Are we really going to be relieved? When will they get here?" Half a dozen women were trying to question him at once.

"Yes, yes, it's quite true." Mr. Harris raised a hand for silence. The women's voices died away.

"Colonel Inglis has sent me to give you all the good news," Mr. Harris announced. "General Havelock's army has reoccupied Cawnpore. He will be marching on Lucknow immediately; we may expect his forces here within a few days."

A woman fainted. Another woman, clad in tattered rags and gaunt as an old she-wolf, was swaying to and fro hysterically, covering her child's face with kisses; the tears were streaming down her face. Some of the women were laughing. Mrs. McLeod, with Ian and Jeannie and me huddled up against her in the crush, was standing rigid as a post, staring at the chaplain.

"Is there . . . do you know if there is any other news from Cawnpore?" she asked. Talk stopped; there was a moment's almost shamefaced silence. Then another woman said, "Yes, what about the garrison of Cawnpore? Is there any news of them."

Mr. Harris shook his head very sadly.

"I'm afraid there is no good news of any of them," he said.

Mrs. McLeod sighed, and turned away, and took us back with her into the little room. Mr. Harris followed us in.

"I hardly know what to say; it's a dreadful thing when good and bad tidings come together. I wish with all my heart I could have brought you some good news of your husband. If there's anything I can do to help . . ."

"You're very kind, but there isn't," Mrs. McLeod answered. "I never really had any hope. And it seems so long since I saw Harry that it might all be part of another life. Everything then was so different. Perhaps things will be better soon. At least I still have my children."

"That is so. They will be a great comfort to you." Mr. Harris sighed.

In a grave and doleful voice, he added, "We must be grateful for any mercies vouchsafed to us in these terrible times."

He had given no details about the fate of the British in Cawnpore, but the sickening story was already known to members of Colonel Inglis's staff. Short of food and water, with many sick and wounded on his hands, General Wheeler, the Commanding Officer at Cawnpore, had agreed to surrender his weakly fortified position in exchange for safe conduct and river transport to Allahabad for himself and his garrison. These terms had not been honored. The garrison had marched out into an ambush in which most of the men and some of the women and children had been massacred immediately. The survivors, 125 women and children, had been shut in a small room and kept there for three weeks. Then on the approach of Havelock's army, they had been cut to pieces with butcher's knives and their bodies thrown down a well. Havelock's soldiers, entering the building, had found the room, with its blood-splashed walls and its floor littered with decomposing flesh and shreds of bloodstained clothing; they had themselves dragged the ghastly remains out of the well.

These events were known in Lucknow, and thin faces hardened savagely as men discussed, in low, muttering voices what they would like to do to any mutineers who might fall into their hands. Many of them had had friends or relatives in Cawnpore.

"I'd hang the lot of them—every one of them. And all the princes and headmen."

"Hanging's too good for those bloody swine. The filthy bloody swine. When I think of young Jim Tucker, and his missus . . . she was only a kid—just eighteen."

There were tears in men's eyes when they spoke of these things, but they were tears of rage.

The siege went on; the firing seemed to continue with an added fierceness. Feelings of hope and hatred animated the defenders. They were anxious to be relieved; they were almost as anxious to kill as many of the enemy as possible before the relief force arrived. Plans were made for a sortie to support the advance of Havelock's army when he reached the outskirts of the city. One dark night Unged, the spy, slipped quietly out of the defenses, and vanished in the direction of the enemy lines. In his hollow stick he carried plans and suggestions for the guidance of Havelock's advancing army.

The days passed. Every day men were killed; women and children died. The question now on everybody's lips was, "When will they come?" Tomorrow, or the day after, perhaps.

"Good heavens above, it's only forty-five miles to Cawnpore. If he left when he said he was leaving, he ought to be here *now*."

"We don't know when he left. And marching to Lucknow from Cawnpore isn't like taking a stroll in the country. I know Havelock, and if he's said he's coming to our relief, you can depend on it, he'll come."

Another dark night came, and Unged, the clever spy, slipped shadow-like through the enemy lines and entered the defenses carrying a letter. Colonel Inglis read this letter and then sent for his post commanders.

"Well, gentlemen, I have just heard from General Havelock. The news is not entirely favorable. General Havelock has won two victories, and reached a position about twenty miles from us. But more than a quarter of his men are down with cholera, he is running short of ammunition, and the enemy are in great strength. In the circumstances he has no alternative but to fall back on Cawnpore, taking his sick and wounded with him. He promises to advance again to our relief as soon as he receives reinforcements."

Colonel Inglis put the letter down on a table and looked round the circle of silent men.

"Thank you, gentlemen. That is all. You may return to your posts."

So the siege went on. The sound of firing was continuous, like waves on the shore. Sometimes it boomed and crashed in great stormy gusts; at other times it died to a mere sullen murmur.

In the Residency the women went about their duties, exchanging few words. Children played, wandering about in groups, dodging in and out of passages and doorways. Their voices were high-pitched but their faces were peaked, and their arms and legs were thin. Their mothers and guardians looked after them as best they could, but nobody exercised any very strict control over them any longer.

"The place is getting to be like a back street in Dublin on a summer night," my father observed, entering the room. "Children playing everywhere, and all the doors open."

"It's like a slum," Mrs. McLeod said. "The state the children are in—they're all in rags. But one can't stop them from playing. They must have a little exercise."

"Let them play and take what pleasure they can in it," my father agreed, smiling. "Let them do anything they want. It's little enough pleasure they have, the poor mites."

And little enough to look forward to, he might have added. During those days death was an ever-present thought in the minds of the garrison. Mothers, sad-eyed, looked at their children playing, and wondered how much longer they would be alive. Some were actually relieved when their children died; now they knew, for certain, that nothing worse could happen to them. Others, like Mrs. McLeod, had made up their minds to kill their children rather than let them fall into the hands of the enemy.

We played, we had lessons, we attended daily prayers, and Mrs. McLeod amused us by drawing pencil sketches in a drawing book. We listened to conversations among the grownups, and talked among ourselves. We knew that death was very close, and it seemed unimportant.

"My father says it'll take weeks for reinforcements to come. And p'raps they won't come. Then what'll we do?"

"Of course they'll come. General Havelock said so."

"But if they don't. My father wouldn't be surprised if General Havelock has his hands pretty full in Cawnpore."

"Then p'raps we shall all be killed. I saw a man killed yesterday. He just fell over and his hat fell off."

"If he only fell over, how do you know he was killed? How do you know he didn't only fall over?"

"Because he didn't get up."

I remember this snatch of conversation very well, because immediately after it, Ian said to me, "What happens to soldiers' muskets and swords when they're killed?"

"I dunno."

"There must be an awful lot of *spare* ones," Ian said. "And I don't s'pose anybody's using them. Why shouldn't we have some? Then we could fight."

This struck me as a very good idea. The same afternoon, while Mrs. McLeod was sleeping, we three children stole upstairs from our semi-basement and made our way out of the building. Nobody was about. The still, heavy heat of afternoon pressed down on everything. We could see trees, their trunks and branches splintered and stripped by gunfire, baking earth, and entrenchments and earthworks branching in various directions. A ragged fire was coming from somewhere in the near distance; it sounded half-hearted.

We began to thread our way along a trench; it was too deep for us to see over the top. "Where are we going?" asked Jeannie.

"I dunno," Ian confessed.

I said, "If we go on long enough we're bound to get somewhere."

"We don't want to walk into the enemy," Jeannie said.

"Don't be silly," Ian told her scornfully. "The enemy are all outside."

We went along a little way, till we came to a broken wooden case, lying in the trench. We stopped and examined this.

"It's only an old wooden box," Jeannie said.

"I can see that," Ian said, and then added, "If somebody stood on it, we could look over the top and see where we're going."

We propped the case against the side of the trench, and held it so that it would not wobble, while Ian got an insecure foothold on the top of it, and raised himself to look over the side of the trench. As his head emerged over the top, there was a sharp spat and a bit of earth flew. Ian jumped down quickly, and grinned in a slightly embarrassed fashion.

"Somebody shot at me," he said. "They missed."

"I think we ought to go back," Jeannie said. "Don't you, Justin?"

I rather agreed with her, but I could not possibly say so. So I said, "No," loudly, and then, "Come on."

We pushed on determinedly some way farther, and came to an intersection in two trenches. A wooden board had letters burned on it, with arrows pointing—Bailey Guard on one side, and Sago House and Cunliffe Post on the other. While we were looking at this board, three ragged and dirty figures approached us along the trench from the direction of the Bailey Guard. They were my father's friend, Lieutenant Aitken, with a couple of loyal Sepoys of the 13th Native Infantry.

"Hallo, hallo, hallo, what have we here?" Aitken said in a tone of amused surprise. "What the devil are you three young wanderers doing in this part of the country? Haven't you heard that this is forbidden territory?"

"We're looking for swords," I explained. "In case we have to fight." I pointed at the board. "The Cunliffe Post. That's where my father is."

"I'm on my way to see him," Aitken said. "I think you three youngsters had better fall in and follow me. This is obviously a matter that needs referring to higher authority."

He grinned at us, and then led the way at a quick pace; we straggled along after him. We passed a long line of defenses which seemed to be unmanned and then, some thirty or forty yards farther on, came suddenly on the post.

The main portion of the post consisted of a shattered bungalow, whose outer wall merged with the wall surrounding that part of the Residency grounds. The wall had been pierced with loopholes, and the parapet and firing step which had been built to reinforce it continued uninterrupted through the bungalow itself. The roof was in holes, with gaping timber showing; the side walls were pitted and crumbling. Around the bungalow, in the depression between the first and second (reserve) line of defenses, ragged pieces of canvas, supported by sticks, had been erected to give some kind of shelter from the sun and rain. Under these canvas coverings men were lying resting, while others, about a dozen at a time, manned the parapet and kept watch on the movements of the enemy. Blackened patches on the ground, and cooking utensils, showed where fires had been kindled and meals prepared.

As we entered the post, one of the men on the parapet fired; his comrade next to him fired a moment later. There was answering fire from the enemy lines. A few bullets thudded against the parapet, and one sang by, high overhead. Aitken raised his voice and shouted, "Meehawl! I've brought you some reinforcements."

"Eh!" My father thrust his head out from one of the canvas shelters. He was lying down, his hands on the ground, his head turned sideways to look up at us. "What the divvle . . ." he said, frowning, and then he crawled out from under the canvas and stood up.

"Where did you find this lot?" he asked. I was very relieved that he did not sound angry.

"Taking their afternoon constitutional," Aitken answered. "They seem to be on a foraging expedition. Looking for weapons."

"In case the mutineers come in and we have to fight," I explained.

Other soldiers were looking out from under their canvas shelters; grinning faces were turned in our direction. One of them was the face of my old acquaintance, Sergeant Mellish.

"Hi there, me young cockalorum," he said. "I see you're still on the active list. That was a fine drink you brought me."

"I'm glad you enjoyed it," I said.

My father laughed. He said, "Look after them for a few minutes, will you, Sergeant. I have to talk to Mr. Aitken; I'll be with you again very soon."

"Come into my bivvyiac, out of the sun," Sergeant Mellish invited. "I have one to meself, being a sergeant, and therefore commanding respect."

"It's because of the smell," said a voice from under another strip of canvas. "There's no decent private soldier can stomach the smell of a sergeant."

"I hear you, Tomlinson, you insubordinate dog," Sergeant Mellish said. "And don't think you won't pay heavily for that remark when we get back to some real soldiering." He grinned at us cheerfully, and made room for us under the canvas. "Not that any of us could be mistaken for a bed of roses," he added. "It comes from not having had any of our clothes off for twenty days."

"I s'pose you've been too busy fighting to undress," Ian suggested.

"We've been doing a bit of that, on and off. It's often a bit quiet about this time of day, but it'll wake up presently."

As if to confirm his words there was an outbreak of firing somewhere near at hand. We could hear the boom of cannon and the thud of shot striking the parapet.

"The Bailey Guard at it," explained Sergeant Mellish. "The enemy have a battery of eighteen-pounders over there." He pointed vaguely in a direction beyond the parapet. "They'll transfer their attention to us soon, I wouldn't doubt."

"Do they kill many people?" asked Ian.

"Not the eighteen-pounders—though they did put a shot clean through a loophole day before yesterday, and knocked a man's head off. What they do is to knock bits of parapet away, and we have the sweat of building it up again. It's Slippery Jim that's one of our principal worries here, in this post. If we could put that fella a couple of feet underground we'd all be happier for it."

"Who's Slippery Jim?" I asked.

"Enemy sniper; he's in one of the housetops. Wait a minute while I show you something. Just stay here and watch me."

He wriggled out of the bivouac, mounted the firing step, and raised his forage cap slowly on the end of his musket. As it cleared the top of the parapet, there came a crack from somewhere in the distance, and a bullet whistled by overhead. Sergeant Mellish lowered his cap; at the same time the men on either side of him fired. Sergeant Mellish jumped cheerfully down from the firing step and came back to us.

"He missed that time," he said. "But he doesn't often. That lad can shoot, I'll tell you."

More shots whizzed overhead and there was a succession of thuds as enemy guns opened on us. Earth spurted from the top of the parapet, making a man duck hastily; there was a crash as a heavy round shot hit the roof of the bungalow, sending chips of stone flying. From a nearby bivouac a voice was raised in protest.

"What did you want to do that for, Sergeant. Now you've gone and started a bleedin' war. And me dreaming 'appily of 'ome sweet 'ome."

"Some people are never happy," observed the Sergeant. "When they're at home they want to join the army, and once they're in the army they start crying for their homes. What's the matter with this. It's what you 'listed for, isn't it?"

"Wot I 'listed for? To be lousy, stinking, dirty, with no bleedin' 'baccy, lyin' under a scruffy bit of canvas in a 'eathen country, surrounded by 'owling budmashes. Blimey, Sergeant, if my best girl was to see me now she wouldn't know me."

"Get along with you, man. If your best girl was to see you now she'd never notice a bit of difference."

Some of the other soldiers laughed. My father and Aitken came out of the bungalow, talking; they seemed unaware of the small bombardment going on. At the entrance to the communication trench they paused for a moment, still talking. Then they parted, and Aitken and his two men made off in the direction of the Bailey Guard.

My father came towards us, and spoke to Sergeant Mellish.

"I want seven men at midnight, Sergeant. They're to assemble at the Bailey Gate, with another party of the 13th, under Mr. Aitken. He'll be in charge."

"Seven men—that'll be six and meself, sir. Is it Slippery Jim?"

"That's it. If we can find him at home we'll settle his activities for good. In any event, we want to blow up the house, so that he can't use that high roof as a sniper's post. If there seems to be any activity in that part of the enemy line, the operation will be canceled. To bring it off successfully, we must achieve complete surprise. Any ideas of your own, Sergeant?"

"M'm. No sir, I don't think so. I think we can bring it off. They're a dozy lot at night; those that aren't awake and shooting are generally asleep." He shook his head sadly. "It all comes from having no real officers."

"I don't think we'll grumble about it," said my father. He turned towards us. "And now what am I going to do with you three?"

That was what we were wondering. My father squatted on his haunches in the sunlight, his arms round his knees, and looked at us thoughtfully. His hard, handsome, rather hawklike features were deeply lined, with a network of wrinkles round the corners of his eyes; I noticed, for the first time that his hair was streaked with gray. His tattered tunic was open at the neck, displaying a patch of dark brown chest. He was not, apparently, wearing any kind of shirt under it. I remarked on this.

"Father, aren't you wearing a shirt?"

"It was crawling," he said. "I washed it, after a fashion, and hung it up, and somebody must have taken a liking to it. I'd already given all my other shirts to the hospital; they needed them." He grinned.

"Now the tunic's as bad. I pass the flame of a candle up and down the seams every night, but they don't mind that at all."

"Mrs. McLeod tried that with some of our clothes," I said with a certain amount of pride. "It didn't do any good. We're all lousy too."

"What! Even the women and children." My father, for the moment, looked astonished. "But why not?" he went on. "They're human after all, the same as the rest of us. Ah well." He rose. "I think we'll all go and have a word with Mrs. McLeod." He raised his voice. "Sergeant Mellish, will you take charge for a few minutes. I'll be back almost immediately."

Mrs. McLeod was angry. Her voice was shrill and complaining.

"This is very naughty of you—very naughty indeed. I've been searching for you everywhere." She turned to my father helplessly. "The children are getting quite out of hand—not only these three. All of them."

"I know that. There've been others wandering around the grounds, finding their ways to the defense posts. But it's in the nature of children to be naughty, and they should be well beaten for it. I'd attend to it myself if I had the time."

He leaned back in the canvas chair, putting his hands behind his head, and went on, slowly, "All the same, when I think about it, I believe I'd just as lief have Justin with me at the post as cooped up inside here. How would you feel about your own children?"

"But . . . what if there's another big attack?"

"There will be," my father said quietly. "That's one thing that's quite certain."

"And you prefer to have Justin with you, rather than leave him with the women. In other words you think . . ." Mrs. McLeod broke off without saying what she thought.

"We'll be all right so long as they don't breach the defenses," I put in. "And if they do that, nobody'll be all right. I expect we'll all be killed."

My father gave me a sidelong glance and a brief smile.

"You watch it, boy," he said. "The way you talk you'll find yourself a soldier in a red coat some day, if you're not careful."

"I *am* going to be a soldier," I asserted.

"I think I understand you, Captain Kelly," Mrs. McLeod said. "If . . . if my children are allowed to visit your post, shall I be permitted to accompany them?"

"That was what I had in mind. You will not be the only ones. There are other women and children at other posts. It is against standing orders, but . . ." My father broke off, smiling again. "Colonel Inglis has very fine eyesight. On his rounds he notices everything which is essential for the defense of the position. Provided that the children are strictly controlled and not hindering efficiency, I imagine that they will escape his observation."

He rose, and looked at each of us in turn.

"They will have to obey orders without argument," he said. "And no playing the fool, or wandering about on their own. That will not be tolerated for one moment." He paused for a moment to let this sink in. "I shall expect you in the morning when you care to come. I think you had all better return here every night."

"Shall we be allowed to fight?" I asked eagerly, when my father had gone. "And shall we have to have lessons?"

"No, you will not be allowed to fight. You will do nothing at all without permission. And you will have to have lessons," Mrs. McLeod answered grimly. In a slightly softer voice she added: "You'll have to be given something to do to keep you occupied."

Chapter 6

"DID you kill Slippery Jim?" I asked.

"I don't know. We killed several of them, and blew up the house."
My father's voice was curt and subdued; there was no smile on his
lips. He turned to Mrs. McLeod. "I've arranged a place for you; it's
the best I can manage. You won't find it luxurious."

"I don't think we're likely to be very particular," Mrs. McLeod
said.

She was looking round her attentively, with frank curiosity. The
post was quiet. A dozen or so men were manning the firing step;
the remainder were under their bivouacs. No grinning faces were
thrust from under the canvas to greet us. I had a feeling of disappointment. Everything seemed unexpectedly dull and flat.

"Here you are," my father said. "This is your place."

Our place was a kind of rough lean-to made of pieces of timber
propped against the inner wall of the bungalow and reinforced with
earth. Immediately outside the entrance a piece of canvas had been
stretched, one end secured to the wall of the bungalow, the other
end supported on two sticks.

"You can sit outside when it's quiet, and go in when things are
lively," my father explained.

There was just room for the four of us in the lean-to; it smelt hot
and earthy. "We shan't be able to have lessons in here," Ian said.
"It's too dark."

"We shall have lessons outside, when it's quiet," Mrs. McLeod said
firmly. "I take it that this is what you call quiet, Captain Kelly."

"Yes, it's quiet enough now. You'll soon know when things liven
up."

"You can hear the cannon balls and the bullets," I said. I added,
"Where's Sergeant Mellish?"

"Sergeant Mellish was killed last night," my father said in a flat,
unemotional voice. "He was a good man. We shall miss him."

"He was the best bloody sergeant in the whole flamin' regiment,"
a voice said from under one of the bivouacs.

"That's enough, Tomlinson. Be silent, sir," my father said sternly.

[48]

"Was it . . . when he was blowing up Slippery Jim's house?" I asked in a whisper.

"No." My father's voice sounded tired. "He came back from that all right. It was afterwards. An enemy shell set fire to something in the bungalow roof; the light of the flames showed up our men working on the parapet. Sergeant Mellish climbed on to the roof to put them out. He was shot through the head."

He was silent, and we were silent for several seconds. Then he spoke matter-of-factly to Mrs. McLeod.

"I leave the children in your charge," he said.

That was our initiation into our new life at the Cunliffe Post. We soon fell into the way of things there. At that time the garrison, reduced by casualties and sickness to fewer than half its original numbers, was simply intent on holding on. Fewer than a thousand men, with some thirty guns, were surrounded by the rebel army of fifty thousand, with 150 guns.

By day about a third of the men, in turn, manned the firing step, while the others rested. At night, under cover of the darkness, the work of strengthening the defenses went on, rations were drawn, the dead were buried. Every night we returned to our little room.

We slept a lot, as everybody did during the long afternoons. There were no lessons; Mrs. McLeod abandoned the attempt to give them to us after the first two days. She did a lot of sketching of the post and its garrison. Her pictures were passed from hand to hand among the soldiers and admired greatly. Sometimes, when he was in the mood, my father would join us, squatting on his haunches, and tell us his stories of old Ireland; and when he did this a circle would form of men squatting or lying on their stomachs, listening with delighted attention to the exploits of Diarmuid or Cuchulain. We were very friendly with the soldiers, who made pets of us and allowed us to clean their muskets, though some of their language shocked Mrs. McLeod. She spoke to my father about it.

"Some of the men can hardly speak a sentence without blaspheming or uttering obscenities. It isn't very nice in front of the children."

"Ah, it won't hurt the children to hear a little rough language; it's a rough life they're living." My father smiled. "You must understand that in times of difficulty blaspheming comes as natural to soldiers as hymn-singing does to women, and it has very much the same effect. It relieves their feelings."

"But if the children ever go into respectable company again . . ."

"They'll never go into more respectable company than they're in at this post. More elegant, possibly, but certainly not more worthy of respect."

Mrs. McLeod compressed her lips slightly.

"I'm not saying anything against the men. I'll admit they have excellent qualities . . ."

"They have. And what more could anybody ask of them at this time, and in this place?" said my father, closing the discussion.

One morning, when we arrived, we found the whole post astir. The bivouacs were empty. Nearly all the men were up on the firing step; every loophole was manned. Some of the men had two, many had three muskets beside them. We could see no sign of my father. Private Tomlinson called to us from the firing step.

"Better take cover, mum, you and the nippers. Things look like getting a bit lively before we're all much older."

"What is it? Are you expecting an attack?"

My father's voice called to us. We hadn't seen him because he was well above our heads, lying on the remains of the bungalow roof, with a telescope in his hand.

"Yes, get the children under cover and keep them there. Don't come out without orders."

"Come, children," Mrs. McLeod said.

We sat in our dark lean-to, excited and a little frightened. Outside there was a silence. Nobody was firing. Once we heard brisk voices; we recognized the voice of Colonel Inglis, the garrison commander.

"Captain Kelly. . . . Ah, there you are, Captain. Your men are all ready; I needn't ask that."

"Ready for anything, sir."

"Have you a good view of their dispositions? What do you see from up there?"

"They're still moving guns, sir. They've brought up another battery of eighteen-pounders and large bodies of men are forming up between the Kaiser Bagh and the old Mess House. It looks to me as if we can expect the main assault between Sago's House and the Bailey Gate."

"There's another large force assembling round the Machi Bhawan," Colonel Inglis told him. "I rather fancy we may expect heavy attacks on two sides of our position. I have a small reserve, but I don't want to use it except in the most serious emergency. Once it is committed I have no other reserves. You understand, Captain."

"Perfectly, sir. So far as this post is concerned, I'm sure we shall manage very nicely on our own," my father said cheerfully.

[50]

"I'm sure of it. I'm depending on it. Good luck to you all," Colonel Inglis said. The men on the firing step raised a cheer as he walked away.

"I hope we shall have something to cheer about when this day's work is finished," said Mrs. McLeod.

My father, kneeling, put his head through the opening into the lean-to.

"Are you all right in here?"

"I imagine you know more about that than we do," Mrs. McLeod answered in a rather bad-tempered voice. "How long do you think this will last?"

"It's impossible to say. You can go back into the Residency if you wish; there's still time." My father reached an arm into the lean-to and gripped my shoulder. "You'll remain here, Justin. I'd like to keep you near me."

"We've no intention of returning to the Residency," Mrs. McLeod said coldly. "If . . ." She broke off and added, "We shall take our chance here."

There was a silence, while my father seemed to be trying to think of something to say. His hand gripped my shoulder. He said, "Well . . ." and broke off, and then added quickly and awkwardly, "Good-by, Justin boy—till we meet again."

He was gone, but I still felt the pressure of his rough, powerful hand on my shoulder. I had a tight sensation in my throat and a smarting in my eyes; I had to sniff and blink to stop myself from crying.

"We must be brave and patient," Mrs. McLeod said in a tone of savage irony. She caught her breath in a half-sob and added, "Oh God, how much longer will this senseless slaughter continue? When will men learn to leave one another at peace?"

We were silent in the stuffy heat, with the sweat trickling down our bodies. We were children, with a heavy load of grown-up knowledge on our young shoulders; we knew that we might all be dead before the evening. Worse than this, emphasizing the closeness of death, was our awareness that our parents had brought us to the post to insure that we should be killed, rather than captured, if the enemy carried the position. We knew this, and we knew the reason for it. We knew what had happened to the captives at Cawnpore.

A great rumble and blast of horrific sound rose suddenly all round us. We seemed to be in the middle of it. The ground on which we were sitting shook; the timbers of the lean-to sprang apart, and earth began to shower down on our heads and shoulders. From outside came a sound of loud, urgent shouting.

On hands and knees, in frantic haste, we began to crawl out of the lean-to; we had to scrabble our way through fallen earth which partially blocked the entrance. We emerged from semi-darkness into bright sunshine which shone on a scene of wreckage. One side wall of the bungalow had collapsed entirely, the remains of the roof had fallen in, and for a distance of about fifteen yards on one side of the bungalow, the parapet had vanished. Where it had stood was a deep crater, with smoke and dust rising from it.

The men had deserted the firestep, and were swarming like ants over the ruins of the bungalow. From somewhere in the debris a hand came out, and a soldier grasped it, and pulled, and my father rose slowly out of the wreckage. He was cursing luridly, and covered with dust; it was in his mustache, his hair, and all over his uniform. His right hand still grasped a broken telescope.

Near the edge of the mine crater three men were lying, one of them partly buried. Only his booted legs were sticking out. Another, on his hands and knees was crawling painfully away, one leg dragging. Mrs. McLeod gave a little cry, and ran to him. We children didn't know what to do, so we stayed solemnly, round-eyed, where we were. Through the jagged gap in the parapet we could see a clear space of about fifty yards across, and beyond that a space crisscrossed with crumbling walls and ruins of houses, none of them more than three or four feet high, and still farther off, perhaps two hundred yards away, the taller, unblown-up buildings lining the narrow streets which led into the depths of the town. These distant streets were jammed full of men, waiting.

My father began to shout orders.

"Jones, and you, Tomlinson, take all the dead and wounded into the reserve trench. Mrs. McLeod, ma'am, I'm going to ask you to take temporary charge of the wounded. You children go with Mrs. McLeod. Now men, we've got to get to work, quickly; we've got to build up some kind of a defense. Come on, all of you, let me see you put your backs into it."

He set the example himself by lifting a huge piece of fallen masonry and plonking it down on the inward edge of the crater. The men worked, their muskets left unattended on the firing step. Some shoveled earth, others brought pieces of stone, an old door, wooden cases filled with earth, anything they could lay their hands on, building up a low wall round the edge of the crater. In the town a gun fired, and then another, and the great thudding and crashing began which we remembered from the previous attack. It seemed that every gun in Lucknow was firing on the defenses, and their fire was badly directed. Instead of being concentrated in overwhelming force on the breach, it was dispersed over the whole length of the defenses.

"This isn't going to hurt us, men," my father shouted cheerfully. "The longer they keep it up, the better. The bloody fools don't know their business. We'll make a point of teaching them."

"Don't stand staring, children," Mrs. McLeod ordered urgently and sharply, and Private Tomlinson said, "Come along, you kids. This way with you." He and another soldier hustled us into a reserve trench; they carried two wounded men in to join us. One was the man we had seen crawling, with the broken leg. The other, unconscious and breathing stertorously, seemed to have half his face and lower jaw smashed in. His neck and the top of his tunic were a sticky mess of blood. We looked; we could not help it, except for Jeannie, who shrank away, covering her face with her hands.

"What am I to do?" Mrs. McLeod demanded despairingly. "I haven't any bandages—nothing."

"You'll 'ave to do the best you can," Private Tomlinson answered abruptly. He and the other man ran back to join the men at the mine crater. The man with the broken leg said feebly, "Don't worry, ma'am; it's all in the day's work." He closed his eyes.

Mrs. McLeod stood for a moment looking utterly helpless. Then, with an expression of grim determination on her face, she raised her skirt and began to pull down her petticoat. "I've got to get some bandages from somewhere," she said. Tugging fiercely, she ripped the petticoat into strips, and approached the man with the head wound.

His mouth hung half open, and his eyes were open, but only the whites of them were visible. He had stopped breathing. As Mrs. McLeod bent over him, four or five flies rose from his bloody face and neck, making her recoil. The man with the broken leg opened his eyes.

"I think he's a goner," he said.

"Oh . . . you mean he's dead. Yes, I . . . I believe he is," Mrs. McLeod said. She looked rather sick.

Three women and two Indian orderlies entered the trench hurriedly, coming from the direction of the Bailey Gate. Their leader was a tall, gaunt woman with white hair and an air of command. She said, "I believe you have wounded here—I see you have. What's that you have in your hand?"

"My petticoat. I was going to use it for bandages . . ."

"We can use it." The woman took the strips of petticoat from Mrs. McLeod's hand, and turned and bent over the dead man. "H'm," she said, and turned from him to the man with the broken leg. "What's wrong with you, my man?"

"It's me leg, matron." The man evidently knew her.

"Let me look. I'll have that medical roll please, orderly."

One of the Indians laid out a role of medical supplies on the floor of the trench. The three women bent down by the wounded man; we heard him gasp, and groan loudly, and one of the women said, "Hold on to my arm. It'll soon be over." Bullets were whistling overhead, and we could hear the constant thud of guns, but we seemed to be away from it in that trench, in a little world of our own. The women rose.

"That's all we can do for you now; we have to go on to the next post," the matron said. "Stay where you are till you're fetched and don't move that leg more than you can help."

Her words were very clearly audible; the sound of cannonading was gradually dying down. From the parapet my father's voice sounded harshly, "Ah, they're coming. On to the firing step, men; man your positions. And wait for it; don't start blazing away. Wait for the order to fire."

From the direction of the city we could hear a wild, high yelling. We all stood, waiting, looking at each other; from our position in the trench we could see nothing of what was happening. I think we all felt we had to see, to know. It was the matron herself who made the first move, edging a few paces out of the trench to a position where she could see the gap in the parapet. We followed her, clustering behind her, peering cautiously as if looking at something forbidden.

Looking outwards through the gap in the parapet, we could see the enemy—long columns of them, with bayonets gleaming and colors flying, emerging from every street facing the position. They came at a kind of trot, uttering a long, high-pitched screaming; but as they met obstacles in the no man's land of rubble and blown-up houses outside the town, the columns broke up, splitting in swirls round different sides of the various obstacles, so that as they came closer they were no longer in columns, but in a vast, irregular wave of men, streaming towards the whole line of defenses. Many of them were firing as they ran; the noise of the firing mingled with the shouting.

On the firestep, our men were standing, but behind the flimsy wall of wood, and earth, and stones which had been thrown round the rim of the mine crater, they were lying down, their muskets cuddled into their shoulders. They were motionless and silent. The great

wave of dark faces and bright uniforms surged on, coming closer
. . . closer . . . and then the front rank seemed to falter and hesitate
for a moment, but only for a moment: the pressure from behind was
forcing it on. We could see the dark faces, the wide-open mouths.

From the left came a crash of firing; the Bailey Guard was engaged. My father, lying behind the low wall, raised himself slightly
and opened his mouth wide in an enormous shout.

"Now men, let 'em have it. Fire."

The crash of the muskets, only a few yards in front of us, was
almost deafeningly loud. In the enemy ranks we saw men stagger
and fall, dropping muskets and scaling ladders; other men tripped
over them. A bright green standard dipped in a dead hand, and
was snatched up again. The dark wave still came on. Another volley
crashed, and men fell and were trampled on; the wave simply swept
over them. Smoke drifted in the bright sunshine. Then my father
and the men with him were on their feet as a press of mutineers
went down into the mine crater, and came up again to attack the
low wall. I saw my father fighting, his tall figure dominating the
breach, his sword rising and falling with remorseless efficiency, with
all the power of his great arms and shoulders behind every cut and
thrust. A man screamed with my father's sword point in his throat,
and the scream stopped suddenly as he toppled backwards, and the
next man received a slashing cut across the neck, and he too toppled; and beside him, my father's men were thrusting, and with-
drawing, and thrusting again with cold and scientific savagery; their
bayonets were well bloodied. Inside a couple of minutes the bottom
of the mine crater was full of dead bodies and writhing men.

And then no more came. The great wave which had surged up
against the defenses had broken and spent its force, and now it was
receding. All along the parapet men were cheering as they went on
firing into the backs of the retreating enemy. A man on horseback
rode furiously among them, haranguing them, striking at them with
his sword, pointing towards the defenses. A bullet hit him, and he
fell from his horse, which galloped away, riderless. In the no man's
land outside the defenses, the enemy dead were lying sprawled;
there were a lot of them. A few wounded men, on hands and knees,
were trying to crawl away in the direction of the town. The sound
of firing lessened.

"Well done, men," my father shouted in his great ringing voice.
"By God, you're a fine lot of fighting villains. 'Tis a pleasure to command you." The men on the parapet turned their heads to grin at
him.

"Horrible. Horrible . . . !" Mrs. McLeod said in a voice that was near to tears. The hospital matron turned to look at her.

"Horrible . . . ! You may think so, but it would have been a good deal more horrible if they'd broken in. Have you forgotten Cawnpore?" she asked harshly. In a slightly kinder voice, she added, "You had better look after your children. Take them back into the trench; they shouldn't be in this exposed position. In fact neither they nor you should be here at all."

"I forget nothing. My husband was in Cawnpore. And I still think all this slaughter is senseless and horrible," Mrs. McLeod answered angrily.

My father turned his head and caught sight of us. He came quickly towards us.

"What are you people doing standing here? Exposing yourselves unnecessarily." As if to lend force to his words, a bullet sang overhead. He went on. "Back with you into that trench, and stay there."

"There are far too many children wandering about and nobody seems to have any control over them at all," the matron complained.

"Do you think so?" my father said politely.

He accompanied us back into the trench. Somebody had covered the dead man with a blanket. The wounded man was where we had left him, sitting with his back to the side of the trench, his legs stretched out in front of him. His eyes had a fevered look.

"How is it with you, Polgenny?" my father asked. "We'll be getting you to the hospital in a minute, while the lull lasts."

"I'm all right sir, except for me leg. I can't seem to stand on it." The man smiled faintly. "They showed us the back seams of their coats, did they, sir?"

"Yes, we beat them back very handsomely."

"If you've no more wounded here, Captain, we'll go on to the next post," the matron said. "You'll send this man to the hospital as soon as possible, will you."

"It will be attended to at once. And thank you for what you've done."

The matron and her party moved away in the direction of the next post. My father turned to us.

"Now I must leave you, and you're to stay here, in this entrenchment. You're not to stir from it: that is an order. It's likely there'll be another attack in an hour, or maybe two hours, and I want the assurance that you'll be under cover. Mrs. McLeod, this will be your responsibility."

"I'll see to it they don't wander," Mrs. McLeod promised.

"It's for your own safety, and my peace of mind." My father smiled, the sternness gone from his haggard, dirty face. "Nobody but a fool exposes himself unnecessarily," he added. "Sensible men use their brains for thinking, not for stopping lead bullets."

My father returned to his men. In a few seconds a very large soldier entered the trench, and smiled at us, and at Polgenny.

"Well mate, feel like a bit of a ride? I've come to take you away."

"Are you going to carry him?" Mrs. McLeod asked.

"That's it, ma'am. Pick-a-back's the style. Now we'll just lift you . . . hup you come . . . arms round my neck . . . that's the ticket . . . hup again . . . and away we go."

Carrying Polgenny pick-a-back, the big soldier trudged away.

We were alone in the trench except for the dead man. The sun burned brightly, and there was no shelter from it. We lay inert on the hot reddish earth, all the energy drained out of us. A continuous sound of firing went on, rising and falling; most of it seemed to be coming from the enemy. Occasionally a ball thudded near us, and we saw dust rising. Once we caught a glimpse of a young officer and four Sikhs, manhandling a small gun past the end of the trench. Soon after midday a soldier brought us some rations—a few morsels of tough salted beef, some hard biscuits, some cold tea. We were glad of the tea.

Early in the afternoon the mutineers made their second attack. It followed the same pattern as the first, beginning with a great clamor of artillery fire, which died away as the enemy columns issued from the town and advanced across no man's land to the defenses. Crouched in our trench, we could hear all the sounds of violent battle, but we could see nothing except the earth on each side of us. A few yards away from us volleys crashed, and men screamed and shouted and fought; we were only separated from it by a wall of earth. We sat, tense, still, rigid with nervous agony, waiting . . . waiting . . . longing for it to stop . . . and it seemed to go on and on and on. Would it never stop?

Then the noise died down. The sound of screaming receded. Mingled with the firing, we could hear cheering. We knew what that meant. Mrs. McLeod gave a deep, long sigh, and breathed the words, "Thank God." I rose to my feet and began to dance about like a madman.

"We've won. We've beaten them back. We've beaten them back," I shouted excitedly.

Two filthy and exhausted men staggered into the trench, carrying another man between them. They laid the other man down on the floor of the trench. He was my father.

His eyes were half open, with a look of pain in them; his two hands were clasped tightly to his left side. One of the men knelt by him and tried to prise his hands away; my father shook his head.

"No, Tomlinson, it's no good. If I let go half my guts will come out." Tomlinson was crying; his tears fell on my father's hands. My father said, "Eh, what's this? Leave me, man; get back to your post. There's work to be done."

I said, "Father!" in a squeaky, terrified voice. He turned his head slowly, as if with an immense effort, to look at me.

"Justin, boy. Justin." His lips writhed in a pitiful attempt at a smile. "It can't be helped, lad. Soldier's luck. Has to happen to every-body sometime."

"Father . . ." I blubbered.

"Take it easy, son. Easy does it." He turned his head to look at Mrs. McLeod. His voice was feeble.

"There's papers at the lawyers—Doyle and Ballinger of Dublin—some money. Justin should be sent to my brother James in Chicago. You'll attend to it."

"I'll attend to it. Is there nothing that can be done for you? Are you sure of that?"

"Sure enough. I'm for the long journey. Soon, maybe, I'll dis-cover . . ." My father turned his head again to look at me, and took a hand from his side, and reached out, and took my hand and pressed it. His hand was slippery with his own blood.

"Justin, boy . . ." he said sadly. His grip on my hand relaxed, and his head drooped sideways. Mrs. McLeod drew me gently away. I buried my face in her chest and began sobbing wildly.

He was buried that night with the other casualties of the day's fighting. Six feet one inch of Michael Kelly, the bold, talkative, kindly Irish fighting man, splendid in his strength and vigor, had been snuffed out like a light in a puff of cold wind, and was laid away in darkness, to the accompaniment of a brief, muttered ritual, under a foot of Lucknow earth.

We stayed in our little room. People came in to see me—Colonel Inglis, Mr. Harris, Lieutenant Aitken. They said kind words about my father, praising his qualities highly: they told me I must be brave, as he would have wished me to be. Their words meant nothing to me; I didn't want to hear them. Like a bereaved puppy, all I wanted was to sit in a corner and howl.

"Try to eat something, Justin."

"I'm not hungry."

"You must try to eat something. It's bad for you to go without food." I stared sullenly at my plate. Mrs. McLeod went on. "We must all try to help each other in these dreadful times. It worries us when you won't eat your food. We're afraid you may fall sick, and be taken away to the hospital."

"I'm terribly worried about Justin," Jeannie said. "When I see him sitting there not eating, it makes me want to cry."

Reluctantly, I began to eat the unpalatable food, and found I was quite hungry.

The days went by. Like urchins the children played in the Residency grounds. It was impossible to prevent them. A few were killed and wounded, but most of us developed the grown-up sense to choose fairly sheltered places for our games, and to duck quickly for cover when the firing became heavy. One place we never visited was the Cunliffe Post. We kept away from that.

The rains came, drenching everything, and when the sun shone the ground gave off a damp, steamy vapor, heavy with the smell of decay and death. The numbers of the sick increased; every night the gravediggers were busy. Early in September the enemy made another full-scale attack. Once more the tattered scarecrows, lining the defenses, fought them and fought them, and finally hurled them back. But it couldn't go on very much longer. Everybody knew it couldn't go on very much longer. Clearly a day was coming when there would not be enough men left to line the defenses.

"Yes, we've beaten them off again," Mrs. Barker said wearily. "And I suppose we may do it again—till one day we shan't beat them back. Perhaps that will be a good thing. Often I can't help wishing it was all over."

"You mustn't think like that," Mrs. McLeod said mechanically.

"Mustn't I?" Mrs. Barker laughed bitterly. "Can you control your thoughts?" She shrugged thin shoulders and went on, "I get tired of dying. Since this siege began I've died at least a dozen times. I feel that's almost too much to ask."

"I know. But we must keep on while we can. We have to think of our children."

"They aren't children. Most of them are more like old men and women. If we ever get out of this—*if* we get out of it, how are they going to fit in with other children? The dear little innocents with their ringlets and their sweetly pretty dresses whom they'll meet playing musical chairs at the vicarage Christmas party."

"They'll soon slip back into the old ways. Children quickly forget."

"Anybody who can quickly forget this place will need to have a damned bad memory," Mrs. Barker said harshly.

"She swore," Jeannie said when Mrs. Barker had left the room.

"She only said damned. That's nothing. I know a lot worse words than that," Ian stated patronizingly.

"Then you're not to use them," Mrs. McLeod said sharply. "It's dreadful to hear children use bad language; it's dreadful to hear anybody use it. I'm talking to you too, Justin."

"I never swear in front of women," I said. "Only in front of men. That's different."

"You must learn never to swear at all. No man who calls himself a gentleman . . ." She broke off, afraid, I think, that what she was about to say might be taken as a reflection on my father. "It's a silly habit," she said.

A day or two later, Jeannie was languid and drooping in the morning, and later in the day took to her bed with her cheeks flushed and her eyes unnaturally bright; she had long attacks of violent shivering. Dr. Fayrer, who came in to see her, diagnosed her complaint as a "low fever" or "ague" which was not contagious.

"Then she can stay in here? I can nurse her myself?" Mrs. McLeod asked.

"Yes. Yes, I think so. In fact, if you feel capable of it, I would prefer it. Our hospital accommodation is very overcrowded."

Jeannie became worse. The fever increased. For hours she lay tossing restlessly on the narrow charpoy, and nothing could be done for her. Sometimes she went away into a queer, delirious dream world of her own, muttering about hills and fields she had seen in a picture book, and looking at us without recognition. Once, in the night, I heard her singing in a queer cracked voice some old Scottish songs which her mother had taught her.

For three or four nights Mrs. McLeod hardly slept at all. She looked like a woman of seventy. Ian and I, subdued and unhappy, stayed in the room. Mrs. McLeod urged us to go out and join the other children, but we had no heart to go. We couldn't leave Jeannie. And she didn't want us to leave her. Even when she didn't seem aware of our presence, she at once noticed our absence.

"Justin, where are you? Don't go away, Justin. Don't leave me."

"I'm here, Jeannie."

"Come and sit by me. I want to be able to see you."

But when I sat by her, she didn't seem to know I was there.

On the fifth night she lay silent and weak, one wasted arm hanging over the edge of the charpoy. That night we all felt that the end could not be far away. Life was slowly leaving her. Lying on my charpoy in the hot room, lit by a shaded candle, I stirred restlessly, unable to sleep for misery. Occasionally I could see Mrs. McLeod, a dark shadow, bending anxiously over Jeannie.

Quite suddenly Jeannie began talking excitedly, pushing herself up to a sitting position, laughing. She stretched out a thin arm towards me and said in a high shrill voice, "Justin, Mama, they're coming. Do you hear them?"

Mrs. McLeod went quickly to her, and urged her back on to the pillow.

"Lie down, darling, and rest. There's nobody coming."

"But I hear them . . . the pipes. And I can see. There's a man on a white horse."

She spoke with such assurance that I sat up and listened, half expecting to hear the squeal of pipes. All I heard was the sound of desultory firing.

"Lie down, dear," Mrs. McLeod urged. She held a glass to Jeannie's lips. "Drink this, and then lie down and go to sleep. You'll be better in the morning."

But we didn't believe that, and she didn't believe it herself.

"I'll lie down, and I'll sleep," Jeannie said with a kind of exultation. "Now I know they're coming, I shall sleep fine." She laid her tired, sandy head on the pillow, and sank immediately into sleep.

She was still asleep when Dr. Fayrer came early in the morning. He bent over her, putting his hands on her forehead.

"Well . . . I really believe the child's better. The fever has certainly subsided."

His touch woke Jeannie. She opened her eyes and smiled up at him.

"I'll be fine now," she said in a weak, confident voice. "I'll want to be well when the Highlanders are here."

"When the . . . ?" Dr. Fayrer stared at her.

"Jeannie had a dream that the Highlanders were coming," Mrs. McLeod explained.

"But . . ." Dr. Fayrer said in an incredulous tone, staring at Jeannie. "Well, I'll be . . ." He suddenly laughed. "This is really extraordinary." He held up a hand and added mysteriously, "Listen. Tell me if you hear anything."

We listened. We heard firing from the parapet. There was a lull, and we heard something else—a low, distant, grumbling sound.

"You hear it, do you," Dr. Fayrer said joyfully. "Unged slipped into the lines shortly before dawn—nearly lost his life, poor fellow. The mutineers fired on him, and our sentries fired on him before he could establish his identity. He brought great news. Brave Havelock and gallant Outram, with a relief force, are scarcely twelve miles away. That sound you can hear is their guns."

Relief. Oh, the heavenly word, bringing luster back into dull eyes and up-tilting in smiles the corners of woefully drooping lips. The end of the siege. The end of the flies—those horrible flies crawling over everything—and of the noise, and the filth, and the nightly fatigue of burying the dead.

The joy and hope, and also the anxiety. Could Havelock and Outram do it? Doubts were expressed. The relief army would have to come from Cawnpore, and it was known that in the approach to the town, facing the Cawnpore Road, the mutineers had built up immensely strong fortifications, bristling with guns. From lookouts on the parapet, they could be seen strengthening these fortifications. Guns which had been pointed towards the Residency were now pointing away from it.

All day there was a lull in the fighting immediately surrounding the Residency. But, in the distance, the sound of firing went on, growing slowly, very slowly, louder. All through the night it continued. When morning came, it was insistent, a loud, steady hammering. Looking from the Residency, we could see the smoke and flame of battle smudging the morning air about a mile distant, in the direction of the Cawnpore Road.

An intense excitement gripped the whole garrison. Children were running about wildly, shouting "Hooray, hooray." Ian and I slipped away from the little room without any difficulty. Jeannie was sleeping peacefully—she was getting better—and Mrs. McLeod, exhausted by long watching, was also sleeping.

That morning emaciated men, their limbs wrapped in bandages, came staggering and limping out of the hospital to take their places on the parapet. No persuasions could stop them. Women and children made their ways to the various posts. Every gun in the Residency grounds was firing, every man who could handle a musket was at a loophole, all firing into the town to keep the mutineers engaged and lend support to the relief army. Anxious eyes peered out through drifting smoke, trying to follow the progress of the battle.

Elation gave way to anxiety as the sound of distant firing seemed to die away. In the town the enemy were shouting hoarsely; their voices held a note of triumph. All the housetops were crowded with riflemen, but few of them were shooting at us. Their fire was directed away from us, towards the east.

Ian and I joined Mrs. Barker and another woman near the Bailey Gate.

"What's happening?" we demanded. "Have you seen any of our soldiers?" We had to shout to make ourselves heard.

"I don't know what's happening. Nobody knows. Here, come over here, you little fool, behind this wall. Do you want to be shot?"

We squatted with the two women in the shelter of a low wall just outside the hospital, not far from the tall arch of the gate. A man climbed up the brickwork of the gate and stood upright on the flat top over the arch, exposing himself recklessly. But many men exposed themselves recklessly that day; some paid the penalty for it.

The man climbed down unscathed and other men clustered round him to hear what he was saying. The word was passed from mouth to mouth.

"There's a devil of a fight going on all round the Begum's Palace."

"The Begum's Palace? But that's away over to the east, entirely in the wrong direction."

"Yes, me boy. We were expecting the attack from the south, and so were the enemy. Outram and Havelock must have marched their men the best part of five miles round the enemy's main defensive position, and they're coming in from the east. The enemy are changing their dispositions as quickly as they can move."

The fighting increased in fury. We could follow its progress by watching the puffs of smoke from enemy muskets as they fired from the housetops at the attacking army. The yelling and screaming and crashing were continuous, and mingled with it we could hear the sound of cheers. The sounds came closer, right up to the wall beside the gate, and every man was firing and every man was cheering.

In through the gateway, riding a white horse, came a dark man, hatless, with blood on his face and his left arm in a sling. The cheering rose to a new intensity; the cry was "Outram! Outram!" Next came a slim little man, scarcely five feet high, and the shouts were for Havelock. And then, pouring through the opening, came the battle-scarred, kilted Highlanders, and the fierce turbaned Sikhs, and the red-coated Madras Fusiliers. There was a wild rush to meet them, and grasp them, and shake them by the hand. Women were crying, children were screaming excitedly, men were crying and laughing and slapping each other on the back. A huge, bearded Highlander snatched me up in his arms and kissed me emotionally on both cheeks.

"Eh, laddie," he told me. "We never expected to find more than your bones."

On November 16 General Outram's small army was joined by another army under General Colin Campbell, and the women and children, the sick and the wounded, were taken by road to Allahabad and thence by river to Calcutta. The six months siege was over.

Chapter 7

CALCUTTA was a city of extremes—of immense riches and gaudy display, and of filthy poverty and the most degrading squalor. The wealthy merchants and highly superior government officials, who lived in elegant mansions surrounded by swarms of servants, inhabited a very different world from the maimed and crippled beggars, who squatted in hundreds along the main streets.

"After living in this town for a few days, I think I begin to understand the mutiny a little better," Mrs. McLeod observed coldly.

We ourselves belonged to an unfortunate class—the refugees. With hundreds of others, we had been welcomed kindly, given other people's castoff clothing, and found reasonably comfortable quarters. Charitably disposed people organized entertainments for our benefit. On two occasions we were taken to parties at the Auckland Hotel, where well-dressed women patted our heads, called us "poor children," and distributed candy and toys. We hadn't really much interest in toys.

We were billeted on Mr. and Mrs. Nixon, a youngish couple who had come to India only a few months previously to teach in some mission school. They were devout, gentle people, full of religious enthusiasm, and I have to admit that we found them terribly boring. They realized this and did not resent it. They regarded our "hardness" as the result of our experiences in Lucknow, and tried always to be understanding and sympathetic.

Mrs. McLeod was often irritable, not only with us, but also with the Nixons. Her intellectual approach to religion made her impatient with their simple, unquestioning faith. Mrs. McLeod liked to think that her religious beliefs were founded on a process of logical reasoning which she could argue about. The Nixons never argued; they did not need to. The truth of their religious beliefs was as clear to them as the sun in the sky.

During this time, as I have discovered from her journal, Mrs. McLeod was being greatly worried by "doubts." The death of her husband, and her experiences in Lucknow, had given her religious beliefs a rude shaking.

This was not her only worry. She was nervous, run down in health, and almost without money, and she did not know what was going to happen to her or to us. Her husband was dead, but owing to some administrative muddle he was not yet officially dead. In the Company's books he was listed as having been on the staff at Lucknow. Because he had been killed in Cawnpore, his name had not appeared in the list of casualties from Lucknow. Because he had only been on temporary duty in Cawnpore, his name was not included in the official list of members of the Cawnpore establishment who had been killed.

Almost every morning she went, on foot, into Calcutta, and spent hours waiting outside offices trying to interview Company officials. As is so often the way with Government offices, one department would refer her to a second, the second would send her to a third, the third would refer her back to the first. She never seemed to get any farther. In the evening, hot, tired, and discouraged, she would trudge back to the Nixons' small house. The only thing she learned with any certainty was that our prospects of leaving the country were slight. Every berth on every homeward bound ship was booked for six months ahead.

"Those men—those *creatures*," she complained bitterly. "Sitting in their offices. All they can think of is their social engagements and their plans for governing the country when the mutiny has been suppressed. Apparently the first thing they propose to do is to hang half the population of Bengal."

"I've heard talk of that kind—far too much of it," Mr. Nixon admitted regretfully. "It ill becomes men in this city—and women too—who have suffered little themselves to display such a vindictive spirit. Surely, once we have pacified the country, our first object should be to found schools in every town and village where the native children can be instructed in the Christian faith."

"From what I've heard, that is precisely what a great many of them are fighting against," Mrs. McLeod answered tartly.

The days dragged by, and it seemed that we were likely to be stuck in Calcutta for months, or even years. Our deliverance came suddenly and quite unexpectedly.

One evening, when we had been with the Nixons for two months, a buggy drew up outside the house. From it descended a very spry young dandy, blue-coated, side-whiskered, fair-haired. He first of all had a brief interview with Mr. Nixon, and then another with Mrs. McLeod, and then I was sent for.

"Is this the boy?" he asked. He looked me up and down; his smile was affable and condescending.

"Your name is Justin Kelly. You are the son of Lieutenant Michael Kelly and Mary Kelly, formerly Mary Lurgan."

"My father was Captain Kelly," I said.

"Captain Kelly. I ask your pardon." He smiled again. "You are, at any rate, the grandson of Major General Sir Horace Lurgan. Pray correct me if I am mistaken."

I stared at him. At that time I had never heard the story of my mother's runaway marriage, and I knew nothing about my grandfather. But Mrs. McLeod knew about it.

"Yes. Justin's grandfather is Sir Horace Lurgan," she said.

"My grandfather! A General. And a Sir!" I exclaimed. "Like General Havelock and General Outram." The news dazzled me. I could scarcely believe it.

"My department has instructions from the Board of Governors in London—or to be more precise, from the Earl of Bracca, who is a member of that board—that everything possible is to be done to assist Captain Kelly or any member of his family who may be in any kind of need or . . . or, er . . . distress. As I understand that the parents of the boy are . . . are unfortunately no longer with us, and as the department is hardly qualified to take charge of an orphan, we have thought it best, taking everything into account, to arrange for the removal of the child into the care of his proper guardians." He looked at me. "How would you like to go home to Ireland, Justin?"

"To Ireland. To my grandfather, Sir . . . Sir Something, the Major General. Ooh yes. I should like to go to Ireland."

"Well, that's where you're going." He turned to Mrs. McLeod. "Obviously the boy will have to be sent in the care of some competent person. He seems to be in your charge. Would you have any objection to accompanying him?"

"I should be very glad to," Mrs. McLeod said quickly, as if clinching a bargain. Then, with a slight hesitation, she added, "I have two children of my own, you know."

"No . . . er, I didn't know. I'm afraid that makes things a little more awkward. The accommodation is very limited."

"I don't want to go unless Aunt Elsie comes with me," I said, and Mrs. McLeod, in a fighting voice, said, "Justin's father put him in my charge. I hold myself responsible for him."

"Indeed. Then perhaps . . . The point is that I have at my disposal a two berth cabin on a vessel sailing for Bristol tomorrow night. I imagine two extra bunks could be fitted in. If you can endure such cramped quarters. . . . You will understand that an opportunity like this may not recur for several months."

"I don't think we shall worry if our quarters are rather cramped," Mrs. McLeod said dryly. "We're not unaccustomed to it."

"No, of course not. In Lucknow . . . It must have been dreadful for you. I think we can promise you something a little better than that. And the sea breezes—very healthy, I believe, though they always make me confoundedly sick. Then we may consider the matter settled; you sail tomorrow. You can be ready in time?"

"We can be ready in ten minutes," Mrs. McLeod said.

"You can. How very remarkable. There are certain small formalities—a few documents to be signed. With your leave, I shall send a conveyance at eleven in the forenoon to bring you to my office, and another in the afternoon to take you to the ship."

"Oh, yes." I saw that Mrs. McLeod was flushing. "The question of money for our passage . . ."

"Oh no, no, no, no, no," the young man said very quickly and rather chidingly, as if such sordid considerations had never entered his mind. "Lord Bracca's instructions . . . that is . . . er, the department is assuming full responsibility for all financial arrangements. You need not concern yourself with that aspect of the matter."

He smiled, and bowed and went away. And we all began to dance and sing like mad people. "We're going home, we're going home, we're going home," we chanted. The Nixons were very happy to hear of our good fortune, and probably rather relieved by the thought of being rid of us. But there were also sobering reflections. Mrs. McLeod's troubles were not yet at an end.

"Where shall we live in England?" Jeannie asked.

"I don't know, Jeannie. I expect we shall go first of all to your Aunt Nellie and her husband in Paddington. If they can have us."

"Is Aunt Nellie nice?"

"Y-yes, I think so. I've never met her; but she's your father's sister, so she's sure to be nice," Mrs. McLeod answered, not very hopefully. "But she and her husband live in a very small house, and they have two children of their own, so we shall have to find a place of our own as quickly as we can."

"Where shall we find a place of our own?"

"I can't tell you, my darling. I shall have to obtain a teaching situation, but it's so long—more than twelve years since I was in England—I don't know how easy or difficult finding a situation is likely to be, or where I shall have to go to look for it. We shall just have to wait and see what happens."

"Why don't you come to Ireland?" I suggested. "If my grand-father's a Major General and a Sir, he must have a big house. They all do. There ought to be enough room for all of us. Do you know my grandfather?" I added.

"No, Justin. I don't know him. But . . ." She paused, looking doubt-ful and slightly embarrassed. "I know very little about him," she went on. "But after all, you're his grandson. I'm sure he'll be glad to have you with him. He can't be expected to want us. We shall have to manage for ourselves. We shall do it."

We had not been happy with the Nixons, but when the actual moment for parting came, we discovered that we were very fond of them. Parting from them was painful. Tears blurred our eyes as we waved to them from the carriage.

"Good-by, Mrs. Nixon. Good-by, Mr. Nixon. And thank you for everything."

"Good-by, good-by, and God bless you. A happy voyage to you all. Mind you write to us; you won't forget, will you. And give our love to England."

It was good-by to the Nixons, and to Calcutta, and also to India.

Chapter 8

THERE is no need for me to describe in great detail our voyage home in the sailing ship *Speedwell*. For the first three weeks we were miserable, tossed about on stormy seas, as the southwest monsoon was blowing, but after that we settled down comfortably enough. Once the rough weather was left astern, Ian and I were allowed to sleep at night on the deck, and that, we felt, was definitely the life for a boy. We heard the wind in the rigging, and the soft swishing as the ship moved through the water. We saw flying fish, and sharks, and wonderful sunsets, when the whole western sky was a glory of red, and gold, and orange, and brilliant dawns, when the sky was a bright blue and all the waves seemed to sparkle with little points of light.

We had lessons. We began to put on weight; the thin, peaked look faded from our faces. Mrs. McLeod wrote in her "journal" and made sketches of the ship and her crew. There was a weekly concert in the saloon, at which Mrs. McLeod played the accompaniments and usually sang a couple of arias from operas by Mozart or Rossini. On Sundays there was a church service, presided over by a returning missionary, a tired, yellow-complexioned man who was recovering from the effects of blackwater fever.

The voyage neared its end, and our excitement became almost unbearable. One morning we saw a faint smudge of land, which slowly became clearer till we could distinguish houses, and fields, and men on horseback.

"It's Ireland," Mrs. McLeod told me.

Ireland! Leaning over the rail, I stared at the cool green fields and darker mountains, overcome by an almost suffocating emotion. All my life I had heard talk of Ireland, and now, seeing it for the first time, I had a great longing for my father and mother and the voices I should never hear again.

"Your first sight of your own country," Mrs. McLeod said, smiling. "You'll always remember this, as long as you live."

I couldn't answer her. With my lips compressed and a lump in my throat I was struggling to hold back my tears.

Having made our landfall, we stood out to sea again and lost sight of the coast. But another day came when we were sailing up a narrowing channel, with land on both sides of us; and on a fine morning in the middle of September we tied up at the docks near Bristol.

There was a great shouting, and bustling, and heaving of ropes as we made fast. Quite a lot of people were on the dockside, kept back by a chain barrier. Some of them were waving to people on the ship, who were waving back.

Two dock officials shouldered their way through the crowd, followed by a tall man, stout, red-faced, black-bearded, whose smart gray trousers, well-cut black coat, glossy hat, and gold-headed cane, no less than his air of confidence, proclaimed his superior station. As this party crossed the gangway, the Captain went to meet them; hands were shaken. The bearded man looked round him curiously, and the Captain spoke to him, pointing towards us.

"Who's that?" I asked. "Is it my grandfather?"

"I don't know, Justin. I shouldn't think so. But he certainly seems to be taking an interest in you."

The Captain and the bearded man came towards us, and the bearded man introduced himself.

"Captain Chandler, Madam, at your service. I understand that you've been kind enough to look after Sir Horace Lurgan's grandson during the voyage."

"Oh . . . yes . . . that is so." Mrs. McLeod sounded a little flustered. She urged me forward. "This is Justin, Captain Chandler. Have you come to meet us on behalf of his grandfather?"

"Yes. That is the situation, though my instructions come from the Earl of Bracca. But I am to take Justin to his grandfather, who is expecting him. How soon do you think he can be ready?"

"He's ready now," Mrs. McLeod answered in a subdued voice. "That is . . . there are a few things in my possession—his father's gold watch, and some trinkets which belonged to his mother. I can hand them into your safekeeping."

"Certainly, certainly. And his baggage . . ."

"I haven't any baggage except this," I said, holding up a canvas bag which held all my possessions. I added, "Are there a lot of rooms in the house where we're going?"

"Why, yes, it's a sizable house. Plenty of room for you, my boy."

"I want them to come," I said, pointing to Mrs. McLeod, and Ian and Jeannie.

"We've been so long together," Mrs. McLeod said in an apologetic and slightly tearful voice. "Through the siege, and in Calcutta, and all through the long voyage." She smiled at me, uncertainly, trying not to cry. "You must go with Captain Chandler, Justin," she said.

"No," I insisted obstinately. "That's silly. If there are plenty of rooms, you must come too."

"I expect Mrs. McLeod wants to go to her own home, you know," Captain Chandler said in a comfortable, patronizing voice.

"She hasn't got a home. She doesn't know where she's going. And she hasn't any money till she gets some from the Company," I said.

Captain Chandler looked very startled, and stared at Mrs. McLeod almost accusingly, and from her to the two shabby children standing by her.

"Is that really true?" he demanded. "Didn't the Company look after you in Calcutta?"

"Everything was so very confused. I went to see a lot of officials, but none of them seemed to know . . ."

"Officials," interrupted Captain Chandler in a tone of great contempt. "They never know anything, except when they know everything—and then they're usually wrong. I think I understand."

He pursed his full lips, and scowled, and went on angrily, "To have endured the siege, and then the voyage home, and nothing at all done for you—upon my soul, I call it a blistering shame. You must allow me, Madam; I shall appoint myself your temporary guardian."

"It's very good of you . . ."

"Not at all, not at all. Got to have somebody to look after you, haven't you? That's plain common sense, isn't it? Come along now; I have a carriage waiting. The horses'll be getting impatient."

Ten minutes later we were all driving along the road to Bristol in a fine carriage drawn by two horses.

"Here we go," Captain Chandler observed cheerfully. "This is your first sight of England, I suppose. You'll find it very different from India." He chuckled. "You'll probably appreciate it better with a good nourishing dinner inside you. We'll see about that as soon as we reach the hotel. A juicy sirloin—not the stringy stuff you get in India, but real honest English beef, with Yorkshire pudding and a dish of roast potatoes. What would you say to that?"

"I think the first thing the children need is baths," Mrs. McLeod said. "And their clothes . . ."

"Rest easy Madam; it shall all be attended to. They shall have their baths, and their dinners, and one of the outfitters shall send up a selection of garments for them to choose from. Under your supervision, naturally."

"You're very kind." Mrs. McLeod hesitated. "You . . . forgive me for inquiring—I understand that you are representing Lord Bracca. You are perhaps his legal adviser."

"What, me a lawyer!" Captain Chandler laughed heartily at the idea. "No, no, no. I'm Lord Bracca's land agent—look after his estates in Ireland, y'know. We were at Eton together—oh, many years ago—and after I left the Army he offered me the position and I took it."

"And Justin's grandfather is a neighbor of Lord Bracca, isn't he. That would account for Lord Bracca's interest in him."

"Never ask me to account for anything that Bracca does," Captain Chandler answered. "He's a law unto himself—always was, even at school." Smiling, his eyes shining with enthusiasm, he went on, speaking with a kind of jovial pride.

"He's a remarkable man—very remarkable. A fine shot, and one of the best horsemen in Ireland, and clever with it—brilliant, you might say. I'm quite convinced there's very little he couldn't accomplish if he really set his mind to it."

"He sounds like a paragon of all the virtues," suggested Mrs. McLeod.

"Not quite *all* the virtues. That would be unbearable in any man." He laughed, to show he was joking, and then continued earnestly, "He's been the best friend I've ever had, and I have an idea he intends to be a good friend to Justin." He turned to me. "He took a lot of trouble to have you found and brought home, and what's more, there's a pony waiting for you when you reach Springhill."

"A pony! Oh, good," I exclaimed. "What's his name?"

"Robin. I picked him for you myself—on Lord Bracca's instructions. You ride, do you?"

"I have, a little. A sergeant instructor gave me some lessons. What's my grandfather like?"

"Sir Horace . . ." Captain Chandler hesitated visibly. "Well, your grandfather's an old man, you know. Lives very quietly. Likes to be left alone a good deal. But you'll find other company at Springhill. Your Uncle Randall and his wife—your Aunt Elizabeth, that is—and your cousin Horace. And there are neighbors. My boy Tom is about your age, and there are the two Corfield children at Woodlawn."

"What, have I got an uncle, and an aunt, and a cousin there too?" I asked. "What does my uncle do?"

"He's in the Army—a Major in the 19th. Surely you knew you had an uncle in the Army."

"I didn't even know I had a grandfather till somebody told me. I knew I had an uncle in America."

"In America? Oh yes . . . yes, of course."

"My father told Mrs. McLeod to send me to him," I added.

"Oh . . . well, that won't be necessary. You're going to your grandfather. If he couldn't have taken you, Lord Bracca was prepared to make arrangements for you himself. But you'll be all right at Springhill. I think you'll like it there."

I sensed a doubt in his voice. He was trying to be very jolly and reassuring about my homecoming, and he wasn't quite succeeding. Mrs. McLeod gave him a hard, suspicious glance and said, "Was there any doubt whether Justin's grandfather would accept him into his household?"

"Oh no, no—no doubt at all," Captain Chandler answered a little bit too eagerly. "As soon as Sir Horace heard that the boy had been traced and . . . and of his circumstances, he agreed immediately that he should be sent to Springhill." Captain Chandler removed his hat, and mopped his brow with a large handkerchief. "It's far and away the best arrangement that can be made—from Justin's point of view, I mean," he explained.

"Is it?" Mrs. McLeod asked pointedly. "Do you really believe that Justin will be happier in his grandfather's house than he would be with his American uncle?"

"Yes Madam, I believe that. What do we know of this American uncle? Very little, I can assure you, and nothing to his credit. In his grandfather's house Justin will receive the education of a gentleman, and in due course, no doubt, will enter the Army. Can you suggest a better future for him?"

"I don't know," Mrs. McLeod admitted helplessly. "I feel a great responsibility for Justin, but what can I do?"

"Your feelings do you great credit, Madam. I'm sure that Justin has every reason to feel grateful for what you've done for him," Captain Chandler said gently. "But frankly, there is nothing more for you to do. Your responsibilities—your very heavy responsibilities—are ended."

"I'm not quite sure of that. Captain Kelly mentioned a firm of lawyers in Dublin—Doyle and Ballinger. If I were to consult them . . ."

"They are Sir Horace's lawyers. Mrs. Kelly left her small affairs in their hands when she married the late Captain Kelly. They are fully acquainted with the plans which have been made for Justin."

[74]

"Oh!" Mrs. McLeod said blankly.

There was an uncomfortable silence, broken only by the clip clop of the horses' hoofs on the dusty road. We children sat watching the unfamiliar trees, and houses, and people, and listening intently. We knew there was division among our elders, and we didn't want to miss a word of it. Captain Chandler, big, and hairy, and elegant in his fine clothes and glossy hat, looked as if he had unexpectedly found himself confronted by a dish which he didn't know how to eat. Mrs. McLeod's expression was glum and brooding. Like many serious and advanced middle-class thinkers, she had a profound distrust of the "aristocracy" among whom she included my grandfather and Lord Bracca. She hated losing any argument, because she always knew she was in the right. Also she was genuinely concerned about my future.

In her journal for that day, which she probably wrote up some time during the evening, she set down her reluctance to hand me over to a grandfather

whose treatment of his only daughter shows him to be possessed of a narrow and unyielding disposition. I cannot help feeling that, despite his protestations, Captain Chandler shares my misgivings. He appears, in himself, to be a kindly and well-intentioned individual, but, no doubt, he is acting under orders which he dare not disregard. What I fail entirely to understand is the behavior of Lord Bracca, who appears to have had Justin traced and brought home for some purpose of his own. But why? What can be his motive? Captain Chandler has tried to convince me that Lord Bracca's good nature is only equaled by his generosity. This I regard as doubtful, though it must be admitted that the most idle and profligate of men (a description which I have heard applied to his lordship!!) are sometimes capable of generous impulses, though they can seldom sustain them. Even so, is a man of such a character likely to be a suitable example for Justin, whose virtues should be encouraged while his errors (rashness, pride, obstinacy) need to be carefully and firmly checked. Captain Chandler has promised that I shall have the opportunity of a personal interview with Lord Bracca in London. I shall, of course, state my views very clearly to him. But some men are impervious to reason, and I fear greatly that he may be one of them.

Such were some of the thoughts which must already have been passing through Mrs. McLeod's mind during the drive from the docks to the hotel, and they are in front of me now, in her faded handwriting, to remind me of incidents which I might easily have forgotten.

We were tired when we reached the hotel, and very conscious of our shabby clothes as we went through the arched entrance into the reception hall. There seemed to be a lot of people about, and all of them were staring at us. At that time the whole of England was eager for first-hand news from India, and reports of the siege of Lucknow had roused patriotic fervor to a high pitch. One of the guests in the hall, an idiotic fat woman in a voluminous purple dress, waved a small Union Jack at us and called out, "Welcome home! And down with the tyrant, Nana Sahib." Mrs. McLeod gave her a look of contempt. Nobody else seemed to hear.

The proprietor, a fat little man, shaped like a barrel, came forward, smiling, to meet us.

"Ah, here you are, Captain. Everything is ready . . ." He broke off, looking astonished, and added, "There are five in your party."

"That's so, Mr. Joll. We'll need an extra room or two."

We went up a wide staircase, and were escorted to our rooms with porters carrying our canvas bags and an escort of chambermaids in blue cotton dresses with white caps and aprons. Tin hip baths were brought into the room and filled with hot water from jugs carried in by the chambermaids. While Mrs. McLeod supervised our baths, Captain Chandler busied himself with other matters. After we had been dried, we were taken into a sitting room where a couple of assistants from a local outfitter had a large selection of new clothes awaiting our inspection.

Then dinner. Clean and freshly clothed, we sat down to the promised roast beef and a big fruit pudding, which were served in a private sitting room. After a long voyage, during which most of our food had been salt beef and pickled pork, the smell of the good soup and meat was wonderful, but we had no appetites to eat it. We were tired and overexcited, I suppose. Only Jeannie made a valiant effort to overeat, and paid for it by being sick almost immediately afterwards.

"The best place for you children is bed," said Mrs. McLeod. And to bed we were sent.

"Doesn't it seem funny to be in a place that isn't always moving about," Ian said to me. "I say, these beds are comfortable, aren't they."

"They're not bad. I liked the ship better."

"So did I, in a way. I suppose we shall all be going to London tomorrow. Captain Chandler's sent a telegram to our aunt and uncle to ask if they can have us. I wonder what'll happen if they can't. I wish we could come to Ireland with you."

"I wish we hadn't left India at all," I said. "I liked our bungalow in Lucknow before the mutiny."

Lying there in the darkened room, I was feeling desperately homesick for the old life, with my father and mother, and Lally, my Ayah. All the familiar places and people were slipping away from me, one after the other. Tomorrow, when the McLeods went to London, my last link with the old life would be broken. I should be alone in a world of strangers.

"It's not much good liking something that isn't there any longer," Ian said philosophically.

The next morning, in their new clothes, and carrying their shiny new portmanteaux, the McLeod family left by rail for London. There was a desperate ten minutes, when the seats were taken, and the luggage stowed in the racks, and we all stood about on the platform, not knowing what to say. There were no tears. We were all brightly and bleakly cheerful.

"We've been a long time together. We shall miss you, Justin. But I expect you'll be happy in your new home."

"I shall miss you," I said.

"Can Justin come and stay with us in London?" Jeannie asked.

"Yes. Yes, as soon as we're settled in a place of our own, I hope he will come." Mrs. McLeod reached out a hand and put it over mine. "Wherever we are, Justin can always come to us if he wants to. We'll be able to find room for him somewhere. Remember that, Justin."

"Good-by, dear Justin."

Jeannie flung her arms round me and pressed her soft lips against my face and eyes. Ian and I shook hands in manly fashion.

"See you again soon," he said. But six years were to pass before I should see him again.

A whistle blew, and a great cloud of smoke billowed across the platform, hiding the departing train. "Good-by," I shouted hoarsely into the smoke. But my words were lost in the puffing of the engine and the rumbling of the iron wheels. I felt Captain Chandler's hand on my shoulder.

"They're gone, my boy. No use in our hanging about. Shall we go back to the carriage?"

I nodded, speechless. The word "gone" had a doleful and forbidding sound. Everything familiar had gone—Lucknow, my father

[77]

and mother, Sergeant Mellish, the Nixons, and now the McLeods, leaving me in a haze of smoke. A breath of wind blew some of the smoke away, showing the empty railroad tracks.

"Cheer up, my lad," Captain Chandler said in a kindly voice. "Look at those railway lines, going forward, d'you see. Going on to all kinds of interesting places. That's what you're going to do. Of course, you'll meet your friends again: there's something to look forward to. Always look forward—never back. The past is finished with —no good brooding about it. I know how you're feeling, old man, but take my advice, forget about the last year. Think of next year and the year after."

He meant kindly, and, of course, he was quite wrong. The past is never finished with. One cannot draw down a curtain. The past is as much a part of the present as the present is of the future. This is a trite saying, and true.

Chapter 9

WE TRAVELED by rail to Holyhead, and then on by paddle steamer to Dublin, where we spent the night. Everything I saw on the journey disappointed me. A slight drizzle was falling as we tied up in Kingston Harbor, and the streets we drove through to the hotel looked drab and cheerless. I longed for the bright sunshine and garish colors, and even the heavy rains, of India. My spirits were low.

"Your first sight of Dublin," Captain Chandler said to me encouragingly. "It's a pity it's raining. It looks better in the sunshine."

"It's not even raining properly," I complained. "Not like it does in India."

"You miss India. So do I, sometimes. I was there, you know, nearly six years. In Madras. I don't suppose you ever got down that way."

"If you liked India, why did you leave?"

"A matter of health. Wounds and fever—I very nearly died. 'Pon my soul, I was a living skeleton when I reached England—had to be carried off the ship. The doctors told me I ought not to go back, and Bracca offered me the position of his land agent, so I took it. That was in '48, soon after he came into the title. I've been with him ever since. Never want to change, if I can help it. He's the finest fellow in the world, is Bracca. You wait till you meet him. You'll see."

"I think that my father was the finest fellow in the world," I said.

"Oh, you do. Quite right that you should. You know . . . did you know . . . he was mentioned in the Commander-in-Chief's dispatches. Recommended for a cross. Doubt if he'll get it, though. Little Vicky has a long memory. She won't forget . . ."

He broke off, looking embarrassed, and then continued, "I didn't know your father. Saw him once, only for a minute, not to speak to. Good-looking man—I remember that."

He paused, waiting. I think he wanted me to talk about my father. He was curious. He had been at Bracca when my mother had scandalized the whole country by running away on her wedding eve, and he wanted to find out what had happened afterwards.

"He was the best-looking man in the Regiment," I said. "And the strongest. The other officers called him Meehawl. They liked being with him. Everybody did. It was always fun when he was there."

"And your mother thought so, too. She enjoyed the fun, did she?"

"Oh yes. And his stories. He used to tell me a story every night at bedtime, except when he was on duty. He was very good at telling stories."

"M'm. Yes, I can easily believe that." He stared at me across the table in the Coffee Room of the Queens Hotel, where we were sitting, and something seemed to be troubling him. "Anyway, they seem to have been happy together," he went on thoughtfully. He shook his head slightly, with a doleful expression on his face. "It's sad—it's very sad," he added.

He sat for a few moments, large and sad, staring down at the white tablecloth, his hairy, well-kept fingers idly playing with a spoon.

"I knew your mother when she was engaged to marry Bracca," he said slowly, as if choosing every word. "She was a lovely girl. She gave Bracca up to marry your father."

He looked at me across the table; his expression was wary and un-easy. And I looked back at him, watchful and suspicious, like a small cat eyeing a big dog of whose intentions it is uncertain.

"You mean Lord Bracca wanted to marry her and she wouldn't have him," I said.

"Y-yes," he agreed doubtfully. "Though it went a bit farther than that. Hang it, the Queen was there to attend the wedding. Only your mother wasn't there for it. She'd gone away with your father."

"Like Grania and Diarmuid?" I asked eagerly.

"Like whoosit?"

"Grania and Diarmuid. She was going to marry the King, only she ran away with Diarmuid, and the King went after them with an army, but he couldn't catch them."

"Yes, yes, I remember the legend. Yes, it was something like that. Only nobody went after them with an army. But . . . well . . . it caused a lot of talk, you know. Bound to."

"Was Lord Bracca very angry?"

"No. Oddly enough, he wasn't. He wouldn't hear a word against your father and mother. In fact, though I don't suppose either of them ever knew it, he did a good deal to help them. But some people were angry."

"Do you mean my grandfather?"

"You're a sharp boy, Justin. Old for your age. A little too old per-haps. Yes, your grandfather was angry. Very disappointed, and very angry." He paused, picked up the spoon, examined it briefly, and put it down again. He looked at me, and went on in a kindly voice, "There are things everybody in the countryside knows, and you don't know. You'd be bound to hear about them from somebody. That's why I'm telling them to you."

"Did Aunt Elsie know about them?"

"Aunt Elsie? Oh, Mrs. McLeod. Yes, she knew."

"Is that why she didn't want me to go to my grandfather?"

"For a youngster you ask the most devilish pointed questions. Yes, I suppose that was her reason. I had a long talk with her last night and another this morning before breakfast. She's a grand woman—there's no doubt of that—but persistent. Very persistent."

I was not impressed by his friendly joviality.

"Is my grandfather a wicked grandfather?" I asked.

"What! Great Heavens, boy, don't start getting ideas like that into your head. Now look, Justin, I'm trying to tell you things that will help you. Perhaps I'm not doing it very well. Your grandfather's not in the least wicked. He's simply an old gentleman—a little crotchety perhaps, and set in his ways, as old gentlemen sometimes are—so don't have too much to say for yourself when you meet him. Leave him to do the talking. D'you see what I mean?"

"Yes. I'm not to talk to him. Aunt Elsie says I talk too much."

"She's a fine one . . ." He suddenly laughed. "I don't mean don't talk at all. Only try to show your grandfather what a fine, well-behaved fellow you are. Then you should get along famously."

He was speaking with the best intentions, but what he said was only confirming my growing suspicion that I was being handed over to an enemy. Lying awake a long time that night, I turned over in my mind all that I had heard, and my feelings were a mingling of defiance and misery. The four walls of the hotel were the walls of a prison.

In the morning there was a round of shopping, and Captain Chandler bought me a lavish outfit of new clothes. I had never owned so many clothes.

"When shall I wear them all?" I asked.

"Well, that I couldn't exactly tell you. There's clothes for this occasion and clothes for that occasion, and so long as you have them you may be confident in all situations. Anyway it's always better to have too much than too little, and Bracca's instructions are that you're to be provided with everything you need."

In the afternoon we left Dublin, traveling on the Dublin, Wicklow and Wexford Railroad as far as Ballinalea. There we were met by my Aunt Elizabeth.

She was a tall, thin woman, with a harassed manner and an air of shyness. I saw her first standing, looking along the small platform, biting her lip; when she saw us she came hesitatingly towards us. Captain Chandler raised his traveling cap with a flourish.

"Ah, Mrs. Lurgan, here we are then, all safe and sound. And this is your nephew. Justin, this is your Aunt Elizabeth."

She looked at me in an almost frightened way. She said, "How are you, Justin?" and made an undecided movement, as if uncertain whether to kiss me or shake hands. We shook hands. Her hand was limp.

"Randall couldn't come," she explained to Captain Chandler. "He had some business in the village."

"He's a busy man, I've no doubt," Captain Chandler answered with a slightly dry inflection.

There was a drive of twelve miles through wild and grand mountain scenery, with great purple slopes on either side of us, and green valleys with streams running through them, and small thatched whitewashed villages, where half-naked children played in the doors of cottages and waved and shouted shrilly to us as we passed. Sitting in the carriage, I watched the passing scene, at first idly, and then becoming more and more fascinated. A mounting excitement grew in me.

"This is more like it," I said suddenly, turning to Captain Chandler. "I mean this is more like what I expected—what my father told me about in his stories."

"Ah, this is nothing. You wait a while till we reach the top of The Gap, up there, and you'll see the whole Vale of Bracca lying below you." He smiled at me. "I'll tell you, Justin, every time I see that sight I know I'm looking at the only place where I'll ever want to live."

The horses were toiling slowly up a long steep hill, with the mountains hiding the sun. Ahead of us was a wide cleft, with blue sky beyond. Captain Chandler put his hand on my shoulder; he had an expectant look on his face. We covered the last few yards and then, as the sun emerged from behind the peak, he pointed with his finger and said, "There now, there it is. What do you think of that?"

From The Gap the roadway dipped sharply, winding down the rugged hillside into the long sunlit valley. The green of the grass was very green; the trees which covered the lower slopes were tinged with gold; there was a bright glitter from the waters of a lake. The road ran right through the valley, climbing away up into the hills on the other side, and another road branched away from it about halfway along, climbing to another gap in the hills towards the south. Round this road junction the village was clustered, the smoke rising lazily from cottage chimneys. Away at the far end of the valley, set on a plateau high above the village, with extensive parklands sloping away down from it, was a gray turreted building with a high surrounding wall. It had a romantic and slightly forbidding air. Everything looked tiny, almost in miniature, from the height from which we were looking across the valley. It was very beautiful.

"Didn't I tell you?" Captain Chandler asked triumphantly.

With his hand on my shoulder, he leaned his great bulk across me, pointing into the distance.

"You see there, that great place at the far end of the valley, high up on the hillside—that's Bracca Castle. The wall you can see running round the outside of the home park is twelve feet high and seven miles long. Now follow my finger: we come down the valley, and there's a house just beyond the village, in there, among the trees. That's Woodlawn, where Major Corfield and his family live. And now see where the road branches off up towards the Fala Gap. About three-quarters of a mile along that road is Springhill, where you're going. It's hidden from us at the moment by a bulge of the hill."

"Where do you live?" I asked.

"Oh, I have my habitation in the Castle, in a building they call the Gatehouse. You'll be able to ride over and see me on your pony."

"Has Lord Bracca given you any idea of when he's returning?" my aunt asked.

"Well, yes. In two or three weeks—that is his plan at present. Of course, he may change his plans."

My aunt flushed. She said defensively, "Randall is not sure whether it would be advisable for Lord Bracca to give Justin a pony. He . . . he would like to discuss the matter with Lord Bracca himself. The pony has been sent back."

"What . . ." exclaimed Captain Chandler violently. He stared at her, and went on in a sorely tried but patient voice, "I told Sir Horace that Lord Bracca was giving Justin a pony. Sir Horace was perfectly agreeable."

"Yes . . . but Randall says the pony is dangerous and . . . and unsuitable for a child."

"That little pony's as docile as a kitten. She hasn't a trace of vice in her."

"She threw Horrie when he tried to ride her," protested my aunt, almost tearfully. "He cut his knee."

"I'm sorry." Captain Chandler paused, looking hot and fierce. "I'll teach Justin to ride the pony," he said. "And if he's thrown and cuts his knee, we'll put some plaster on it, and he'll get straight back on the pony and ride her again." He turned to me. "Won't you, Justin?"

"I was thrown once in Lucknow, and cut my lip," I said. "My father said that everybody gets thrown some time."

"Exactly," Captain Chandler said. My aunt bit her lip and said nothing.

In a kind of stiff silence, we drove through the village. Men and women at cottage doors touched their hats and bobbed to us as we passed. Captain Chandler acknowledged these salutations. At the road junction we turned south, and drove for another mile up a steadily increasing incline.

An entrance, with wrought-iron gates, and a small lodge standing beside them, opened on to a rutty, half-mile-long drive, with the big red house standing at the end. As the carriage approached, a man and a small boy, followed by a woman, came out of the front door of the house and stood on the steps, waiting for us. The small boy waved, and my aunt waved back at him.

"Horace seems to have recovered from his fall," Captain Chandler said.

"It wasn't very serious," my aunt admitted.

"Is my grandfather there?" I asked.

"No. That's your Uncle Randall and your cousin Horrie, and the lady behind them is Miss Smithson, the governess," my aunt told me.

The group on the steps came down to meet us as we stepped out of the carriage. My uncle said, "Ah, here you are. And this is Justin, is it?" He was a small, thin man, with fierce pale blue eyes, wispy graying hair, and a fussy, impatient manner. He stared at me frowning, as if I were a problem he had to solve instantly, but I was to learn later that this frown was meaningless. He habitually frowned when speaking to give an air of weight and decision to his utterances.

"You are Justin, aren't you?" he demanded.

"Yes sir."

"Then speak up, boy. Answer when you're spoken to. This is your cousin Horace. Say how d'you do to your cousin, Horace."

"How d'you do, Justin," Horace said shyly. He was a small, frail child, a good inch and a half shorter than I was, fair-haired, with big blue eyes in a thin face. He smiled at me, timidly but with an unmistakable offer of friendliness.

"Hallo," I said.

"You children had better go inside. Miss Smithson, will you take the children to the nursery," my Uncle Randall ordered. "Will you come in for a few minutes, Chandler. There's a small matter I'd like to discuss with you."

"Not now, I think, thank you. I shall call in the morning about ten. There's a small matter I'd like to discuss with Sir Horace. Perhaps you'd be kind enough to tell him."

"Come along, children," said Miss Smithson, taking our hands.

The interior of the house had a shabby and neglected look. In the large hall, which we entered first, the plaster was faded, and cracked in places, the carpet was trodden and threadbare, a big tiger skin in front of the tall marble fireplace was shabby and moth-eaten. Over the fireplace was a stag's head, with branching antlers, and one glass eye missing. A small table had part of a leg broken off and was supported by two books. There was a slight smell of dust and decay.

We mounted a broad, creaking staircase to the nursery, and I remember my first impression was that everything was red. The wall paper was a faded red, the long curtains were a dull purple, the carpet was red with a blue pattern, and a large table in the middle of the room was covered by a red baize cloth. On this table were an exercise book, some pencils, and an elementary arithmetic primer.

"Do you have lessons?" I asked.

"Yes," Horrie answered. "Every morning. In the afternoon I rest, and then, if it's fine enough, Miss Smithson takes me for a walk. Sometimes we go to Woodlawn and I play with Rose Corfield. Tony —that's her brother—won't play with us because he's too old. And he's at boarding school, most of the time."

"Do you go to see Captain Chandler?"

"No. Mama says that Tom Chandler's rough. She doesn't like me to play with him. It's because he pushed me and I fell over. I don't think he meant me to fall over."

"Do you often fall over?" I asked. "You fell off my pony, didn't you."

"Yes. It was because the pony was a bit fresh. When I tried to gallop I fell off. I didn't hurt myself much."

"It was very naughty of you to ride a strange pony like that, and Dooley should never have let you try," Miss Smithson said. She turned to me. "Horrie's a little delicate. He'll grow out of it, but at present he mustn't do anything rough or violent. You must remember that, Justin."

"I don't want to be delicate," Horrie said. "I'd rather be the same as everybody else."

"So you shall be if you do what you're told," Miss Smithson promised. "Now Justin must wash after his journey. Look at those grubby hands."

I was taken into the room which I was to share with Horrie and Miss Smithson washed my hands, sponged my face, and tidied my hair and clothes. She was putting the finishing touches on me when my Uncle Randall entered. He looked hot and angry about something.

"Sir Horace will see Justin now. Is he ready?"

"Yes. I've just finished tidying him."

"H'm." He looked me up and down. "Those clothes are new, aren't they. And all those other clothes you've brought. They all have Dublin labels on them. Did Captain Chandler buy them for you?"

"Yes."

"Then confound his impertinence. What right has he . . . who does he think he is? I wish Captain Chandler would remember his place; he's Lord Bracca's paid servant."

"I think Lord Bracca told him to buy them," I suggested.

"I don't remember asking your opinion." He stared at me frowning and went on, "Your father has evidently failed to teach you how a boy of your age should behave. That, I suppose, is not altogether surprising. If you're going to stay in this house you'll have to learn to keep your opinions to yourself till you're asked for them. We don't want any of your sergeant's mess manners here."

"My father was a Captain and the best soldier in the regiment," I said defiantly. "He'd have put you into his pocket and walked away with you."

"What! Do you dare to answer me back. I can see that you need a lesson immediately, and you shall have one."

He stepped forward, took me by the shoulder with his left hand, and with his right hand he slapped my face, not very hard, but fairly sharply. I tore myself from his grip, seized the hairbrush with which Miss Smithson had been brushing my hair, and hurled it at his head. It missed, and crashed into a mirror over a dressing table, splintering the glass.

He said, "Oh, would you," in a startled voice, and seized me, and began slapping me again, viciously this time. In return, sobbing with rage, I kicked his shins as hard as I could. I must have kicked pretty hard, because he released me and bent over to rub his leg. I dodged round a small chair and then, as he came after me again, I slipped like an eel through the doorway and went clattering away down the creaky stairs. Behind me I heard him shouting, "Come back. Come back at once. Do you hear me?"

I reached the hall and paused for a moment, like a hunted animal, looking round me. I could see three closed doors, and one open doorway. Above me there was a clamor of voices. I heard my aunt say, "Randall, what is it? What's happening?" and my uncle's answer, "Just wait till I get hold of him."

I ran through the open doorway, and then stopped abruptly. I was in a study, with paneled walls, two of which had glass-fronted bookcases. Three shabby leather chairs were grouped round an arched fireplace. In front of the window, at the far end of the room, was a large desk at which an old man was sitting. I stood looking at him, and he looked at me.

He was tall and gaunt, with a harsh, wrinkled face, a large, aquiline nose, light flinty blue eyes, set under bushy eyebrows, and white wavy hair. He sat quite still, his thin lips pressed together, his eyes cold. From outside the room I heard my uncle's voice call, "Where's he gone? Did you see which way he went?" The old man opened his mouth and called, "What's the meaning of all the noise? Come in here, Randall, and stop shouting."

My uncle and aunt entered looking flushed and bothered. My uncle said savagely, "Oh, there you are," and then, to the old man, "He's nothing better than a savage. A wild animal. I suppose it's only what might have been expected but . . ."

"Be quiet," said the old man. He sat back in his chair, his bony hands on the desk in front of him. He looked at each of us in turn, coldly and without favor. He didn't want any of us; we were an affliction he had to put up with. He pointed a long finger at me.

"You, boy. I want the truth. What have you been doing?"

Half-sniveling, I answered defiantly, "He said something about my father. My father was a better man than he is."

"I had to correct him for impertinence," my Uncle Randall protested. "I merely remarked that he needed the training which his parents had failed to give him. He flung a brush at me and kicked and struggled like an animal."

"The boy's parents are dead," the old man said harshly. "There was no necessity to refer to them at all. You know that very well."

"I wasn't impertinent," I said. "I only said I thought Lord Bracca told Captain Chandler to buy those clothes. You asked me if Captain

[87]

Chandler bought the clothes." I gulped and added, "You said Captain Chandler was impertinent, but you didn't hit him. And you wouldn't 've hit me if my father had been alive. He'd have soon set you to rightabouts."

"It's ridiculous," my uncle said angrily. "Chandler's bought the boy two whole trunkfuls of clothes—the most expensive clothes, from Bramley and Oakshott. The kind of clothes we would never think of buying for Horrie."

"Is that a matter which concerns you?" my grandfather asked.

My uncle flushed, and frowned, and looked very confused, like a small boy in the presence of a stern master.

"But it's an insult," he protested. "An insult to you."

"Fiddlesticks," the old man said sharply. He paused. "Justin can expect little from me except a roof. Everything I have will go to you, and then to Horrie. If Bracca chooses to take an interest in Justin, I don't consider that I have any right to object."

"But why should he take an interest in him? He's never even seen him."

The old man, my grandfather, made a slight gesture with his hands as if to indicate that he neither knew nor cared.

"I think I have made my opinion sufficiently clear," he said. "Unless there is some further observation which you wish to make."

Without waiting for any further observation, he turned to me.

"You will remain for a few moments, if you please. I have to speak to you."

He waited till the door had closed behind my aunt and uncle. Then he said, in a cold, deliberate voice, "This will be your home for the next few years. I trust that you will be happy here. That will depend on yourself."

I didn't know what answer I was expected to make, so I said nothing. My grandfather leaned back in his chair, folding his arms.

"You will be given the training and education necessary to fit you for an honorable career. I imagine that, when you are old enough, you will wish to enter the Army."

"Yes," I said. "Like my father."

He gave a little nod.

"I understand that your father was an excellent soldier," he said politely. After the slightest pause, he continued, "For the present you will take lessons from Miss Smithson; you will remain in her charge till we can find a suitable school for you. I shall not expect to hear any complaints from her about your behavior."

"Can I have my pony?" I asked.

[88]

"Your . . . pony, did you say?"

"The pony Captain Chandler sent for me."

"Yes, yes," he said impatiently. "You'll probably need riding lessons; Dooley can give them to you. He has little enough to do. Miss Smithson will arrange it. You may return to her now."

"Thank you, sir."

I turned and went out. As I reached the door I glanced back. My grandfather's chin had sunk on to his chest: he was staring fixedly at the desk in front of him. He looked old and grim.

After tea, at Horrie's insistence, I was taken round and introduced to the rest of the household. There were seven of them, not a large household staff for a place the size of Springhill, in those days, when servants were about two for a penny. In the kitchen regions we met Smannel, the butler, and Mullen, the coachman, both old soldiers who had served under my grandfather. Also Mrs. Smannel, who combined the offices of cook and housekeeper, Alice, the housemaid, and Florence, the kitchen-maid.

We went out by the back entrance to the stables, where I met Dooley, the groom, and Fergus, the stableboy. These two lived in a kind of loft over the harness room, with an old brown retriever named Andy to keep them company. Finally we visited the small cottage where Venn, the gardener, lived with his wife and his twenty-two-year-old son, who also worked in the gardens.

After this round of visits we returned to the nursery, and Miss Smithson read to us till about quarter to seven. Then our hair was brushed, and we were smartened up for the ritual of saying good night. This took place in the drawing room, where my grandfather, my uncle, and my aunt, in their evening clothes, were waiting for the butler to announce dinner.

There was a little awkwardness on this first evening. We entered the drawing room, and I didn't know what I was supposed to do, and Miss Smithson didn't know what I was expected to do. Horrie went to his grandfather, and kissed him, and then his father, and then his mother. I stood still by Miss Smithson. My grandfather, his back to the fireplace and his hands behind him, glanced towards me and said in a voice of almost stern politeness, "Good night, Justin." I answered, "Good night, sir." My aunt said, "Good night, Justin," in a timid voice, and again I answered, "Good night." My uncle said nothing. He didn't even look at me. His expression was sulky.

We returned to the nursery, and had our supper of warm bread and milk. Then we went to bed. Miss Smithson kissed me good night.

Chapter 10

NOBODY could have described the household at Springhill as a happy and united Victorian family circle. The house itself was shabby and gloomy. My grandfather kept very much to himself. Except for dinner, he even had his meals alone.

Except in the evening, at the ceremony of saying good night, I seldom met my grandfather face to face. It was understood that I was to keep out of his way, and Miss Smithson saw to it that I kept out of his way. When we did meet, he was polite, as he might have been to an unwelcome guest.

What else can I find to say about him after all these years. He was proud, rigid, and narrow-minded. He despised weakness of any kind, and scorned sentiment. As a landlord, he had the reputation of being exacting, but scrupulously fair, and during the great famine he had remitted the rents of his tenants and had done his best to feed them, at his own expense. In consequence he was respected, even if he was not greatly liked. I doubt if he ever wanted to be liked. His nature seemed to be a mixture of intense pride, a stiff, formal courtesy, and a strong sense of duty.

Nobody respected my Uncle Randall or my Aunt Elizabeth. My grandfather's attitude to them made it clear that he regarded them both as fools, and neighbors, villagers, and servants all seemed to share his opinion of them. My uncle's trouble was that he wanted to be considered important. He longed to be like my grandfather, inspiring awe and exercising authority, and this made him fume and bluster a lot, and sometimes he issued rash orders which he had to cancel immediately afterwards on my grandfather's instructions. When thwarted, or snubbed by my grandfather, he sulked, and went about with an aggrieved expression, but nobody took much notice of it. Nobody took much notice of him at all. My aunt was probably the only person he ever succeeded in impressing, or frightening. She was an amiable woman, but hopelessly timid and incompetent. It was no secret that my uncle married her for her fortune of £500 a year. I sometimes wonder why she married him.

If I have seemed to describe an unhappy and dismal household,

I can also say that, for a long time, I was not unhappy in it. Within a couple of days of my arrival I had settled down and was finding life full of interest. Most of my time was spent with Miss Smithson and Horrie.

Miss Smithson, scarcely eighteen herself, was the daughter of a hard up English country parson. She was a fresh-complexioned, sturdy, good-tempered young woman, who enjoyed playing with us and made us laugh.

I liked her from the beginning, and Horrie was devoted to her; within a day or two he was almost equally devoted to me. He had an eager, affectionate nature, which responded instantly to a smile or a friendly suggestion. He needed somebody to love and admire, and his parents were inadequate to these needs.

I was soon on friendly terms with all the servants, and especially with Jerry Dooley, the old groom. On the second day after my arrival, Captain Chandler brought my pony and gave me a riding lesson in the meadow behind the house, with Miss Smithson and Horrie and Dooley looking on. First he took me round on a leading rein and then he allowed me to ride by his side.

"All right," he said approvingly. "You'll do famously. You've been well taught, I can see."

"Dooley will take me riding," I said. "My grandfather said he could."

"He must bring you to the Castle to meet my son Tom. Tomorrow afternoon perhaps, if it's fine." He paused, looking at Miss Smithson. "What about Horrie? You might drive him over in the dog cart."

"I shall have to ask Major Lurgan about that, Captain Chandler."

"He won't let me go," Horrie said in a resigned voice. "He'll say it'll be bad for me."

"I'm sorry. But there's no reason why Dooley shouldn't bring Justin. I'll have a word with Sir Horace about it."

The following afternoon, very proud in my new riding clothes astride my pretty gray pony, I rode to the Castle escorted by Dooley. Horrie watched my departure from the nursery window, and waved to me as I went. The afternoon was warm with mellow September sunshine, the turf was springy under the horses' hoofs. Avoiding the road, we rode across the hillside, over grass, along narrow paths twisting through bracken and between trees. A feeling of happiness bubbled up in me till I could have burst out singing.

"This is what I like," I said.

"You're right surely; there's a lot to be said for it," Dooley agreed, his dark-skinned, solemn monkey face crinkling in amusement at my enthusiasm. "It'll be a change for you, after India, I'm thinking."

"Yes. I liked India, but I think I'm going to like Ireland too. Were you ever in India?"

"Was I, you ask? Me that passed eighteen of the best years of my life marching and fighting over the whole length and breadth of the country."

"Were you in many battles?"

"Ah, I was in a bit of fighting here and there, on the northwest frontier, and down in Burma. That was before you were born."

I was delighted that Dooley had been in India. It seemed to establish him as a firm ally. But everything was delightful that afternoon: the sunshine, the golden tints in the trees, the movements of my pony between my thighs, the quiet village straggling in the valley below, and, in the distance, like something out of a medieval romance, the walls and turrets of Bracca Castle standing against the skyline.

As we approached nearer, mounting a steepish slope, the outer wall of the Castle seemed to become higher and higher, a gray impregnable mass, with projecting towers, barring our way. On the outside of this wall was a deep ditch, with a little stagnant water in the bottom of it. At one point a lowered drawbridge spanned this ditch, and led into a great arch over which was built the Gatehouse, the tall, twin-towered building where Captain Chandler lived. We had evidently been seen coming. As we rode over the drawbridge, Captain Chandler and a boy of about my own age emerged from a doorway leading into the arch and stood waiting for us.

"Here you are then. Welcome to Bracca." In a voice that echoed hollowly through the arch, Captain Chandler shouted, "Shamus! Where is the confounded man? Ah, there you are. Take the horses and look after Dooley. Come on in, Justin—this is my son Tom. Lead the way, Tom, will you?"

We went through a narrow entrance leading from the arch directly onto a narrow, winding flight of stone steps, with dark walls on either side. The middles of the steps were worn down by the passage of thousands of feet over hundreds of years; the air was impregnated with a slight smell of antiquity and damp stone.

"It has to be single file. The staircase is built that way so that it can be defended more easily," Captain Chandler's voice told me from behind my back.

The staircase ended in a spacious landing with doors into several living rooms. The one we entered had paneled walls; the heavy mahogany furniture, comfortable saddleback chairs, and long plum-colored damask curtains gave it an air of Victorian opulence. In one of the chairs a buxom, red-headed, ruddy-complexioned woman was sitting doing some needlework. She laid it down as we entered.

"Here's Justin, my dear," Captain Chandler said.

"Come here, Justin Kelly, and let me look at you," she said, in a voice deep as a man's. But she sounded friendly enough, so I went closer, and she gave me a large, hard hand and stared me up and down like a dealer examining a horse.

"He's the image of his father," she declared. "And the same bold be-damned-to-you look in his eye." She smiled, robbing the words of any offense. "I knew your father when he was in camp here in the Home Park. We used to talk in the evening sometimes, down there, under the arch. I'd quite a fancy for him meself, I can tell you."

"Really, my dear . . ." Captain Chandler protested half-heartedly. Mrs. Chandler laughed and rose from her chair.

"What would you like to do, Justin?"

"I'd like to see the Castle."

"That shouldn't be difficult. You can see it from this window."

She put her hand on my shoulder and took me to a window. I saw wide lawns, and terraced gardens, and pergolas with rose trees growing over them, and peacocks, looking disdainful, and in the middle, rising to a sheer height of ninety feet with its five circular towers projecting from the walls, was the great Keep. One had to turn one's head to glance along the full length of its battlemented surface.

"Impressive, isn't it," Captain Chandler said. "This ground between here and the Keep is called the Outer Bailey, and the Keep itself is built all round a kind of great courtyard called the Inner Bailey. The idea was that, if the outer wall and the Gatehouse were carried, everybody could take refuge in the Keep."

"Were there any famous sieges?" I asked.

"None at all. Disappointing, isn't it. In the early days I suppose that anybody who had any idea of besieging the place came and looked at it, and then decided to go somewhere else. Let's go and take a walk round, shall we, and you'll be able to see things for yourself."

There was too much to see in one afternoon, but I saw the great banqueting hall, where two hundred could sit down to dine, and the huge drawing rooms, and the library, and picture gallery, and the stables, where fifty horses were kept. I had a huge tea in the Gatehouse, and afterwards Tom and I played and wrestled for a while on the lawn, and were fairly evenly matched. When we were tired, Mrs. Chandler refreshed us with home-brewed beer and meat sandwiches; and then, in the deepening twilight, I rode back with Dooley across the hillside. The afternoon had been lovely and unforgettable.

Three days later there was another outing. This was a more formal affair. My aunt and uncle were to drive over to take tea with Major and Mrs. Corfield, and we children were to play with the Corfield children. Miss Smithson was not to be included in the party.

There was a lot of washing, and hair brushing, and arranging of clothes, so that we should do Miss Smithson credit. At half past two we were ready and waiting, looking our best. And then my Uncle Randall entered.

"Is Horrie ready?" he asked.

"Yes, Major Lurgan. Both the children are quite ready."

"*Both* the children?" My uncle looked at me and then looked at Miss Smithson. For a moment he said nothing. And Miss Smithson said nothing; she didn't know what to say.

"Is Justin going somewhere?" my uncle asked. "To his friends the Chandlers, perhaps?"

"But I thought . . . I was under the impression . . ." Miss Smithson was flushed and stammering. "Mrs. Lurgan told me that the children were to be ready by half past two, and I naturally concluded . . ."

"Your natural conclusions don't interest me greatly," my uncle interrupted. "It's time Horrie and I were going. Come along, Horrie."

"I want Justin to come too," Horrie objected.

That was quite the wrong thing to say. My uncle turned on him bad-temperedly.

"What you want is neither here nor there. It's quite time you learned to do what you're told. Come along now, and let's have no more of this nonsense."

He took Horrie firmly by the arm and led him from the room. Miss Smithson and I were left facing each other. Miss Smithson turned her head, looking at the doorway through which my uncle had gone, and there were dislike and contempt in her expression. She turned back to me.

"I'm sorry, Justin; it was my fault. I thought you were both going. I hope you're not very disappointed."

"I'm not disappointed. I didn't want to go," I said.

Through the open nursery window we could hear raised voices below. I went to the window. The carriage was outside the front door, and my aunt and uncle were about to enter it. The disturbance was caused by Horrie, who was protesting tearfully to his mother.

"I want Justin to come. Why can't Justin come? Miss Smithson said he was coming."

"Miss Smithson must learn not to exceed her instructions," my uncle said, and my aunt added, "Horrie, do stop crying. You'll disturb your grandpapa. Now get into the carriage like a good boy. Justin can come another time."

"I don't want to get into the carriage. I want to stay here with Justin."

"Stop it, do you hear? Do as you're told and get into the carriage." My uncle took Horrie by the arm and shook him slightly, and with that Horrie raised a terrible howl. And then my grandfather came out of the house.

"What's going on here? What's the meaning of this disturbance?" He glanced at Horrie. "What are you doing to the child?"

"I want Justin to come, and papa won't let him," Horrie sobbed.

"Won't let him?" My grandfather turned and looked at my uncle. "Why won't you let him? What's he been doing?"

"I wasn't aware that he was included in the invitation," my uncle said, looking sheepish.

"Not included? Who said he wasn't included? Do you imagine I want the Corfields to think I'm trying to hide him? Of course he must go. Kindly tell Miss Smithson to have him made ready at once."

My grandfather turned and walked back into the house. My uncle looked angry and crestfallen; my aunt seemed to be on the point of tears. Mullen, the coachman, stood by the carriage door, stolid and impassive, as if he had not heard a word. I turned to Miss Smithson.

"I don't want to go," I said. "I won't go."

"Yes you will, Justin. We've had quite enough trouble about this already; we don't want any more." She gave me a rough, friendly slap on the shoulder. "You'll go and behave nicely to please me, won't you?"

"M'm. I'll go to please you, if you like. But I don't want to go to their silly old tea party."

Oh, the drive to Woodlawn in the silent carriage, with my uncle sulky, pointedly ignoring my presence, my aunt pale and downcast, and Horrie, tearful but triumphant, sitting beside me tightly clutching my hand. Woodlawn was a largish manor house with spacious rooms and everything in them bright and polished.

Major Corfield, tall and thin and rather precise, and Mrs. Corfield, small and fair, with the remains of prettiness still haunting a lined and withered face, engaged my aunt and uncle in polite and animated conversation. We children were sent into the garden to play with the Corfield children, Rose and Tony, under the care of the Corfield governess. And there, for the first time, I fell in love.

Rose Corfield was extremely pretty, with a delicious pink skin, long curling ringlets, and big, laughing blue eyes. She had a soft pretty voice, and a slightly arch manner.

"What shall we play?" she asked. She gave me a smiling look. "Justin shall choose because he's a stranger here. What shall we play, Justin?"

I was dazzled. I had never seen anybody so pink and white and delicious.

"What do you generally play?" I asked.

"You can leave me out," Tony said. "I've got some things to see to. I'm making a ship." He was a tall, fair boy of nearly thirteen, and he was offended because he had been banished from the company of the grownups and sent to play with us kids. I have always imagined that his parents' reason for sending him out of the drawing room was that they and my aunt and uncle wanted to discuss a subject not quite suitable for his young ears. They wanted to talk about me.

Tony went away, his hands in his pockets, whistling to show his independence. Horrie and I and Rose played sedately (Horrie was not allowed to run about) under the supervision of the Corfield governess. I was initiated into the game of croquet. But what I remember chiefly about that afternoon is Rose's pretty, wide-skirted, white dress, with a pattern of forget-me-nots on it, her ringlets and big blue hair ribbon matching her blue eyes, her cajoling ways, and her laughter. We had tea with the grownups, very much on our best behavior, and after tea Rose was encouraged to sing a little song to us (*Pitter patter pitter patter raindrop man*) and my aunt and uncle said how sweetly pretty, and what a clever child she was. Then Horrie recited a poem (*The boy stood on the burning deck*) and received his share of praise. I was asked if I had any social accomplishments, and replied that I hadn't, which seemed to surprise nobody except Horrie, who said, "But Justin knows lots of songs." That was fairly true because, during the voyage home, Mrs. McLeod had given me and Jeannie and Ian almost daily singing lessons. I said hastily, "I don't remember any," and nobody urged me to remember any.

That evening, at the good night ceremony, my grandfather, with

[96]

formal courtesy, told me that in five days time I should be going away to school.

"I trust that you will be happy there, and I shall hope to receive favorable reports of your progress."

The five days passed quickly. On the last morning but one of my stay at Springhill a letter arrived for me from London. It was from Mrs. McLeod.

My dear Justin,

After all the bustle and rush of the last few days, at last I can sit down and write to you. I can best begin, I think, by saying that we are all well, and hope you are too, and happy in your new home. We think of you a lot.

Now for our news. We are still with my sister-in-law and her husband, but will very shortly be moving into the upper part of a house in Westbourne Grove. The ground floor of the building is occupied by a haberdasher's shop, which is not quite what I should have wished, but we have our own entrance, and our quarters are spacious and pleasant, with a very elegant drawing room, where I hope to give music lessons to a few private pupils. I already have the promise of three pupils, who will come to me as soon as we are settled in.

Ian and Jeannie are to attend a small day school in the neighborhood, and I have been fortunate enough to obtain part-time employment for three days a week in the same school, instructing some of the children in the rudiments of music. So, as you see, we have little to complain of. Indeed, everything has turned out far better than I could have hoped, and this, I must tell you, has been largely due to the kindness of Lord Bracca.

I have had two interviews with Lord Bracca in his London mansion in Grosvenor Square. On the first occasion I confess I was somewhat intimidated by the grandeur, not to say extravagance, of a great nobleman's mansion, but when I was shown into his lordship's presence I found him to have a great charm and natural courtesy of manner which put me immediately at my ease. He was most kind and considerate both in providing me with letters of recommendation which have proved most useful to me, and in arranging my affairs with the Company. He professed the deepest interest in you and asked me many questions about you and your mother and father, and our life in India. He gave me to understand that he intends to see you himself shortly after he returns to Ireland, and I am sure that you will find him, in the best sense of the word, a true noble-man—kindly, possessed of the highest degree of intellect, and entirely without undue pride or affectation. I feel myself that it is a great pity he does not devote his undoubted talent to some form of public service, but that, I fear, is a matter on which I am hardly in a position to give him advice.

Well, Justin, I must close now. There is still a great deal to be done. Ian and Jeannie join me in sending you our love. We shall hope to hear from you soon and learn how you are faring.

Most affectionately yours,
Elsie McLeod.

I showed this letter, with great pride, to Miss Smithson and Horrie, who were suitably impressed. Then I had to take it to the stables and show it to my friend Dooley. He read it slowly, sitting on an upturned case in the harness room, his booted legs thrust out in front of him, his wrinkled face close to the writing paper, tracing the words with a forefinger.

"Well, well, young gentleman. There's great news for you surely. You'll be having Lordy himself coming to see you."

"Lordy? Is that what you call him? Does he know?"

"That's what we call him among ourselves, and I wouldn't doubt that he knows. Not that he'd be likely to worry his head about anything we'd call him."

"Aunt Elsie—Mrs. McLeod, who sent me that letter—thought she wasn't going to like him. But she does like him."

"Ah, sure she'll like him, if he wants her to. Men, women and children, they all like Lordy—except them that don't like him."

"Who doesn't like him—except my Uncle Randall? Do you like him?"

"Whether I like him or not is of no account at all. There's many that like him, and with reason, I'll not deny it. He's a fine dashing horseman, and a better landlord than most, and very free and open-handed in his ways." He looked at the letter, and folded it carefully, and passed it back to me. For a moment he looked unde-cided, watching me while I placed it carefully in one of my pockets. Then he added, "I was the man that carried the letter from your mother to your father the night she went away with him. She came to me, here in this harness room, at nine o'clock on her wedding eve, and she says, 'Dooley, there's a letter I want you to deliver and wait for an answer,' and I found your father in the camp in the Castle grounds and he read the letter and wrote an answer, and I brought it back to her, and in the morning they was both gone. You'll have heard about that."

"I know my mother ran away. Why did she run away?"

"Ah," said Dooley, in a somber and mysterious voice. "That's it. Why did she? She had a reason, I've no doubt—the same reason, maybe, that makes some of the men and women in the village cross themselves when his shadow falls on them, and he riding across the country on his horse."

"What nonsense, Dooley," said Miss Smithson's voice from the doorway. "You oughtn't to tell Justin such tales." She turned to me. "Come along Justin, your luncheon's ready. We're waiting for you."

"What did Dooley mean about people crossing themselves when Lord Bracca's shadow falls on them?" I asked as we were crossing the stable yard.

"He's a silly old man, and he was talking a lot of rubbish. You mustn't take any notice of it."

"But why should they cross themselves?"

"No reason at all. I've told you, Dooley was talking a lot of superstitious nonsense. Come along now and get those hands washed; you can't sit down to table with hands like that."

I could get no more out of her, so in the afternoon I tried to find Dooley to ask him some more questions. But Dooley was keeping out of my way. Possibly he felt that he had said too much already.

Early the following morning my aunt took me to Bray, just outside Dublin, to the Glenside Academy for the Sons of Gentlemen, and handed me into the care of the headmaster, The Reverend Septimus Alton.

Chapter 11

GLENSIDE was a small school, with about thirty-five to forty boarders, varying in age between eight and fourteen. My memories of it are pleasant. Mr. Alton, the headmaster, was a kindly man, though he could be stern when he had to. The boys in his charge were well fed and well looked after.

In fact, school life presented few difficulties to me. It was like being at anchor in a safe harbor after the storms and turmoils of the previous year. Without being industrious I had my father's retentive memory, and some of his aptitude for athletic sports. These things helped, and the fact that I was a Lucknow boy, and had seen real fighting, gave me a certain prestige among the other boys and even with Mr. Alton and Mr. Penny, the assistant master. "Tell us about Lucknow," was a frequent request in the dormitory after the candles had been put out.

Three weeks after my arrival at the school, Mrs. Alton came abruptly one morning into the classroom. She was a small woman, dowdy but energetic, with wispy gray hair, sharp features, and a slight, dark mustache. Her temper was hot. She was given to administering sudden sharp slaps to boys who annoyed her, but she could also be impulsively very kind. Behind her back the boys called her Mrs. Whiskers.

On this occasion she looked flustered and excited. She said, "I'm sorry to interrupt you, Mr. Penny. I must ask you to spare Kelly for a few moments. He has a visitor—an important visitor. The Earl of Bracca wishes to see him."

I rose from my desk. Mrs. Alton looked at me and went on, "Kelly! Your hands! And your hair! Come along with me quickly. You can't see Lord Bracca looking like that."

She whisked me upstairs to the dormitory, and flanneled my face and hands, and brushed my hair, and tidied my clothes.

"That's better—a little. How you manage to get your clothes into such a state I really don't know. Now mind you behave properly. Don't forget to address Lord Bracca as 'my lord.'" At that moment she caught sight of herself in a glass, and exclaimed, "Oh my goodness—I'm nearly as bad as you are. You must wait a minute now while I straighten myself."

She straightened herself, and we went down to the fussy, lace-curtained drawing room, where Mr. and Mrs. Alton sat in the evening and sometimes entertained people to tea. Nobody was there. This seemed to dismay Mrs. Alton considerably.

"They're not here. Where can they be?" she said in a surprised voice, and then, "Oh dear! Mr. Alton must be showing him the school. With everything at sixes and sevens, and nothing prepared."

That was what was happening. A minute later we heard Mr. Alton's booming voice in the passage which led from the classrooms to the headmaster's private quarters.

" . . . plenty of fresh air, plenty of exercise, and plenty to keep them occupied. Work and play in reasonable proportions. That is the system I practice."

"How right—how very right you are. Indeed, I agree with you entirely," a grave, melodious voice answered. Then they entered the room, and I saw Bracca for the first time. I had never seen anybody quite like him.

He was a tall man, slightly over six feet in height, broad-shouldered, narrow-hipped, and strikingly handsome. His hair, worn a little long, and inclined to curl, was very fair. His eyes, set wide apart under a broad forehead, were an unusually brilliant blue. His features were regular, and of a Grecian symmetry—at Eton, I was told, he had been nicknamed Apollo—but his expression, in repose, was melancholy, and though he had a charming, ready smile, I seldom heard him laugh aloud. Despite his height he moved very lightly and easily; it was impossible to imagine him making an awkward or clumsy movement.

There were other things I was to learn about him as our acquaintance developed. Like my father, he had an extraordinary memory; he never forgot a face, or a conversation. He was a brilliant shot and an expert swordsman. A thin scar on one side of his throat was a relic of an attempt which he had made, as a very young man, to kill himself; nobody knew why. His voice had honey in it; he had a voice of extraordinary charm and persuasion, quiet and beautifully modulated, very flattering to the listener.

Mr. Alton and Bracca entered, and Mr. Alton put his hand on my shoulder and said, "This is Justin Kelly, my lord. He's settling down very well among us, I'm happy to say."

"That's good. How do you do, Justin. I've been looking forward to meeting you."

He gave me a slight, friendly smile and held out a hand. I took it and answered, "I'm very well, thank you, sir. I mean, my lord."

"Mr. Alton has kindly given permission for me to take you to my house in Dublin for luncheon, if you'd care to come. Would you?"

"Thank you, sir."

"Then shall we go?"

We went off in style in a fine carriage, with a cocked-hatted coachman and groom on the box, two footmen behind, and two well-trained spotty Dalmatians running under the carriage. The whole school was at the windows to see us go.

"Do you like your school, Justin?"

"It's all right."

"And your masters—Mr. Alton, the headmaster."

"He's not bad."

"An excellent description of him, I would say. You know I've met your friend Mrs. McLeod."

"Yes. She wrote and told me. She went to your house to talk to you."

"Yes, she certainly talked. She gave me a lot of kind messages for you. She told me you are very like your father. I think she was right."

I looked at him squarely. I said, "I want to be like my father."

"He was a fine man—one of the best. I had a great admiration for your father, and for your mother. Now he's been awarded a posthumous cross; that is something I think you don't know yet. In fact it hasn't been officially announced. I'm very glad to be the first to tell you."

"He *has* been given a cross? Captain Chandler told me he might get one."

"He has it. The Queen has approved the award. I was told just before I left London. I expect you'll have to come to Dublin Castle to receive it from the Viceroy. You can stay in my house if you like."

I was elated. Now, I felt, nobody could say another word against my father. He had a Victoria Cross from the Queen.

"Does my Uncle Randall know?" I asked.

"Not yet. Nor your grandfather. No doubt they'll be delighted." His lips twitched faintly. "Perhaps you'd like to tell them yourself."

"Yes. On Sunday, when I write my letter. I'll tell Mr. Alton, too. You haven't told him?"

"No, I haven't. You tell him yourself. I expect he'll be pleased."

And he was pleased. He made a speech to the whole school, followed by a reading aloud of part of the noble oration of Pericles over the Athenian dead, and finishing with the announcement of a special half holiday.

We drove into Dublin, talking easily. Bracca's smile, his air of friendly attention, his quiet questions and comments gave me the feeling that here was a grownup to whom I could say anything I liked with the absolute certainty of being understood. I told him I disliked my Uncle Randall.

"Why bother?" he asked. This idea was new to my childish mind, and I stared at him. He gave me a little sidelong glance and a slight smile. "Next time you see him, take a really good look at him," he advised me. "Then try to imagine to yourself what it must be like to be like him."

"I should hate to be like him." I added, "Don't you dislike anybody?"

"Not very much. But I don't like many people very much either. I liked your father and mother."

"I like you," I said.

"That's good. But I wouldn't overdo that either. It's not always a good thing to like people too easily—or too much."

Was he warning me against himself? If so, he was talking over my head. Anyway, it was already too late, and he knew it. With his splendor and his charm, he had come into my life like a dazzling vision, and I was completely under his spell and was to remain under it. He had that effect on a lot of people.

We reached the fashionable quarter of FitzStephen Street where Bracca House was situated. It was a graceful, Georgian building, with tall, arched windows and a pillared entrance. We entered a big hall, in which the first thing that struck me was the walls and ceiling, decorated with painted figures from Greek mythology, floating in a kind of sky of pale blue. A footman took our hats. A butler addressed himself to Bracca.

"Mrs. Lindford has called, my lord. She was most insistent on waiting for you. I have shown her into the library."

"In the library. Thank you. Come along, Justin; let's go and see the lady."

He put a hand on my elbow and guided me towards a door which a footman opened. In the book-lined library a tall, handsome woman was standing with her back to the fireplace, looking frightened, and angry, and also impatient. She made a swift movement towards us as we entered, and then stopped it when she saw me.

"Well, Kitty, this is a pleasure. May I present Justin Kelly, a young friend of mine."

She made no attempt to greet me. She said in a hard, angry voice, "Is he one of yours?"

"No, not one of mine. The son of some old friends. How are you, Kitty? You're looking very well."

"I'm not looking well," she burst out angrily. "And I haven't come here to bandy compliments, either. I've come to tell you that Jack knows everything."

"That's always been one of his favorite delusions." He smiled his brief smile at her. "I suppose he's being rather tiresome."

"You suppose . . ." She gave a bitter, rather dramatic laugh. "He received a letter by the afternoon post, and he didn't say anything then, but he looked at me queerly, and started drinking, and then, after dinner . . . he was so violent, I had to lock myself in my room . . . and he banged on the door and threatened to shoot me, and you . . . and then he went away and started drinking again, and this morning I left the house first thing and caught the first train to Dublin." She brought all this out in a rush of words, and then added viciously, "I know who wrote the letter. It was Teresa Fletcher—another of your discarded mistresses."

"That's scandal, my dear. Quite untrue, of course. But I can see you're upset, and we must have a talk and see if we can straighten things out."

"How can we straighten things out? Jack swears he's going to shoot you."

"That would be one way of straightening them out so far as I'm concerned. Though Jack, if I remember rightly, is not a very good shot. But we'll talk about it when you're rested, and I've finished entertaining my young friend. Where are you staying, Kitty?"

"At the Queens Hotel. I haven't any clothes with me; all I brought was a traveling bag. I dared not stay to pack."

"Wretched for you." He stepped to a long, tasseled bell cord, and pulled. Instantaneously, it seemed, a footman entered. Bracca said, "The brougham, at once, please, Walters. Mrs. Lindford requires to be taken to the Queens Hotel." He turned back, smiling, to Mrs. Lindford. "Now you go and rest, my dear. You're looking terribly tired; we can't have that, you know. And I'll come and see you later, when you're a little recovered."

"But . . ." She glanced at me, and back to Bracca, and looked as if there was a lot more she wanted to say, and all the time he was taking her quite easily towards the door. They left the room together; the murmur of their voices died away in the hall.

Bracca returned to the room within about a minute. It was

[104]

evident that nothing had happened to cloud his normal serenity. He said, "I think a glass of sherry would be pleasant. What do you say, Justin? I'm expecting our mutual friend Harry Chandler at any moment. He'll be joining us for luncheon."

As he was speaking, the sherry was brought in, and while he was pouring it Captain Chandler arrived. He greeted me heartily.

"Ah, Justin; it's good to see you again. Are you enjoying school?"

"Yes, thank you, sir."

"That's first class; I'm glad you're enjoying yourself." But Captain Chandler seemed to have something on his mind. He turned to Bracca.

"I think I should tell you, Rupert, there's a certain lady in Dublin. I've just heard. I think she wants to see you."

"She's seen me, my dear fellow. She was here when we arrived. Apparently she has something she wants to talk about—which is not entirely unusual. I've arranged to call on her at seven this evening."

"At seven? But Rupert . . . you can't have forgotten. Or have you changed your plans. I understood you were catching the steam packet for Holyhead this evening."

"Oh, my immortal soul." Bracca contorted his face into an expression of anguish, closing his eyes and raising a hand to his forehead. "What a wretch I am. How could I have forgotten? It's unpardonable of me. What shall I do?"

He opened his eyes, and looked at Captain Chandler over the top of his wineglass.

"Be a good fellow, Harry, and go and see her for me. Give her my most humble—my most abject apologies. Tell her how much I look forward to seeing her some other time. You'll do that for me, won't you?"

"Me go and see her? Dash it all, Rupert, that's rather a tall order. If I go to see her, with a story like that, when she's expecting you, she'll probably scratch my eyes out. You know what she's like when she's angry."

"A little soothing syrup, a few compliments, and she won't be angry any more. You'll manage her very nicely. I'm sure you will."

"Why is she so angry?" I asked innocently. "Is it because she's a discarded mistress?" They both turned and looked at me, and under their gaze, I colored, feeling that I had made a fool of myself. So I added, "I don't really know what a mistress is."

"What have they been teaching you all this time at that school?" Bracca smiled his brief smile. "A mistress, Justin, is a woman who professes to give you all she has—which may sometimes be more than you want. All she asks in return is a long nourishing drink of your heart's blood three times daily."

I didn't understand him, but because he was smiling, I smiled too, knowing it was all a joke. "But how do you discard a mistress?" I asked.

"Ah! That's a problem which has been perplexing the world's most brilliant intellects since the days of Adam and Eve. A discarded mistress is rather like a cold in the chest. You may think you're rid of it, but you can never be sure it won't come back and give you some more trouble."

"You shouldn't talk like that to the boy," Captain Chandler protested, laughing. "If he repeats any of it, it may get him into trouble at school."

"He won't repeat any of it. I have the greatest confidence in Justin. He'll never repeat anything I may say to him in private conversation. Will you, Justin?"

"No sir—I mean my lord. I promise I won't."

"No, no, never promise anything. Making promises may get you into all kinds of trouble." He put a friendly hand on my shoulder, and smiled down at me. "And don't worry whether to call me sir, or my lord. I think you'd better just call me Bracca."

We went in to luncheon; and if I was slightly awed by the splendor of the paneled dining room, the glitter of the glass and silver, the attentions of the flunkeys who waited on us, the lavish magnificence of the food, and the presence of the two older men, I can also add that I enjoyed myself greatly. Everything was wonderful and exciting. At one time the conversation touched on Mrs. McLeod, and I said, "I had a long letter from her. She's going to give music lessons."

"So I understand," Bracca said. "Indeed, she gave me one. Most instructive."

His air was so grave and bland that I almost believed he meant his words seriously. Captain Chandler smiled. He said, "She was very favorably impressed by her pupil. She wrote to me too. I must confess I'd been wondering whether she'd succumb to your blandishments. It seems that she did."

"What blandishments?" Bracca asked. "She came to talk to me, and I listened to her. At one time the conversation turned on music and the teaching of music, and she favored me with an interpretation of a Beethoven sonata on my drawing room pianoforte. She played it, as I remember, with great correctness."

"She used to play the pianoforte on the ship," I said. "And sometimes she sang."

"What a charming voyage you must have had. Do you like music, Justin?"

"M'm . . ." I was doubtful. "I liked the songs my father sang," I said.

"I expect I know some of them. We'll sing after luncheon, shall we?"

After lucheon we gathered round the highly decorated gold and black piano in the Chinese drawing room, and he sang to us. His voice was a light, stylish baritone, with a good deal of feeling in it. He sang first of all the songs I remembered—*The Harp that once o'er Tara's Walls* and *She is far from the land where her young hero sleeps,* and then continued with some more recent melodies, fairly newly arrived from America—*Way down upon the Swanee River* and *My old Kentucky Home.* I stood by him, appreciating the tuneful melancholy of the songs, and watching with fascination the light, easy way his strong fingers moved over the keys. Some day, I decided, I too would play and sing.

He sat back on the music stool and let his hands fall on his thighs.

"Enough, I think. Did you enjoy it, Justin?"

"Yes sir . . . I mean . . ." I was too shy to say it.

"Bracca," he said. He smiled. "Some day I'll take you to the opera, and you shall hear Grisi and Mario. That will really be singing. Now I must take you back to the school."

Back at the school I was eagerly questioned by the other boys. What was Lord Bracca like to talk to, what was the inside of his house like, what kind of food had I eaten? All expressed envy and admiration of my outing except one. Cardwell, who had been mildly friendly as a big boy can be to a small boy, asked me, "What did you think of Lord Bracca, young 'un?"

"He's a corker," I answered with enthusiasm.

"You think so. My pater's met him; he doesn't think so. He says he's an unmitigated cad."

I was hurt and disappointed that Cardwell should fail to appreciate my new hero, and, of course, I didn't believe him.

Chapter 12

AFTER THAT FIRST MEETING I did not see Bracca again for two years. When I arrived at Springhill for the Christmas vacation, I learned that there had been a scandal of some kind, and that Bracca was abroad. He stayed abroad; from time to time I had news that he was in Rome, in Athens, in Alexandria. He was always a great traveler.

Horrie gave me the first news of the scandal, though he knew little about it.

"I think he shot somebody," he told me. "I heard my papa and mama talking about it. I couldn't hear anything else."

I tried to get more news, at first without success. Miss Smithson wouldn't tell me anything. "I know nothing about it and I don't want to know," she told me. Dooley was not more helpful. "What Lordy does is no concern of the likes of me. Let him go his own way, wherever it may lead him."

Finally I appealed to Mrs. Chandler.

"Did Bracca shoot somebody?"

"He did so. He fought a duel on the sands at Calais with Colonel Lindford, and shot him in the lung. It wasn't a nice business, and the less said about it the better. Except that if I had my way with Kitty Lindford, I'd take my riding crop to her."

"My dear, at the moment she's sitting by the bedside of a husband who's still critically ill," Captain Chandler protested.

"And she proclaiming her shame at the top of her voice to all the world, like the heroine of an Italian opera." Mrs. Chandler gave a derisive snort. "As for Colonel Lindford, everyone knows he had the right to challenge half a dozen men at the least, so why did he have to pick out the best shot of any of them. It was the creature herself who egged him on to it; you can depend on that. There'd have been little glory in it for her if her husband had been fighting about her with any plain Tom or Dick."

"Yes, yes, there may be something in what you say. It's all a pity—a great pity." Captain Chandler sighed dolefully. "If only the women would leave Bracca alone," he complained. "But they won't. They run after him like . . . like . . ."

"You needn't tell the boy what they're like," Mrs. Chandler said. "He'll find that out for himself in good time, I dare say." She gave her deep laugh, and slapped me heartily on the backside. "Run along with you. Standing about here, and engaging me in gossip, like an old hen wife."

There were children's parties during that Christmas holiday. The Corfields gave one (Rose looked enchanting in a pink dress), the Chandlers gave one; even my aunt and uncle gave one. But I missed the last two of these parties.

There were also presents. On the day I arrived at Springhill, I was summoned to my grandfather's study. He sat at his big desk, remote and glacial, with my school report spread out in front of him.

"So you're with us again for a time, Justin. I have examined your school report. Your headmaster has no fault to find with you. I am glad of it."

I said nothing. After a pause, my grandfather went on, "Tomorrow your aunt and uncle and Horrie, with Miss Smithson, will be going into Wicklow to buy Christmas gifts. There are probably people to whom you will wish to give something; in fact, you should do so. It is an established social custom. This sovereign should cover the cost of whatever you may wish to buy. You may take it."

He laid a golden sovereign down on the front edge of the desk. I took it.

"Thank you, sir."

"I advise you to make out a list. Put down the names of people to whom you intend to give presents, and the amount you propose to spend on each. Miss Smithson will help you."

"Yes sir."

"That is all. Oh, there will be no need for you to buy presents for your aunt or uncle, or for me. A pictorial card, I think, will be suitable—as a small act of courtesy, you understand."

"Yes sir."

"Very well. You may go."

The presents were heaped round a small Christmas Tree in the nursery, but were not opened till after church and our midday Christmas dinner. There was quite a pile for me—a prayer book from my grandfather, a handkerchief from my aunt and uncle, a clockwork railroad set from the Chandlers, a pencil case from Horrie, a scarf from Miss Smithson, a sketch book (to remind you to keep up with your drawing), a game called "Lotto," and another case of pencils from the McLeods, and, best of all, a beautiful new saddle from Bracca. In the afternoon we went to the Corfields at Woodlawn, and stuffed ourselves with Christmas cake and crystallized fruit, and played games.

On Boxing Day morning, with Captain Chandler and Tom, I went to a meet of the West Wicklow foxhounds, and that ended my Christmas festivities and nearly finished my career. Trying to jump a stone wall, I came a most frightful cropper, and was taken back to Springhill, unconscious, on a cart. For the next ten days I was in bed with slight concussion, a wrenched knee, and a badly bruised shoulder. My pony, luckily, was unhurt.

"No thanks to you," Captain Chandler told me. "It needed an experienced rider to take that jump. Don't make the mistake of confusing foolhardiness with daring, Justin. For one thing, it's not being fair to the horse. If you expect to trust your horse, your horse must be able to trust you. Always remember that."

I remembered it.

The holiday ended, and I said good-by to friendly Horrie and kind Miss Smithson, who would be on their way to Bermuda, with my aunt and uncle, very soon.

Then there was school again. Latin, geography, scripture. Roast beef with cabbage and potatoes, and rice pudding. Sharp nipping mornings when the cold seemed to penetrate right through our skins as we got out of bed, and there was sometimes a thin film of ice on the water in which we washed. But the classrooms were warm, with bright fires in them. Prayers in the morning and evening, and church twice on Sundays. Mr. Penny saying, "Kelly, you will write out twenty times: *I must pay attention and not fidget while in class.* I should like it written, and not merely scribbled." The days becoming longer, and the first signs of spring beginning to show.

In April I went back to Springhill for the Easter holiday, and there were no Horrie and Miss Smithson to greet me this time. Dooley met me at Ballinalea, and told me my grandfather was in bed with a bronchial chill. I wasn't greatly interested.

"How's Robin?" I asked.

"Ah, Robin's fine. I've been exercising her against your coming. And the Captain was at the house yesterday to ask after your granddad, and he said Master Tom is home, and for you to ride over and see them whenever you have the inclination."

"I'll go tomorrow."

The big, dingy house seemed cheerless and empty without Horrie and Miss Smithson. The hall was dusty; the stag's head had lost its remaining eye. I had a meal of boiled eggs and bread and butter in the nursery, waited on by Alice, the housemaid.

After I had had my tea, my grandfather sent for me. I found him lying, propped up by pillows, in a huge brass bedstead, a woolen scarf round his shoulders, and a flannel nightcap on his head. His hollow cheeks had a bright flush in them; his voice was weak and wheezy.

"So you're here again, Justin."

"Yes sir. I'm sorry you're ill."

"Very kind of you." He closed his eyes for a long moment, and then opened them again. "Mrs. Smannel has instructions to look after you and attend to your wants. You will avoid giving her any unnecessary trouble."

"Yes sir."

"Your school report was reasonably satisfactory. Your handwriting appears to be your weakest subject. You must improve it."

"Yes sir."

"You will find a sovereign on that dressing table for your holiday expenses. That is all. You may go." He closed his eyes again tiredly and turned his head away. I took the sovereign and went.

The holiday turned out very well. After one more meal in the nursery, I insisted on having the remainder of my meals in the kitchen, with Mrs. Smannel, and Smannel, and the other servants. I enjoyed their company a great deal.

"Come along now, Master Justin. Yer dinner's ready."

"What is it today, Mrs. Smannel?"

"Boiled bacon, with cabbage and potatoes. A dish fit for any Irishman. Get enough of that under your belt and you'll be fit to go anywhere and do anything."

"He's fit enough for that now," observed Smannel, who had a hearty kind of jocularity when not performing his butler's functions. "Who's your sweetheart, Master Justin?"

"Alice, and Mrs. Smannel."

"And what have I done?" asked Florence, the kitchen-maid. "Why would I be left out?"

"You can be my sweetheart on Sundays."

"Two for the week and one for Sundays—that's a fair allowance for any man," commented Smannel. "And what will you be doing in your spare time, Master Justin?"

"Riding horses."

"It's a good life you have in mind for yourself. I can see that."

As servants go, I think they were a pretty lazy lot; I know the house was never really properly clean. But they were all genial and good-humored people, and not all their talk consisted of crude jokes about sweethearts. In the evenings, when the kerosene lamp was shining on the kitchen table, and the fire burning brightly in the big iron range, the men would smoke their pipes (Mrs. Smannel allowed smoking in the kitchen after the dinner had been served) and there would be talk about the villagers, the local gentry, and about political events. I remember that one evening the talk came round to the great famine of 1846–49.

"Them was terrible days," Mullen said. "I tell you, below there in the village you could find maybe two or three dead in one cottage, and three or four in the next, and nobody at all to give them decent burial."

"Why did they die?" I asked. Smannel took up the story.

"First it was the potato crop that failed, and all the grain in the country already sold and going across the sea to England. There was talk of forbidding the sending of foodstuffs out of the country, but nothing came of it, because, it was said, it might have interfered with trade. So there was no food left for man nor beast, nor even for the little children."

"After that it was the sickness," Mullen said. "The way a man would lie down in a ditch, or the shelter of a wall, and that would be his last resting place. The smell of the dead and the dying rose up to the heavens."

"That was like Lucknow," I said.

"Lady Lurgan, your grandmother, started a soup kitchen," said Smannel, taking up the story. "But it was little enough she could do. The food was not to be had, even for those with the money to buy it. Every morning many were turned away. It would have broken your heart to see it. Then herself took the sickness, and died of it inside twenty-four hours, here in this house. 'I'm not feeling very well, Smannel,' she says to me. 'I think I shall lie down for a while.' 'Will I call the doctor?' I asked, and she says, 'No, never mind the doctor. He has enough on his hands. I shall be better by the morning.' But in the evening the General himself went to find the doctor, and in the morning she was dead."

"That was like Lucknow too," I said. "Only there wasn't any siege here. Why couldn't somebody bring food in?"

"So they did, after the Parliament in London had spent two years or more talking about what was to be done, and doing nothing at all. When they sent food the dead was already numbered in their hundreds of thousands, and there was nobody left to eat it. In the end they sent enough food to choke the whole population, but the help came too late. I remember, when I first came here, you'd see twice the numbers of men and young girls in the village you'd see now."

"But . . . didn't Lord Bracca do anything?" I asked uneasily. "He wouldn't let anybody starve."

"Him," Mullen said. He gave a laugh. "It's little that one ever cared whether his tenants lived or died. He was a hard, bitter man, and well hated by all who knew him."

I couldn't believe this. I wanted to argue, but had nothing to say. Mrs. Smannel saw my expression.

"That was the old lord, the uncle of the one that's here now," she explained. "This one is a different kind of a man altogether."

"Better, or worse?" Dooley asked harshly. He glanced round the circle pugnaciously, as if challenging opposition. "Better, or worse?" he repeated.

"Be easy, now." Mullen laughed. "The way you talk sometimes, anybody'd be thinking you was after joining the Whiteboys or what is it they call it now—the Fenian Brotherhood. Lordy's a fine gentleman and a good landlord, and that nobody can deny, though it's the Captain does most of the ordering and managing for him on the estate."

"I'll not be after joining the Whiteboys or any other sort of boys," Dooley said obstinately. "But it's my belief that it would be better for some people if they'd never been born. Call him a fine gentleman if you will, but I'm telling you there'll be no luck nor good fortune in it for any that has dealings with him."

He was talking at me, and I knew it, and this caused a coolness between us for two or three days. We became stiff and formal with each other. But we were the best of friends again before the end of the holiday.

"That's foolish talk," Mrs. Smannel said severely. "And I'll have none of it in my kitchen. Anyway, it's time Master Justin was in his bed; the clock has struck nine. Time we was all thinking of our beds."

I spent most of my days with the Chandlers, riding and practicing jumping with Tom Chandler; the days went by all too swiftly. Then there was school again, the warm summer term, with sunlight streaming through the classroom windows, and cricket, and swimming in the sea, and then the long summer holiday, from the middle of July till the middle of September. My grandfather was well and about again by this time, but the pattern of the previous holiday was repeated. It suited both of us. I kept out of his way, and he did not interfere with me, though whenever we met he stopped for a moment to inquire courteously how I was doing. It wasn't till later, when I overheard people commenting on the way I was being brought up, that I realized there was anything unusual in the situation.

So the months and years slipped by, school alternating with holidays, with no special events to mark their passing. Bracca was far away, a distant, almost legendary figure, though I was reminded of him at every Christmas and on every birthday by presents which arrived for me from foreign cities.

Towards the end of my summer holiday in 1861, I came down to breakfast one morning to find a stir of excitement among the servants. There was news, and Mrs. Smannel was bursting with eagerness to tell it to me.

"So here you are—ten minutes late for your breakfast, as usual. Some day you'll be down on the stroke of eight, and I shall fall dead with surprise. But never mind that now; sit down while I tell you something. There's somebody you're going to see today, or maybe tomorrow. Can you guess who that may be?"

I had arranged to be at the Gatehouse at ten to go riding with Mrs. Chandler and Tom. Who else was likely to be there? The Corfields had been in England on a visit for some weeks. Perhaps they were back.

"Rose Corfield," I said. "Or Tony."

Mrs. Smannel laughed.

"You and your Rose Corfield. No, it's somebody quite different you'll be meeting very soon. His Lordship is back."

"What! Lord Bracca?"

"Lord Bracca himself. He arrived at ten last night in a hired carriage from Ballinalea, without as much as a hint or a message to say he was coming. There was a fine to-do from all accounts—men and women running here, there and everywhere. But all his Lordship wanted, so he said, was a bottle of wine and his bed."

"Why didn't he tell anybody he was coming?"

"That's it: why didn't he? And he bringing no baggage or servants with him at all, when you know the way his Lordship travels. Not a stitch except what he stood up in. Maybe you'll be hearing something at the Gatehouse this morning."

They were all agog with curiosity, and so was I. But as I rode across the hills towards the Castle, urging my pony on, I had the excited, nervous feeling one gets before an important occasion which may prove to be a flat disappointment. *Supposing he doesn't like me any more,* I thought, and then, what was even worse: *Supposing I don't like him.* That, I knew, would be a great disaster for me. It would be as if a god had fallen from his pedestal.

I hitched my pony to a post outside the arched gateway and pulled the iron chain which actuated the Chandlers' door bell. Tom himself opened to me.

"Hallo, Justin. I expect you've heard, haven't you? Lord Bracca's back."

"Yes, Mrs. Smannel told me. Have you seen him yet?"

"No. He came when I was in bed. Papa's with him now. I say, I don't think we shall be able to go riding with Mama this morning. I hope you don't mind."

I hadn't any wish to go riding. All I wanted was to see Bracca.

Chattering, we mounted the stairs, and entered the main living room. Mrs. Chandler met us there.

"Good morning, Justin. Of course, you've heard. I expect it's all over the village by this time. No riding for us this morning."

"Shall I see Lord Bracca?"

"Well, I don't know. If he has any sense he'll stay in bed for the next day or two. I told him so last night. But it's no good giving him advice. He does what he pleases."

"Why ought he to stay in bed? Is he ill?"

"He didn't look at all well to me, but, of course I only saw him for two or three minutes. And he was dog tired." She made a sound that was halfway between a sigh and a laugh. "I wonder what he's been up to."

"He'd come to Wexford, in a little ship, from some place in Spain," Tom informed me. "Then he took a special train to Ballinalea and a carriage here. He hadn't had his clothes off for a week. And Papa thinks that somebody must have taken a shot at him, because he has a scar on his forehead, and it's hardly healed."

"Stop gossiping, Tom. And don't go telling any silly stories in the village. Not that it will make much difference if you do. People always talk, and the less they know the more they generally say."

We heard voices on the stairs—Captain Chandler's deep voice, and then the mellow persuasive voice which I remembered instantly, the moment I heard it. Then they came in.

"Stephanie, my dear. Your servant, Madam. And Tom, and Justin.

How delightful this is—to be surrounded by all my friends. I declare I was never so happy."

"Go on with you," Mrs. Chandler said in her deep, rough voice, and then added anxiously, "I believe you ought to be in bed."

"In bed? I've been in bed most of the night. A man can't spend the whole of his life in bed. Though I don't really see why he shouldn't, if that is his inclination."

Already I was held fast by the spell again, fascinated as a rabbit. The voice "with honey in it," the handsome, rather melancholy features, lit up by the occasional brief smile, the flash of the bright blue eyes, the grace of movement—all these things, no doubt, played their part. There was more than these mere physical attributes in Bracca's charm. It was said of Edmund Kean, the actor, that when he came on to the stage "something happened to the audience." When Bracca came into a room, something happened to the people in the room: they became immediately aware of him. But there was never any obvious effort on his part to gain attention. Everything he did or said seemed unstudied and natural, and he could talk with ease to anybody, and listen with an air of attention to anybody. Perhaps that was part of his magnetism. His manners were perfect.

He saw me watching him, and gave me his brief smile, and I smiled broadly back at him. Mrs. Chandler said, "Sit down, Rupert, and tell us about yourself. But first of all you must have something; we still have some of that old Armagnac Harry brought home three years ago. I think you're looking tired. You need a bracer."

"Then I'll certainly have some of your old Armagnac, if you'll join me. Though I hope I shall find the air of Bracca sufficiently bracing for a while. It's good to be home again."

"It's good to have you. I hope you've come for a long stay." The Armagnac was brought, and poured for the grownups. Mrs. Chandler said, "What were you doing in Spain? We thought you were still in Egypt."

"No. I found Egypt rather oppressive in the hot weather, so I decided to take advantage of an invitation I'd had from some people I'd met in Rome, in the spring, to stay with them on their estate in northern Spain. A largish estate near Llanes, about fifty miles from Santander. I stayed with them . . . oh, it must have been for about two weeks—and then at two o'clock on a warm afternoon, while I was taking my siesta, my host suddenly tried to murder me."

"Tried to murder you?"

"And very nearly succeeded." He raised a hand and touched a livid red scar that ran into his hair on the left-hand side of his forehead. "I was quite unarmed at the time; I had to escape by jumping from a window. Then he set his servants on to hunt me—a most harassing experience. I hid in some woods till dusk, and then managed to make my way to the seashore. They were still after me—I could hear them—but there was a schooner anchored in the bay, and I swam out to it, and managed to haul myself aboard. The crew were French; at first I think they thought seriously of throwing me back in again. But they relented, and bound up my head, and I had a talk with the captain, and the upshot was that I offered him a thousand pounds to take me to Ireland. Of course I had no money with me, but after a certain amount of argument, he consented, and brought me to Wexford. An uncomfortable voyage; it took nine days, and I had to sleep on the deck because my cabin smelled so abominably. The rest I think you know."

"But . . . what a monster! What made him try to murder you? Was he mad?"

"Quite mad. A raving bedlamite. And he seemed such a quiet, harmless fellow. A great pity. Such a tragedy for his wife, too. She was charming."

"His . . . oh . . ." Mrs. Chandler said. Captain Chandler gave her a warning look, and she said no more.

Bracca turned to me.

"How's school life, Justin? How are Cardwell and Roche?"

"Cardwell's left. He's gone to school in England. Roche is still there. He was twelve last term."

"And you'll be twelve next May. Shades of the prison house . . . but you look very happy on it, I must say. What about you, Tom? I suppose you'll soon be going to Eton."

"Next year. And after I leave school I'm going into the Horse Artillery."

"A good choice. Within a few years the Artillery may easily become the most important arm in the services." He turned to Mrs. Chandler. "Perhaps I might entertain the boys this morning—or they might entertain me. Unless they have some more pressing engagement. I shall give them luncheon. And I hope you and Harry will dine with me this evening."

"You won't let them tire you."

"I think not. I am more likely to tire them. First I must make the grand tour, and see who has come and gone in my absence. After that we may find something more amusing to do."

We walked from the Gatehouse across the lawns and gardens to the great Keep, and followed Bracca while he made a tour of the

[117]

whole vast establishment. Everyone there were servants, and he seemed to know all of them personally; his memory for names and faces was infallible. In the library we met Mr. Grimshaw, the tubby, spectacled librarian.

"Well, Grimshaw, what have you new for me? There must be quite an accumulation of books. I shall expect to do a lot of reading during my stay."

"Quite an accumulation, my lord. The monthly parcel has arrived regularly from Quaritch and I've arranged all the new volumes in order for your inspection. If your lordship would care to glance over these shelves . . ."

"Yes, certainly. I'm all eagerness to see what additions you've made. Ah, it appears that Mr. Dickens is still busy. A very industrious author, Mr. Dickens." He stretched out a hand, took a volume from a shelf, and glanced at the title. "*A Tale of Two Cities*. Really, Mr. Dickens must have been traveling. Have you read this, Grimshaw?"

"Yes, my lord. A most brilliant and original work."

"You think so. I wonder if I shall agree with you. I am not, in general, enthusiastic about the work of Mr. Dickens. The conditions he describes undoubtedly exist; it is his characters with which I find fault. Those refined slum dwellers, who speak as if they had taken lessons in elocution—so very genteel. *I assure you, lady, that I am extremely sensible of the consideration you have shown a wretched and unworthy woman*—no, no, Grimshaw; that is not how they talk."

He replaced the volume and selected another. "*The Virginians*, by William Makepeace Thackeray. Now there is a man who can write about real people, though I imagine he will never improve on *Vanity Fair*." He replaced the volume and took another. "Ah, what have we here? *The Ordeal of Richard Feverel*, by George Meredith. Have you read this one, Grimshaw?"

"I have scanned it, my lord. The writing appears somewhat uneven."

"Uneven. As uneven as the mountains in the moon. But brilliant, Grimshaw, brilliant. I read the book in Italy. The name of the author was unknown to me, but I am convinced that it will soon be widely known."

"The author is not entirely unknown, my lord. He has written two previous books—a volume of poems, and a fantasy entitled *The Shaving of Shagpat*. Such notices of them as I observed were somewhat unfavorable."

"Get them, Grimshaw—order them from Quaritch in our next consignment. I shall be interested." He turned to me. "Do you like reading, Justin, or are you too busily occupied with other forms of entertainment?"

"Last term I read a book called *Charles O'Malley, The Irish Dragoon*," I answered. "It's in the school library."

"By Charles Lever, one of our home-brewed authors. I met him last year in Italy; he's our Consul at Spezia. An amusing fellow—rather like one of his own characters."

"I liked *The Irish Dragoon*," I said.

"I agree with you. Any time you wish to read, the library is here, you know, entirely at your disposal. You need ask no permission, except of Mr. Grimshaw, and I don't imagine you'll encounter any difficulties from him."

"I shall be delighted, my lord." Mr. Grimshaw smiled at me. "Any time you care to come. You will almost always find me here."

"And now," Bracca said, as we were leaving the library, "there is still over an hour before the time for luncheon. How do you think we should entertain ourselves? What would you say to a little pistol practice?"

We thought it was a wonderful idea. Like all boys we longed to play with firearms, and neither of us had ever fired a pistol.

The pistol was a derringer, a small, single-shot affair which fired a percussion cartridge, and we did our practicing in a dried-up portion of the moat under the castle wall. A target, marked with a bull's-eye and surrounding rings, had been set up.

"The first thing is to load. You will note how I keep the pistol pointing downwards, and away from myself, and from you. There, you see the cartridge is in the breech. Now I shall cock the pistol by drawing back the hammer. That is not strictly necessary, but it makes the pull on the trigger lighter. I'll take the first shot; you watch how I do it."

He merely raised the hand containing the pistol. There was a sharp crack as the cartridge exploded. The bullet hole was in one edge of the bull.

"But you didn't aim," I said.

"You think not." He smiled his brief smile. "A pistol, or a repeating revolver, is a very different weapon from a rifle. With a rifle you usually shoot lying down, or standing in an entrenchment. You close the disengaged eye, you get your backsight and foresight in line, you take careful aim, and you fire. That does very well for a rifle, but a pistol is intended for much quicker, closer work; you must learn to aim it merely by pointing it."

We spent a very happy and instructive hour practicing pistol shooting, though neither Tom nor I succeeded in so much as hitting the target. But there were to be more lessons in the future, and in time we both became pretty good shots.

Five days later I returned to school, and, for once, I was reluctant to go. I said so to Bracca.

"But I thought you liked your school, Justin. You're quite happy there, aren't you?"

"Y-yes, I s'pose so. It's not bad. But by the time I come for Christmas I expect you'll be gone."

"It's possible. I may get a fit of restlessness, and decide to go away, though I hardly think I shall do so before Christmas. At the moment I feel the urge to vegetate for a while." He smiled. "But let me give you a piece of advice. Never allow yourself to become too attached to any one person. It can only lead to disappointment."

"I'm not attached to any one person. I like Captain Chandler, and Mrs. Chandler, and Rose, and Tom, and Dooley—lots of people. But I like it best when you're here. Everybody does."

"Not quite everybody. But never mind that. Go back to school and enjoy yourself as well as you can; at your age you should not find it difficult. Take the utmost from every moment that passes, remembering that regret is a folly and hope a delusion. Then you should do very well. I expect to be here at Christmas, but you mustn't depend on it."

He was there at Christmas and gave a lavish house party. For a week the Castle was thronged with visiting "society"; there were balls, dinners, hunting, and other entertainments. My grandfather had no Christmas celebration that year, but for the three days of the Christmas festivities I went to stay with the Chandlers and had a very jolly time indeed. My present from Bracca was a beautiful little chestnut mare—seven years old, and a real sweetheart, with the mildest eye, and the most gallant and charming disposition. Even Dooley was impressed.

"Ah, the little beauty. The darling horse. By what name will you be calling her?"

"Cleopatra. She's by Pompey out of Queen of the Night."

"Then she'll be from Major Scrope's stable at Kildare. And Lordy will have paid the best part of three hundred guineas for her—or more." He shook his head gloomily, and then brightened. "Ah well, there can be no evil in the little horse," he added.

During the first week in January Bracca took me to Dublin to hear a visiting Italian opera company from London in a performance of Bellini's *La Sonnambula*. Piccolomini sang the part of Amina to a packed and wildly enthusiastic audience. After the opera a cheering crowd unharnessed the horses from her carriage and drew her back in a triumphal procession to her hotel.

"Quite an ovation," Bracca observed. "How did you like the opera, Justin?"

I had been thrilled by it, but as much for the glitter and excitement, the flowers and curtain calls, as by the singing, which I was too young to appreciate.

"I liked it very much. It must be wonderful to be a great singer. Is she the best singer in the world?"

"She wouldn't be pleased to hear you express any other view. I think, perhaps, Grisi was even better in the role. And there was another—perhaps the best singer who ever lived—who excelled either of them. As a young man I had the privilege of hearing her twice. Her name was Malibran."

"What a funny name. Was she Irish?"

"No. Her father was Garcia, the Spanish tenor, who was also the best teacher in the world. At the age of sixteen she was already singing principal roles. She was a superb singer, an incomparable actress, a gifted painter . . . and above all, she was intensely alive. When she made her entrance you felt that every hair of her head had a separate life of its own. She died suddenly in St. Petersburg when she was only twenty-eight." He paused, and added, "Perhaps she was lucky."

"Lucky? Because she died?"

"Why not? She probably lived more in her twenty-eight years than most people would live in a hundred and twenty-eight. If she were alive now, she'd be fifty—an old singer, with her voice gone, and probably very fat." He smiled, and made a slight grimace, and continued, "Perhaps my thoughts tonight are slightly colored by a tragedy in my own life. I'll tell you about it, in confidence, of course. Yesterday I was forty."

It seemed very old to me. With childish clumsiness, I said, "Forty. Then you're older than my father. He was thirty-nine."

"Yes. He was thirty-nine when he died. And your mother was even younger—scarcely twenty-nine. But no doubt they had what they wanted." He gave a short laugh. "It would have been different if your mother had married me. I could have given her everything —except what she wanted. And she could have given me nothing except an uncomplaining patience which I might have found very difficult to bear."

"Is that why she ran away?" I asked.

"Partly. And there was your father. I think she might have gone through with it, and married me, if she hadn't met him. And if a woman hadn't told her something about me and another woman —something that happened to be perfectly true. The evening before she ran away she came to me to ask if it was true. I told her it was. Then I told your father to escort her home. I wondered if they'd reached any decision. And they did."

"You weren't angry." I remembered Captain Chandler had told me Bracca hadn't been angry.

"No." He spoke negligently, as if referring to something of little importance. "I was curious to see how it would all turn out. I was even curious to see you, the result of this—romance. And here you are, the image of your father, ready to dive into life like a swimmer. And I'm forty."

"Forty's not old," I protested. "My grandfather's seventy."

"Old enough. At forty a man begins to realize that there's nothing he'll ever do that he hasn't done before—except one thing, of course. You know, Justin, there are men in India—you may have seen them —who spend their lives sitting cross-legged under trees. The sun burns them, the rain drenches them, and they don't notice. They do nothing; and yet in their own way, so I have been told, they live more intensely than you or I could ever dream of doing."

"They don't have much fun, do they?"

"I think perhaps they do. They have knowledge—a knowledge which can't be learned from books—which enables them to view the activities of humanity as nothing more important than the antics of a conglomeration of blue-bottomed monkeys frenziedly chasing their own tails. They're right, as you'll discover. How often does one cheat, and lie, and plot to get what one wants, only to find when one has captured it that all one is grasping is the tip of one's own tail."

He raised fingertips to his mouth, and yawned, and I yawned in sympathy. The time was almost midnight, and I was feeling very sleepy. He rose, still yawning.

"All the same, I doubt if I shall end my days sitting under a tree. As for being forty, I think you may be right. As you point out, forty is not so very old. Perhaps I should postpone these somber reflections till I'm forty-one or even forty-two."

"Or fifty," I suggested.

"Oh no, not fifty. The mere thought of being fifty sends a cold shudder down my spine. I think I shall have to go to bed."

He escorted me to my room, and said good night. As I was undressing, I heard the sound of carriage wheels in the roadway outside. I looked through the window and saw Bracca leaving the house. I have no idea where he went. The following morning we returned to Bracca.

The only other event I can remember during that Christmas holiday was my first fight with Tony Corfield. This was only important because it gave me my first real inkling of some of the talk that went on about me, and of the way some people resented the favor shown me by Bracca.

There had been a fall of snow during the morning. During the afternoon, Tom and I were busy in a field beyond the village, pelting each other with snowballs, when we saw Tony and Rose Corfield coming along the lane. Tom said, "Shall we give them a volley?" I said weakly, "Oh, I dunno," because I didn't want to throw snowballs at Rose. Tom, shrewdly guessing my reason, said, "Why not? Is it because it's Rose? You're a bit soppy about her, aren't you?"

"I'm not," I said indignantly; and to show how unsoppy I was, I scooped up a snowball, and advanced to the low wall that bordered the field, and let fly. The snowball hit Tony on the side of the head, knocking his cap off.

He came at the wall, and over it and grabbed me. I struggled, but he was sixteen, and much heavier and stronger than I was. He rolled me over in the snow, and then grabbed a handful of it and crammed it down the back of my neck.

So far everything had been good-humored; I was laughing while I was struggling. When he had crammed the snow down my neck, he stood away and said, "That'll teach you to throw snowballs at your betters."

Sitting on the ground, digging snow out of my collar, I said, "You're only bigger, not better. Someday I'll be as big as you and then I'll put snow down your neck."

"I'm bigger and better," he said. "My father's a gentleman; yours was only a sergeant. You should remember that, even if you do happen to be Lord Bracca's little pet. Your grandfather knows it. That's why he makes you dine in the servants' hall."

He spoke coldly and viciously, as if he had a personal spite against me. I sat for a moment, quite dumbfounded, and then, with a rush of hot blood to my head, I scrambled to my feet and went for him.

I don't believe he wanted to fight me. At first he used his superior weight and strength to push me away. But when I succeeded in hitting him in the mouth, he began to hit back in real earnest, and half a minute later I was sitting on the ground again with a black eye and a bloody lip. My head was reeling dizzily.

"You asked for that, and I hope you like it," Tony said in a harsh, tense voice. His face was pale, and there was a speck of blood on his lip. He turned away abruptly and vaulted the wall, and I started to rise with some intention of going after him. Tom grabbed me by the arms and said, "Don't be a fool, Justin." As Tony and Rose walked rather quickly away, he added, "He's jealous because Bracca gave you that hunter. He always was a stinker."

Mrs. Chandler, who bathed my lip and eye, asked me no questions, but no doubt she questioned Tom when I had gone. The next morning, when I met Bracca, he looked at me with a smiling amusement.

"Well, Justin, you seem to have copped a shiner. A real beauty, if I may say so. I gather you've been taking on someone a little over your weight."

"He said something about my father."

"So you had to go for him and get yourself a swollen eye and a thick lip. How do you know that wasn't exactly what he wanted?"

"But . . . what else could I do?"

"Smile, Justin. An amused indifference is by far the most effective answer to an insult. Far more effective than fighting—especially if you're quite certain to be licked."

"You've done plenty of fighting. I know that."

"I suppose I have, though it's usually the other fellow who's done the challenging. And I take some pains to insure that I'm a fairly good shot. As a precaution, you understand—people are so touchy. Some of them will challenge you on the slightest provocation. But if you're going out of your way to tackle overweight customers like Tony Corfield, I recommend you to learn to use your mauleys. You may have to fight him again some day, and you'll want to lick him next time. I think we might arrange that. I'll have a word with your headmaster and find out if he has any objections."

He had a word with Mr. Alton, and the result was that during the remainder of my stay at Glenside a professional pugilist named Frank Heffernan came to the school from Dublin once a week to give me boxing lessons. Far from objecting, Mr. Alton became enthusiastic about boxing as a subject, and sent letters to all the parents offering to give their children, at a small extra fee, a course of instruction in "the noble and manly art of self-defense." A dozen boys joined the class, and we had some rare old set-tos in the gymnasium.

When I arrived at Springhill for the Easter holiday, Bracca had gone.

"To Brazil," Mrs. Chandler told me. "Of all the countries to choose. Full of fever and bloodshed and the Lord knows what. Or so I've heard. And what d'you think he told me when I asked him his reason for going to Brazil?"

"What did he tell you?"

"Because he'd never been there. That was his reason."

To me it seemed then, and still seems, a very good reason.

This time Bracca was away for three years.

Chapter 13

WHEN I WAS THIRTEEN I was taken from Glenside and sent to school in England. The school chosen for me was a new one, built and endowed by public subscription as a memorial to the late Duke of Wellington, and intended to provide an inexpensive education for "the orphan children of indigent and meritorious officers of the Army." It had been opened, with great pomp, by Queen Victoria and the Prince Consort, in 1859, and the first master was a strikingly handsome thirty-year-old clergyman, who had been picked personally for the position by the Prince.

When I first went there the school was still unfinished—a huge red building in the style of a Louis XV chateau, dumped down in a vast area of lonely Berkshire moorland. With the other new boys I gave my name to a red-coated porter, handed in my trunk, and was instructed how to find my dormitory. I was inspecting this place, bouncing up and down on the bed to see how hard it was, when the door opened and two boys entered.

"You're Kelly, the new boy."

"Yes."

"I'm Dawkin and this is Jones Major. Lawton's told us to show you round."

"Lawton? Is he a master?"

"No." The scorn in Dawkin's voice indicated his opinion of masters. "Lawton's captain of the cricket team and prefect of this dormitory. Every new boy gets shown round on his first day. After that he has to find his way for himself."

On this first afternoon of the summer term, the whole school seemed to have turned out and to be walking in twos and threes round the quads, each new boy escorted by two bigger boys. As we walked my two companions asked questions—where did I come from, what games did I play—and imparted odd scraps of information.

"That's Thomson over there; he's in the sixth, and a prefect, but he's a stinking swot. Ah, there's Lawton—look, over there—and that's Trench with him. Lawton's the fair one, but Trench is in the cricket eleven too."

Two big boys were approaching us, one fair and the other dark. It was the dark boy who caught my attention.

"Trench?" I said. "Was he ever at a school called Glenside?"

"I dunno. He's a fellow countryman of yours."

"I think I know Trench," I said.

I had stopped, and was staring, and I saw Trench glance in my direction, and then pause. He came towards me, frowning, followed by Lawton.

"Haven't I seen you somewhere before? What's your name?"

"Kelly. And it was at Glenside. You left the term after I came."

"Kelly—of course, now I remember. The Lucknow boy. That's right, isn't it?"

"Lucknow boy?" Lawton asked.

"He was in the siege," Trench explained. He turned back to me. "Who was cock of the school when you left?"

"Well . . . I was."

"You!" He sounded quite disgusted. "Well, you're not cock of the school here. Here you're just a scrubby little new boy, lower than a duck's arse, and that's almost as low as you can get. You'd better understand that."

"Yes, Trench." But I grinned, and then he grinned back.

"How was old Alton when you left? And Penny—the virgin's dream of bliss."

"They were just the same."

"I'll bet they were. What was your best game at Glenside—cricket or football? You must have been good at something to be cock of the school."

I had learned caution. I said, "Oh, I dunno. I was about average at football and cricket. I think I was best at boxing—not that I was really any good."

"Did they teach boxing?" Lawton asked.

"Yes. There was an instructor from Dublin who used to come to the school."

"They didn't have that in my time," Trench said, and Lawton said, "So you're a boxer, are you? I'll remember that."

They nodded and moved away; and Dawkin said: "Have you been taught boxing?"

"A little."

"Then you can box with me tomorrow and give me a wrinkle or two. Will you?"

"If you like."

So straight away, on my first day at the school, I acquired a ready-made reputation as a fighter, and for the rest of my time there I had to live up to it. I took one or two beatings, but Heffernan had done his work pretty well, and in most of the many fights I had, I found that I was able to hold my own.

Mr. Alton and Mr. Penny also seemed to have done their work well. After an examination by Mr. Neve, my tutor, I was assigned to a form of boys most of whom were two or three years older than I was. But this may not have been due so much to my own knowledge as to the plain proud ignorance of the other boys.

There were some two hundred of them, mostly from poor army families, and they presented, in the mass, most of the characteristics of unusually warlike Zulus. Book learning was something which they had been brought up from their cradles to despise. Fighting was to be their chosen trade. They were a rough lot, and under a weak master they could easily have degenerated into an undisciplined rabble. Dr. Benson was not a weak master.

The first time I saw him was in Chapel on my first evening and I remember it very well because he reminded me instantly of Bracca. There was a superficial likeness between the two men—the tall figure, the fair hair, worn slightly long, the handsome, classically-molded features, the blue eyes, the fine speaking voice. But no two men could have been more different. Bracca was quiet, casual, amused, and inclined to dismiss things which displeased him with a shrug. Dr. Benson was not casual, nor amused, and he was never quiet. Whenever he appeared the thunder rolled and the lightning could be seen. And when admonition failed, he had a very powerful right hand with a cane.

After my first three weeks at Wellington College, I stopped taking anything in the school with any real degree of seriousness. I found the uniforms absurd, the customs stupid, and the lessons, given by bored masters to large classes of inattentive boys, extremely dull. Except at mathematics, for which I had some talent, and English, which interested me, I scarcely did any work at all.

Dr. Benson could find excuses for a stupid boy, who was unable to learn, but for a boy who could learn, and wouldn't, he had little toleration. And when that boy was also unpunctual, unrepentant for his misdeeds, and inattentive in Chapel, there was only one thing to do with him—flog him till he saw reason. So I was flogged regularly, and if I were to say I didn't mind the floggings, I should be exaggerating. It would be more accurate to say that I became used to them, and regarded them as a rather painful inconvenience.

I knew I had to go to school somewhere before I could be grown-up and independent, and I accepted the necessity.

Bracca returned to Ireland for a short visit a few days before the end of my Easter holiday in 1864. I rode over to see him the day after he arrived, and found the Chandlers with him.

"Justin! How tall you are, my dear fellow. Of course, you're fourteen. That probably accounts for it. Sit down and tell me about yourself."

"There's nothing much to tell. What was Brazil like?"

"Devilish hot. Charming people, though—some of them. I went on from there to the United States, as I expect you know. Though with this Civil War going on there, they can hardly be called United."

"What is your opinion of the war, Rupert?" Captain Chandler asked.

"I'm quite positive that the North will win."

"Are you? The general opinion seems to be that the South can hardly lose. All the talk is of Southern victories."

"London's a long way from the Potomac River. With every month that passes the Northern armies grow stronger, the Southern armies weaker. In spite of his victories, General Lee is hard pressed."

"I must admit that you surprise me."

"Did you see any fighting?" I asked.

"A little. The Union authorities allowed a few neutral observers to accompany their armies, and by the good offices of Colonel Freeman I was able to join them for a time. I witnessed the attack on Fredericksburg." He turned to Captain Chandler. "By God, Harry, you should have seen it. The fire power of the modern rifle—it's positively terrifying. Burnside launched his huge army in a frontal attack on Lee's smaller army, and was repulsed with the most hideous losses. His men fought well—they fought very well—but they were helpless against men fighting from prepared positions. The Irish Brigade in particular made a magnificent charge, and left half their number on the field."

"The Irish Brigade?" I asked. "Which side were they on?"

"Those I watched were on the Union side. But there are a great many Irishmen in the Confederate armies too."

"You mean they're fighting against each other. Why are they doing that? I thought the war was all about slaves."

"It's a war for freedom, Justin. The men on the Northern side are fighting to abolish the foul curse of slavery, and the Confederates

[129]

are fighting with equal enthusiasm to free their states from the brutal tyranny of the Northern industrialist. And the politicians who contrived the war—well, I suppose they're too busy making speeches to do much fighting."

He rose, smiling. "Come on out, Justin. Let's go riding and see if we can break our necks on horseback. I'd like to observe what progress you've made since my last visit."

We rode across the hillside and talked. He said, "How do you like Wellington College?"

"It's not bad. Most of the boys are English. I like them well enough."

"I suppose the great majority will be going into the Army. Do you intend to enter the Army?"

"Why, of course. My father was in the Army."

"You know you couldn't possibly have a worse reason for entering the Army than merely because your father was in it."

"But . . . my father liked being in the Army. He often said so."

"So did mine. It was his world, and it was taken for granted that it would be my world. I took it for granted myself—as you're doing."

"Didn't you like the Army?"

"For seven years I was most abominably bored. I had too little to do and not enough money to spend. I thought most of my fellow officers were ignorant clods, and they regarded me as a conceited pup. I've no doubt we were both right. In my early days some of them objected to my habits of reading and listening to music, which they considered effeminate and unsoldierly. To convince them of my manliness I had to break several of their heads and sleep with quite a number of their wives and daughters. Terrible women, rather like army rations; I still shudder sometimes when I think of them. But in those days I was too poor to afford attractive mistresses."

Such views, coming from Bracca, bewildered me. There was something wrong somewhere, and I wanted to put my finger on it.

"But . . . if you didn't like the Army, why did my father like it? He wasn't an ignorant clod."

"Your father was a man of unusual wit and imagination, who was also a born soldier. That happens sometimes, though rarely. I never was a soldier. Your father knew that. He and I understood each other extremely well."

"Captain Chandler told me you were a very good soldier."

"Harry would say that. He may even believe it. I could ride, and use my weapons with some skill, and even command a company, but after three months in the Army I looked on the whole thing as a lot of plain tomfoolery. Almost my happiest moment in the Army was when I heard my uncle and cousin were dead suddenly, and that I was rich and my own master."

"Were you glad they were dead?" I asked incredulously. "Just because you wanted their money."

"I was overjoyed." He glanced at me and smiled; his bright blue eyes held an amused expression. "I believe you're shocked."

I was. I had seen death at Lucknow, but in Mr. Alton's school, and at Wellington, we were taught to speak of it with reverence and a certain pious gloom. One didn't express delight at anybody's death.

As I watched him, Bracca's face became sad and grave. He sighed. In a solemn and slightly whining voice, he said, "The unhappy deaths of my poor uncle—the miserable old blackguard—and my unfortunate cousin—the snarling, sour-faced hypocrite—filled me with a sorrow which even the news that I had inherited a title and a large fortune could not dispel." He looked at me, and his expression was so doleful and sanctimonious that I couldn't help laughing.

"There, you see. You don't believe a word of it."

"Oh well, if they were as bad as that . . ."

"A mean, dingy couple, Justin, I assure you. But never mind them. We were talking about you."

"Yes. But if I don't go into the Army, what can I do?"

"You could be a poet. Or keep a brothel. Or marry a rich old widow. You could even go to America. You have plenty of time in the next two or three years to make up your mind what you want to do."

"My father meant me to go to America. I have an uncle there."

"I know—the play actor. Your father often spoke of him, and while I was in America I had the curiosity to see if I could trace him. It proved unexpectedly easy. He'd been invalided out of the Irish Brigade after being badly wounded at Bull Run. Now he's managing a hotel in Chicago."

"What's he like?"

"Like? Why, if your father was an eagle, I think your uncle is probably a turkey. A very fine turkey. You can imagine him as a tall, red-faced, smiling man, with a cigar in his mouth and a flower in his coat. Genial, talkative, and, I should say, fairly shrewd. And a sound Irish patriot. He was uncertain whether to flatter me because I'm a lord or denounce me because I'm a landlord. He managed to do both."

"He manages a hotel? What's it called?"

"The Mackinaw House. A smallish place, but it has quite a reputation as a resort of actors, journalists, and sporting men. I spent an amusing evening there with your uncle and aunt."

"My aunt? What's she like?"

"Her name is Zoe. She's a stout, jolly woman, with dyed hair, and a laugh that sets the glasses ringing. You'll like her."

"Will I?" I said, half laughing, and half disappointed. "They both sound awful to me."

In my mind I could picture myself introducing a fat aunt, with dyed hair and a laugh that set the glasses ringing, to Rose Corfield, or some of the boys at Wellington College. The picture made me uncomfortable. Bracca was watching me smiling, his eyes mocking me. He knew exactly what was passing in my mind.

"Don't be such a damned snob, Justin," he said. "You should feel proud of your uncle."

"Why?"

"Because he had the courage and imagination to strike out for himself and make his own way in the world. If he hadn't he wouldn't be the manager of a reasonable hotel, with a cigar in his mouth, and a flower in his coat, and amusing friends to drink with in the evening. He'd be a potman now, serving porter in a dirty little saloon in Glenaly, or a farm laborer, without an idea in his head outside his own parish. He'd be as bad as your Uncle Randall."

I laughed. "My Uncle Randall isn't exactly a potman or a farm laborer."

"He isn't exactly anything. He's a notable example of a man who went into the Army because it was expected of him, when his natural vocation was to be a pimp, or a process server. Go into the Army if you want to, but be sure you do want to. And now let me see if you can ride."

He galloped away from me at a cracking pace, and for the next twenty minutes I had a hair-raising ride. On we went, faster and faster, over a wide ditch, down a short hill, and then across a level stretch with a fence in the distance and a stream on the far side. I felt a sickening little flash of fear as I saw Bracca's great steeple-chaser nine or ten lengths ahead of me rise like a swallow; but there was no stopping now, and as I settled myself more firmly in the saddle I felt an upward, thrusting motion between my thighs as my game little mare went at the fence, and then there was a bright flash of water and white stones below me, and an awful moment as the far bank crumpled under Cleopatra's hind legs. But she recovered her foothold almost instantly, and we were safely over.

Bracca had reined up and was waiting for me. I heard him laugh, which was a rare sound.

"So you followed me over. Some day you may be a horseman. I think the time has come for you to have another horse."

"Oh no," I protested. Looking back at the jump, I knew I should never have tried it if I had not been dared. I knew, too, that I deserved no praise. It was my clever horse who had taken me over. I felt a warm gratitude to her.

"I like Cleopatra better than any horse I know," I added.

"Better than this one?"

I knew that was a joke. He was riding a great black thoroughbred which had won two steeplechases and cost twelve hundred guineas. I laughed dutifully.

"Quite as much," I answered.

"Oh, you do." We turned our horses' heads in the direction of home, and he went on, "When do you go back to school, Justin?"

"On Wednesday. That is, I go by the packet on Tuesday evening. I have to be there on Wednesday afternoon."

"I'm going on Monday. You can come with me if you like, and spend a day and a night in London."

"Can I? I've never been in London, except just to pass through it." An idea came into my mind, and I added, "Perhaps I could see the McLeods. I haven't seen them since we came home from India."

"The McLeods? Oh yes, the music mistress and her children. Certainly you can see them; you can see anyone you like. I'll speak to your grandfather and make the necessary arrangements."

We rode on in silence. I was going to London with Bracca, which delighted me, and I also had the happy, buoyant feeling which comes from having done something rather daring. As we approached the Castle I was wondering, perhaps a little boastfully, what the Chandlers would say when I told them I had jumped the Tiernan Water.

Mrs. Chandler was waiting for us under the Gatehouse Arch. As we slowed our horses to a walk, she came to meet us.

"By God, Rupert, you ought to be shot," she said in her bluntest voice. "I was watching from an upper window; I saw you take Justin over Tiernan Water. That was a damnably senseless thing to do. The boy might easily have broken his neck."

"You're quite wrong, my dear." Smiling, the reins held loosely in his hand, Bracca sat on the big horse looking down at her. He went on blandly, "I didn't take Justin over. If he risked his neck, he did it on his own responsibility. Justin's reached an age now when he decides for himself whether or not he'll jump, or which way he'll jump. Haven't you, Justin?"

"Yes," I said.

"Rupert, what poppycock. You knew very well he'd follow where you led."

"He knew what he was doing. And here he is, safe and sound. What's more, he's won himself a horse."

"A horse. What horse?"

"This horse—Persephone. I think she should suit him very well." He looked at me. "Come and ride her tomorrow if you feel inclined. I think you'd better stable her here for the present, as you're going back to school so soon. You can claim her and take her away when your summer holidays begin."

Without waiting for any thanks, he raised his hat to Mrs. Chandler and rode away from under the arch. I remained where I was; I was lunching with the Chandlers. Mrs. Chandler stared after Bracca, an expression of exasperation on her face. Captain Chandler came round a corner of the arch and joined us.

"Did you have a good ride?" he asked me.

"Harry, Rupert took Justin over Tiernan Water. And now he's given him Persephone," Mrs. Chandler said.

"What!" Captain Chandler stared at her. "You say he's given Justin Persephone. Has he, by God."

"Harry, it's senseless. First to do his best to kill the boy, and then to give him the best horse in his stable. I don't grudge Justin the horse but it . . . it's unsuitable. A boy of fourteen riding a twelve-hundred-guinea steeplechaser."

"You may be right, but it's no good arguing about it with Rupert. You know what he is."

"Sometimes I think he really has sold his soul to the devil," Mrs. Chandler said. "But you're right about one thing. It certainly does no good to argue with him."

That night, when I joined the servants in the kitchen, I noticed a new arrival. Florence, the kitchen-maid, had left to be married, and her place had been taken by a slim, impudent-looking young girl, with a mass of curly red hair and a broad ingratiating grin. I don't think I spoke to her that evening. While the others bombarded me with questions about Bracca, she sat quietly at the back of the circle, as befitted her newness and her lowly station. But every time I caught her eye, she grinned.

Her name was Tessie Flaherty.

Chapter 14

"IF you feel inclined for a gentle stroll in the Park, and then, perhaps, up Bond Street, I'll accompany you," Bracca said. "Walking is as good a way as any of seeing London on a fine May morning. But if you have an unquenchable longing to visit the Zoo, or the Houses of Parliament, I'll ask Curling to take you."

"I'd like to walk," I said. "Who's Curling?"

"Mr. Curling, my invaluable secretary. A charming old fellow, with the face of an angry monkey and a habit of taking snuff. You're wise to avoid his company. I do so myself whenever I find it possible."

I laughed and said, "Then why do you have him as your secretary?"

"Partly from habit; I've known him a long time. But he's also very useful. He looks after my affairs in England when I'm away, as Harry Chandler looks after them in Ireland, and has an eagle eye for my interests. He deals with all my most disagreeable correspondence. He interviews people whom I don't want to see. He buys pictures and ornaments for me with infallible judgment; he's very learned on such subjects. He has no interests in life whatever outside my affairs, and he dislikes nearly all my friends. So do I, for that matter. It forms a kind of bond between us."

We left the house and walked towards Hyde Park. Park Lane was gay with glittering carriages, drawn by sleek horses, and driven by skillful top-hatted coachmen. The women in these carriages wore light summer dresses and boas, and carried brightly colored parasols in slender, white-kid-gloved hands. They looked very rich and fashionable, and made me feel like a coarse country boy. But being with Bracca gave me confidence. He seemed taller, more distinguished, handsomer than any of the men.

As we strolled along, continually raising our hats to his acquaintances, he kept up a light commentary on the people we passed.

"Who was that you raised your hat to?"

"The woman in the ancient barouche with the two plain girls? That was Lady Ditchling and two of her daughters. She has seven of them, all unmarried. A dreadful situation for her. There's a story that she offered them as a complete harem to a visiting Persian Prince, but he declined on the grounds that they reminded him more of bulls than bulbuls."

We had approached the railings bordering the Row, and were watching the riders exercising themselves and their horses. A small woman in a black riding habit reined in her horse abruptly and waved to us. She was accompanied by a beefy, muscular man, with heavy black whiskers and the expression of a supercilious ox. The woman hailed us.

"Bracca, you bad penny. Have you turned up again?" She edged her horse up closer to the railings, and added stridently, "My God, what are you doing with that schoolboy? You haven't by any chance changed your religion."

"How are you, Lily. You're looking very pretty. A little stouter, perhaps, than when I saw you last."

"You bloody swine, Bracca." Her voice was coarse, but she had an extremely pretty face and the most beautiful eyes I had ever seen, very large, a deep violet in color, with an expression of gaiety and almost childlike innocence in them. She turned to her companion.

"Did you hear what he said? Did you hear the scoundrel insult a defenseless woman? And you call yourself a man. Why don't you get off your horse and knock him down?"

"I never met a defenseless woman," the beefy man said in a drawling voice. "And if I got off my horse he might knock me down." He smiled, and his face lost the expression of a supercilious ox and became quite genial. "Haven't seen you for a long time, Rupert. Somebody told me you were dead."

"That was only a wish." Bracca turned to me. "Justin, I want you to meet two old friends of mine, Miss Wilton and Lord Hammersley. Mr. Kelly from County Wicklow, my friend and neighbor."

Lord Hammersley said, "How d'you do, Mr. Kelly," and Miss Wilton said, in an affected Irish brogue, "Justin Kelly is it, from County Wicklow. The top of the morning to you, Mr. Kelly. And you're a neighbor of Lord Bracca. Now what kind of a name would his lordship be having in your vicinity? He's known as a black-hearted villain, I'll be bound."

"He is not then. After St. Patrick himself he has the best name in the whole of Ireland. Excepting among those who say he's sold his soul to the devil."

I saw Bracca smile his brief, sudden smile. Hammersley gave a loud guffaw. He said, "Good for you, my boy. He had you there,

Ninepins." Miss Wilton, or Ninepins, laughed, and it was a joyful silvery sound.

"I think I like you, Mr. Justin Kelly," she said. "How old are you?"

"Fourteen."

"Fourteen. Oh my God, I was hoping you were at least sixteen. Never mind—I can be patient. I'm sure we shall be friends. Come and see me on your sixteenth birthday, and I'll give you a present. Will you remember that?"

"I'll remember, Miss Wilton."

"Call me Ninepins. All my friends do except Bracca—and he's no friend of mine. I hate the bloody man." She smiled at Bracca. "I'm not going to invite you to come and see me because if I do, you won't. I'll make Ham bring you one evening."

"I'll bring him," Lord Hammersley said. "Against my better judgment."

"Darling Ham, you never had any judgment. Your only assets are a magnificent physique and an unlimited bank balance. But money isn't everything, is it, Justin." She winked at me, and her expression was that of a mischievous little girl. "Don't forget to come and see me on your sixteenth birthday."

When they had ridden on, I said to Bracca, "Who is Miss Wilton?"

"She's our most celebrated *Traviata*." I looked puzzled, and he added, "If you'd like it in plain English, she's a whore."

"A . . ." I hesitated on the word. "A whore?"

"At the very top of her profession. At present her protector seems to be Hammersley; before him there was Dalloway, and before him the Comte DuPlessis. All highly eligible; poor Lady Ditchling would give up her prospects of Heaven to marry one of her daughters to any of them. But they prefer Lily, or Ninepins, as her friends call her."

"Why do they call her that?"

"One night at Astleys she picked up a bottle and threatened to knock down a group of young guardees like a row of bloody ninepins. So I've been told. It could easily be true."

"I wish I'd been there." I laughed. "What do you think of her?"

"She has the tongue of a fishwife, the mind of a child, the heart of a lion, the body of an Aphrodite, and the eyes of an angel. A magnetic creature, as many men have found—including yourself, I can see. You must certainly visit her on your sixteenth birthday. It should be an interesting experience."

"I don't suppose she'll remember. Anyway, she doesn't know my birthday."

"Then you must make her remember. You'll never get anything you want by sitting and hoping for it. But wait till you're sixteen, and then see how you feel. Now we'll go and look at the shops."

We took a hansom cab to Bond Street and looked at the shops, and Bracca made a few small purchases for himself and bought me a pair of ivory-backed hairbrushes. After luncheon Bracca had business of his own to attend to, but he had arranged for the McLeods to be brought from Westbourne Grove to spend the afternoon with me. Long before three, when they were due to arrive, I was waiting impatiently in the hall for them.

Punctually at three the doorbell jangled. Anticipating the butler, I ran to the door to open it. They had arrived in style, in one of Bracca's carriages, all dressed in their best—Mrs. McLeod crino-lined, pink-bonneted, and wearing a feather boa, Jeannie in blue silk, Ian in an Eton suit. There was a moment of awkwardness as we all examined each other.

"Justin! Good gracious, how you've grown. Quite the young gentle-man, I declare. I should hardly have known you. Am I still allowed to kiss you?"

She laughed and kissed me, and behind her Jeannie and Ian were looking at me shyly. They were both still sandy-haired and freckled as I remembered them, but Jeannie, at fourteen, was a sturdy, plumpish girl, covered with puppy fat, while Ian, nearly two years older, was still angular and bony, and hardly taller than Jeannie. I topped the pair of them by a good three inches.

"Come on upstairs," I said. "We're going into the Fragonard room, and there'll be tea presently. Lord Bracca says he understands you have to go home soon after five, and a carriage has been ordered, but he's hoping to be back in time to see you before you leave."

"Yes, I mustn't be late. I have a private music lesson with an important pupil at half past five," Mrs. McLeod said, as we were mounting the stairs. We entered the room and waited while Mrs. McLeod examined the paintings and pointed out their merits to us. She was still the same old Mrs. McLeod, didactic, self-opinionated, and for an hour the party limped painfully, while she monopolized the conversation.

"Now tell us about yourself, Justin. What have you been doing this long time; it's nearly eighteen months since you wrote. I suppose you see a lot of Lord Bracca."

"Not very much. He's away most of the time. I see him when he's at Bracca."

"But you're staying with him now, in London. You must be quite one of his favorites."

"I'm staying with him because I'm going to Wellington College tomorrow."

"Wellington—not Eton," Mrs. McLeod said in a tone of slight surprise. "Ian gained himself a scholarship entrance to Westminster School. He's been there a year now. Haven't you, Ian."

"Yes, Mama."

"Do you like it?" I asked.

"Yes, it's all right."

"He likes it very well," Mrs. McLeod told me. "Though I think he could work harder. Jeannie's still at the school in Bayswater, and is making excellent progress with her singing. I teach her myself. What do you do at school, Justin?"

"Oh, we have lessons and games—football and cricket." I looked at Ian. "Do you like cricket?"

"Ian likes cricket but doesn't care greatly for football," Mrs. McLeod said. "That is so, isn't it, Ian?"

Without waiting for his answer, she turned to me. "Not that games and sports have any real importance compared with study. I'm sure Lord Bracca would agree with me."

"Yes," I said politely. "He thinks study's very important. Especially things like music and books."

The reunion looked like being a horrible failure; I was beginning to wish I hadn't suggested it. Ian and Jeannie sat stiffly on the edges of their chairs, hardly able to get a word in, while Mrs. McLeod talked on and on. But when tea came, with a lot of complicated little French pastries, stuffed with cream, and almonds, and other things, the atmosphere became more earthy, and soon we were in the middle of a *Do you remember* conversation about Lucknow, and Calcutta, and the people we had known. We were all chatting quite merrily when Bracca entered, a few minutes after five o'clock.

"Mrs. McLeod—how pleasant to meet you again. I recall a most interesting discussion about music, though I expect you've forgotten that years ago."

Mrs. McLeod blushed, and looked pleased and gracious.

"Indeed I haven't, Lord Bracca; I remember our two meetings very well. I was saying so only a few moments ago, wasn't I, Justin? May I introduce my two children, Ian and Jeannette."

"Ian and Jeannie. I've heard so much about you two that I feel I almost know you already." Bracca sat down, smiling at the children, and stretched out his long legs easily. "I'm going to ask you to grant me a favor—with Mrs. McLeod's consent."

They stared at him, wondering what favor he could possibly ask them. He looked at Mrs. McLeod.

"I know you have an engagement to keep, and I'm obliged to go out. A committee meeting—inconvenient, but rather important. I wonder if Ian and Jeannie would be kind enough to stay for a while and entertain Justin at dinner." He looked towards Ian and Jeannie. "I'm sure you'll have plenty to talk about, and the absence of grown-up company won't seriously inconvenience you."

Mrs. McLeod looked at him blankly for a moment; I think she was a little hurt by not being included in the invitation. He went on, speaking as if everything was already settled, "The children will be home with you by nine. Mr. Curling, my secretary, will escort them, and will hand them over to you personally. I think you will be interested to meet Mr. Curling—a profound scholar and a great connoisseur of *objets d'art*. He was once my tutor, and still treats me very sternly when he thinks the occasion demands it."

"I'm sure you were a very apt pupil," Mrs. McLeod said archly.

So that was settled, and Mrs. McLeod went home alone. Bracca saw her to the carriage and came back to us.

"I have to go and dress. The house is yours. Dinner will be served at seven, and you'll be told when it's time to go home. Look after your guests well, Justin. See they have all they want."

"Can we go anywhere we like?" I asked.

"If you go anywhere you shouldn't, somebody'll soon tell you." He smiled at Ian and Jeannie. "I'll wish you good night now. I hope we shall meet again."

We were alone, and it was quite like the old days in Lucknow. At once we all became very animated. Ian and Jeannie were full of curiosity. We went into the drawing room, the dining room, the billiard room, chattering like parrots, pausing to examine and touch anything which took our attention. We went into a long, rather narrow room known as the Gallery.

In the middle of the room were three long glass-topped show-cases lined with velvet. One of them contained a collection of gold snuff boxes, another held Japanese sword guards, and the third held a collection of small Chinese ornaments, mostly of carved jade. Round the walls were shelves on which at intervals were placed bowls, vases, statuettes, and porcelain ornaments arranged according to their ages and countries of origin.

"What are all these things?" Ian asked.

"Lord Bracca calls them Mr. Curling's collection. He owns them but Mr. Curling buys them for him."

We walked round idly, not very interested. There was a graceful vase on one of the shelves, decorated with a pattern of leaves and a butterfly on a glazed, creamy background.

"That's pretty," Jeannie said. "Can I look?"

The vase was above her head. She reached upwards to take it from the shelf, and it slipped through her fingers and fell to the floor and broke into three pieces.

"Clumsy," Ian said.

"Oh dear," Jeannie said. She looked at me in acute distress. "What'll I do, Justin? Will he be very angry?"

"I don't know," I said. We stood staring down at the broken pieces in dismay. "I suppose I'd better tell somebody," I added.

Reluctantly I went and found a tall stockinged and powdered footman, who came back with me into the Gallery.

"So you've broken one of them things." He shook his head, concerned, but sympathetic. "I'm afraid I shall 'ave to inform Mr. Curling. He never lets nobody touch anything in 'ere except himself."

He went away, and we waited. We were becoming more and more frightened. Jeannie was trying hard not to cry.

Mr. Curling came in, evidently in a great hurry. I hadn't met him before, but I should have recognized him at once from Bracca's description—"the face of an angry monkey."

"What's this, what's this, what have you done?" he said very rapidly, in a high voice, and then his voice rose a whole octave higher as he saw the vase and exclaimed in a tone of sheer anguish: "Oh! What *have* you done. You've broken the Tz'u Chou vase."

He went on his knees, as if falling by the body of a loved one, and picked up the pieces and looked at them, and then glared up at us with positive hatred.

"How did you do this? How did you do it? Were you playing with it?"

"I wanted to look at it. It slipped through my fingers," Jeannie said in a muffled voice.

"T'cha," he said. He rose and went on angrily, "Stay where you are. Don't touch anything. Don't dare to touch anything else. I shall have to tell Lord Bracca about this."

Jeannie was crying. Ian and I stood dumb and pale. There was a wait of about half a minute and then Bracca and Mr. Curling came in. Bracca was half dressed; over black evening trousers and a stiff white shirt, he was wearing a thick green silk dressing gown.

"What's all this?" he asked. "Something broken, I hear." He glanced down at the pieces of the vase. "Oh, that," he added.

"They were playing with it," Mr. Curling said in a voice of pure venom.

"We weren't," I said, and Jeannie, crying, said, "I only wanted to look at it and it slipped through my fingers."

"Nothing to cry about, my dear," Bracca said. "It was an accident; it might have happened to anyone. It doesn't matter in the least."

"Doesn't matter?" Mr. Curling said in an outraged voice. "The Tz'u Chou vase. It's nine hundred years old, and quite irreplaceable."

"If I thought that I should go out and hang myself immediately," Bracca said. "Nothing's irreplaceable, Curling. The vase is nine hundred years old, you say; it's lucky to have survived so long. Somebody had to break it some time, and I'm not in the least sorry. I never liked it."

He reached out his hands, and picked Jeannie up, holding her close to him in the crook of his right arm, and smoothed her hair back from her forehead with his left hand. He said gently, "Never cry about anything broken, Jeannie. Forget about it and think of something else." Then he kissed her wet eyes, and her lips, and smiled at her, and lowered her to the floor again.

"So we'll all forget this trifling incident, shall we," he added. "Oh, and one other thing. I shall be obliged if nobody will make any mention of it to Mrs. McLeod. I want it to be completely forgotten."

We all stood watching as he went out of the room. And from that moment Jeannie was his devoted slave.

"Well," I said, in a tone of relief. "He didn't seem to mind very much, did he?"

"No, he didn't mind," Mr. Curling agreed, in a voice of intense bitterness. "A beautiful object has been destroyed by three stupid children, and Lord Bracca is indifferent. Throw it away, and buy something else."

He turned from us as if he couldn't bear the sight of us any longer, picked up the broken pieces, and hurried with them from the room. Ian gave a deep sigh.

"I'm glad we haven't got to tell Mama," he said. "She'd have gone on about it for days."

"I hope Mr. Curling won't tell her," Jeannie said. "He looks mean enough."

I heard afterwards that he said nothing whatever to Ian and

Jeannie during the drive to Westbourne Grove, and was barely civil to Mrs. McLeod when he handed them back into her care. So she never knew about the broken vase.

The following afternoon I returned to Wellington.

Chapter 15

I GREW TALLER and stronger, but no wiser. At Wellington College, without bothering to work hard, I easily obtained the usual removes from one form to another, and I invariably headed my form in mathematics. This did not impress Dr. Benson, who was a classical scholar, and who despised mathematics. My relations with him remained uncordial. But during my last year I played football for the school, and was made a prefect; and my tutor advised me to enter the engineers rather than the infantry.

"In the engineers," he told me. "You'll find your mathematics will come in very useful."

During the holidays I rode, and visited with the Chandlers, and sometimes I went out to dinner parties, or other social functions. Whenever I could, I tried to put myself somewhere near Rose Corfield, but I very seldom succeeded. At infrequent intervals I met Bracca, and my resumed friendship with the McLeods went on. It became my custom, on my way to and from Wellington, to spend a night or two nights in their house in Westbourne Grove.

They lived plainly, but comfortably enough, in an atmosphere of strenuous and high-minded culture. This was promoted by Mrs. Mc-Leod, who was becoming more energetic and more and more self-opinionated as the years went by. She was prospering in her profession of music teacher. At all hours of the day, and often late into the evening, the house was filled with the sounds of piano and singing lessons. She was an exacting parent, and, staying in the house, I could see how she often irritated her children, and especially Jeannie, with her domineering and bossy ways. But she was always very kind to me.

At Springhill my grandfather kept to himself, and left me to come and go as I pleased. There were times when the Chandlers and Bracca were all away from Ireland, and then I would go riding alone, taking sandwiches with me, and often spending a night in some small farm, or village inn. I rode alone along winding tracks over the hills and through the valleys on my great black mare, Persephone, or the small chestnut, Cleopatra.

My relations with the Smannels and Dooley and the other servants remained very friendly, but with a slight difference. I was no longer regarded as a child in the house, to be told what to do and what not to do. An invisible dividing line had been crossed, and though I still sat with them and talked with them, I was no longer quite one of them. I had become the boss's grandson, the young master.

The only one of them who did not recognize that my increased size gave me an increase in authority was Tessie, the eighteen-year-old kitchen-maid. She treated me with complete disrespect, mocking me, laughing at me, and sometimes playing jokes on me. On my sixteenth birthday she threw a rotten apple at me which hit me in the back of the neck.

I had had a solitary birthday; the Chandlers and Bracca were all in England. There had been presents sent by post—a gold sovereign purse, containing ten pounds, from Bracca, a silk scarf and some gloves from the Chandlers, the poems of Wordsworth from Mrs. Mc-Leod, and a leather wallet from Ian and Jeannie. After breakfast I had saddled Persephone and ridden most of the day, eating my sandwiches, with a pint of porter, at a small inn on the slopes of Mullaghcleevaun.

I had returned home, hungry as a wolf, and had just finished stabling Persephone, when the apple hit me. I knew at once who had thrown it; I turned quickly, and was just in time to see Tessie's thin figure sprinting away round the corner of the stables. I went after her like a rocket.

The stables were L-shaped. When I reached the corner of the L, and looked along the bottom, there was no sign of Tessie. But she couldn't have got clear away; she hadn't had the time. The door of one of the loose boxes was open.

I went to it and entered. She was there, standing in the middle of the floor, her hands on her hips, laughing.

"I've got you now," I said. I was expecting her to dodge, or make a dash for the door, as she had on previous occasions when I had chased her.

She stood quite still. I took her by the arms and said, "Now what am I going to do with you?"

She didn't try to draw away, or struggle. "An' now what are you going to do with me?" she said in a mocking whisper. She was leaning against me, looking up into my face, her lips slightly parted. I only had to bend my head.

When I kissed her, she thrust her belly urgently against mine, and flung both her thin arms round my neck, holding my face close to hers. I was surprised, and excited by the softness of her lips, and her close clinging body. My pulses were pounding. With both arms round her, I crushed her to me till I could hear her ribs crack.

"Ah," she gasped. "Let me go, Justin. It's destroying me you are."

I loosened my grip, and took a hand from behind her back, and gently touched one of her breasts. She put a hand over mine and pressed my hand to her. I could feel the soft mound under my fingers. My fingers tightened on it.

"No, Justin, no." Her voice was a whisper. She tugged at the hand that was on her breast. "Not now. Wait. I'll slip into your room tonight."

I was so surprised that my grip on her loosened altogether. She gave a low laugh, and wriggled away out of my arms. "Tonight, when it's dark," she whispered. Then she was gone.

I had a dazed, solemn, almost frightened feeling as I went to the door of the loose box, and saw her vanish into the back door of the house. She was the first girl I had ever kissed, except Jeannie (who somehow didn't seem to count) and tonight . . . But she didn't mean it, I told myself. She had only been joking. She couldn't have meant it. I found some reassurance in this thought. I wasn't certain that I wanted her to come.

I entered the kitchen, and had my supper, and sat talking for a while to Mrs. Smannel, and Dooley, and the other servants, and she hardly looked at me the whole time. At about half past nine there was a general stirring, and pushing back of chairs, and we all went to bed.

I lay in bed, in my dark room, wide awake, and wondering. She wasn't coming. I knew she wasn't coming. But every little creak or sound in the house made me raise my head expectantly. A long time passed.

Finally I turned on my side, and thrust my head determinedly into the pillow, and closed my eyes. I should go to sleep; that was my firm intention. But it was no good closing my eyes, because I didn't sleep.

A loud creak caught my attention, and I sat up and turned my head. The door was opening. She came in, a slim white shape in the darkness, and closed the door carefully, and came quickly to the bed. I heard her whisper, "Move over, will you; make a bit of room. Ah, I'm as cold as the hind legs of a frog."

But she wasn't cold when she slid in beside me, rubbing herself against me like a cat, purring with pleasure. She was warm and eager and willing, her arms hot round my neck, her slim, writhing body supple and ardent, her lips thirsty against my lips.

"Ah . . . ah . . . ah . . ." she said, in soft, crooning gasps of ecstasy. "Ah, Justin . . . Justin . . ."

Later, when she was lying quietly beside me, with her head on my shoulder, and her fingertips gently exploring my face, she said, "You didn't expect anything like this on your birthday, did you?"

"No, I didn't. Though . . ." I broke off.

"Though what?"

"Nothing."

"Though what? Tell me."

"Well, there was somebody asked me to come and see her on my sixteenth birthday."

"And who would that be? Not that whey-faced Miss Corfield?"

"No. And she's not whey-faced. But if you want to know who it was, it was somebody called Ninepins."

"Ninepins. What sort of a name would that be for a woman to have? Who is she?"

"She's a . . . a friend of Lord Hammersley. She was with him when she came and spoke to us. It was in London; I was with Lord Bracca."

"A friend is it? And he calls her Ninepins. What kind of a friend? Is she his fancy woman?"

"Well . . . I suppose some people might say so."

"Only some people?" She laughed softly. "And she asked for you to come and visit her on your sixteenth birthday. Was she pretty, Justin?"

"Yes. I . . . I didn't really notice very much."

"You didn't notice." Her tone was softly mocking. "Are you sorry you didn't go? Would you rather be with her than with me?"

"No. I'd much rather be with you."

"Me brave boyo. But you have to say that, don't you? What was she wearing?"

"A black riding habit. She was riding, in the Row, when we met her."

"And had she pearls round her throat, and jeweled rings on her fingers. Diamonds and rubies and the like?"

I laughed and said, "I didn't really notice. But I expect she has plenty of jewels."

"So will I have when I go to London. Fine silks and satins, and

[147]

jewels on my fingers, and servants to wait on me, and my own carriage to ride in."

"It sounds a good idea. And when are you going to London?"

"When I have the money saved. It's a slow business, surely. I'll need ten pounds to take me to London, and I have five already. So I'm halfway there."

"So you are. But silks and jewels don't grow on trees, even in London, Tessie. There are plenty of poor people in London, the same as here."

"There's plenty of poor people everywhere, and I'm one of them in this place. But there's plenty of rich people in London—men who'd think nothing of giving a girl a hundred pounds, or two hundred, or maybe more, if they liked her. The way your Ninepins gets her jewels and her riding habit. What she can do, I can do. Anyways, I can try."

"But . . ." I broke off, speechless. It seemed to me that she was telling me calmly, and as a matter of everyday interest, that she proposed to become a whore. She gave a little wiggle, and stretched out her legs; her hair brushed my mouth.

"I'm no beauty, but the men like me," she went on thoughtfully. "There's not a boy in the village I couldn't have by crooking my finger—or even old Smannel, or Mullen. So why wouldn't I find somebody in London—somebody rich like that lord who was with your Ninepins? Tell me that."

"But . . . but it would mean that you'd have to sell yourself . . . that . . . that . . ."

"And what else have I to sell? Why wouldn't I sell myself if I get what I want?"

"You'd hate it, Tessie. Selling yourself to any man . . ."

"Not any man. Only somebody I fancied. And why would I hate that? What I hate is when there's no men. When I've nothing to do but wish I had the feel of a nice fellow's arms round me, and his mouth on my mouth."

"You . . . you like men . . . I mean, just men."

"I love them. Without them I have the weight of the world on my shoulders, and a dead heart in me. And that's the frank truth of it. But tonight, with the arms of my darling holding me, and the warm tide of love in my body, I feel light as the air."

"That's all very well," I said rather sourly. "But from what you've said, it seems to me you have rather a lot of darlings."

"You think I'm a bad girl. A bad, wicked girl. You do, don't you."

"I . . ."

"Yes you do. Say it. Say you think I'm a bad, wicked girl."

She put her lips against mine, and blew gently, and then turned her head slowly from side to side, rubbing her lips along mine, thrusting the tip of her tongue in between my lips, and her hands were busy in my back and ribs, while her body was undulating against mine like a warm snake.

"Say it . . . ah . . . ah, Justin . . . Ah, me darling . . ." The last words faded in an ecstatic sigh.

After she had left me I lay for a while, half exultant and half ashamed, the fragrance of her body still lingering in my bed. Next morning, at breakast, I was a little embarrassed about meeting her, but she grinned at me frankly. Her smile had an added sweetness, and her eyes were bright and happy. She looked, as she herself had put it, as if she were floating on air.

There were only three nights left of my holidays, and she came to me on two of them.

"Justin." Her voice was a little whisper. "Say you love me."

"But what about you, Tessie. How many men do you love?"

"Only you, me darling." She nibbled along the top of my shoulder, and gently bit the lobe of my ear, and brushed her lips across my lips. "I love you, I love you, I love you. Does that satisfy you?"

"I love you, I love you, I love you. But you won't love anybody else while I'm at school, will you? I'll be home again in July."

"How do I know, me darling? Who's to tell what may happen to-morrow? Maybe I'll love the old General. Or Mr. Dooley." She gave a little giggle. "I'll not love anybody else while you're at school, Justin. I'll be counting the days till July."

On the last night of my holiday, as she was leaving me, I took her hand and pressed into it five of the sovereigns which Bracca had sent me on my birthday.

"Here's a present for you, Tessie. Something to remember me by."

"What is this?" She spoke sharply. "Is it money you're giving me for coming into your bed?"

"No, it isn't. I wouldn't give any girl money for coming into my bed. It's five pounds I'm giving you because I'd like you to have it."

"Five pounds." The sum seemed to startle her. "Where did you get five pounds? Everybody knows what your granddad gives you."

"Lord Bracca gave me ten pounds on my birthday. I'm sharing it with you."

"Is it to help me get to London, so I can find a rich lover?"

"Good Lord, no. That's the last thing I want you to do. Buy yourself something pretty—something you'll like."

"I'll do that. A fine length of pink silk, for a dress. Would you like me in pink silk, Justin?"

"Yes . . . I mean, no. Not pink, with all that red hair. Green silk, Tessie. And then if you can get the day off and go to Dublin, I'll meet you and take you out."

"Will you? And me in my green silk. Won't I be the proud girl, in my fine silk, with my cavalier on my arm." She chinked the money gleefully. "Five pounds. And it's taken me the best part of a year to save four. I'll always love you for this, Justin. Even if I love somebody else, I'll still love you a little bit. Will you always love me?"

"I'll never forget you. I can promise you that, Tessie."

"Never forget me. That's it. That's what I want. You'll love other girls, and I'll love other men, but you'll still be thinking of Tessie Flaherty from time to time, and I'll be thinking of Justin Kelly, and remembering the good times the two of us had."

We kept one part of the bargain; we didn't forget each other. But my pretty plan for taking Tessie out in Dublin in a green silk dress came to nothing because my Uncle Randall retired from the Army. He had been stationed in Aldershot since his return from Bermuda in 1864. In June 1866 he left the Army altogether and came with my Aunt Elizabeth and my cousin Horrie to live at Springhill. They were there when I arrived towards the end of July for my summer holiday.

Everything was different. The days when I could come riding home in the evening, and say, "Mrs. Smannel, me old darling, is there anything to eat in this house," and have a meal prepared for me, were gone. Meals were at regular hours, and in the dining room; we dressed for dinner, which my grandfather also attended. My uncle believed in "keeping servants in their places," and one of the first things my aunt asked me was to stay out of the kitchen.

"I know you won't mind, Justin," she said, in her frightened, appealing way. "It's . . . your uncle says that the servants have got quite out of hand. No proper household accounts have been kept, and there's been the most wicked extravagance. Of course your grandfather never bothers about such things."

But I soon noticed that, under my uncle's and aunt's supervision, the house was no cleaner, and the food was worse and less plentiful in the dining room than it had been in the kitchen.

I will say that neither my aunt nor uncle attempted to interfere much with me. The only change, apart from having my meals in the dining room, was that if I intended to be out for a meal, I was expected to let my aunt or Smannel know.

"It makes it so much easier if we know how many there are going to be," my aunt explained.

Horrie, thin and spectacled, was still the mild sweet-natured boy whom I had met on my arrival from India. It would have been impossible for me to dislike him, but we had very little in common. Like me, he was only at Springhill for a summer holiday. At the end of August he would return to England, not to Eton, as had been planned, but as the private pupil of the Rector of a parish in Devonshire. It had been decided that he was too delicate for either school or the Army; he was going into the Church.

And Tessie . . .

The nature of all the new arrangements was explained to me on the first day of the holiday, before I had any chance to see her. But that night, when all the house was quiet, I heard my bedroom door creak, and she came slipping into my room.

"Justin, me darling. Justin, Justin, Justin. Take me in your arms and hold me tight, me darling. Ah Justin, I've been longing for this day." Every word was punctuated by a kiss.

Later, we lay talking, and I spoke about the changes in the house.

"It's damnable. They've asked me to stay out of the kitchen."

"That Major Randall. Him and his: 'You'll please understand that I prefer to have things done my way.'" Her voice, as she spoke these words, was a passable imitation of my Uncle Randall's. She paused, and then added, with a giggle, "And him trying to snatch a kiss from me out beyond in the dairy."

"What, my Uncle Randall!"

"Himself, the old cluricaune. 'You're quite a nice little girl,' he says, and then . . . I had to burst out laughing."

"Well I'll be damned. The leery old devil."

"Ah, you never know with these old men. Let's not waste the time talking about him."

We did not waste time talking about him.

I was with the Chandlers all the following day, and did not return to Springhill for dinner. That night Tessie did not come to my room. I didn't attach any vast importance to this, but, in spite of my aunt's injunction, I made a point of going through the kitchen on my way to the stables in the morning. I did not see Tessie.

In the harness room I saw Dooley, and stopped to wish him good morning. After a few preliminary remarks about the weather, I said as casually as I could, "I haven't seen Tessie around this morning. I hope she's not sick."

He gave me a sly glance. His voice was as dry as an old twig.

"If you didn't see her that's hardly surprising, considering she's left the house."

"Left the house? When?"

"Yesterday morning, soon after you went out. Your uncle told her to get her things packed and be gone."

"But . . . why?"

"No reason was given that I know of. If you need to know the reason, maybe you'll ask your uncle. No doubt he'll tell you, if you ask."

"M'm, I see," I said doubtfully. His sly, knowing look made me uncomfortable. I couldn't avoid a feeling that Tessie's dismissal was a result of her visit to my room the previous night.

"Do you know Tessie's home address?" I asked.

"I do not. But if it's writing to her you're thinking of, I could get her address. Mrs. Smannel will have it."

I rode away that morning in a worried and perplexed mood. If Tessie had been dismissed for sleeping with me, I wasn't in a position to protest about it.

That evening I tackled Horrie. I said, "What's happened to little Tessie, the kitchen-maid. I haven't seen her around."

"Tessie—oh, that one. My father had to discharge her. I don't know why." I thought his voice sounded cold.

The only other person I could question was my uncle, and I made up my mind to do so. I wanted to know. The next morning we were alone together for a minute in the dining room.

"I haven't seen Tessie about," I said. "What's happened to her?"

I saw him flush angrily. He said, in a vicious tone, "That little slut. I found she'd been lifting her skirts to half the boys in the village. I got rid of her."

There was another blank wall. What he said might be true, or it might not. Watching him, to see if it would make him flush, I said, "Only the boys. Not the old men." But he was flushed already.

I obtained Tessie's address from Dooley, and wrote to her, asking what had happened, and whether she needed any help. The days passed, and then the weeks, and I went back to school without receiving any reply.

But during my next holiday, just before Christmas, I had a letter from her. It was from a London address. I don't recall the exact words, but it went something like this.

Darling Justin,

I am with a man who says he knew you in Lucknow and knew your father but you might not remember him, his name is Corporal Tomlinson but he is not in the army now, he sells paper in the streets.

Darling Justin, you said you would help me and I wonder if you can. I have not been lucky, and things are bad, and Corporal Tomlinson has been sick, and there is not even money for a bit of coal. I have been out flower selling in the place of a girl who has the fever, but yesterday I only made sixpence profit, and I had to give half to the girl who has the fever because it is her pitch.

If you can help me I shall be grateful and if you can't, well, better luck the next time.

If you write you had better address the letter care of Mr. Tomlinson, and then it will reach me.

Your loving,
Tessie Flaherty

Tomlinson! My mind went back to the heat and stench of Lucknow, and I remembered him instantly. The funny little man, full of cockney jokes and quips, who had helped to carry my father's dying body into the reserve trench. But he hadn't been joking then. I remembered the tears running down his dirty face and falling on my father's hands, and my father's voice: "Eh, what's this? Leave me, man; get back to your post." I hadn't seen Tomlinson since that day.

And Tessie. Poor Tessie didn't seem to be doing as well as she had hoped in London. I counted up my money, and found that I had nearly four pounds; I sent three of them to her. She did not acknowledge my letter.

I didn't worry about it. Once the money was sent off, I hardly gave Tessie another thought. At Christmas parties, and at the great ball at Bracca Castle on Boxing Day, Rose Corfield had smiled at me—a little distantly, perhaps, but she had smiled. And I had danced with her.

When Rose smiled at me, no other woman had any place in my mind at all. And what had happened between me and Tessie was quite unimportant. A mere incident, such as might happen to anyone. Best forgotten.

When I returned to Wellington in January 1867, my thoughts were full of Rose.

Chapter 16

IN MARCH 1867 there was an attempted Fenian uprising in Ireland. Plans had been made for men to gather secretly in the hills, and, at a given time to march out, storm police barracks, and capture towns and villages.

At the time for the gathering of the rebels, snow was falling in Ireland as it had not fallen within living memory. It went on, day after day. Roads were blocked, mountain passes choked up, towns and villages were isolated. The rebellion was literally buried in a huge snowdrift.

In one or two places attacks were made on police barracks, but they were unsuccessful. Some of the rebel leaders, including a Colonel Bourke, late of the Confederate Army, were captured. For his part in the rising, Colonel Bourke was tried and condemned to death, but was afterwards reprieved.

Another event of that wild March was the Farnborough Rail crash, which attracted little attention. It was an unimportant accident. In thick mist the locomotive of a goods train ran into the rear coach of a passenger train which was standing at the platform in Farnborough station. One passenger in the stationary train was killed, and three were fairly seriously injured.

I was one of the injured.

The official pretext for my trip to London was to see a dentist; but I had arranged to lunch with Bracca. The morning was raw and cold, with thick patches of mist in many places.

The train was late starting, and crawled along slowly, stopping at intervals. At Farnborough there was a long wait. I was in a compartment in the rear of the train, looking at dim figures moving about in the mist on the platform, and waiting impatiently for the train to go on. A man and a woman were standing near the door of my compartment.

I saw a look of terror come suddenly into the man's face. He gave a hoarse yell, "Look out, look out!" and grabbed the woman violently by the arm and jerked her away from the train. I was about to open the window to see what was the matter with him, when the whole of the compartment seemed to heave up abruptly under me. I fell sideways, sprawling across one of the seats, and heard a great grinding and crashing all round me, and then something hit me hard on the head and I lost consciousness. When I came to I was in a hospital in Farnborough, with a broken arm, a broken leg, and concussion. The morning after the crash, with a doctor and two nurses in attendance, I was put into a horse ambulance and taken to Bracca's house in Grosvenor Square.

I was sick there in some luxury, with two starched nurses who took turns to rustle round my bedside attending to my wants, and two doctors, who came twice daily to hold consultations over me. As soon as I was sufficiently conscious, I began to have visitors. Bracca came in to see me. He showed his usual unconcern.

"I understand that you're likely to survive," he said. "Indeed, the doctors tell me that with luck you'll escape any deformity except a scar on your forehead. You'll be able to explain that you obtained it in a duel with a Russian Prince in Athens. That kind of explanation always appeals to women."

"It's very good of you to have me here."

"Not in the least. Your presence will cause me no inconvenience whatever. When you're well enough to leave your bed you may use the Fragonard room to receive your friends."

The McLeods came, bringing grapes. Mrs. McLeod was very concerned, and bossy, and questioned the nurse on duty very closely about the treatment I was receiving. I had the impression that she was quite prepared to take over the duty of nursing me herself. But in the end she seemed satisfied that I was being well looked after.

"You must do what the doctors and nurses tell you, Justin," she informed me. "Then you'll get well quickly."

The McLeods were my most frequent visitors, but they did not always come together. Ian, who had left school and was working in a law office in The Strand, sometimes came in on his way home from work. Jeannie occasionally came in alone during the afternoons, when her mother was busy with music lessons. When I was well enough to leave my bedroom and lie on a chaise longue in the Fragonard room, she would often entertain me by playing and singing to me.

With the approach of her seventeenth birthday she had lost most of her puppy fat and was a well-proportioned girl, still sandy-haired and freckled, but strong and clear-eyed, with an air of "hills and heather" about her which she disliked; she would have preferred to

[155]

look frail and frilly. When I wanted to tease her, I called her a bonnie lassie.

One afternoon, when I was lying on the chaise longue in the Fragonard room, and Jeannie was singing to me to her own accompaniment, Bracca entered the room. He came in very quietly, and waited, motionless, just inside the doorway, till she had finished her song.

"That was charming," he said.

She turned quickly on the piano stool, and saw him, and looked very confused.

"Oh! I didn't know you were there, Lord Bracca."

"Do sing again. I enjoyed that very much. You sing well."

"Oh, I don't."

"Oh, you do." He sat down, smiling at her. "You persuade her, Justin."

"Sing *The Last Rose of Summer*," I urged. It was one of my favorite songs at that time.

There was no need for Jeannie to be shy about singing in public. She had sung at church concerts, and Choral Society concerts in Bayswater. But I could see that she was nervous as she turned to the piano. She sang *The Last Rose of Summer*, and followed it with Schubert's *Ave Maria*.

"Thank you very much. Are you going to make singing a career?" Bracca asked.

"Not singing. Teaching. I shall have to help Mama."

"Teaching's a noble profession—so I understand. But with a voice like yours . . . ? Have you thought of the opera?"

"Mama would never let me. She thinks opera singers . . ." Jeannie hesitated.

"Are sometimes a little irregular in their habits," Bracca said. He smiled, and raised an eyebrow slightly, and the irregularity of opera singers became something quite unimportant.

"One mustn't judge them quite as one judges ordinary people," he went on. "The gods, if one can believe the old stories, were also a trifle unconventional in their love affairs at times."

"I'd love to meet some of them," Jeannie confessed. "Lotti, or Piccolomini, or the new one, Adelina Patti. Do you know any of them?"

"I've met most of them. And I know Mr. Lumley, the manager of the Italian Opera. But if your mother disapproves . . ." He shrugged regretfully.

"She does," Jeannie said ruefully.

"A pity." He paused. "But I wonder . . . If you'd be interested, I think I might help to get you one or two small engagements to sing."

"To sing? Where?"

"In private houses, at evening parties and the like. Nothing important, I'm afraid, but it would be a professional engagement. There'd be a small fee—something trifling—three guineas or so—and you'd have the opportunity of meeting people. Some of them might even be useful to you if you ever intend to make singing your career."

"Oh, I'd love that. And I don't see why Mama should mind. Do you think I sing well enough?"

"Quite well enough. And you look charming, which is equally important. You should wear white, I think. A simple white evening gown, not too frilly."

"An evening gown. You mean a low evening gown. But I haven't got one," Jeannie said in dismay.

"Then you must get one. If you don't, you'll feel dowdy and provincial, and the other women will think you so. And arms and shoulders like yours should not be kept hidden. But I think that can be easily arranged. My cousin, Joan Satterley, has a daughter about your build who has far more clothes than she can possibly wear. The same Mrs. Satterley is giving an evening party some time towards the end of the month; I forget the exact date. You shall make your debut at it. What about an accompanist? Will you accompany yourself?"

"I expect Mama will want to accompany me. If she allows me to go," Jeannie said.

"That's what mothers are for—to accompany their daughters, even though the daughters don't always appreciate such attentions. Will you broach this subject to your mother, or would you like me to speak to her?"

"I wish you'd speak to her. She'll take a lot more notice of you."

"Very well; I'll do so. Now I think we might have some tea, and afterwards I hope you'll sing for me again."

I don't know what Bracca said to Mrs. McLeod, but Jeannie told me afterwards that, far from objecting, her mother was delighted by the idea of Jeannie singing at evening parties under Bracca's patronage.

"You may meet all kinds of people—the highest in the land," she told Jeannie excitedly, and added at once, "Not that that's important. And we'll put your fees into a savings account. You never know when a small reserve of money may be useful."

Some three or four days after the meeting between Bracca and Jeannie, I was lying on the chaise longue reading a book which I had found on one of the shelves. It was Swinburne's *Poems and Ballads*, which had recently made quite a sensation.

Bracca entered, and I put the book down. He came towards me and glanced at it.

"Swinburne—I've met him. A ridiculous young man with a squeaky voice and a mop of red hair. But he has an imagination; his flesh tints are particularly colorful. You can almost smell them."

"I've never read anything like these poems before," I said.

"A lot of people would agree with you. There was a tremendous outcry when they first appeared. But I haven't come in to discuss Mr. Swinburne's erotic trifles. I've some rather unfortunate news for you. Harry Chandler's dead."

"Captain Chandler . . . dead." I stared at him, trying to adjust my mind to this abrupt announcement. "But . . . how . . . ?"

"I don't know all the details. Apparently his horse fell and he broke his neck. Fortunately death seems to have been instantaneous. I shall have to cross to Ireland immediately. It's a most damnable nuisance." He paused, and a slight smile touched his lips. "And that it should be Harry, who was always lecturing me about riding recklessly. And now . . ."

"It's going to be horrible without him," I said.

"Horrible. Oh no. There'll be a big funeral, with a good deal of keening, and other barbaric fuss, and I shall be put to the trouble of finding another agent."

His words seemed to me to be brutally callous.

"But . . . don't you care? He was your friend."

"He's dead, Justin. A dead man has no friends. What can he do for them, or they for him? As for Harry, he enjoyed his life, and his death was swift. He could have felt nothing more than a twinge— no worse than having a tooth taken out. I hope, when my time comes, I may be as lucky."

"It isn't so lucky for Mrs. Chandler and Tom."

"No. But in six months, or a year . . . Tom will be at the Military College; Stephanie will have found something to interest her. She may even marry again, if she can catch another man. She's the kind of woman who likes having a husband."

He turned from me, and stared for a few moments gloomily out of the window.

"I don't want to go to this damnable funeral," he added in a voice of sudden, weary irritation. "I could murder Harry for having killed himself at such an inconvenient moment. Why couldn't he have waited till I was abroad somewhere?"

He turned back towards me, and suddenly smiled.

"By God, I'm in a black mood today. I hate the whole world, and principally I hate myself. When I'm buried, don't come to my funeral, Justin. Get drunk, sleep with a woman, go out riding, but stay away from my slightly stinking remains. Will you do that?"

"You're not dead yet," I said.

"There's no need to remind me of that. I'm constantly being made aware of it. Well, I must go. I'll order a wreath to be sent in your name to the funeral, and if you care to write a note of condolence to Stephanie, I'll take it with me. But you must do it at once. I shall be leaving within an hour."

I wrote a letter, and he took it. When he had gone I sat for a long time, feeling dull and miserable, thinking of the kindly friend whom I should never see again. And, for the first time in my life, I found myself almost disliking Bracca.

"Rupert has been very kind—more than kind," Mrs. Chandler told me. "Poor Harry saved very little, but Rupert has arranged things very comfortably for me. Tom will be able to enter the Army, and I shall have a little house near Windsor, where he'll be able to come and see me."

"I wish you weren't leaving," I said.

"I love this place. But I don't know that I'd care to stay here now. You must come and see me and Tom in England, Justin. Will you be returning to Wellington?"

"No. I was leaving this summer in any event."

"Then I suppose you're looking forward to going to Sandhurst."

"I don't know. There's been a bit of a mess-up. I should have gone in September, but my name wasn't entered. Apparently nobody thought about it. The result is, I may have to wait another year before I can get in."

"What a pity. Couldn't Rupert do something? Have you asked him?"

"No. And I don't want to. He doesn't really think it's a good idea for me to go into the Army. And I'm not sure I do either."

"Not go into the Army. But why not? I hope Rupert hasn't been putting a lot of silly ideas into your head. What do you want to do?"

"I don't know what I want to do; that's the trouble. I only know I don't want to spend more than a year doing nothing at Springhill."

"I can understand that. But . . . don't be guided too much by Rupert, Justin. He can be a bit of a monkey sometimes, you know."

"A monkey?" I smiled at the comparison. "He can be a bit of a devil. I realize that."

"He can," she answered. "Harry and I were as fond of him as anyone could be, but he used to frighten us sometimes. You never know what he may do."

"I don't suppose he knows himself," I suggested.

"He does know. Rupert always knows exactly what he's doing. And when he gets up to any mischief—bad mischief sometimes—he does it because he means to do it. I don't know why. There's a cold, wicked streak in him somewhere; there is in all the FitzStephen family." She broke off, flushing. "I know I shouldn't say these things after he's been so generous. He's always generous. But don't trust him too much, Justin."

This conversation took place at the beginning of the second week in June, the day after my return to Ireland. At the end of that week Mrs. Chandler left for England, and Mr. Lashwood, the new agent, with his wife and small daughter took over the Gatehouse. They were pleasant enough people, but very busy with their new life, and they were not the Chandlers. I could not foresee myself ever becoming very intimate with them.

I was pretty well again by that time; my bones had knit soundly, and the doctors in London had told me that all I needed to complete my recovery was to take things moderately easily for a few weeks. There was no reason for me to take things other than easily. I had nothing to do.

At Springhill I was treated with formal courtesy by my grandfather, and a kind of sullen civility by my uncle. We had little to say to each other. My aunt, thin and faded, went about the house furtively, like a sick mouse. I think she would have liked to be a little friendly with me, but I, young and proud and inconsiderate, made it clear that I preferred to be regarded as someone altogether outside the family circle.

For a few days I was very much on my own. Apart from Mr. Grimshaw, the librarian at the Castle, all my friends were away. The Chandlers had gone to Windsor, Bracca was in London, Horrie in Devonshire, Rose and Tony Corfield were in England (though I was never friendly with Tony). There were plenty of people with whom I exchanged nods and a few friendly words—the Church of England parson, the priest, the doctor, and all the villagers, but all these were mere acquaintances. I looked forward to a lonely time till August, when Bracca planned to return for a stay, and the Corfields and Horrie would also be coming back to the village.

I first heard about the newcomers at dinner on the third evening after my arrival. My uncle was speaking about them.

"I met the man who's taken Hazel Lodge this afternoon. A one-armed feller—calls himself a Captain. I suppose he may have some right to the title; I don't know. He's not a gentleman."

"I've heard he was in one of the American armies in the Civil War," my aunt said, in her thin, tired voice.

"Everybody's heard that," my uncle answered crushingly. "It may be true or it may not. I shouldn't be surprised if the feller's a Fenian agent. I wonder Bracca let him have the place."

The subject did not interest my grandfather, and was dropped. But my curiosity was roused. I sought out Dooley.

"I'm told there's a newcomer at Hazel Lodge. Do you know anything about him?"

"Ah, sure I know about him. It'd be a month or six weeks or more since he came to Hazel Lodge, and it standing empty this last twenty years. Captain Fay, late of the Union Army, he calls himself, and he has the loss of an arm to prove it. He has a young daughter with him; you'll see her riding through the village sometimes on a gray pony."

"So he has a daughter. What's she like?"

"She's just a young girl. I've no doubt you'll be seeing her. Though it might be a wise thing on your part to keep clear of this same Captain Fay—the Soldier, they call him in the village—and his daughter."

"Why d'you say that? What's wrong with them?"

"Who knows?"

"That's what I'm asking you. Who does know? Do you think the man may be a Fenian?"

"I know nothing. I wish to know nothing. I mind me own business."

"That's a great lie, Dooley. You know more of everybody's business than any man in the district. Tell me now, is he a Fenian?"

"I know nothing of what he is. Which of the horses will you be riding tomorrow? Will it be Persephone or Cleopatra?"

"It will be Cleopatra. I might take a ride past Hazel Lodge and see what there is to see."

Hazel Lodge was a small, solitary house on a by-road about three quarters of a mile outside the village. The morning after my talk with Dooley I rode slowly past it and noticed that it had a new, spruce air. Windows had been mended, woodwork painted, and some attempt had been made to tidy the small front garden. But my reconnaissance was unsuccessful. I caught no glimpse of either of the inhabitants.

Living so near, I was bound to run across them sooner or later, and the first meeting occurred in another two days time. I was on Persephone, heading towards Springhill through the Fala Gap, when I saw, at the roadside, a girl kneeling on the grass verge with a pony's forehoof tucked into her lap. I reined up and dismounted, and she glanced up at me.

"Can I help?" I asked.

"It's nothing. I guess I can manage. He has a small stone under his shoe."

She was trying to get it out with a hairpin. I took a clasp knife from my pocket, and said, "Let me," and she said, "Look out he doesn't kick you, then," and yielded her place to me. In a moment the stone was out.

"I think that'll be all right."

"Thanks."

Standing by our horses, we looked curiously at each other. She was young—not much more than sixteen, I guessed—but a fine, long-limbed girl, with a natural healthy grace about her. Her hair, which was black, hung in long plaits down her back; her eyes, the darkest shade of blue velvet, were set under finely arched eyebrows. Their expression, as she examined me, was honest and candid, and yet slightly suspicious. She wasn't quite sure of me.

I liked her at once, and I smiled at her. With a little reluctance, she smiled back.

"You'll be Mr. Anthony Corfield, of Woodlawn?" she suggested.

"I will not. I'll be Mr. Justin Kelly, of Springhill."

"Why, of course. How silly I am. I should've guessed that at once, by the horse."

"The horse."

"The black. Everybody knows her. Wherever I go they all tell me about Mister Kelly and his black steeplechaser. I reckon you're one of the sights of the countryside."

"Well, that's very gratifying. I'd no idea I was talked about."

"Oh, but you are. I've heard a whole lot about you. You were in a railroad smash, weren't you? Are you all right now?"

"Quite all right. But I'm told that the locomotive that hit me will never be the same again."

We both laughed at this simple joke, because we were in a mood

[162]

for laughing. We mounted our horses, and began to move slowly on, side by side. I said, "How do you like Ireland?"

"I love it. It's what I always wanted—to come to Ireland—and now I'm here I'm so happy I could sing all the time."

"Do you like it as much as your own country?"

"This is my own country. There's not a drop of blood in me that isn't Irish. I'm as Irish as you are."

She spoke forcibly, with a flash of indignation which made me smile. I said, "I was thinking of you as an American. You are American, aren't you? I mean, you were born there, and your father was in the American Army. That's only what I've heard."

"I was born in Richmond, Virginia. But my father and mother were both Irish. You don't have to be born in a country to belong to it."

"You're quite right. I was born in India, but that doesn't make me an Indian."

"Your father was in the English Army," she said severely, as if blaming me for something. "And you talk more like an Englishman than an Irishman."

"I expect that's because I was at school in England. You talk like an American. But we're still both Irish, aren't we?"

"I guess so." She laughed, friendly as a puppy again.

"I've often thought I'd like to go to America. Tell me about Richmond."

"It was a nice place. My father worked on a newspaper there, and we had a lot of friends. But we had to leave when I was ten." She paused, looking perplexed and a little unhappy. "It was the war," she explained. "My father was an abolitionist. We went to Chicago, where my mother came from, and he joined the Union Army."

"And your mother . . . ?"

"She died last year. That's what made my father decide to come to Ireland. He didn't care for Chicago after mother's death, and we couldn't go back to the South. So . . . so we came to Ireland."

I realized that I was stirring up unhappy memories. In an effort to turn the conversation onto a more cheerful topic, I said encouragingly, "But you like it here. What do you do all the time? Do you ever go to Dublin?"

"We were there two weeks while my father was looking for a house. It had to be cheap, and it had to be fairly near Dublin; he may want to use some of the libraries there. He wants to write a book about the war, but it's very difficult for him with only his left arm. He's had to learn to write from the beginning again."

"It must be difficult. Have you made many friends here?"

"Everybody's quite friendly except . . . except some people." She turned her head and looked at me, giving me a challenging glance from her beautiful eyes. "People like you," she added.

"Like me? Am I unfriendly? I didn't know."

"I don't mean you yourself. But haven't you got an uncle—a Major Lurgan?"

"I have. What has he been doing?"

"He spoke to my father in the village last week—and called him Fay. And expected my father to call him sir, or your honor. I'm not certain which." She gave a schoolgirl grin, and continued, "I don't think he'll talk to my father again."

"Don't hold me responsible for my uncle's doings," I said. "But look, I'll tell you what. When I meet your father I'll call him your honor, and he can call me Kelly. How will that do?"

She laughed. "And what will you call me?"

"That's an important question, Miss Fay. What other names have you?"

"Only Mollie. That's what my friends call me." She flushed. "I haven't really any friends here," she admitted. "They nearly all stop to have a word, and pass the time of day, but there's no one to talk to, if you see what I mean. Not like there was in Chicago."

"I see what you mean. The Chandlers were my best friends, and since Captain Chandler died and the others left Ireland, I've been pretty much on my own. I don't suppose you ever met the Chandlers."

"I met Captain Chandler. My father had to see him about renting Hazel Lodge."

"Is it comfortable? The house, I mean."

"It's all right now. What it'll be like in winter I don't know. I hope it won't be too bad, because my father still isn't very strong."

"Get a good peat fire going," I said. "Then you'll be warm enough."

We were approaching Hazel Lodge. At the garden gate we stopped, and she looked at me doubtfully, plainly hesitating. Then she said, "Come in if you'd care to, and meet my father." She paused and added, "But don't if you don't want to."

"I'd like to."

We entered by the front door directly into the living room. It was a fair-sized room, white-walled, and stone-floored, with a stone fireplace. The furniture was very simple—a large oak table, an oak dresser with crockery arranged on its shelves, three plain wooden chairs and two small armchairs, and two rush mats which partially covered the floor. A door at the far end led into the kitchen and scullery, and against the back wall of the room a wooden staircase slanted upwards giving access to the upper story of the house.

At the table, which was covered with papers, a man was seated, writing. As we came in, he rose, laying down his pen. He was of medium height, thin-bodied and thin-faced; he had a shock of iron gray curly hair, and deep-set dark eyes with an expression of tired discontent in them. His features were deeply lined; his thin mouth drooped slightly downwards at the corners, adding to his expression of discontent. His eyes examined me with surprise in them, but not, I thought, any pleasure.

"I brought a visitor," Mollie said. "Father, this is Mr. Justin Kelly."

"How do you do, sir?" I said. As I said "sir" I saw Mollie smile briefly, and immediately assume a straight face again.

"I'm glad to know you, Mr. Kelly." His voice was soft and courteous, with a slight drawl in it. He offered me his left hand, and then indicated a chair. "Will you sit here. You'll take a cup of tea with us, I hope. Or perhaps something more powerful. A little whisky."

"Tea, for me, thank you."

"I'll make some hot dripping toast," Mollie said. "Do you like hot dripping toast, Justin?"

"Very much."

She went into the kitchen, leaving the door slightly ajar. I could hear the clatter of crockery, and then her voice singing sweetly and softly.

> Down de meadows am a'ringing
> The darkies' mournful song,
> While de mocking bird am singing,
> Happy as de day is long.

The Soldier was clearing his papers from the table. He smiled the twisted, rather mirthless smile that I was soon to know well, and said, "Mollie seems to be pleased about something. She must have enjoyed her ride."

"That's a pretty song. Is it a Southern song?"

"In sentiment only. It was written by a Pittsburgh man named Stephen Foster, some time before the war. Hasn't it reached this country yet?"

[165]

"I expect it has, but I haven't heard it. Didn't Stephen Foster write *Way down upon the Swanee River*? I know that one."

"Yes, it's by the same man. He died a couple of years or so ago, quite young. The drink was his trouble. The booze. Mine is that I've lost an arm. You may have noticed."

"Yes . . ."

"That's all right. Don't pretend not to notice. And don't try to help me with anything, either. I hate it." He smiled his twisted smile. "And don't take any notice when I'm irritable. I usually am."

He put his papers into a drawer in the dresser and closed the drawer, and sat down facing me.

"What brought you to this house?" he asked.

"Why . . . Miss Mollie brought me here. We met . . ."

"Miss Mollie? Aren't you being rather formal considering that she called you Justin? But she probably hasn't the advantages of your superior education. In fact she has very little education at all. The war's partly responsible."

"Are you being irritable now?" I asked.

"I suppose I am. I've been writing all the afternoon, and it's still slow work with my left hand. I think of a sentence and before I've done half of it I've forgotten the rest."

"Mollie tells me you're writing a book about the war in America."

"Yes. Not so much the war as a whole—simply the experiences of one individual who took part in it. I want to put down my own feelings and impressions from the day when I left my friends in the South to join their enemies in the North, till the day after the war when I took a short trip back to the South and saw what my new friends in the North had done and were still doing to it."

"Do you mean you think you fought on the wrong side? Weren't you fighting to abolish slavery?"

"I've come to believe that any side in war is the wrong side. I'm convinced that anybody who fights, for any cause whatever, is a fool who ought to have his head examined."

"You don't sympathize with causes—the Fenian cause, for instance."

"Is that what you've heard?" He spoke with a kind of bitter savagery. "Then let me tell you what I think about the Fenians. I regard them as worse than fools; they're criminal pests. What good can they do with their stupid bomb outrages, and their petty shootings? They're the kind of Irishman I most despise—the blabbering, loud-voiced kind, who use the word patriotism simply as an excuse for stirring up trouble."

Mollie came in with a tea tray. She said seriously: "What's father talking about? Is he getting argumentative?"

"Ha," the Soldier said. "Now there's a little Fenian in the making. She believes in Ireland being an independent nation."

"And what's wrong with that?" Mollie asked. "Why should Ireland be governed by the English?"

"Because there's no room in the world today for small independent nations," her father answered.

Mollie gave me tea, and a plate with toast on it. I said to her, "Whose side were you on in the American war?"

"Why, the Union side. The same as father."

"So you believe in independence for Ireland, but not for the Southern states of America."

"But that's quite different. Ireland and England are two different nations. The North and South in America are the same nation."

"That was the Northern argument, and they killed 200,000 Southerners and devastated half a continent to prove it," the Soldier said. He hunched the shoulder from which no arm hung. "And this was my contribution to the argument. It taught me my lesson—to keep out of that kind of trouble in the future. A little late, perhaps. Not even the Fenians would be likely to want a one-armed cripple in their ranks."

I didn't know what answer to make to this remark. Feeling rather uncomfortable, I said, "I remember Lord Bracca saying that the soldiers on both sides were fighting for freedom and that the politicians who caused the war were far too busy making speeches to do any fighting."

"I think that sums it up. Freedom is the catchword—the big lie that makes men fight." He paused. "You know Lord Bracca fairly well, I believe."

"Yes. Have you met him?"

"I have. It was quite an education." The Soldier smiled. "He came into this—this hovel and asked if there was anything we needed done. You'll notice that the windows and roof have been repaired. He talked to me—a shabby ex-soldier minus a flipper—without the slightest trace of condescension. He made me feel that he considered me worth talking to—not like some of the jumped-up military men we seem to have in this district. And he talked sense. He was thoroughly well informed even about such subjects as the Civil War in my country."

"It sounds very like him," I said. "And I think he is fairly well informed about the American Civil War. He saw a little of it, you know."

"Yes, he told me he was at Fredericksburg and witnessed the charge of the Irish Brigade. I was in that charge. We took an awful whipping that day."

"I have an uncle who was in the Irish Brigade—not very long though. He was wounded at Bull Run and invalided out. His name is the same as mine—Kelly."

"That'd be a very uncommon name in the Irish Brigade, the name of Kelly," the Soldier said dryly. "I dare say, between them, the different regiments could have mustered a company of Kellys. Do you know which was his regiment?"

"No. I don't know him at all myself; I've never met him. But Lord Bracca has. He met him in Chicago; he's running a hotel there. You may have heard of it—the Mackinaw House."

"The Mackinaw House, you say. Then your uncle would be James Kelly, the actor."

"Yes. Do you know him?"

"Every Irishman in Chicago knows James Kelly. And every newspaperman and actor knows the Mackinaw House. We were there ourselves, weren't we, Mollie, for ten days, after we sold our home and before we sailed for Europe. And you say James Kelly is your uncle. In God's name, how do you happen to be Jimmy Kelly's nephew?"

"His brother married my mother. That's the only explanation I'm aware of."

"His brother. Ah yes, I seem to remember him mentioning a brother one day. Was he in the English Army?"

"He was. He was a Captain, like you. He and my mother both died in Lucknow."

"So that's it. And then you were brought back to your grandfather's house. But you're still Jimmy Kelly's nephew. What do you think of that, Mollie?"

Mollie smiled.

"I thought there must be something like that about him," she said.

Chapter 17

DURING the following weeks I saw a lot of the Fays. This was partly because there was no other companionship available for me, and partly because I liked them. Everything about them was new and interesting to me—their informality, their American accents, even their clothes. For riding Mollie usually wore a tweed skirt, a dark gray shirtwaist blouse, with a red silk handkerchief round her neck, and was bareheaded. This costume was considered slightly improper by some of the local people, who were accustomed to see women riders properly "habited."

"We're freaks of nature in this place," the Soldier told me. "Neither peasant nor gentry, nor even trade. And as we don't attend either church or chapel, we're unbelievers into the bargain."

"Are you an unbeliever?" I asked.

"Quite the contrary. I believe that what is true is rational, and what is rational is true. There you have my simple creed. I belong to no church."

The weather was warm that summer; the days drifted by carelessly in a haze of sunshine. Mollie shared my liking for little-frequented tracks and untrodden byways. Sometimes we would ride for hours without meeting anybody. And then we would enter a village and see the ragged women sitting in the doorways; and the ragged children would come out with shrill cries, clustering round us, begging for pennies.

"I hate it," Mollie said to me on one occasion. "Why should all these people have nothing, and Lord Bracca so much."

"I don't know. But we're not on Bracca's land now. You only need to look around you to see that. The landlord here is Sir Roderick Dennis of Togher—he's what they call an absentee landlord."

"I don't care whose land it is. It ought to be taken away from him and given to the rightful owners, the people who live on it." She paused. "How much land does Lord Bracca own?"

"A good many thousand acres in County Wicklow, and more in Kildare, and streets of houses in Dublin—to say nothing of land in England and more houses in London. He even owns land in America."

"While these people are nearly starving. You've only to look at them."

"They have a bad landlord. Bracca isn't a bad landlord. Any of his tenants will tell you that."

"You won't hear anything against him, will you. He's an angel in your eyes."

"An angel! Bracca!" I laughed. "He's no angel."

"But he's your best friend, isn't he. You'd never do anything against him."

"Why should I?"

"That's what I said: you wouldn't. Not even for Ireland."

"You mean I ought to take his land away and give it to somebody else. I doubt if he'd let me."

"Now you're laughing at me. It doesn't make you mad when you see these people with nothing and Lord Bracca with everything."

"You can't blame him because there are poor people in the country. I suppose there are rich and poor in every country. Aren't there any poor in Chicago?"

"Yes, there are. But it seems different, somehow. It's not Ireland." She paused, and then added with unusual earnestness, "There's nothing I wouldn't do for Ireland. Even if it was something I hated doing."

This conversation occurred between us, but was not typical of our usual talks. Mostly we chattered lightly and inconsequentially, laughing a good deal, enjoying the warm air, the riding, and each other's company. Sometimes we quarreled, but they were only small quarrels; we very soon made friends again. Our quarrels usually ended in laughter. And if my liking for her was a little patronizing, I think it was because of her pigtails. They made her seem like a schoolgirl in my eyes, and not the growing young woman she really was. She was a friendly companion, of whom I was fond, but all my thoughts of women were focused on Rose Corfield.

It was not expected that my rides with Mollie and my visits to Hazel Lodge would pass unremarked by the people at Springhill. But for ten or twelve days no mention was made of them. Then, one evening, I came in two or three minutes late for dinner. After I had made my apologies, my uncle said, "I suppose you were delayed by your new friends—the American Soldier and the oddly dressed girl you seem to take such pleasure in riding with."

"They didn't delay me. I just didn't notice the time."

"You must find their company very entertaining not to notice the time."

"Yes."

"And you've been lending the girl one of your horses, haven't you. You go riding everywhere, all over the hills together, just the two of you."

"Yes."

"They must appreciate your friendship. Especially as nobody else in the district seems anxious to know them."

"Who else is there? The Corfields and Lord Bracca are all away."

"I don't imagine Major Corfield or Lord Bracca would ever consider meeting them socially—though I understand that Bracca isn't always very particular about his acquaintances. I was thinking of people like Dr. Daly, and the Lashwoods."

"Have they told you they don't want to meet the Fays?"

"What is all this, Randall?" demanded my grandfather in the tone of irritation which he reserved for my uncle. "Do you know something against these people? If so, say it, and stop blathering."

"I know nothing about them," answered my uncle in his sulky voice. "That's the point—does anybody know anything about them? Where they come from, or what they're doing here."

"Captain Fay's father was a doctor in Limerick. His parents died in the famine of '47 and he went to America. He got married in Chicago, and then went to work on a newspaper in Richmond, Virginia. Mollie was born in Richmond. He went back to Chicago before the Civil War; his sympathies were with the North. After the war started he joined the Union forces, fought in several engagements, reached the rank of Captain, and lost an arm at Chancellorsville. Does that answer your questions?"

"I suppose he told you all those things himself," my uncle said.

I noticed that blue, knotted veins were standing out sharply on my grandfather's bony forehead and the back of his parchment dry hands. An unbearable exasperation was mounting in him. But my Uncle Randall wasn't looking at my grandfather. He was looking at me.

"Of course he told me himself," I agreed. "He told me other things, too. About my uncle. He knows him well."

"Your uncle . . . ?" For a moment Randall didn't seem to know what I was talking about. I imagine he'd forgotten I had any relatives on my father's side.

"My Uncle James, in Chicago. He used to be an actor, but he gave that up when the war began and joined the Union Army. Now he's managing a hotel. Quite a well-known one, I believe."

"How very interesting," said my uncle, with a kind of sly relish.

[171]

"He's evidently risen in the world, like your father. I suppose he finds his well-known hotel a great change from the dirty little wayside beerhouse he was born in."

I heard my grandfather draw in a sudden breath; his exasperation had reached a culminating point. And I, too, suddenly lost my temper. It was my uncle's silly sneering face and silly sneering voice that did it.

We always had wine at dinner, and Smannel had just refilled my glass with claret. I picked up the glass and threw the contents in my uncle's face.

He gave an outraged gasp, and started back, rising and knocking his chair over behind him. Red wine dripped down from his face on to his white shirt front. My aunt rose with a little distressed yelp, and began to dab at his shirt front with a table napkin. He thrust her aside roughly.

"You . . . you . . ."

He said no more. He was looking at my grandfather. My grandfather, his hands relaxed on the table in front of him, was leaning back in his chair, laughing. His laughter was almost noiseless, merely a succession of slight, wheezy gasps through his opened lips. With a sense of shock it occurred to me that this was the first time I had ever seen him laugh.

"Well, Randall, and what are you going to do now?" he asked.

It was plain that my uncle hadn't the slightest idea what to do. He dabbed at his face and shirt front with a damask table napkin, and made tcha-ing noises, and looked furious and helpless.

"When you've completed your toilet, perhaps you'll sit down again, and we can resume our dinner," my grandfather said.

The remainder of the meal passed in silence. Smannel served us; we ate mechanically. Nobody spoke. When it was over I went to my room. The time was not yet nine o'clock, and I had no wish to go to bed. Nor had I the inclination to do anything else.

I sat and brooded, in a mood of disgust and black fury. With self-pitying resentment, I considered my unlucky position. For another year I might be stuck where I was, at Springhill, with the "family." And what a family. My grandfather, a desiccated image, with scarcely a particle of warm blood in him; my uncle, mean as a weasel and spiteful as a stingray; and my pathetic aunt, who didn't count for anything one way or the other. My family, indeed! They had disowned my mother, hated my father, and had nothing but dislike for me. How could I get away from them?

With boyish longing I thought of pretty, fair Rose Corfield, and my heart ached in me. *Oh Rose, if only I could run away with you as my father ran away with my mother.*

"*Rose, Rose my darling, let's run away together.*"

"*Justin, do you mean it?*"

"*Of course I mean it. Rose, say you'll come with me.*"

"*I'll come Justin. Where shall we go?*"

"Yah," I said, and punched my pillow, because I knew it was only a silly daydream. Anyway, Rose wasn't in the country yet; she wouldn't be coming to Woodlawn till the end of the London season in about two weeks time. But Mollie was there, and in the morning I went riding with her, quite cheerful again.

"I suppose all your fine friends will be coming to Ireland soon, and then we won't be seeing any more of you," she remarked to me two or three evenings later, when I was having tea with her and her father in Hazel Lodge.

"The Corfields are coming on the twenty-sixth and Bracca on the twenty-seventh; he'll be staying the whole of August. But you'll still be seeing me."

"Will there be a lot of parties and entertainments?"

"Bracca will be having quite a lot of people to stay at one time and another and there'll be garden parties, picnics, dinner parties. The Corfields are giving a dinner on August the second for Mrs. Corfield's birthday; that's a yearly event. Even my grandfather may give a dinner, though that'll mean getting out all the glass and silver, which is put away, and hiring a special chef and powdered footmen from an agency in Dublin."

"And will Lord Bracca be at the Corfields' party on the second of August?" the Soldier asked.

"He's almost certain to be."

"What time does a party like that begin, and what time will it finish?"

"The cards will say seven-thirty, for eight o'clock. That'll mean we'll get there at about a quarter to eight. As for what time we'll leave, that'll rather depend on what time Bracca decides he wants to go home. It won't be before eleven, but I doubt if it'll be much after. He's not given to staying very late at our country entertainments."

"Does everything in this part of the world depend on the whim of Lord Bracca?" Mollie asked.

"He's the big fish in our small pool. Where he leads the rest follow."

"You're content to follow a man like Lord Bracca, with better men, like Thomas Reardon and William Kelly—your own namesake —lying in Kilmainham jail?"

"What have Reardon and my namesake been doing to land themselves in Kilmainham jail?"

"Stirring up trouble," the Soldier said. "Mollie has a sentimental admiration for such people which prevents her from appreciating the greatness and magnificence of Lord Bracca."

Mollie frowned and bit her lip, and did not answer. That was all, then.

There are times in a man's life when, under a cloudless sky, invisible forces are mustering round him. Events, as yet in the future, are quietly taking up their positions, waiting the opportunity to happen. And the man goes on, strolling unconcernedly into the well-laid ambush.

But afterwards, when the dust of the catastrophe has settled, he can understand, in clear recollection, the underlying significance of many things which, at the time, seemed to have no unusual meanings at all. He can link them together to form a recognizable pattern. And then, if he wants to, he can say, "So that was it."

I can remember that, two days after my conversation with the Soldier and Mollie in Hazel Lodge, the two of them went on a three-day visit to Dublin.

"To check dates," the Soldier told me. "I was all through the Civil War, but if I as much as get the date of a skirmish wrong, every little prig who writes reviews for a newspaper will pounce on it to try to prove that the whole book is a mass of lies."

When he returned, he seemed satisfied.

"I think I got what I wanted," he told me. "I may have to go again to fix a few final details. What have you been doing?"

"Only the usual. Riding around."

"Any news of your friends? No alteration of plans? You're still expecting them at the end of the month?"

"I haven't heard anything. But I think their plans are fairly definite."

Mollie said nothing. She seemed to be in a saying-nothing mood. When we rode there were long silences between us.

"Is there something on your mind, Mollie?"

"No. What should there be on my mind?"

"I don't know. You might be in love. Did you fall in love with somebody in Dublin? I believe that's what it is."

"Don't be silly, Justin." She flushed and sounded cross.

I was riding with her on the twenty-eighth of July, when we met

Rose and Anthony Corfield. This happened about a mile outside the village, at a point where two tracks converged. We all stopped.

"Justin! I was wondering when we should see you. We arrived yesterday; did you know? You had a bad accident, didn't you, but you look all right now. You must tell me all about it. How are you?"

"I'm all right, Rose. May I introduce Miss Fay—Miss Corfield, Mr. Corfield."

I was feeling slightly embarrassed, afraid that Tony Corfield might be inclined to curl his lip a little at Mollie; he was greatly given to curling his lip. But he greeted her very civilly; indeed, there seemed to be quite a gleam of interest in his eyes. Rose gave Mollie a swift glance up and down and turned back to me.

"You ride with me, Justin; there isn't room for four of us on this narrow track. Tony shall escort Miss . . . Miss . . ." She seemed to have forgotten the name. "You'll come back to tea with us, of course, won't you," she added. "I want you to tell me everything."

We left Mollie at Hazel Lodge and I went on with the Corfields to Woodlawn. Then there was tea, drunk from paper-thin Japanese cups, and thin bread and butter with strawberry jam, and small sandwiches with tomato in them, and little cakes. And there was conversation.

"Now tell us all about yourself, Justin. Are you quite recovered from your accident? Where did you find the odd-looking girl?"

I laughed.

"How many questions do I have to answer at once? Yes, I'm quite recovered from my accident. And the girl is Mollie Fay, but I don't think she's odd-looking."

"Oh Justin, she is. Those clothes. And her hair. She'd be a scream in London. Wouldn't she, Tony?"

"Yaas, I dessay." Tony, twenty-one, and a Cornet in the 7th Hussars, affected a drawling, patronizing way of speaking. "I wouldn't say she's bad-looking, all the same," he added condescendingly.

This remark evidently surprised Rose greatly. She turned a blue-eyed, wondering stare on me.

"Oh, do you think so. But she's so sunburnt. Like a native. And those horrid pigtails. Do you think she's good-looking, Justin?"

"Well . . . yes." I didn't want to seem to admire Mollie too much, so I added hastily, "Of course, she's very young."

"I thought she looked rather like a squaw, with that brown skin and those pigtails." Rose laughed gaily, to show that this was only a joke; she looked very pretty when she laughed. "I expect she's very nice," she added. "She must be if you and Tony admire her so much."

Tony raised an eyebrow and looked superior. I said, "I think you'd like her if you knew her," to which Rose answered, "Do you," in a slightly amused voice. Major Corfield said, "Her father doesn't seem such a bad fellow—not at all bad. I had a few words with him in the village this afternoon. He was apparently a Captain in one of the American armies. Quite interesting." He glanced at Mrs. Corfield. "We might perhaps have him to tea some time, with the parson and the doctor."

"Yes dear. We might, perhaps, some time," said Mrs. Corfield.

When I left the Corfields I was filled with elation mingled with a kind of guilt. Rose had asked me to ride again with her and Tony the following day. And the day after that I was going to see Bracca.

I had to call at Hazel Lodge on the way home to pick up my horse Cleopatra. Mollie was not there.

"She's gone into the village for something; I don't know what," the Soldier told me. "She asked me to thank you for the loan of the horse."

"That's all right. Thank her, for me, for her company." I paused, guiltily. Usually when I parted it was to make another appointment. I hardly knew what to say.

"I hope she'll come riding with me again soon," I said. "I'm going to the Corfields tomorrow, and on Tuesday I have to go to the Castle."

"I'll give her your message," said the Soldier.

On Monday I rode with the Corfields—with Major Corfield and Rose this time. Tony did not come. The ride was disappointing. Major Corfield kept me so busily engaged in talk that I hardly had a word with Rose. I had a suspicion that he had only come along to prevent me from riding alone with her.

On Tuesday I lunched at the Castle with Bracca and his widowed cousin, Mrs. Satterley, who had come for a month to act as hostess for him. There were only the three of us at luncheon.

"This is the lull before the storm," he told me. "Next week the guests start arriving, and for the rest of the month the house will resemble a railway terminus. Joan will have to do all the entertaining. Talking of entertaining, your young friend Jeannie McLeod is having quite a success. Isn't she, Joan?"

"The little Scots girl with the awful mother." Mrs. Satterley, a large, self-confident brunette, smiled at me. "She has a lovely voice

—at least, it would be if it were properly trained. She should go to Garcia; you must try to persuade her."

"Her mother gives her singing lessons," I said.

"I know she does. I don't think she should. But I can hardly tell the mother that."

"I doubt whether Justin would altogether care to either," Bracca said. He smiled at me. "I understand that you've become acquainted with my new tenants at Hazel Lodge. Fairly well acquainted. You find them interesting?"

"Yes. I like them. They're different from the other people round here. Their ideas are interesting."

"They have ideas, do they?" observed Bracca. "A house in this district with ideas in it, and a good-looking daughter—I don't wonder you find them interesting. What are their ideas?"

"I don't know." I laughed, and tried to remember something the Soldier had said. "Captain Fay says that what is true is rational, and what is rational is true," I repeated.

"In other words, the truth for him is what he believes to be true. Look out for him, Justin. These people with simple faith in their own reasoning powers can be dangerous. Whatever they do, they're always convinced that they must be right."

The next day, Wednesday, I had nothing to do, so I went to Hazel Lodge to ask Mollie to come riding with me. Her manner was subdued, and she received me coldly.

"I have a lot to do today, and you have plenty of friends to go riding with."

"I haven't anybody today. Come on, Mollie; why won't you come riding with me? You're not offended about anything, are you?"

"Why should I be offended? Do I have to go riding with you whenever you choose to crook a finger?" She spoke angrily, and then paused, and added more gently, "I think it would be better if I didn't go riding with you again."

"But Mollie, why?"

"I think it will be better," she answered obstinately. "You stay with your friends, and I'll stay with mine. That will be better for both of us."

"How will it be better? I choose my own friends, and you're one of them."

"No." She shook her head. "We can never be friends, Justin. I know that very well. And I'll not go riding with you any more."

I couldn't persuade her, and I left Hazel Lodge more disappointed than I had expected to be.

On the next day Dooley was taken suddenly sick. On my return in the afternoon from a solitary ride, I found him lying unconscious on the harness room floor.

"Dooley!" I bent over him and grasped his shoulder. His stertorous breathing made me think he was drunk, and I took a sniff of his breath, but there was no sign of liquor on it. "Dooley!" I said again, and I went and fetched water and dashed it on his face, but it had no effect. So then I put my arms under his knees and shoulders, and lifted him easily—he was an old man, and very light—and carried him to the kitchen. All the servants came crowding round me.

"Mother of God, what is it?" "Is it Mr. Dooley; what would be wrong with the poor old gentleman? Did he have a fall, now?"

"I don't know what's wrong with him," I said. "I found him lying on the harness room floor." I put Dooley down on the kitchen table, and continued, "Get him into a bed somewhere here in the house; he can't be sick in that old loft over the harness room. I'll fetch Dr. Daly."

"I'm thinking it'll be a kind of an apocalyptical fit," declared Mrs. Smannel. "Didn't me old father have one, and him in his seventy-third year. He never spoke or moved again."

"Never mind your poor old father. Get Dooley into bed, and don't try to revive him with whisky or brandy—not till the doctor comes. And one of you'd better tell my grandfather."

I had to chase Dr. Daly over four or five miles of country, from cottage to cottage, before I could bring him trotting back to Springhill on his little cob. Dooley was still unconscious. After examining him, the doctor confirmed Mrs. Smannel's diagnosis.

"It appears to be a cerebral apoplexy. I've taken a pint of blood from him; beyond that the only treatment is absolute rest and quiet. And his head must be kept raised on a pillow to allow the blood to flow away from the brain. You'd better send for me at once if he recovers consciousness."

"Do you think he'll recover?" I asked.

"It's impossible to say. If he does, there may be a partial paralysis. I shall call in and see him again this afternoon."

I sat with Dooley myself for part of the morning, till arrangements had been made for a couple of village women to come to the house and take turns at sitting by his bedside.

After luncheon, feeling rather glum and not really knowing what to do with myself, I rode across the hillside to the Castle. Bracca and Mrs. Satterley were both out, but I passed an hour chatting with Mr. Grimshaw, the librarian. When I left, instead of taking my usual path back to Springhill, I made a detour to pass close to Woodlawn. There was just a chance, a remote chance, I knew, that I might meet Rose.

The gardens at the back of Woodlawn were bounded by a strip of woods which ran across the gentle slope of the hillside. I knew that Rose sometimes walked in these woods. When I reached the woods, I dismounted from Cleopatra, and walked, letting the horse follow me. As I walked, I peered down the slope, between the trees, trying to spy out what was happening in the Woodlawn gardens.

Then, to my joy, I saw her coming towards me along the path. She had on a light, full-skirted summer dress; a wide-brimmed straw hat dangled by two strings from her right hand. The sunlight, threading between the green branches, glinted on her fair hair, and a small spaniel dog was running in front of her. She made a very pretty picture.

"Justin! This is a surprise. Imagine meeting you here. Are you on your way to the house to see Tony?"

"No," I said. "I . . . I didn't come to see Tony." My speech sounded awkward and stumbling, and I was conscious of it.

"Oh dear. If it's papa or mama you want to see, I'm afraid they're both out. I do hope it's nothing important. Could I take any message?"

"I was hoping I'd see you," I confessed.

"Were you?" Her eyelids fell, veiling her eyes, and then she looked up at me in a coy and roguish way. "Why poor me?" she asked. "Surely you'd much rather meet your American friend. She's much prettier than I am. I know you think so."

"There's no one prettier than you. I . . . I'd do anything for you."

I reached out and took her hand. She did not try to draw it away.

"Quite the knight errant." She gave a little, half-mocking, half-inviting laugh. "Would you go out and fight dragons for me, Justin?"

"Rose . . . Let me kiss you."

"Oh, Justin." She sounded shocked, but not very shocked. And she was smiling. I stepped closer to her, and put an arm round her, and she made a little token resistance, but not much. I kissed her cheek clumsily, and then her forehead. Her hair smelled like new-mown hay.

"You mustn't," she murmured; and then I kissed her lips, and they were soft and willing, and her body yielded limply against mine.

"Oh Rose," I said devoutly. She laughed softly, and her lips parted.

"You know you oughtn't . . ."

She stopped speaking; and then suddenly she became stiff as a poker in my arms, and began struggling violently. And then she began to scream.

"Stop it. Stop it you brute. How dare you?"

Utterly dumbfounded, I released my hold on her. She thrust herself away from me, her color high, and her expression a mingling of fear and anger. I heard a shout behind me, and half turned, and as I did so a heavy walking stick came down with a painful thwack across my shoulders.

It was Tony Corfield. His face was pale, his eyes blazing with anger. He raised the stick again, shouting, "You cad. I'll teach you to insult my sister." The stick came down again, but this time I jumped swiftly aside, so that the blow missed, the stick merely whistling through the air in wasted effort. Eager and bloodthirsty, Tony came on after me, raising the stick again.

"By God, I'm going to give you the thrashing you deserve," he said.

This time, as he swiped at me with the stick, I grabbed it, and twisted it from his hand, and threw it away among the trees. We grappled for a moment, and I pushed him away; and then as he came on again I hit him a heavy blow with my left fist, full on the mouth, and then gave him the old Tom Sayers cross with the right under the chin. He went tumbling over backwards among the ferns.

"Oh, you brute," Rose shrieked. "You horrible brute."

Tony rose, blood streaming from his mouth, and came recklessly at me again. I stood planted, waiting; and a memory of our first fist fight flashed into my mind. Then, as a big boy, he had given a beating to a younger and smaller boy. I remembered that, and as he came at me I measured him carefully and met him with another right, solidly planted, smack on the chin. He went down again.

"Go away, go away," Rose sobbed in a shrill, hysterical voice. Her face looked distorted and ugly.

I stood for a moment, trembling slightly, watching the two of them. Tony was trying to sit up; Rose went to him and helped him. I turned, and mounted my horse, and rode away.

The sunlight seemed wan and bleak when I emerged from the wood. My pulses were pounding, and a black mist fogged my brain. All I could see in it was the sly, frightened expression on

Rose's face when she caught sight of her brother over my shoulder, and started to struggle and yell for help. Had that been Rose, my angel, my beautiful blue-eyed dream girl, with the smiling lips and the soft golden hair? It undoubtedly had, and my mind was reeling and groggy at this revelation of the perfidy of women. *"Fool"* my mind said to me with savage bitterness. A fool was exactly what I was. A half-witted fool without the sense to distinguish between honey and poison.

Blood was running down my knuckles where Tony's front teeth had gashed them, and this gave me a little angry consolation. At least I had knocked the curl from that fine fellow's lips; he wouldn't be smiling with quite the same insolent superiority for the next day or two. I bound a handkerchief tightly round my hand to stop the blood from dripping onto the saddle and onto my clothes.

After a while I dismounted from Cleopatra and sat down on the grass in the shelter of some bushes. As the first violence of my rage ebbed, certain coldly practical considerations were forcing themselves on my attention. There was the dinner party at the Corfields' that evening. Obviously I couldn't go to it. Well, very obviously I couldn't. And then . . . ?

Rose and Tony Corfield would have their version of what had happened in the wood. Whatever they chose to say, I should be unable to contradict it. Any attempt I might make to explain anything, or to try to justify myself, would only make my position worse.

I scowled, and swore, and thought: *Ah, to hell with all of them. Let them say what they like. I'll leave them all. I'll leave the bloody country.*

If I was to be judged guilty, as I was certain to be, I would be guilty with a scornful laugh and an air of defiance. But I wouldn't stay at Springhill, to be condemned by my grandfather and uncle, and cold-shouldered by the Corfields. I'd go to America, even if I had to work my passage. My mind played with thoughts of working my passage—how did one set about doing such a thing? I didn't know, but I'd do it somehow.

The sun was beginning to dip behind the tops of the distant hills when I remounted my horse. I rode slowly, in no hurry to get back to Springhill. On the way I passed Hazel Lodge. The Soldier was standing at the garden gate in front of the small house, looking anxiously up and down the lane. He hailed me.

"Have you seen Mollie?"

"No, I haven't seen her."

"Ah well, I expect she'll be back." He glanced at the bloodstained handkerchief round my right hand and added, "Did you take a toss?"

"No," I answered. Then I grinned in a rather sickly way and said, "Well, maybe I did. It's nothing."

"Why don't you come inside and take a little something. You'll be doing me a favor if you will. By God, I could use a drink myself."

"Then we're of one mind, because a drink is just what I need at this moment." I slipped from my horse and followed him into the house.

He motioned me to a chair, and poured two stiff tots of whisky. But he didn't sit down himself. He took his glass and wandered nervously about the room with it. I took a long thirsty swig at my glass and found I'd finished it. But the strong spirit had a bracing effect on me; I found myself feeling better. The Soldier put down his glass and refilled mine.

"Is the hand paining you?" he asked. "Or maybe you have some other injury."

"I've no other injury. Apart from the bite on my hand I've seldom felt better. And the hand will heal soon enough."

"Did you say bite? It was a dog, was it? You need to be careful with a dog bite. You should pour a little whisky from the bottle onto it. They say it cleanses the wound."

"I wouldn't want to waste your whisky. I'll put something on it when I get home."

"As you please. How is your man Dooley? I was sorry to hear he was taken sick."

"Yes, poor old Dooley. He was conscious this morning, but his left arm and leg are paralyzed, and his speech is affected. The doctor says it may pass away from him—or it may not. But there'll be no more riding for him in any event."

"What will he do then? I suppose there's some poor law establishment, or institution that will take him."

"I don't know. But why would he want to go into an institution?"

"What else will there be for him? I don't suppose your grandfather will want to keep a sick, useless old man."

"What? Oh yes, he will. Dooley's one of his old soldiers." I laughed. "He'll be far more likely to send me away."

"So Dooley gets the reward for being a faithful and loyal servant. That's a good thing to hear." The Soldier smiled his bitter, twisted smile, and poured more whisky into my glass. "And why would they want to send you away?"

"Because I'm not a loyal and trusted servant, and they hated my father and mother, and dislike me. And I don't care a lot for them either." It was the whisky talking; I raised my glass and drank some more of it. "I'm thinking I'll go anyway. I might go to America."

"You could do worse. There's often I wish to God I was there." He sighed, and for a moment he looked haggard and anxious. "Or that I'd left Mollie behind with your Uncle James when he offered to take her," he added.

There was a sound of hoofs outside, and he looked round with an expression of relief.

"And here she is," he said.

She came in. She hesitated when she saw me, and flushed, and then, without speaking, she crossed the room quickly and began to climb the stairs. The Soldier called after her, "Hey Mollie. Aren't you going to pass the time of day with Justin?" His voice did not sound natural. He gave a short, uneasy laugh, and added, "I wonder what's wrong with Mollie." His smile was false, and his face looked sad and sick.

I finished my drink, and rose. So now Mollie wouldn't even speak to me, and my first reaction was one of defiance. All right: nobody had to speak to me who didn't want to.

"I'll be on my way," I said.

"Well, if you must . . ." the Soldier said. But I knew he wanted me to go.

I lurched a little as I made for the door. The three stiff whiskies, taken in my excited state, had hit me hard. I swerved again as I approached Cleopatra, but I managed to scramble onto her back. As I rode, keeping my seat with difficulty, the ground under my horse seemed to be swaying, and I had a tendency to see double. To see things as they were I found it necessary to close one eye.

By sheer determination I managed to get Cleopatra into her stable and take the saddle off her. I called the stable boy to groom and feed her. Lurching like a stricken ship, I made my way into the house, clutching at things as I went. In the hall I found my grandfather and aunt and uncle, in evening clothes, looking impatient. My grandfather spoke: "Justin. Are you aware of the time?"

"No," I said. And I clutched at the banisters at the bottom of the stairs. My two grandfathers, and two uncles, and two aunts stared at me, their figures merging in a kind of haze.

"By God, he's drunk," my uncle said in a scandalized voice.

"Drunk as a fiddler's bitch," I agreed solemnly, and I closed my eyes, while everything seemed to swirl; and then I turned and began to make my erratic way up the stairs. When I reached my room, I flung myself onto the bed.

I felt awful.

Chapter 18

I WOKE UP in darkness. My head was aching slightly and the whisky had left a sour taste in my mouth. For a few moments I lay wondering muzzily where I was. Then, as my brain cleared, I realized that I was stretched out on my own bed, still in my riding clothes.

I grunted, and swung my legs over the side of the bed, and lit a candle. By its light I consulted my watch. The time was nearly nine.

There was a fluttery feeling in my stomach, and I was very thirsty. I thought a cup of strong tea, and then, perhaps, some food, was what I needed; I remembered I had eaten nothing since luncheon. I splashed water over my face in the handbasin, and dried myself, and then went to my bedroom door. It was locked on the outside.

A shock of hot anger went through me, and then I laughed. *My uncle,* I thought. *All right, Uncle Randall! All right you miserable, mean, spiteful, bloody little bastard!* Probably he had given orders to the servants not to answer if I pulled the bell cord. I could almost hear him saying, "Let him cool his heels in there till the morning without any dinner. A little solitary confinement is what he needs."

And did he really think I was going to stay locked in my room like a bloody convict? Getting out presented no difficulties. I knotted my sheets together, tied one end round the leg of a heavy mahogany dresser, and let the other end dangle from the window. Then I climbed down the sheets as far as I could go, and dropped about ten feet into a soft flower bed at the side of the house.

I entered the house by the back door, and went through the scullery into the kitchen. The servants were all sitting taking their ease by the light of a kerosene lamp; a soft haze of tobacco smoke was in the air. When I entered they all looked round. There was a scraping of chairs as they rose.

"All right; don't disturb yourselves," I said. "Except that I'd like a little food and something to drink."

Smannel looked very embarrassed.

"Well, Master Justin, the Major gave orders . . ."

"Never mind the Major. I'm giving the orders to this garrison at present. Bread and cheese and a bottle of wine will do if you've nothing better handy, and if you don't want to get it for me I can find it for myself."

"There's some cold bacon," suggested Mrs. Smannel. "Or I could fry you some eggs, or maybe a chop if you'd fancy that."

"You're a darling, Mrs. Smannel. The only woman I could ever really love. Bacon will do beautifully—bacon sandwiches. And don't forget the bottle of wine. I shall take them out onto the hillside and eat them under the stars."

"Bacon sandwiches and a bottle of wine, is it?" Mrs. Smannel said cheerfully. "We're all likely to be hanged for this, but I wouldn't want to see you go without your dinner, and you tired after your ride this afternoon."

They were all smiling, and their smiles indicated that they knew everything, and were on my side. I had to smile back at them. But I wasn't feeling much like smiling.

Taking my sandwiches and wine, I walked away from the back of the house. The night was still, with a faint warm wind blowing; the sky overhead was bright with stars. As I climbed diagonally up the sloping hillside, I could see the faint lights shining in the valley below me. One after another they went out, as the occupants of cottages went to their beds. But across the valley I could see lights shining in Woodlawn, and high up, at the far end of the valley, there were lights in Bracca Castle.

As I walked on, alone in the night, a great despondency filled me. I felt that I was an outcast, a lonely wanderer, hounded by fate and misjudged by my fellow men. In that house across the valley my aunt, and uncle, and the Corfields and their friends were dining; no doubt they were talking about me. Condemning me. Having a fine time telling each other how unspeakable I was. And Mollie, too. I should never ride with Mollie again. The reflection deepened my melancholy.

I must have walked the best part of two miles before I stopped on a wooded slope above the roadway which led to Bracca Castle. Below me the road, edged by a stone wall, twisted sharply in an S-bend round the side of the hill, and then dipped steeply into the valley. Higher up, and a mile away, the lights of Bracca Castle were hidden from me by the trees. There was a winding, hardly used pathway through the woods, which continued upwards and beyond them, winding more and more steeply, higher and higher, till it reached a small precipitous gap which faced towards the south.

Sitting in the shelter of a beech tree at the side of the path, I opened my wine and took a swig from the bottle. The slightly harsh, red taste of the wine was comforting; it seemed to be what my jaded nerves were demanding. I smacked my lips over it, and held the bottle up, and looked at it appreciatively, and took another swig. A-ah, that was good. The fluttery feeling left my stomach, and already my thoughts were taking on a more lively tinge. Tomorrow . . . why was I worrying about tomorrow? I was Justin Kelly, son of Michael Kelly, wasn't I? Well then, what reason had I to be gloomy?

I opened the packet of sandwiches, and took a bite of one. The sandwiches were good, too. I suddenly discovered that I was hungry.

I had just finished my first sandwich when a sound attracted my attention. A horse whinnied, and then I heard a noise of movement somewhere above me in the woods. I listened, puzzled; what could any horseman be doing at ten at night, coming into the woods from the direction of the Aroca Gap? The sound came closer, and I picked up my bottle and my sandwiches and slipped away from the footpath, hiding behind a tree.

Faint starlight gleaming between the branches showed me dark shapes coming closer. There were nine or ten of them, mounted and armed, their horses walking, making a rustling and a slight jingling noise as they threaded their way in single file along the narrow, overgrown pathway. At the head of this somber procession, leading them through the woods, was Mollie Fay.

Mollie! I thought with a shock of surprise. She passed within a few feet of me, looking tired and unhappy on her small pony leading the dark line of men. I had to know what was going on, so, keeping a parallel track, I stole down stealthily after them. At the edge of the wood, near the wall bordering the S-bend in the road, they halted, clustering round Mollie in an irregular circle. She spoke in a low voice which was not quite steady.

"This is the place. You'll be able to find your own way back over the top."

"We will, surely," one of the men said, and another asked, "How long will we have to wait?"

"I don't know," Mollie answered. "He's likely to leave Woodlawn soon after eleven."

"It'll seem long," the second man said. "The time passes slowly when you're waiting."

"Never mind that now," the first man said. "You be getting back to your own home, girleen, the way you and your da will both be asleep in your beds and will know nothing of this night's happenings if the police or others come round to you asking questions."

"Yes," Mollie said in a subdued voice. "I've done all I can do."

She rode away, a small figure on a small pony, vanishing instantly into the darkness. The man who seemed to be the leader of the party dismounted from his horse; the others followed suit. The leader gave directions.

"One of us will need to look after the horses. That will be you, Shamus. We'd best take them up the path to the far side of the wood; we don't want them frightened by the shooting. There will be four of us behind the wall on one side of the road, and five on the other. That should be plenty for what's to be done. We shall see the carriage lights, and the horses will be toiling slowly at the top of the rise."

"I'll be glad enough when this night's work is done," one of the men said.

The word FENIANS was blazing across my astonished mind in big fiery letters. I knew about Fenians, I had talked about them, but like many people in the district I had always regarded them as stupid and criminal elements who committed senseless outrages in other counties. It was a startling shock to realize that these men were here, almost on my own doorstep, and that they had come to kill somebody. They had come to kill Bracca.

With the greatest caution, I began to move away, putting my feet down very delicately, afraid that a breaking twig or a rustling branch would betray my presence. The sound of the men's voices faded, and I began to feel safer. When I reached the clear ground above the belt of woods, I started running.

I had to run nearly two miles in my riding clothes to reach Springhill, and a lot of the going was pretty rough, over heather and ferns. When I staggered into the stable yard my legs were leaden, I was dripping with sweat, and my breath was coming painfully, in wheezy gasps. I yelled hoarsely for a sleepy stable boy to come and help me, and saddled and bridled Persephone.

Then I was away again, galloping down the road and through the village towards Woodlawn. When the door opened in response to my jangling peal, I said impatiently: "I must see Lord Bracca at once."

"Er . . . yes sir." The Corfield butler looked at me doubtfully. He evidently thought I was rather oddly dressed for an evening call. After a perceptible hesitation, he added, "I will inform his lordship."

But I was too impatient to wait for him. In my excitement I followed hard on his heels across the hall to the drawing room. A sound of music came from within. As the door opened I had an instant picture of the cream and gold room, brilliantly lit by wax candles. Mrs. Satterley was at the piano, with Bracca turning the music pages for her, and round the room, on the spindly Sheraton furniture, women, rising white-shouldered like Venuses out of the seas of muslin, and stiff, white-shirt-fronted men, were listening in attitudes of polite attention.

The music stopped. All round the room everybody seemed to stiffen, and turn. Rose's mouth was open; she was staring at me with blank, frightened astonishment. My grandfather was frowning, his eyes flinty under his bushy eyebrows. My uncle and Tony Corfield both rose to their feet. I noticed that Tony's lower lip was swelled up like a puffball.

"I came to speak to Lord Bracca," I said. I looked at Bracca. "There are about a dozen armed men behind the walls at the bend in the road on the way to the Castle. They're waiting there to shoot you on your way home."

"A dozen, did you say?" Bracca asked. He looked amused; his lips twitched faintly. "Thank you, Justin. I am obliged to you for letting me know."

There was a kind of rustle all round the room. Mrs. Corfield said, "Armed men! Oh dear!" and my uncle said angrily, "What is this nonsense? How dare you come here with such a story. You're drunk again."

I didn't answer him. I said to Bracca, "I was there in Crackley Wood, above the corner, and I saw and heard them."

"I don't believe a word of it," my uncle said.

"Perhaps you'd like to take my place in the carriage and drive as far as the corner?" Bracca suggested gently.

"Be quiet, Randall," my grandfather said in the voice which he reserved for my uncle. He turned towards me.

"How does it happen that you saw and heard these men? What were you doing in Crackley Wood?"

"I was drinking a bottle of Burgundy and eating a bacon sandwich. I heard the men coming from higher up—from the direction of the Aroca Gap. They passed within a foot or two of me."

Another man took up the questioning. He was short, red-faced, fat, normally rather cheerful. I knew him slightly—Colonel Colquhoun, the Resident Magistrate.

"Were they on horseback?" he asked.

"They were."

"And they came from the direction of the Aroca Gap—from the south."

"So far as I could judge."

"Did you recognize any of them?"

"No. It was very dark, and I couldn't get too close. I should think they were all strangers."

"You didn't, I suppose, notice if one of them had an arm missing."

"I didn't. But I shouldn't think so. I couldn't see their faces, but they all seemed to have the right number of limbs."

"You just said you couldn't see them," my uncle pointed out. "Now you say you could see them. Perhaps you knew they were going to be there. Possibly your friends the Fays told you."

"Yes," Tony Corfield said. "You haven't really told us yet what you were doing in that wood. Drinking Burgundy and eating bacon —that's a likely excuse."

"What else would he have been doing in a wood?" asked Bracca. He looked at Tony, smiling, and Tony flushed, and opened his mouth, and shut it, and said nothing.

"I don't care a damn what any of you believe," I said. "I've told you what I have to tell you; you can do what you like about it."

I turned with angry dignity, and crossed the hall, and left the house, slamming the front door after me. I never knew if anybody came after me, or tried to call me back. I was on my horse and away.

I had another errand. During the talk in the Corfields' drawing room I had mentioned nothing of Mollie's part in the ambush because, to my untutored mind, fresh from Wellington, that would have seemed like "sneaking." But my indignation against both her and the Soldier was hot, and I intended to let them know it. All that talk of the Soldier's about the foolishness of fighting, and the criminal folly of the Fenians . . . oh, he had codded me along in fine style, and a lot of good it had done him. I had a vindictive wish to tell him just how much good it had done him.

I rode up to Hazel Lodge, thrust open the garden gate with my foot, and advanced to the front door. A light was shining in an upper window. I kicked the front door and shouted, "You, in there. I want to talk to you."

A window opened and the Soldier's head was thrust out.

"Who is that . . . ? Oh, it's you. I was just settling down for my first beauty sleep. Come again in the morning."

"It's not far to the Constabulary Barracks," I said. "Barely two miles. Maybe you'd rather I'd talk to them about your plans for tonight."

"What's that? Now just wait a minute. I don't know what it is you have on your mind, but I'll be down."

I dismounted, and waited. In a few seconds he came down. He had pulled a pair of trousers on, and tucked his nightshirt into them.

"Will you step inside?"

A candle in a brass candlestick was burning on the table. The Soldier motioned me to a chair, but I did not sit down. I preferred to say my piece standing.

The Soldier spoke heavily.

"What is all this you're saying about a plan and the Constabulary?" His voice was calm, but I could see that he was not calm. His eyes were worried and fearful.

"I've just left Woodlawn, where I've been to warn Lord Bracca about the ambush set for him. The men hiding behind the wall. Maybe you've forgotten." I was mighty sarcastic.

Mollie came down the stairs into the room. She was fully dressed. Her face was pale, and the glance she gave me was full of hatred. She looked like a cat about to spring.

"Do you know what the boy's talking about?" the Soldier asked her.

"I was in the wood," I said. "I saw you and the men. I heard what you were saying."

"Do you think this will help you with Rose Corfield?" Mollie asked. Her eyes glowered defiance at me. "You never were a true Irishman. And what are you now but an informer?"

"I'm not a cowardly murderer. I don't skulk behind walls to shoot unsuspecting people. That's a fine, brave patriotic thing to do."

"Ah, you children," the Soldier said in a weary voice. He turned on me, suddenly vehement, gesturing with his one arm. "Can't you understand that this is war. You kill because you must, to further your own cause. It may be one man in an ambush, or ten thousand men in a battle. The principle is the same."

"Even when that one man happens to be the best landlord in this part of the country."

"Yes," he answered roughly. "If he's a good landlord all the more reason for killing him. A bad landlord is doing our work for us."

"And you don't call that murder. You don't mind bringing your daughter into it?"

"I do mind. Do you think I wanted Mollie to take part in this business tonight? The man who should have guided the others over the hills couldn't come. I had to let Mollie go. There was no one else."

He turned away from me, his arm falling to his side.

"Why should I try to justify myself to you? How long have we, do you think, before the police come?"

"I don't know. I didn't tell the R. M. and Bracca that I'd seen Mollie with the men. But you're suspected; I can tell you that. Your work here is finished. If you want to escape arrest I advise you to be away out of this place before the morning."

"Thank you. I'm sure your advice is very good. But how are we to escape, with only one small pony between the two of us. If we could get as far as Wicklow . . ." He paused, looking at me intently. "I wouldn't want Mollie to be sent to jail," he added apologetically.

I opened my mouth and was going to speak when Mollie interrupted. She said, "No," violently, and repeated it: "No." Then she came away hurriedly from the foot of the stairs, and went to an oak writing desk; she had her back to me. She pulled open a drawer, and turned. There was a big repeating revolver in her right hand.

"Stand still," she said in a quick urgent voice. Watching me, pale and rigid, she added, to her father, "You hold him here. I'll take his horse and ride and warn the men."

She took her glance off me for a moment. I lashed out in a sudden backhand swing with my riding crop, hitting her hand sharply. She gave a cry of pain, and the revolver fell from her hand. I stepped forward, bending, to try to grab it from the floor, and she bent forward at the same time. Our two figures collided.

She thrust at me with all her strength, to push me aside; my hands were too full of her to search for the revolver. I wasn't sure exactly where it was. The table lurched as we swayed into it, and the candle fell and went out. In the darkness, faintly outlined against the light from the window, I saw the Soldier moving, his arm raised with an ebony ruler in his hand. But he could only hover around undecidedly; he dared not strike for fear of hitting Mollie. I swung Mollie round bodily, at the same time wrenching my right arm free, and plunged towards him, swinging my right arm. My right fist caught in a heavy clout on the side of his face, sending him staggering backwards into a small chair, which tipped over as he fell into it. He was a lightly built man, and having only one arm handicapped him.

Mollie was still struggling like a mad thing, kicking at my ankles and battering at my face, and she was a strong girl. I got a grip of her right wrist, and then her left, twisting her arms behind her back, and holding her helpless, hard up against me. With one foot I sought for the revolver, and touched it, and put my foot on it.

"You'd better give up, Mollie," I said. "It's no good."

She stopped struggling. Her head sank on my chest and her body went limp. I could feel her heart thumping against my chest.

"Let me go," she said in a small, choked voice.

I released her, thrusting her slightly away from me, and bent down quickly, and picked up the revolver.

"Pick up that candle and light it," I said hoarsely. "And don't try anything else, because if any murders are going to be committed here, I shall be the murderer."

"The pistol won't fire," the Soldier said in a tired voice. "The trigger's defective."

I pointed the revolver at the ground and pressed the trigger. Nothing happened. The trigger was defective.

The Soldier relit the candle, which shed a dim light in the room. Mollie was leaning against a post at the foot of the stairs. She looked exhausted. Her pigtails had come undone and her hair was in disorder. She was watching me.

The Soldier picked up the fallen chair and sat in it, uttering a deep sigh. He too looked as if all the energy had been drained out of him. And that was how I felt—as if my limbs were weighted.

"Your hand's bleeding," Mollie said in an odd, dispassionate voice. I looked at my hand. Blood was running from the cut which Tony Corfield's teeth had made in my knuckles. How long ago had that been—only a few hours. It seemed like an age.

"One of you can ride the gray pony. The other can ride in front of me, on Persephone. I'll take you as far as the outskirts of Wicklow," I said.

It was as if a little current of life had touched both of them. Their heads seemed to come up. The Soldier gave a short, hard laugh.

"You may get into trouble if it's ever discovered that you helped us," he said. "I suppose you've thought of that."

"I'm in trouble anyway," I said.

"I don't want his help," Mollie said. "I'd rather hang."

"I wouldn't," the Soldier said. "And it's me they'll hang. You're too young."

"Go without me, then. I'll not escape and leave the others to be taken."

"Don't be childish, Mollie. What good will it do to allow yourself to be captured? Aren't things bad enough already?"

"When you've finished arguing, perhaps you'll let me know whether you're coming," I said.

"We're coming," the Soldier said. "If you'd allow us to join you outside in about three minutes. We have to collect a few possessions."

I looked at him doubtfully, and he added, "I'm not thinking of playing you any trick; you have my word for that. What I want is a brief word alone with Mollie."

I shrugged, and left the house, and went to my horse. In a few seconds I saw wisps of smoke coiling up out of the house chimney. They were burning something. I did not care what they were doing.

We rode away, the Soldier on the small pony, and Mollie, in the crook of my arm, in front of me, on Persephone. I avoided the roads and kept to narrow pathways winding across the slopes of the hills. Our progress in the darkness was slow. Out there, in the cool night, with the black shapes of the hills round us and the faint stars overhead, we could have been the only people in the world. Mollie's head was against my shoulder, but her face was averted. I could not see her expression. After a while my right arm began to ache.

Once, in the far distance somewhere behind us, we heard a faint crackle of shots. The sound continued raggedly for about half a minute, and then died away. A little later I could feel rather than see that Mollie was crying, and trying to hide the fact that she was crying. I wanted to say something to her, but could think of nothing to say. What could I have said?

At a point about three-quarters of a mile from Wicklow Town I signaled a halt.

"This is where I'll leave you. You'll find the road into Wicklow there, at the bottom of the field. A few minutes should take you into the town."

"We shall manage very well now, thank you," the Soldier said.

Mollie slid from Persephone's back, down to the ground. For a moment she stood looking up at me, and I sat on the horse looking down at her. Again I wanted to say something but could say nothing. Mollie's head drooped, and she turned away from me; and I pulled my horse's head round and started the long ride back.

A dim gray was showing in the sky when I rode into the stable yard at Springhill. Everything was quiet. I stabled Persephone and rubbed her down, and then propped the yard ladder against the wall of the house and climbed back into my bedroom through the window. The sheets were still hanging from the window, as I had left them, but the door of the room was unlocked with the key on the outside. I shifted it to the inside and locked the door again.

I didn't bother to remake the bed. I simply took my clothes off, letting them lie where they fell, flung myself down on the mattress, and pulled a blanket up round me. I must have gone to sleep almost at once.

Chapter 19

I WOKE from a confused dream of Mollie, and Dooley, and the Soldier, and a lot of Fenians, to hear someone banging on my bedroom door. I went to the door and opened it. Smannel was there with a tray.

"I brought you a bite of breakfast. And your grandfather's compliments, and he'd be obliged if you'd see him in his office at nine o'clock."

"That will suit me very well. I'll be wanting a word with him too. What happened last night, Smannel, about the Fenians?"

"Ah, there was a bit of a brush. A trooper has a flesh wound in the arm, and one of the Fenians is captured. The rest got away. That's the story as I have it."

"It sounds like a very bloody engagement, with little harm done on either side. How's Dooley this morning?"

"He's poorly, Master Justin, very poorly. All the night he seemed to be tormented with something in his mind; I think it'd do him a deal of good if only he'd the power of speech, and could tell it. Father O'Gorman is with him now."

"I'm sorry he's no better."

"He's quieter this morning; I think the end is not far away."

Poor old Dooley, I thought sadly, as I cracked my first egg. But there it was. The Chandlers had gone, the Fays had gone, and now Dooley was on the point of making a longer journey. And I was going too. More than ever, my determination about that was strong. Yes, I would leave the whole boiling of it. I wouldn't spend another night under my grandfather's roof.

I had enough money to take me to London and leave four or five pounds over. And once in London I would look around, find some work to do, stand unaided on my own feet. No one would need to help me, and I would be my own master. It was a matter of the greatest importance to me that I should accept help from no one.

My grandfather was sitting at the big desk under the far window in his paneled study, or "office" as he preferred to call it. He looked up as I entered, a gaunt old man, stiff as an icicle, thin-lipped and cold-eyed. With one bony hand he motioned me to a chair. But I was in a mood of brash defiance, and I intended to make it plain.

"I'll stand if you don't mind," I said.

"As you will." His voice too was thin and cold as an east wind.

He put his elbows on to the desk, pressing his fingertips together, and went on speaking slowly and quietly.

"You came into the house drunk yesterday evening. I have no particular comment to make on that, except to recommend you to exercise more care in your consumption of alcohol. What I have to speak to you about is an incident of which Major Corfield informed me privately when I visited him last night. You know what I'm referring to."

"Yes."

"Have you anything to say? Any explanation you'd like to offer?"

"No."

"H'm. No, I suppose not." He paused, contemplating his fingertips; it was a long pause. Then he went on deliberately, "I think it might be a good thing for you to pay a visit to England. Stay there for a while. When you go to Sandhurst . . ."

"I'm not going to Sandhurst," I interrupted. "I'm not going into the Army at all. But I'm not staying here either. I intend to leave this house, and once I'm gone I'll not be coming back."

To my surprise, he smiled. It was the faintest smile, merely a slight loosening of the corners of his lips.

"I won't argue with your decision. In fact, I agree with it. There are other places in the world which you might find more congenial. I'm thinking of, for instance, Australia."

"You mean in a convict settlement. I imagine I should feel quite at home there."

He ignored the remark.

"A friend of mine has a cattle station in New South Wales—or rather, his son has it now. The life, I understand, is agreeable and not unremunerative. You would, of course, have to go as a pupil for a term of years, at the end of which arrangements could be made for you to buy a station of your own."

"Thank you, but I have no intention of going to Australia."

"You haven't. You're not even prepared to consider the suggestion?"

"No."

"Very well." He put his hands on the desk, and leaned back in his chair, looking at me. "What are you going to do, Justin? You say you're not going into the Army. You refuse to consider my suggestion of Australia—quite a reasonable suggestion, I think. Have you any ideas of your own about what you want to do?"

"What I want is to get away from this place. That's the first thing I intend to do."

"Yes, yes; I understand that." He spoke impatiently, and then gave a deep, exasperated sigh, and added, "Why do you stare at me like that? In God's name, boy, what have I done to make you hate me so much? Have I ever ill-treated you, or been unfair, or done you any injury? Have I?"

"No," I admitted. "You've always been fair—considering that you hated my father, and disowned my mother, and never wanted me here. But that's all right; now you can be rid of me. I'm going."

"I did not hate your father. Where did you get such an idea? I never even knew the man. And I did not disown your mother. She was always my favorite—always—till she deliberately repudiated me, and everything to which she should have been loyal."

"By marrying the man she wanted to marry instead of the man you wanted her to marry?"

"By dishonoring her pledged word. By making her name, and mine, a scandal and a byword throughout the whole kingdom. You accuse me of not having wanted you here. I admit the accusation. When you first came your presence reminded me of the most painful episode in my life. I did my best not to let that influence my behavior towards you. If I failed I can only say that I'm sorry."

I laughed.

"You have no need to apologize to me. It was my mother you failed, by being ashamed of her. My mother never did anything to be ashamed of in her life."

"You are entitled to your own opinions. You must allow me the privilege of having mine." His hands pressed on the top of the desk; he rose stiffly, and edged round the desk, and walked, with the painful slowness of an old man, towards the door. He did not look at me as he crossed the room. I went to the door and opened it for him.

"Thank you." He stepped forward into the doorway, and then paused and looked back at me. "I shall not presume to advise you further about your future. You will let me know, shortly, I hope, what plans you have made."

He moved away from the doorway across the hall, and took a stick from a stand; he was going for his usual morning exercise in the garden. My uncle entered the hall by the front door, his limbs jerking like an excited puppet's, his pale eyes snapping with excitement.

"They got away," he announced. "When the police went to the house this morning, they found them gone." He paused importantly, and then brought out the next sentence with great emphasis and relish. "Some traitor must have given them warning."

"Eh," my grandfather said. He took an old tweed shooting hat from the stand and put it on his head. "What the devil are you talking about?" he demanded.

"I'm talking about the man and woman at Hazel Lodge. Justin's friends. They've run away. The police are after them."

"What about it? You don't expect me to run after them as well, do you? For heaven's sake, Randall, stop chattering like a monkey and leave the police to manage their own business. I'm sure they can do very well without your help."

My grandfather pushed open the front door and went on out of the house. I turned and began to go towards the stairs, but my uncle came after me.

"Just a minute. Oh, no you don't. You're not going away yet. I want a word with you. I want to know where you went after you left Woodlawn last night."

I turned to look at him. I had to be calm, and I knew I had to be cautious. The little rat was going to get me into trouble if he could.

"What are you talking about? Where do you think I went?"

"I know where you went. You went to warn those people—those friends of yours. You're a traitor—a traitor to your country. There are severe penalties for that kind of thing. You realize that, don't you?"

"Why don't you stop chattering like a monkey. You heard what your father said. I went to bed last night after I left Woodlawn."

"That's a lie. I can prove it's a lie. You were not in your bed at one o'clock this morning. I went and looked."

"My bedroom was locked when I came in. I slept in the room next to it till early this morning. And if you call me a liar again I shall knock you down."

I was hunching my shoulders, scowling down at him, overtopping him by a good four inches. I was frightened, and fright made me angry. I went on, "You're always at my heels like a snarling cur, yap, yap, yap, yap, the whole time. That gob of yours needs stopping, and I'll do it if I hear any more from you."

To my relief, he looked unsure of himself. His glance shifted and he couldn't meet mine. I laughed, and turned aside from him and went on up the stairs.

Once inside my room I began to look hastily through my belongings, putting essentials to one side. I wanted to get away as quickly as possible. I was kneeling on the floor, stuffing shirts into a traveling bag, when Smannel entered.

"Lord Bracca has called to see you, Master Justin. I've shown his lordship into the drawing room."

"Damnation. I suppose I shall have to see him."

Bracca was standing in front of the fireplace, tall, fair, and handsome in his beautifully cut riding clothes. He looked at me gravely, and his composure irritated me. It was all very well for him to be composed. I was not composed.

"Good morning, Justin. You seem to have saved my life last night. A most embarrassing position for me. I must try to thank you."

"You needn't."

"That relieves my mind a great deal. I hate thanking people." The corners of his mouth twitched. "You'll forgive me mentioning it, and don't think I'm quarreling with your notions of amusement, but why choose a public path in broad daylight, where anybody passing could see you. Couldn't you at least have taken her aside into some bushes?"

"I suppose you all had a fine time talking about it at dinner last night."

"At the Corfields' dinner table? My dear boy, do you imagine the Corfields would regard the rape of their only daughter as an enlivening subject for debate over the fish?"

"I didn't rape her." I was angry and impatient, and his amusement wasn't improving my temper.

"Very disappointing for you. But just as well, I think. She might have been a great nuisance afterwards. Quite a pretty girl, Justin, but shallow. Shallow as a puddle. Such creatures can become very tiresome."

"Thank you for telling me."

"You seem a little out of humor this morning. You musn't take this affair seriously. A mere incident—far worse for the Corfields than for you. But never mind them: what about you? I've just been talking to your grandfather in the garden. Your plans seem to be a little vague. Have you any?"

"I'm leaving here today." I paused, hesitating, and then added, "My uncle's doing his best to get me sent to jail. He says I warned the Fays that the police would be coming for them this morning."

"I hope you denied it firmly." Bracca's voice was sharp and quick. He was no longer trifling.

"I told him he was a liar."

"That was sensible. How soon can you be ready to leave? In half an hour?"

"Yes . . . but do you think the police are likely to arrest me?"

"There's a risk of it, while their blood is up—if they can find you. You had better go to England immediately. I shall take you to Wicklow myself, and set you on the train for Dublin. How are you for money?"

"I've plenty."

"If you need any in London, you may draw on Curling. But we can settle that while we're on our way. I shall return here for you in half an hour."

"You . . . you won't get into trouble yourself if they find you've helped me to escape?"

"What nonsense is this? You're not escaping. You're going on a visit to England. In any event, I think I know how to deal with trouble."

Everything went off without any hitch. Bracca saw me onto the train for Dublin, and that evening I caught the steam packet for England.

Chapter 20

"I WON'T take less than three pounds," I said.

"I couldn't do it, guv'ner. I'd be losing money meself." The slicked down, greasy little man behind the counter turned the watch over disparagingly. "Tell you wot. I'll tike a chance an' make it two pound five."

I was selling one of my watches—one which Bracca had given me on my birthday some years before—and I was angrily conscious that I was going to be swindled. But I had no real idea of the value of the watch.

"Three pounds," I repeated.

"Come off it, guv'ner. I'd like to oblige a fine young feller like you—but three pounds. There ain't much call for this sort of watch, you know. If I was to say two pound ten . . ."

"Give me that watch back," I said sharply, and I reached out my hand to take it. He stepped quickly back, away from me, behind the counter.

"'Ere, 'ere, no need to be so 'asty, young feller. You shall 'ave your three pounds, though it's takin' the bread out of the mouths of me wife an' kids."

He paid three gold sovereigns onto the counter, and I took them up and left the pawnshop. In the Euston Road carts and vans were lumbering along noisily, and the sidewalks were crowded with men and women going about their business. They looked limp and bedraggled in the afternoon heat. I joined the passing procession, walking listlessly, my hands in my pockets, jingling my three gold coins. The heat and stink and dirt of London were oppressive after the green freshness of County Wicklow. I had learned bitterly the difference between being in London with friends and money, and being in London without friends and almost without money.

For eleven days I had tramped the streets, visiting banks, warehouses, shops, factories, looking for work. Nobody wanted me. I had answered advertisements. Nobody had replied. Now I had sunk to pawning things to pay for my food.

I turned out of the Euston Road into a narrow street called Tolman Street, and turned again into a grimy building with a sign over the door which said:

THE ARKLOW HOTEL

Inside, at the reception desk, a severe-looking woman with gray hair piled high on her head, a white starchy blouse, and a black skirt, sat doing accounts. I spoke to her.

"Any letters for me this afternoon, Miss Jenner?"

She made a pretense of looking into a row of pigeonholes.

"Nothing this afternoon, Mr. Kelly."

"Thank you, Miss Jenner."

I went up to my third-floor room, unlaced my boots and stretched myself out on the bed. The long, blank, lonely evening lay ahead of me. At six, or a little later, I would leave the hotel and wander about the street—Tottenham Court Road, Oxford Street, Regent Street, Piccadilly, The Strand. With the coming of dusk the gas lamps would be lit; hansom cabs and carriages would disgorge their passengers into restaurants and theaters; gaudy gin palaces and pubs would be crowded with drinkers; and in almost every doorway and corner the prostitutes would be soliciting the male passers-by. Mostly they were pitiful, shabby creatures, whose reason for selling what they had to sell was simple: they needed the price of a meal. Few of them could have been called truthfully "Daughters of Joy."

Lying on my bed, I slept for a short while. When I awoke, the light was beginning to fade. And now what? Go out, walk the streets, have a meal at a cheap eating house, come back to the hotel, go to bed. The same tomorrow and the day after, till I had pawned the last of my possessions.

An idea which had come into my mind three or four times during the past days hardened into a determination. In my bag was a small leather-bound address book given to me one Christmas by Mrs. McLeod. I found the book, and looked up the address I needed.

> Miss Tessie Flaherty
> c/o Corporal Tomlinson
> 12, Lemon Lane
> Seven Dials,
> London

Corporal Tomlinson, my old Lucknow acquaintance. If he was still there, he might be able to give me some advice about looking for work. In any event, we'd be able to talk about old times, which would be better than walking aimlessly about the streets. I was longing for someone friendly to talk to.

The walk to Seven Dials from the Euston Road scarcely took me ten minutes, and, after a couple of inquiries, I found Lemon Lane. At the first sight of it I almost turned back.

In the street, littered with bits of torn newspaper and other rubbish, barefoot children were playing, their cries and yells rising shrilly on the twilit air. The tall houses were dingy, with chipped and scarred paintwork and missing windowpanes. In the open doorways of most of them, women were sitting on the front steps. They had a slatternly air.

I looked, and hesitated, and then gritted my teeth and went on. There were two women sitting on the doorstep of number 12, one of them a bulging fat creature, enormously red-faced, with bare feet thrust into tattered carpet slippers, and the other a pale young girl of sixteen or so, with the frail, pathetic look of a consumptive. I raised my hat to them.

"Corporal Tomlinson? Does he live here?"

The fat woman jerked her thumb over her shoulder.

"Third floor back you'll find 'im. If 'e's 'ome."

" 'E is," said the thin girl. "Come in an hour ago. Fair wore out, 'e looked. It's the 'eat," she explained.

"You better go up if you want 'im," the fat woman said. She squeezed her large body slightly to one side. "Make a bit of room, Liz, and let the gennelman pass."

I squeezed past them into a smell of moldy wood and sweaty clothing, and found myself confronted by a flight of bare wooden stairs. They creaked as I climbed upwards, and the banisters were wobbly. On the third floor was an uncarpeted landing with three doors leading off it. I knocked on the door which led into the room facing the back of the house. A voice inside called, "Who's that? Come in."

The room was barely furnished, but quite clean. A strip of old carpet partially covered the floorboards, which looked as if they had been fairly recently scrubbed. A plain deal table, a white painted cupboard, a woven basketwork chair, a plain, wooden chair, a narrow black bedstead, a coal scuttle, and an upturned packing case, on which had been placed a tin jug and basin and a small kerosene stove, comprised the rest of the furniture. A man was lying on the bed. He raised himself on one elbow to see who it was as I entered.

"Corporal Tomlinson?" I asked.

"That's me." He stared at me, a small, shriveled man in a faded gray shirt and old trousers. He was much smaller than I remembered him, and much older.

"Who the . . . I know you, guv'ner. I seen you before somewhere, ain't I?"

"Justin Kelly is the name."

"Justin Kelly! Gawd Almighty!" He swung his legs with alacrity over the side of the bed. "Well, blimey, if this ain't a surprise. 'Ere, take a seat, sir."

He grinned broadly, showing gaps where several front teeth should have been, and turned the basket chair towards me, dusting it vigorously with his hand.

"Thank you. How are you, Tomlinson? It's a long time since we met."

"It is that—though sometimes it seems only yesterday. You remember Sergeant Mellish—'im wot was knocked off by a sniper."

"I remember him very well. He was a friend of mine."

" 'E was a good feller, old Mellish. One of the best. There was a lot of good men bit the dust there, in them entrenchments at Lucknow."

We spent about ten minutes remembering the events and people we had known in Lucknow. Then Tomlinson said, "Well sir, wot are you doing in London, if I may ask. Have you left school now?"

"I've left school and left my home in Ireland. I'm looking for work."

"Wot kind of work? Ain't you going into the Army, same as your father, the Captain?"

"No, I'm not. What I want is some kind of work, and I'm damned if I know how to find it."

"There's many can say that, sir. You wouldn't think of bein' a doctor or a lawyer, would you?"

"Those jobs need a long training, and that needs money. I haven't any. I must find a job as soon as I can. Any job, to keep me going. I don't care what it is."

"But . . . wot about your grandfather, the General, an' your uncle, the Major. Won't they do nothin' for you?"

"Nothing at all. I don't want them to. I suppose Tessie told you about them. What's happened to Tessie? Is she still here?"

"No. Left 'ere three or four months ago, in the beginning of April." He grinned, showing the gaps in his teeth. "She's a corker, that kid. A real fizzer if ever you see one."

"How did you happen to meet her? And what's happened to her now?"

" 'Ow'd I meet 'er? Why, I met 'er in the doorway below, where she was shelterin' from the rain. Cold an' wet an' 'ungry, an' sobbin' 'er bleedin' 'eart out. She'd nowhere to go, an' no money. I brought 'er in an' give 'er a cuppa tea, to warm 'er like, an' she spent the night in front of a bit of fire I 'ad in the grate. I wasn't too well meself; I was startin' an attack of the shakin' ague. I gets it often in the winter when the chill gets into me bones. In the mornin' I was real bad. She stayed with me, an' tried to look after me a bit, but we 'adn't no money except a few coppers she picked up 'elpin' the flower girls, and pretty soon we 'adn't no grub nor coal. In the end she wrote to you, and you sent 'er some money. Then we was all right—almost in the lap of luxury, you might say. She took the room next to this one, and we lived for the best part of a month on that money. By the time it was gone I could git around again, and she found 'erself a job waitressing in a restaurant in The Strand. That's where she came to meet the cove she's with now."

"You lived the best part of a month on the money I sent—on three pounds. How on earth did you manage that?"

"We reckoned we was bleedin' lucky." He grinned. "Blimey, there's eight rooms in this 'ouse, and I doubt if you'd find three quid among the lot."

"Do you think I could live for a month on three pounds?"

"You . . . ?" He laughed. "It wouldn't be wot you're accustomed to. Where are you living now?"

"In a cheap hotel near Euston Station. Bed and breakfast two shillings and threepence. Then there's food—a shilling for lunch, and a shilling for dinner, and, of course things like omnibus fares, papers, baths—it's threepence a day at the hotel for a bath."

"I pays two and ninepence a week for this kip," Tomlinson said. "And if I can spend sevenpence or eightpence a day on me food I don't reckon to starve. Then there's etceteras—soap, a bit of 'baccy when I can afford it, and I 'ave to try to put by a shillin' or two for the winters."

"What kind of work do you do?"

"Want to see?" He bent down and hauled, from under the bed, a tray with raised sides and a wide cloth band which enabled him to hang it in front of him from his shoulders. On this tray were packets of cheap stationery, a few bottles of ink, blotting paper, pens, pencils.

"'Ere you are, sir. D'you want to write a letter to your best girl? Time she 'eard from you, I'll lay. A nice packet of paper and envelopes—only a penny. Ain't got a pen? Then look at this. Real relief nib—only a ha'penny. Wot's that—you don't know 'ow to write? That's easy. I'll write the letter for you."

He thrust the tray back under the bed.

"I do, too; I write letters for 'em for a penny a time. Got me own regular clientele."

"If . . . if it's not a rude question, how much money do you make?"

"Well, I ain't no bleedin' Rothschild. If I can knock up ten or eleven shillings a week in the summer, and seven or eight in the winter, I don't grumble. Bless you, there's thousands worse off than me. You only 'ave to look around you."

"Seven or eight shillings a week—it doesn't seem very much. Couldn't you get a regular job of some kind? Something that would pay you a little better."

"Jobs ain't so easy to get. And if I get a regular job and fall sick— then I lose the job. I ain't so strong as I was, you know. But with this, if I 'as a bad turn, I goes to bed, and when I'm better I carries on where I left off. It don't cost me nothing being in bed, except the rent. I ain't 'ungry when I'm sick."

The thought came to me: shall I be like that some day? Shall I end up selling stationery in the streets, with only a shilling or two between me and starvation?

"I'm thinking of going to have my dinner in a few minutes," I said. "Come and have some with me."

He shook his head, smiling.

"I ain't dressed for dining out. Thanks all the same." He paused. "Tell you wot. Can you eat fried fish and chips and drink beer?"

"Quite easily."

"Two penn'orth of fish, a penn'orth of chips, and a jug of beer. Between the two of us."

"It sounds all right."

"Then you 'ave your dinner with me. That is . . . don't if you don't want to."

"I do want to. I'd like to."

"I'll send young Alfie Baker to fetch it. Just stand easy a minute while I write a note."

He sat down at the table and wrote a note, and then left the room, taking a jug with him. I heard his voice on the stairs calling, "Alfie. Is young Alfie there?" A voice lower down took up the cry. "Alfie. Mr. Tomlinson wants you." In a few seconds he returned.

"Fish and beer comin' up." He took two tin plates and a couple of glasses from the cupboard, and put them down on the table. "I ain't got much crockery, the reason bein' I don't use much. We'll 'ave to make do." He grinned and added, "Like Lucknow."

"That'll be all right." I had been thinking while he was out of the room, and I went on, "You said this room costs you two shillings and ninepence a week. Could I get one like it?"

"You could. There's the room next door, where young Tessie was." He paused, shaking his head. "No, it wouldn't do. Not your style."

"Why not? This room is as good as my cubicle at Wellington College. And it's clean."

"That's only 'cos I give it a lick of the old Army spit and polish once in a while. You should 'ave seen it when I come in. I 'ad to burn two sulphur candles to drive out the bleedin' bugs." He shook his head again. "You wouldn't like it."

"I don't like where I am now, and I'm spending too much money. Unless I cut down I soon won't have any at all. Is there any chance of seeing the room?"

"That's easy enough. It ain't locked. No 'arm in looking, I s'pose." He took a candlestick from a shelf over the fireplace, and struck a match. "Might as well 'ave a bit of a glim. It's gettin' dark."

Carrying the candle, he led the way into the passage and pushed the door of the next room. It opened with a creak, and we entered. Candlelight showed four patchy and discolored walls, a dirty floor, a single uncurtained window. Dust lay thick over everything. There were gray ashes, months old, in the fireplace.

"There's no furniture," I said.

"No. Mrs. Marrable could lend a few sticks—she 'as a lot of stuff in that basement. We 'ad some things from 'er when Tessie was 'ere— that made the room thrippence a week more. If she'd stayed we was going to slap a coat of whitewash over the walls, same as I've done in my place. It brightens it up a bit."

"Yes." But I felt a sinking of my spirits; the bare, cheerless room depressed me. For the sake of something to say, I went on, "And it's been empty since Tessie left. Where is she now?"

"I told you, she picked up with this cove while she was waitressin' —a coal merchant, Fred Symonds by name. Oodles of tin—got 'is own coal carts all over London; you can see 'em anywhere. 'E's set 'er up in a room in Greek Street—thirty bob a week, an' 'er rent paid for 'er, an' nothing to do." He grinned. "Well, not a lot to do. Nothing that don't come quite natural. I still see 'er sometimes. Might be seein' 'er t'night."

"You think she might come here to see you?"

"She might. Depends on whether 'er feller wants 'er, or whether 'e'll be spendin' the evenin' respectable with 'is wife an' kids."

"Oh! I see. She told me she was going to get herself a rich man some day. What's he like?"

"I never seen 'im. She don't bring 'im 'ere." He turned his head, listening. "Blimey, I believe she's 'ere."

We went on to the passage outside the room. From the bottom of the stairs there came a sound of excited voices. A small urchin, ragged and barefooted, came up the stairs carrying a jug and a parcel wrapped in old newspaper.

"I got your fish an' chips an' beer, Mr. Tomlinson, an' delivered your note. Miss Flaherty come along with me. She brought me in a cab. She's below now, 'avin' a word with mum an' dad."

"All right, son; stick them down on the table."

The boy put the jug and the parcel down, and went. We waited for a few seconds. There was a sound of quick light feet on the stairs, and a laugh, and Tessie came through the doorway in a whirl, bringing with her a strong smell of mignonette. She dumped a basket down on the table and flung her arms round me.

"Justin, me darling."

She was all-alive-o, vibrant with vitality, hugging me, kissing me, laughing, all at the same time. Clasping her in my arms was rather like hugging an amorous and excited electric eel. I kissed her back very willingly, and Tomlinson hovered round the two of us, smiling his half toothless smile, looking like a benevolent old image.

"Tessie, my sweetheart. Here, let me have a look at you, when you've finished eating me. Let me give my eyes a treat."

She withdrew from me, laughing, and did a little twirl, raising one hand in the air and looking at me coquettishly over her shoulder. She had on a dress of some flimsy material, high at the neck, tight-waisted, long-sleeved and crinoline-skirted, with a wide pattern of black and white stripes running all the way down. With this she was wearing white gloves, with a pattern in black on the backs of them, and a small flat black and white hat, with a black feather sticking from it. Round her neck she was wearing a long chain of large black and white beads. The whole effect was a little gaudy, but drew attention to the enticing lines of her figure, and her bright air of being delighted with herself made her look delightful.

"D'you like me, Justin?"

"Lovely, Tessie. Beautiful. I'll bet there isn't another girl in the whole town to come anywhere near you."

"Maybe you 'aven't noticed," Tomlinson said. "I'm 'ere too. The name's Tomlinson, in case you've forgotten."

"So it is, me old corporal, and if you'll look in that bag you'll find a pork pie and a little bottle of gin I brought to comfort you in your afflictions. And I wasn't neglecting you. I was only wanting to find out how Justin likes me with me clothes on."

She plonked herself down on the bed, her skirt billowing round her, and went on talking quickly.

"I had your three pounds, Justin, and thank you. Now tell me, how did you leave Wicklow? How's your uncle—the black-hearted old villain—and your old grandfather? And your friend they call Lordy—Lord Bracca. And old Smannel, and Mrs. Smannel? And how long will you be staying in London? I want to know everything."

"He's come to live in London," Tomlinson said, uncorking the gin. "He's thinkin' of takin' the room next to this one, where you used to live."

"And what the devil would be the use of that room to him, and me not in it?" she asked impudently.

"It's true enough, Tessie," I said. "I've left my old home and all my relations and friends in Wicklow. I'm on my own from now on."

"Did you quarrel with them? I wouldn't wonder at it. And are you never going back?"

"I quarreled with them. And I'm never going back."

"Let's all 'ave a drop of this beer," Tomlinson suggested. "With a drop of this gin in it. An' we can 'ave a two-course dinner—fish an' pork pie."

"It's for the two of you," Tessie said. "I'll not be wanting any. I've had me dinner."

Tomlinson dished out greasy helpings of fried fish and potatoes on the tin plates, and handed me a glass of beer liberally spiked with gin. I took a good swallow, and almost brought it up again, it was so horrible. But Tomlinson evidently liked it. He smacked his lips and grinned broadly.

"A'ah. A nice drop of wallop with a good stiffener of mother's ruin. That does me a power of good."

"Drink hearty, old gentleman, and quench your thirst, till we see the steam of it rising out of your ears," Tessie said. She turned to me. "And what are you going to do in London, Justin?"

"I'm trying to find myself some work. Any sort of work. It doesn't seem to be easy."

"Did you quarrel with all of them? You didn't quarrel with Lord Bracca, the one that gave you the fine horse."

"No, I didn't quarrel with Bracca. But I'm not going running to him for help."

"Why wouldn't you want help from Lord Bracca? Isn't he the best friend you have in the world? That was how I heard the story in the kitchens at Springhill."

"I suppose that's true enough. But I don't want any help from him."

Tomlinson, pouring himself some more beer and gin, said, "Wot's that? You got a man like Lord Bracca be'ind you, willin' to 'elp, an' you won't let 'im. Gorblimey, you must be a mug."

"All right, I'm a mug." I paused, trying to find words which would make them understand, and then went on, "All my life I've been paid for by somebody else. My food, my clothes, my schooling, even my horses were all paid for by other people. I've finished with all that. In future I mean to pay my own way."

"So you can look the whole world in the face and spit in its eye," observed Tessie, smiling. "I'm thinking it was more than just a quarrel with your uncle drove you from Ireland and turned you against your own friends. Wasn't it?"

She paused, waiting for me to answer, and I did not answer. She went on, half mockingly, "So you want to work for your own keep, and not live on other people. That's different from me, now. I want to live on other people, and not work. And what do you think of that."

"Well, that's your business. I wouldn't argue with you about it."

"Did you ever try working, Justin—the way I worked in your grandfather's kitchen in Springhill. Three shillings a week, and all I liked to eat—I'll say this, the food was plentiful. And then, at the end of it, I was put out of the house like an empty bottle, and without a character, because your uncle thought I'd been into your bed and I wouldn't go into his." She shook her head decidedly. "There's no independence to be found in work, Justin—not when you have to go cap in hand for the work. The only independence is in having money, or in knowing those who will give it to you. Or will help you to find the work you want."

"Like your Mr. Fred Symonds, with 'is bleedin' coal carts," put in Tomlinson, with his mouth full of fish. He leered at me across the table, and poured himself more beer and gin. "She's a smart girl, is young Tessie. You better listen to 'er. She 'as it all worked out, pat."

"So it seems." I smiled at Tessie. Trying to switch the subject away from myself, I asked, "What sort of a man is your coal merchant? Handsome and dignified, I hope."

"Is it me immoral life you'd be after discussing?" She grinned at me, with a mischievous flash of her blue eyes. "Now what will I say

[211]

about him. He's certainly a fine, dignified sort of a feller, with a great habit of looking at his watch, as if all the time in the world was in danger of escaping from him. But it's little joy he has in his life, the poor man. His wife doesn't understand him, his childer won't obey him, he isn't made of money as some think, meaning Tessie Flaherty, and his workmen are up to all manner of dodges—falling sick with the consumption, or breaking their limbs—just to spite the poor man. It's a hard life he has, surely."

Her speech gave me a feeling of distaste. I didn't think she ought to be the man's mistress, and take his money, and mock him behind his back.

"You sound very fond of him," I remarked.

She detected the irony in my voice, and stiffened like a cat. I saw her fists clench in her lap. She stared at me, her expression hard and challenging.

"Maybe you think I should be doing honest work for my living. Working as his servant—he told me he has three of them in the house. So I'd have to give him what he wants from me without him paying for it, or be discharged without a character, the way I was by your own uncle." She paused. "You want work, do you? There's work for a man in Fred's coalyard—the place of a man who was taken sick yesterday. I'd like to see you doing that work."

"Where is the coalyard?" I asked. "I'll apply for that work tomorrow."

"Don't you be a mug," Tomlinson said. He swallowed a long draught of gin and beer. "It's a bloody awful job, coal 'eaving. A mate of mine tried it once. Bleedin' near killed 'im."

"If other people can do the work, I can." I spoke to Tessie. "So will you give me the address of the coalyard?"

"He's right, Justin. It is killing work. You'd be a fool to take it."

"Then I'll be a fool."

"As you will. I'll say a word to Fred and make sure he gives you the work. You'll need to be me cousin, Timothy Flaherty from Wexford, come to England to make his fortune." She paused, smiling; it wasn't a very friendly smile. "When all's said, it can do you no harm to try your talent at honest work."

She rose.

"I must be away to my own work now. Himself will be coming in to see me on his way home from the Liberal Committee meeting. I'll be letting you know more tomorrow about the work in the coalyard—if you haven't changed your mind."

"I haven't any intention of changing my mind," I said.

Next morning I received a note from her telling me to report to Mr. Rees, the foreman of the coalyard, on the following Monday morning.

Chapter 21

THE WORK was murderous at first. I was working in the coalyard itself, which was in a railroad siding not far from Euston Station. Cars full of coal came into the siding and were unloaded onto huge mounds of coal dotted about the yard. This coal, in turn, was shoveled into sacks, which were stacked on long flat carts drawn by powerful horses, and taken away to be delivered to customers. My wages were twelve shillings and sixpence a week.

Mr. Rees, the foreman of the gang, was a short, immensely broad, dark-eyed, dark-skinned Welshman, with a close-cropped bullet head and wiry stubble all over his face. He took me in hand immediately.

"You are from Ireland, are you not?" he asked in his sing-song voice. "What was you doing before you came here?"

I had to say something. I said, "I was working on a farm."

"On a farm?" He sounded surprised. "Man, but your hands are soft for a farm worker. You will have trouble with those hands."

He watched me working for a few minutes and then said, "You are using your arms too much. It is not the strength of the arms that gets the coal on to the shovel, look you—it is the swing of the shoulders. Now watch me, and I will show you."

He showed me, and I tried to follow his instructions. On that first day I was tired by breakfast time. At midday, when we stopped for an hour for dinner, I couldn't eat. I needed to lie down and recover in the shelter of a wall. When the whistle blew for us to resume work I was so stiff that I could hardly move, and my hands were already covered with blisters. But I had to go on shoveling, because Rees wouldn't leave me alone.

"Come on man, swing those shoulders. Put your back into it. We've no time for idlers in this yard."

I thought he was a brutal bastard, but he was speaking the plain truth. The coal had to be shoveled, and he had to see that it was shoveled. That was his job.

At six, when knocking-off time came, I was sick and dizzy, with barely the strength to reach my lodgings and stagger up to my room.

Once in my room I collapsed on to the bed and lay still. My whole body was aching, and my hands were very painful. I felt I should never be able to move again.

Tomlinson came into the room and bent over me. He spoke in a hoarse whisper, as if in the presence of death.

"'Ow's it goin', matey? 'Ow are you?"

I stirred reluctantly, and grunted, and looked up at him. "Oh, it's you. I'm all right."

"I brought you a cuppa char. 'Ere, sit up mate, an' drink this. It'll do you good. 'Ad anything to eat today?"

I drank the hot tea greedily, because I was very thirsty. It helped a little.

"Plenty more in the pot. I'll get you some. 'An there's 'alf the pork pie left. You'd like a bit of that."

"I could do with a drop more tea. I'm not hungry."

"Must 'ave somethin' to eat. Keep your strength up."

He left the room, and was away for some minutes. When he returned he brought Tessie with him. I was sitting on the edge of the bed, ruefully examining my hands by the light of a candle. Tessie smiled at me doubtfully, as if not quite sure of her welcome, and then came quickly towards me.

"Justin . . . your hands. What have you done to them?" She sat beside me on the bed, and took one of my hands in hers. Her lips were quivering distressfully, and there were tears in her eyes.

"Ah, why did I let you do it? It's all my fault. I should never have let you take the work."

"Nonsense, Tessie. I did it entirely of my own free will. And I've earned a day's pay. Do you realize that? The first money I ever earned in my life."

"Justin, you must give it up. I never really meant for you to work in the coalyard. It isn't your sort of work at all."

"Who says so? Just because I have a few blisters on my hands. . . . They'll harden in a day or two. I'm all right. I like the work very well."

I laughed at her, not feeling much like laughing, and found myself wishing she hadn't come to see me.

"I brought you a little sup of whisky, Justin. Will you take it now?"

"An' you must eat a bit of the pork pie," Tomlinson put in. "You can't get along without eatin'—nobody can. Stands to reason, don't it?"

"I must go downstairs and wash before I do anything else. I'm as filthy as . . . well, as a coal shifter."

When I had washed, and eaten the pork pie, and we had shared the whisky, Tomlinson made an excuse and left us. I didn't really want him to go. I wasn't eager to be left alone with Tessie.

"You're tired, aren't you, Justin."

"A little."

"Then lie down and take your ease. There, put your feet up on the bed. I'll stay with you for a while."

"What about your coal merchant?"

"I'll not be seeing him tonight." She stretched herself out beside me on the bed, and stroked my cheek with the tips of her fingers. "You've turned against me, Justin. You don't like me any more."

"That's not true, Tessie."

"It is true." She wriggled closer to me, lying on my chest, looking down at me. "You liked me in Ireland, but you don't like me now. You think I'm a bad girl."

"I know damned well you're a bad girl. That doesn't mean I don't like you."

She gave a little laugh and cuddled closer, while her fingers, gently insinuating, began undoing buttons. Her lips were moist and soft; her body was pliable; and she smelled of mignonette. But afterwards, when she had tidied herself and gone, I lay limply on the bed, aching in body and rueful and sick at heart. The candle shone dimly on the table with the remains of the pork pie and the empty whisky bottle beside it; and contemplating myself and my surroundings, I could only see a shabby, sweaty fellow lying in a sordid room after making love to a coal merchant's fancy woman. Where was the fine, confident fellow who had ridden about the Wicklow Hills with Mollie Fay? Where too, I wondered, was Mollie, whom I had only begun to value truly when I had lost her. Mollie, I thought, and thinking of her I closed my eyes and made a grimace. I would have hated her to see me at that moment.

Soon I slept, and then it was morning and I rose stiffly and went to work.

Within a week or two I was used to the work. My hands hardened. The muscles of my back and thighs and shoulders became accustomed to the effort of swinging the heavy shovel. But there were things I could not get used to. One was the coal dust, which got into my hair, and into my clothes, and became ingrained under my skin. And my room had bugs in it. I fought against them with evil-smelling candles which Tomlinson bought for me, and with carbolic and whitewash. Sometimes I thought I was rid of them. For ten days or

[216]

two weeks at a time I would sleep unbitten. Then I would wake up one morning to find a patch of tell-tale blotches on an arm or a leg, and the battle with the bugs would begin all over again.

All my valuables—my father's watch, my studs, my cuff links, and even the two good suits which I had brought to England, were in pawn. This was not because I needed the money, but to insure their safety. Tomlinson insisted on it.

"You can't take 'em to work, and if anybody was to know there was a gold watch and gold links in this place, you'd lose 'em before you was a week older. Stick 'em in pop, where they'll be safe, and keep the money on you. And don't tell nobody you've got it."

At six every morning except Sunday, a "knocker-up" came into the house and banged on my door. I paid him two pence a week for this service. At half past six I went to work. At about seven in the evening, when I returned, Tomlinson usually had a galvanized bucket full of water heating for me on the kerosene stove. I discarded my working clothes, washed, shaved, and changed into a clean suit, suitable for a working man, which I had bought for £1 in Holborn. By the time I was washed and changed, Tomlinson would have a meal ready—usually fried herring, or sausage, or a slice of liver, and a pot of strong tea. On Saturdays we sometimes had a pint or two of beer at a local pub, and then went on to the Middlesex Music Hall, where in a beery, boisterous, smoke-thick atmosphere, we could hear red-nosed comedians cracking smutty jokes, and full-chested sopranos singing songs about young heroes who had died bravely on the battlefield.

On Saturday nights, till a late hour, the street was always boisterous, full of drunks shouting, singing, and sometimes fighting. But on Sunday mornings there was a deathly hush over the whole district. The street, littered with the debris of Saturday night, would be empty. At about ten, in a slowly mounting chorus of doors opening and voices calling, the street would begin to awaken from the Sunday morning "lie-in."

The days passed, and grew shorter; the weather became colder. At the yard we had to stop work at five, and more men were taken on to keep deliveries up to date, but our wages were docked by one shilling and sixpence a week because of the shorter hours. The winter evenings seemed interminably long and dreary, and my spirits sank to a very low ebb.

I had the feeling of being hopelessly trapped. The very nature of my job prevented me from looking for a better one. With the grime of the coalyard on me, nobody would think of giving me work as a clerk or salesman. But if I gave up my job I might not find another one at all.

"I think I'll stick it till the spring," I told Tomlinson. "Then I'll chuck it up, and get one of my good suits out of pawn, and try for something better. If I can't find something then, I'll go to sea, or enlist."

"You know your own business. The winter's no time to be out of work and 'ungry, I can tell you that. What I can't understand is why you don't go to one of your posh pals, and git them to find you something. It ain't reasonable to be so foolish."

"It's a heavy life, surely," Tessie said. "And let's hope there's something better in store for all of us."

She was bored and unhappy with her coal merchant. Every eight or nine days she would come in with a nip of gin for Tomlinson and some old magazines for me, and we would share our troubles.

"Ah, what a man. Always wanting to know how I've spent every minute of me time. Where was I in the morning, where was I in the afternoon; did I speak to anybody, did anybody speak to me? And him full of his own troubles, with his wife, and his childer, and the men at the yard—and then he'll want to know, do I really love him. What would you do with a man like that?"

"I know what I'd like to do with him for docking my wages. Doesn't he ever take you out anywhere, to a theater or a restaurant?"

"Take me out? He'd be feared to walk down the street with me, in case anybody should see him and tell his wife."

"I can see that he's a highly respectable gentleman."

"He is, surely." She gave a doleful little sigh, and shook her head. "I wish you were rich, Justin. Think of the two of us, you in your fine clothes, and me in my silks and diamonds, going to take our dinners in a splendacious great hotel, with waiters darting here and there to open doors and pull out our chairs, and flunkeys bowing all around us."

"Silks and diamonds—is that all you want? Are they really so important to you, Tessie?"

"It's having the money to buy them that's important. Everything is better if you have money. Even love is better. Tell me something that you want, Justin. Something that you can have without money."

"I don't think I really know what I want. I only know what I don't want."

"What you want is money, me darling. It's the one thing you need."

"Perhaps you're right, Tessie. Though it isn't always the rich who are happy. Look at your coal merchant. He doesn't seem very happy."

"And would he be happier, do you think, with an empty belly and no roof to cover him? The rich may not always be happy, Justin, but the hungry and homeless are always unhappy."

In the weeks that followed, I was unhappy enough without being either hungry or homeless. November was a month of cold rain and sleet, and working in the yard in the splashing rain, a hot sweaty body, in cold soaking clothes, was a misery that sometimes seemed hardly endurable. Oh, the relief of getting back to my lodging at the end of the day.

"God, what a bloody afternoon. I'll swear it never stopped for a moment. Is that a drop of hot tea you have there, Tommy?"

"That's wot it is, mate. Thought you might need it. You'd better git them clothes off as soon as you've 'ad it, an' 'ang them in front of the fire."

He looked pinched and very old. His cheerfulness was a painful fake. The cold got into his thin blood, making him shiver, and the continual rain kept him indoors and prevented him from selling his stationery. Day after day he earned as little as 5d or 6d; some days he earned nothing at all. A frightened expression came into his eyes, and I noticed that sometimes his hands were a little shaky.

"You haven't eaten anything today, Tommy. There's all the food still in the cupboard that I left there last night."

"I couldn't be bothered. Wasn't 'ungry."

"That's what I call a bloody lot of nonsense. If the food's there it's meant to be eaten. I've brought in some sausages tonight, and you're going to have some. Where's that frying pan?"

"It's nice of you, kid, but you shouldn't do it. I c'n manage. I don't want you to spend your money on me."

"Ah, don't talk such rot. I've seventeen quid round my middle, tucked away in my belt."

One evening in the middle of December, while he was cooking herrings for our supper, he gave a gasp, and clutched his chest, and then fainted. He remained unconscious as I took his clothes off him and got him under the blankets; his lips had a blue tinge. When I found I couldn't revive him, I ran down the stairs to the front room where Mrs. Baker lived.

"Mrs. Baker. Would you let Alfie run an errand for me? I want to send a note to Miss Flaherty. And could you tell me the address of the nearest doctor."

"Alfie, Mr. Kelly wants you to take a note for 'im." I gave the boy the note, and a penny, and Mrs. Baker went on: "I 'ad Dr. King, from round the corner, in Chepstow Street when I 'ad Alfie. Is it for Mr. Tomlinson?"

"Yes. He's unconscious. I think he ought to have a doctor at once."

"Unconscious, is 'e. That's bad. That's very bad. I do 'ope it ain't nothin' catchin'. 'Ere, you nip back upstairs an' look after the old gentleman, while I go an' find Dr. King. 'E may be 'ome, or 'e may be in the Freemason's Arms. 'E knows me, the doctor does."

Tessie arrived before the doctor, and busied herself tidying the room and putting a kettle on for tea. Tomlinson's eyes were open, and he was conscious, but only just.

"Wot 'appened. I 'ad a pain . . . Gawd, I thought I was dyin', an' then . . ."

"You lie still, old soldier. Don't try to talk. Just take it easy till the doctor comes."

"Wot, you called a sawbones? Lot of bleedin' fuss . . ." His eyes closed tiredly.

Dr. King was elderly and shabby, with a gruff, abrupt manner. His reddened nose, bloodshot eyes, and whisky breath proclaimed his story.

"H'm. I think I can see what's wrong with you, my man. But I'd better take a look at you. You two can wait outside; I'll be with you in a few minutes."

He joined us in a few minutes and said, "Is either of you related to him?"

"No. I don't think he has any relatives. We're his friends. What's wrong with him?"

"Quite a lot. But it's his heart that's responsible for his present condition. Is there anybody who can look after him?"

"Yes," Tessie said. "I can."

"He must do nothing—absolutely nothing. He'll need to be fed, washed, everything. You understand that."

"Yes."

"Very good. Then one of you will sit with him during the night. If he seems to be getting worse, you may send for me. But if he dies before you send for me, you needn't send for me till the morning. I'll give you a prescription which you can have made up at the pharmacy."

"And what food is he to have?" asked Tessie.

"Oh . . . warm bread and milk, with a little brandy in it, if you can get any. That will be quite enough for him at present."

I went out and obtained the milk and brandy and had the prescription dispensed. Tessie gave Tomlinson his medicine, and a little bread and milk while I was changing my clothes, and when I entered the room again she had a herring and a pot of tea ready for my supper.

The brandy and medicine had revived Tomlinson a little. He talked to us in a feeble voice.

"Wot did the old sawbones say. Did 'e tell you I was due for me ticket?"

"He didn't think you were at all bad. All you need is a little rest."

"A little rest? A bleedin' long rest." He gave a ghost of a laugh. "You don't 'ave to tell me," he went on. "It's me ticker, ain't it. This ain't the first time it's 'appened—not by a long chalk. It 'appened once when I was with you, Tessie. Don't you remember?"

"That was the hunger," objected Tessie. "You'll remember we'd neither of us had more than a dry crust to eat for two days." She glanced at me. "It was just before your money came."

"It wasn't the 'unger. I got used to bein' 'ungry." He closed his eyes, and sighed, and was silent for a few moments. Then he opened his eyes again. "Ah, wot's the odds?" he murmured. "There ain't no 'arm in bein' dead. It can't be no worse than standin' about on the pavement day after day, waitin' for the bit of luck that don't never come."

"We'll have none of that talk," Tessie said. "Go to sleep now. You'll be better in the morning."

"I'll be better," he agreed in a faint whisper. He smiled at us. "It's been nice 'avin' you two kids 'ere. I been 'appier since you been 'ere than I been for years. I'd like you to know I love you—both of you."

"Will you stop talking, you old image," said Tessie in a choked voice. She went to him, tears running down her cheeks, and tucked in his blankets, and bent over and kissed him. "There now, go to sleep. And there'll be one of us sitting here by you in case you'll be wanting anything."

He slept. The room was quiet. After a while Tessie said to me, "Why don't you go and lie down, Justin. I can watch by him."

"I'll stay with you."

"No, you go and lie down. There's no sense in the two of us watching, and you have a heavy day's work tomorrow. You must have some sleep."

"I won't do that. But I'll fetch my pillow and stretch out on the floor here for a while. Then I'll be with you in case I'm wanted."

I was tired after my day's work. I stretched out on the floor, and went almost immediately into a doze. Once I heard a sound of whispering, and started up on one elbow, to see Tessie bending over the bed. She turned and smiled at me, and motioned me to lie down again. Then I must have fallen into a much deeper sleep, because the next thing I remember is Tessie shaking my shoulder, and a faint light of dawn coming in through the window.

"Justin. Justin. His . . . his breathing. It . . . it's stopped."

"What!" I rose quickly and went to Tomlinson. His features were composed in an expression that was still and peaceful. He was not breathing.

"He's gone, Tessie," I said gently. "I think he went very easily. He has no more troubles now."

"God rest his soul," she said, and crossed herself. She was weeping, and I found that tears were running down my own cheeks.

She went on her knees by the bedside and began to say a prayer.

Chapter 22

TOMLINSON DIED on a Thursday morning. He was buried on the following Saturday afternoon, and I dug into £7 of my hoard of money to give him an oak coffin, black plumes, and two carriages. From his Army discharge, which I found among his few possessions, I learned that his age was forty-seven. I had always thought of him as an old man.

The people from the house rode in the two carriages, and, to my surprise, about fifteen unexpected mourners turned up on foot, most of them bringing small wreaths or bunches of flowers. There was a good deal of weeping as the solemn service was read at the graveside, but afterwards the mourners cheered themselves with beer and ham sandwiches in my room. Mrs. Marrable, the landlady, pronounced Tomlinson's epitaph.

"'E was a cheery old buffer," she said. "Never no trouble in the 'ouse, an' always a smile an' a kind word for everyone. I'm glad 'e 'ad a good send-off."

Sunday was a black day. Tessie did not come to see me, and Tomlinson's room was silent and empty. I found I was missing the old man terribly, and in the evening, in sheer desperation, I went into a pub and had a couple of strong slugs of whisky to try to revive my spirits. I had had nothing but a piece of bread and cheese to eat during the day, and the whisky had the effect of sending me to bed slightly drunk.

On Monday morning I reached a record new depth of misery. Swinging my shovel, I found myself almost envying Tomlinson. What was the point in prolonging a hopeless and dreary existence? Surely anything, even death, was better than spending my whole life throwing lumps of coal from one place to another.

I was so sunk in my gloom that I hardly noticed when, halfway through the morning, there came a sudden pause in the rhythm of the men working round me. Everything seemed to slack off for a moment. Then I heard a calm, musical voice speaking close behind me.

"May I interrupt for a moment."

I turned my head quickly, and there was Bracca. He was standing easily, one hand on his hip, looking at me, his lips smiling, his eyes gleaming with amusement. Everyone was staring at him, and he did not mind. Like a leading actor, he was accustomed to being stared at.

"Oh, hallo," I said.

"How are you, Justin? You're looking very well. And what an interesting occupation. Good for the muscles, I imagine."

The yard manager and Taffy Rees came hurrying towards us. The manager spoke to Bracca. His manner was obsequious.

"Good morning, sir. Is there something I can do for you?"

"Why, yes. I should like you to discharge one of your men. The man you see there, on the coal heap."

The manager looked mystified for a moment, and then turned on me fiercely.

"What have you been doing? What have you been up to? Come on now, out with it."

"You'd better ask Lord Bracca," I said. All my gloom had vanished abruptly. I suddenly felt extraordinarily lighthearted. A broad smile spread across my face. Bracca was smiling back at me.

"It's nothing very serious," he said to the manager. "I only want to take him to luncheon."

"In these clothes?" I asked.

"My dear Justin, all your things were sent from Ireland to Grosvenor Square the day after you left. Everything there is ready for you."

I looked at the shovel in my hand, and then I threw it down on to the coal heap. It fell with a clang. I said, "I'm sorry, Taffy, but you're a man short."

"But . . ." Rees said, and then stopped. He did not know what to say.

"Will Justin's absence mean more work for the rest of you?" Bracca asked pleasantly. "Perhaps this will adjust the situation." He took from a leather case a five-pound note which he handed to Rees. Then he turned to the manager. "Thank you very much; you've been most obliging. If you're quite ready, Justin."

Bracca's private hansom was waiting outside the yard gate. I tried to sit as far from him as possible; I was afraid to touch him. He was so very clean and I was so very dirty.

"What brought you to the coalyard?" I asked.

"You did. Didn't it occur to you, when you decided to disappear so abruptly, that somebody would start looking for you?"

"I wasn't sure. I thought it was quite likely that nobody would bother."

"You do yourself an injustice. We bothered quite a lot." He smiled. "When you left, your grandfather and I thought you were going to Grosvenor Square. We both wrote letters to you there. More than a week passed before we heard from Mr. Curling that you hadn't arrived. We made inquiries from the McLeods, and the Chandlers; they hadn't seen you. We didn't suspect that you'd been murdered or kidnaped—we thought your disappearance was an act of your own will—but we wanted to find you. There was a certain delicacy about putting the matter in the hands of the police; your uncle suggested that you might have found some means of joining your friends the Fays. We thought there might be some truth in his suspicions."

"There wasn't. The Fays have no friendly feeling for me, I can assure you."

"No? You surprise me. We didn't know that, so we put the task of finding you into the hands of some very discreet inquiry agents. They tried everywhere to find you, even as far away as America. We thought there was a possibility you might have gone there, to your uncle."

"I might have done that if I'd had the money for my passage."

"Instead you hid yourself very successfully in a coalyard—till yesterday, when a very amusing young friend of yours paid me a visit and told me where you were."

"What . . . ? Do you mean Tessie Flaherty?"

"I do. Really Justin, I must congratulate you. To have formed such an entertaining companionship while working in a coalyard—I can only attribute it to sheer genius."

"You liked Tessie."

"A clever little girl. I imagine she will go far in her profession. From what she said I gather that, unlike her, you have conceived an intense passion for honest toil."

The light tone, the slightly raised eyebrow, the smile in the blue eyes, made me feel that he considered my behavior ridiculous.

"That wasn't it at all," I protested hotly. "I didn't want to live on my grandfather any more. That was all. I wanted to manage my own affairs."

"You were angry, weren't you. With Rose Corfield, with your grandfather, your uncle, the Fays—with everybody. But was it necessary to bury yourself under a mound of coal? I think that was a little over-dramatic."

"Do you think I liked working in that coalyard? I did it because I didn't want to starve."

"But why on earth should you have starved? After all, you know, you're not quite a pauper. There's your mother's money—enough to keep you in a moderate degree of comfort. Nobody ever had the slightest intention of withholding it from you. Surely you must have realized that."

"My mother's money? What money?"

"Your mother's small private fortune; she had it from an aunt, I believe. The capital is left in trust for you till you're twenty-one—the trustees are the Dublin lawyers, Doyle and Ballinger. The income, which is at your disposal, amounts to about two hundred and forty pounds a year."

"Then . . . do you mean that I have two hundred and forty pounds a year of my own? That I've always had it, ever since I came back from India?"

"Yes. I'm surprised that you didn't know. I'm sure your grandfather thought you knew. Incidentally, there's an accumulation of several years income lying in an account in the Bank of Ireland—slightly over two thousand pounds. That is in addition to the capital sum which forms the trust."

I had the sensation of being a man in a dream, who knows he is dreaming and will wake up presently. I looked at Bracca, and saw that he was smiling; and I could hear the clip-clop of the horse's hoofs on the roadway, and on both sides of the hansom were the shop windows of Piccadilly, bright with things to buy—and in a joyous flash it entered my mind that now I was in a position to go into those shops and buy anything I wanted.

"Well . . ." I said, and I laughed. "Well, I'll be damned. And there was I working in that bloody coalyard."

"You'll be able to dine out on that story for the rest of the winter," Bracca said. "But now the first thing is to get you clean and reasonably clothed, and notify various people of your return to the fold. The McLeods, and Chandlers, and your grandfather."

The well-trained footmen and butler showed no surprise when I entered the house with Bracca in my grimy coal shifter's clothes, though I'll bet there was some talk about it below stairs. My room was ready for me, my clothes laid out, waiting. Never had carpets felt so soft underfoot, hot water so genial, or clean linen such a heavenly blessing.

When I had scrubbed and dressed myself, there were letters for me to read. The only one of importance was from my grandfather, written the day after my departure from Ireland.

[226]

My dear Justin,

During our interview yesterday morning I made a proposal for your future which you rejected as unacceptable. I have no further proposals to make regarding your choice of a career. You will doubtless decide for yourself where your inclinations lie. But there are certain observations, and some advice which I would ask you to consider.

When you first came to Springhill, after the deaths of your parents, I took steps, in conjunction with Messrs. Doyle and Ballinger, to have myself appointed your legal guardian and to assume responsibility for your upbringing and education. There are certain moneys left for you in the trusteeship of Doyle and Ballinger, and with these I have only concerned myself to the extent of trying to insure that they should come to you completely intact, both with regard to the capital, and the income which might accumulate during your schooldays. The capital, of course, could not be drawn on without some kind of court order; the accumulated income, I calculated, could be used for the purchase of your commission when the time comes for you to enter the Army. But you have decided not to enter the Army, and this money will now be available for other purposes.

My final advice to you is that you should employ this accumulated income in fitting yourself for some honorable profession.

I am arranging with the trustees for the income from your mother's estate to be paid to you in regular quarterly instalments, and for a sum of £100 to be forwarded to you for your immediate requirements. Any additional sums which you may need will be paid to you at the discretion of your trustees, and I can assure you that this discretion will not be exercised unreasonably.

I have given orders that all your personal belongings shall be packed and dispatched to you at Lord Bracca's London residence. I understand that you wish the two horses to be returned to Lord Bracca's stable. This is being done.

You will be sorry to hear that poor Dooley died this morning. His end was peaceful.

In conclusion, may I express the sincere wish that your future may be both happy and prosperous.

> Believe me,
> Your affec: grandfather,
> Horace Lurgan.

Reading the lines, I could almost see my grandfather, stiff as a poker, sitting at his desk slowly writing them. As I folded the letter, and placed it in my wallet, I thought, with an unexpected touch of melancholy, *I shall never see him again.*

Bracca had excused himself from an invitation to lunch out, and we had luncheon together. I had many questions to ask him.

"What happened after I left Ireland? The Fays weren't caught, were they?"

"No. They got away out of the country. The last I heard of them they were in your uncle's hotel in Chicago. But that was two months ago."

"In Chicago? Did the police come to Springhill after me?"

"I rather anticipated them by calling on the District Inspector to discuss the affair with him. In the course of the conversation I mentioned how grateful I was to you for saving my life, and told him I'd sent you to England to conduct some business for me. He took the hint. And your grandfather had a very plain talk with your uncle about his habit of opening his mouth too wide." Bracca smiled. "Once they'd cooled down a little, the authorities weren't very anxious to catch Fay and his daughter. A one-armed American soldier and a pretty girl of seventeen—half the country would have sympathized with them. Young Mr. Swinburne would have written a poem about them. And anyway, there was no very clear proof against them."

"What about the Corfields? Are they still at Woodlawn?"

"Rose has gone on a visit to an uncle in Malta. She'll probably marry a naval officer. That, I believe, is the object of the visit."

"I've just read the letter from my grandfather. I expect you know what's in it."

"Yes. He's concerned about your future. Genuinely concerned, I may say. He spoke about it to me."

"Now I have the money, I'd like to go to America."

"To Chicago?" Bracca asked blandly. He shook his head. "Not a good idea. I'm positive that neither your grandfather nor your trustees would consent. In their place I know I wouldn't."

"Why not?" I asked resentfully. "You once said you thought America would suit me."

"Not yet. If you go there now with your pockets full of money, either it will be taken from you by a sharper, or you'll spend it within six months. And then what will you do? Shovel coal?"

"Do you think I'm quite a fool?"

"Not quite." His eyes, bright and mocking, made me feel a fool.

"Every year thousands of people go to America. Unskilled laborers, who obtain work felling trees, plowing land, shoveling coal. You would be a fool to add yourself to their number. Go to America by all means, but learn something first—law, medicine, engineering— something that you can sell at a good price."

"M'm. Yes, I see what you mean. My tutor at Wellington College told me I ought to be an engineer. You think I should join some engineering firm and get some experience before I go to America."

"Certainly I do, if you like that idea. There are enormous possibilities for trained engineers in America. New roads to be constructed, railroad systems to be developed, docks, reservoirs, factories to be built, the half of a continent to be opened up." He paused, smiling, and then continued. "Think about it; there's no immediate hurry. And now for the rest of the day. I have to go out this afternoon, and this evening we dine with Joan Satterley; she's anxious to thank you for saving her life. Is there anything you want to do this afternoon, or would you rather relax with a book?"

"I'd like to settle up with my old landlady, and get my studs and links and my father's watch out of pawn." I hesitated. "And . . . I . . . I suppose I ought to find somewhere to live. I know you don't mind having me here . . ."

"Stay as long as you like; it won't worry me in the least. But I agree that you should have a place of your own. There's no hurry about that either. I shall be going abroad within the next two or three days. You can stay here and look about till you find something."

I went out that afternoon and settled accounts with my landlady, redeemed my jewelry from the pawnbroker, and then took a cab to Greek Street to see Tessie.

In answer to my ring the door was opened by a dark heavy woman with thickly coiled black hair, leering, sardonic features, and a slight mustache. She looked as if she was familiar with all the evil in the world, and approved of all of it.

"Is Miss Flaherty in? Can I see her?"

"She's not in, and you can't see her. She's gone." Her voice was rich and oily, and her words came to me with a strong whiff of garlic.

"Gone? Gone out, do you mean? I suppose she'll be back."

"I said gone. She went in a cab first thing this morning. You're the third feller that's been here looking for her. One's the bearded gent that used to come in the evenings. The other's the young chap that used to come in the afternoons." She grinned slyly at me. "Is your name Mr. Kelly, by any chance?"

"Yes. That's my name."

"Then there's a message. She told me that if Mr. Kelly was to call, I was to give him a kiss for her, and tell him she'd see him again some time, maybe." She opened the door more widely. "You'd better come inside if you want the kiss."

"Well . . . thanks very much, but . . ."

She gave a guffaw of coarse laughter, breathing a cloud of garlic in my face. The door closed.

I walked slowly away, uncertain whether I ought to feel angry, or sad, or to laugh. When I told Bracca what had happened, he smiled.

"Vanished, has she? In a cab. Life is like that." He shook his head gravely, and quoted:

> *"Come my Celia, let us prove*
> *While we may, the sport of love.*
> *Time will not be ours for ever . . .*

"She's probably proving the sport of love with three other men by this time," he continued. "You'll have to find yourself three other women. It shouldn't be difficult."

"I don't want any other women. I'm going to be an engineer."

"A good resolution. I wonder how long it will last."

"It'll last," I said.

He left for Paris three days later. I found myself comfortable rooms in Ebury Street, and I wrote to my grandfather and my trustees telling them that I proposed to study civil engineering for the next three years, and that when I was twenty-one I intended to go to America. Both approved of my decision, and Mr. Doyle gave me a letter of introduction to a firm of civil engineers in London, in which his own brother-in-law was a partner. The result was that I arranged to pay a premium of £300, and to enter the offices of McNulty, James, Ritchie, and Kierney, Civil Engineers, for a period of three years' training.

I spent Christmas with the Chandlers, and New Year's Eve with the McLeods. On January first I began my new life as an engineering pupil.

Chapter 23

McNULTY's was an important concern. Its headquarters occupied the whole of a large block of offices in Westminster and it had engineering projects as far afield as India, Canada, Australia, and the Argentine Republic.

At the time when I joined, the firm had some thirty young future engineers in training. Most of these were dispersed about the country on various projects known as "sites." I was one of a batch of six new trainees, who all came in at the same time. Four of them were English boys who had come straight from school. Their training period was to last for five years. The other, Joe Bowden, had come from Toronto, and was to return there when his training was finished. Like me, he had agreed to stay for three years.

"It's not long enough," Mr. McNulty grumbled to me when he interviewed me. "You'll not learn anything worth knowing in three years."

"I have to go to America to join a relative when I'm twenty-one," I lied. "I want to get as much training as I can before I go."

"H'm." He stared at me, frowning doubtfully, and I understood that he was undecided whether to take me or not. "Ah well, maybe we'll be able to give you a grounding," he said. "Though that'll depend on how hard you choose to work."

The first year was a little like being back at school. On three days every week we attended science lectures at University College. Our attention at these lectures was stimulated by the fact that we had been told that, unless we reached the College's "Intermediate" standard in science within a year, we would never become engineers.

On the other three days of the week, and during the College vacations, we went to the office. There we received instruction from Mr. Jackson, an old engineer, near his retirement, who was in charge of the firm's library and records. Under his charge we learned such practical things as surveying and leveling and making out ground plans, and every month he would bring out from the records some project already completed by the firm, and make it the subject of a series of lectures, setting us small problems as he went along, and then showing us the correct solutions. In addition to these daytime activities, there were evening classes twice a week.

"How do you think you're going to like it?" Mrs. McLeod asked me at the end of my first week with the firm.

"I like it very much so far. I think I shall go on liking it."

"You don't miss the life in Ireland. The riding and shooting, and the gay parties at Bracca Castle."

"There weren't really very many gay parties, you know. Anyway, I don't have much time to think about them. I'm too busy."

"And the Fenians," put in Ian. "Though there seems to be no need to go to Ireland to find them. That business in Clerkenwell last month . . ."

Halfway through December the Fenians had exploded a barrel of gunpowder under the walls of Clerkenwell prison, in London. Six houses near the prison had collapsed, twelve people had been killed, and more than a hundred injured. For this crime four men and one woman had been arrested. In the trial which followed, three of the men and the woman were acquitted; the other man was hanged.

Whenever anybody spoke to me of Fenians, I found myself on the defensive. I said, "That was a bad business. I've little sympathy with the Fenians myself, but then I wasn't in the famine, and I'm not a poverty-stricken tenant with an absentee landlord."

"I agree with Justin," Mrs. McLeod said in her didactic voice. "I've no sympathy whatever with murderers and assassins, but I think the government is greatly to blame. If they devoted less time and money to unnecessary wars in China and Afghanistan, and paid more attention to the conditions of people in places like Ireland, we shouldn't have these horrible outrages."

"Let's get rid of Lord Derby, and Disraeli," Ian put in. "And make Mr. Gladstone Prime Minister. Then we'd have peace abroad, prosperity at home, no more trouble in Ireland, and everybody would be happy." He glanced at me, smiling. "I hope you're a sound Liberal, Justin."

"I've never thought about it."

"But you must," insisted Mrs. McLeod seriously. "You're a man now; in a few years you'll have a vote. You must be able to exercise it with a due sense of responsibility."

"In a few years I'll be in America," I said.

"Why are you so determined to go to America?" Jeannie asked. "What's the particular attraction?"

"Oh, I dunno. I feel that it's the place for me. I know Ireland isn't."

"What's wrong with England?" Ian asked.

"Nothing, if you're English. I happen to be a bloody Mick."

They all looked very startled. Ian grinned, Jeannie gave a gasp of astonishment, Mrs. McLeod stared for a moment and then said, in a tone of the severest disapproval, "Really, Justin. Do you imagine you're still in the coalyard?"

"That's what they used to call me in the coalyard."

"Surely you're not going to be influenced by what was said to you by a lot of ignorant workmen."

"But they're right. That's precisely what I am. I belong to the same nation as the men who shot the policeman in Manchester and killed all these men and women in Clerkenwell."

"That's silly," objected Ian. "I belong to the same race as Mac-Heath, but that doesn't make me a highwayman. And you're not a Fenian." He smiled, to show it was a joke. "Or are you?"

"No. If I were I should stay in Ireland. I hate the Fenian ideas of shooting people from behind walls, and exploding kegs of gunpowder in the streets of London. But if I met a Fenian on the run, with the police after him, I'm pretty sure I'd help him to escape. That's partly my reason for going to America. I feel I don't belong anywhere—not in Ireland nor in England. I'm looking for a new country."

"You'll probably end up a millionaire," Ian suggested.

"I hope so. Jeannie will be a celebrated prima donna, and you'll be Lord Chancellor. And when we're old we'll all meet and talk over the old times."

"And how much happier we were when we were young and poor," Jeannie suggested.

"I can't see Jeannie becoming a prima donna unless she practices harder," Mrs. McLeod put in, in a good-humored tone, but meaning it.

Jeannie did not answer. With me and Ian she was frank and natural. In her mother's presence she was usually silent.

That year in London was a happy one. For the first time I was doing work which really interested me. My lodgings were comfortable, the landlady kind, the food good. There were three lodgers, all young men; the other two were Joe Bowden, my fellow student at McNulty's, and Rodney Millard, a young medical student. We each had our own bedroom and shared a common sitting room, and the three of us got along very well together. We worked hard, and argued fiercely. Sometimes we made up parties with Ian and Jeannie and a girl cousin of Millard's to go to theaters or concerts, and on weekends we often got together for picnic lunches and country walks in Windsor or Epping Forest.

My outlook was changing. At McNulty's I was meeting people who did things—men who had built railroads, and viaducts, and reservoirs—and I found their company greatly to my liking. I looked forward eagerly to the day when I should be able to do some real engineering on a "site."

This happened at the end of the year, when I was sent to a harbor construction project in Scotland. At the same time Joe Bowden was sent to a railroad extension in Wales. A new batch of pupils would be coming into McNulty's in the New Year.

There were farewells to be said.

"Come back any time you like, Mr. Kelly," my landlady told me. "Even when all the letting rooms are taken I always have a spare room for a friend."

"I'll miss you, Justin. And Joe," Jeannie said. "It's been a lovely year—the best year I ever had. Will you remember to send me some Scottish heather?"

"I will. And I'll be back in a year telling you what a fine engineer I am. By that time you'll be able to sing that top C."

"I won't. My singing doesn't get any better. Mama isn't at all pleased with me."

When all my good-bys were said, I caught the Scotch Express for Invercairn, and reported myself to tall, burly, genial, and bearded Mr. Butt, the Chief Resident Engineer on the new harbor site.

"Come to work with us, have you. Well, we'll try to see that you do."

Now I began real engineering, and my working time was filled with plans and drawings, and working section and level books, and progress reports, and water pressures and velocities, and pipes and aqueducts and embankments and foundations and stone and brick and cast iron, and all the organized activity of work in the process of erection. During the long Scotch evenings I worked hard at my books—there was little else to do—and when the days grew longer I sometimes went fishing or climbing with the other engineers.

I stayed on the harbor site for a year, returning to London just in time for the Christmas of 1866. It had been arranged that I should spend my Christmas with the McLeods.

"Justin, how lovely to have you back with us." Jeannie kissed me warmly. "How long are you going to stay?"

"Nearly a month. I have to sit for an exam early in January. Then I'm off to Lancashire to a job on a pumping station. You're all looking very well."

But they weren't all looking very well. Mrs. McLeod was full of her usual energy, Ian was his ordinary quiet friendly self, but Jeannie often had a tired look on her face and an anxious expression in her eyes. She wasn't very happy. The irritation between her and her mother was becoming acute, and she was having serious trouble with her voice.

"It gets tired, and my throat aches," she told me. "And I keep going all thin in the middle register. Then, if I get over that, my high notes start cracking. I'm almost afraid to sing in public any more."

"Perhaps your voice needs a rest," I suggested.

"That's what Mrs. Satterley and Lord Bracca think. He was at her house last week when I tried to sing there, and he brought me home afterwards. He told Mama he thought I needed a rest, but she won't listen, even to him, when it's about singing. You know how Mama is. Nobody knows more than she does about music."

"Well, I suppose she ought to know quite a lot about it."

Jeannie looked at me, and compressed her lips, and then, half crying, burst out vehemently, "Justin, she doesn't know anything about it. She . . . she doesn't even understand music. That's one thing I've found out."

"Oh, come Jeannie. Isn't that a bit hard. Considering the years she's been teaching music . . ."

"I don't care. She doesn't understand it. She doesn't even care about it. Justin, three weeks ago we went to the Hanover Square Rooms —the Philharmonic, with Joachim playing the Beethoven violin concerto. Do you know what Mama did? While Joachim was playing, she sat beside me and *hummed*."

"Nodding her head in time to the music. I've seen her do it myself. I suppose it drove you almost mad." I laughed. "But Jeannie, she was only doing it so that all the people round her should realize that she knew every note that was being played."

"I don't care why she did it. Nobody who cares about music could sit and hum while Joachim was playing. Mama only knows music like you know arithmetic." She paused, with lips quivering and tears in her eyes. "I don't know what to do. Sometimes, when she's giving me a lesson, I find myself actually hating her. It's a horrible feeling."

"Poor Jeannie. Perhaps Mrs. Satterley's right about mothers not teaching their own daughters. Look, Jeannie, if it's a question of money . . . I have quite a lot, you know, if you want to have lessons from Garcia."

"How nice of you, Justin." She put an arm on my shoulder and gave me a quick kiss on the cheek. "It isn't money. But Mama wouldn't let me go to anybody else. You know Mama."

I heard the other side of the story from Mrs. McLeod.

"I'm worried about Jeannie, Justin. She seems to have lost all her enthusiasm. I wish I knew what was wrong with her. Sometimes I have to force her to practice."

"She's been having trouble with her singing, hasn't she?"

"Singing isn't easy, Justin, if you want to sing really well. All singers have their troubles, and the way to cure them is to persevere and sing yourself out of them. That was what I was taught when I was a girl." She sighed. "I wish she wouldn't see so much of Mrs. Satterley. I'm sure that woman has a bad influence on Jeannie."

"Oh, I shouldn't think so. She's done quite a lot for Jeannie, hasn't she?"

"Yes, unfortunately. And, of course, she's related to Lord Bracca. That makes it very difficult for me to do what I would wish, and stop Jeannie from seeing her. You're both going to her house tomorrow evening, aren't you?"

"Yes, but I don't think Jeannie really wants to go. She doesn't want to be asked to sing."

"What's the good of her going out to places like that if she doesn't sing?" demanded Mrs. McLeod rather crossly. "Perhaps Jeannie imagines she's being temperamental. I think she's merely being stupid."

"I suppose one can't always feel like singing," I argued weakly.

"Nonsense, Justin. Do you always feel like engineering? A professional singer has to sing whether she feels like it or not."

Two days after Christmas I had an unexpected meeting. Coming out of a shop in Piccadilly, I almost ran into Tessie, who was entering. We both paused in the shop doorway, and looked at each other, and laughed.

"Well . . . Tessie. How are you? No need to ask that, though. Furs, silks and . . . yes, pearls. Are they real, Tessie?"

"Still the same old Justin. I knew I should meet you again. Take a look at me." She preened herself for my admiration, laughing at me with pride and self-satisfaction. "And what do you think of me now?"

"You look wonderful, Tessie. As if you'd stepped straight out of the window of an expensive shop." And, to be factual, she did.

"You're looking different yourself from what you did in the coal-yard. How's engineering?"

I was surprised that she knew about the engineering. I said, "It's going along very nicely. I like it."

"And when are you coming to see me? I have me own little house now, in Maida Vale, and a servant, and me own horse and trap."

I had no intention of going to see her, so I said, "You know what happens when I go to see you. I find you've vanished like a puff of smoke. Where did you go when you left Greek Street so suddenly?"

"To Paris." She seemed slightly surprised by my question. "But it was no good. Ah, he was old. Like a clock in a handsome case, with the springs wore out. Hardly a tick in him. And he dyes his hair, Justin. Did you know that he dyes his hair?"

"He?" I said.

She did not seem to notice my interjection. She prattled on gaily, "So after two weeks I left him and ran away with a painter. He had money too. He took me to Rome, and Florence, and Venice and Athens. I've seen some fine sights, I can tell you. My friend now is a young chap I met in Athens. He's rich, too. His father owns a whole shipping line, no less."

"You're a clever girl, Tessie. Bracca said you were. Did you have it all planned in your mind before you went to see him?"

"I had nothing planned when I went to see him except doing you a bit of good. But when we'd finished talking about you, and he said, 'I'm going to Paris in two days or three; how would you like to come?' what was I to answer. It was a chance, wasn't it? You wouldn't be blaming me for taking it."

"I wouldn't be blaming you at all." I laughed. "I'm very glad you've done well for yourself."

"But you won't come to see me," she said shrewdly. "I'll not hold it against you. And maybe it's as well. A girl in my position can't afford to get herself talked about—not too much. Tell me, do you still see Lord Bracca? Is he still your friend?"

"Yes. I haven't seen him for more than a year. He's been away, and so have I. But I expect I'll be seeing him next week when he returns from Ireland."

[237]

"No need to say anything about meeting me, d'you think?"

"I won't even mention you to him."

"It'd be as well so. No need to rake into what's past. I'm thinking I shouldn't have told you what I did."

"Bracca will never know that you told me."

"The address is 3, Aubrey Villas, Maida Vale—but I'll not be expecting you. So it's good-by now, Justin. We'll meet again some time, maybe. That was the message I left for you last time, wasn't it."

"Good-by, Tessie. Look after yourself."

She gave me the old broad, mischievous grin. "I'm doing that all right. Never you fear."

Then we parted, and I wandered idly along Piccadilly turning over in my mind what she had just told me. *So that's why she disappeared*, I thought. *She went to see Bracca, and on a casual impulse he reached out a thumb and finger and flicked her away to Paris.* I remembered his words about her. "Vanished, has she? In a cab. Life is like that."

It didn't matter. It was a trivial episode, of no importance whatever, I told myself. But why had he done it? I could imagine what he would say if I mentioned the incident to him. He would smile. He would say, "My dear fellow, any man who can't keep a girl deserves to lose her." But I hadn't really wanted to keep her. I grinned a little slyly as I thought, "But he didn't keep her very long either."

I went to luncheon at Grosvenor Square during the following week. We were only a small party—Bracca, Mrs. Satterley, Mrs. Satterley's daughter and her husband, a Captain Somers Cox of the Scots Fusilier Guards, and myself. Bracca was looking pale and tired, and walking with the aid of a stick. He had, he told us, taken a bad toss the day before leaving Ireland.

"Entirely my own fault. I deserved to break my neck and only twisted my knee. Killed the horse; they had to shoot the poor brute. Ought to have shot me as well for damned bad riding."

"Was it wise to travel so soon?" Mrs. Somers Cox asked.

"Oh, I think so. I was bored, Betty, most intolerably bored. When you're bored the only remedy is to go somewhere else. It may be as bad, but at least it'll be a little different."

"How long do you propose to be bored in London?" Mrs. Satterley asked in her lazy, slightly insolent voice. "Have you any plans?"

"None at all. I'm almost in a state of suspended animation.

Nowhere to go, nothing to do, and the clock ticking." He spread out his hands and smiled with all his old charm. "Do you notice the old man in the corner sharpening his scythe?"

"You seem to be in a morbid state of mind, Rupert," Mrs. Satterley said. "Anybody might think your days were numbered." She smiled, and added with a slight touch of malice, "I'll predict that you'll live to be a hundred, and end your days being wheeled along the Brighton sea front by a devoted nurse."

"The oldest inhabitant," put in Betty Somers Cox. "And everybody will say how wonderful you are for your age, and remember how wicked you were when you were young."

"What a horrifying prospect. Death would be vastly preferable."

"Oh, I dunno," observed Captain Somers Cox cheerfully. "I suppose a time comes when we all have to slow down—to sit back quietly in our corners and watch the youngsters taking the hurdles we used to jump ourselves. It's only natural, ain't it?" He laughed. "My old guv'ner's eighty-one, and he's as merry as a grig."

"An admirable old gentleman," agreed Bracca. "But I doubt if I'm capable of his state of cheerful resignation. I have the conviction that when a man loses his capacity for action, and a woman her charm, they might as well be dead." He smiled at me. "What do you think about it, Justin?"

The question took me by surprise, and I laughed uneasily. I had been watching Bracca, trying, without staring too obviously, to make up my mind whether his hair was really dyed.

"I don't really know. In some ways I suppose it's better to be dead than decrepit. I may not always think like that."

"Thank you, Justin. Your support encourages me. But I haven't heard your news yet. You've been in Scotland, and you're going away again very soon. Where are you bound for this time?"

"Lancashire. I shall be leaving London on the twelfth."

"And how are your friends—Mrs. McLeod and the charming daughter who sings so delightfully. I hope you'll bring her here one afternoon to sing to me—to charm away the melancholy induced in me by this confounded knee. That is, if you think she'd care to come."

"I know she'd like to. It will have to be on a Saturday or a Sunday. Those are my only free afternoons."

"Next Saturday then. A week today."

But Jeannie was not to sing for Bracca on that Saturday, nor for many Saturdays afterwards. On the Wednesday following my luncheon with Bracca, Ian went to bed complaining of a headache and pains in his stomach. He was the first of twenty cases of typhoid fever which occurred in the district during the next few weeks.

On Thursday Jeannie and Mrs. McLeod both went down with the same complaint.

All of them were critically ill, and I was alone with them. With the doctor's help I hired a nurse to come in, and some of the neighbors came in too to help with cooking and housework. On Friday morning I sent a note to Bracca explaining the situation.

Within an hour of receiving the note he was at the house, and before midday on Friday another nurse and a housekeeper had been engaged, his own doctor had visited the patients, and all my things had been removed from the house to Grosvenor Square.

"You'd only be in the way in a house full of sick people," he told me.

"I don't know how to thank you . . ."

"Then don't try. It isn't really necessary." He smiled. "It's been no bother to me, you know. All I've done is to issue a few orders. Somebody else has to do all the work."

Ian died on the ninth of January, and was buried on the twelfth. Mrs. McLeod and Jeannie were both too dangerously ill at the time to be told of his death. They knew nothing of it till three weeks later. I put off my departure for Lancashire for a day to attend his funeral, and would have asked permission to put it off further, but Bracca dissuaded me.

"What good will it do you or them if you hang about in London? There's literally nothing you can do now. Come back in a month or five weeks, and then go and see them, and they'll be able to appreciate your visit."

I was able to leave my work for three days at the end of February, and made a brief visit to London. Mrs. McLeod and Jeannie and I had a sad reunion.

"Thank you for all your letters, Justin. They were a great comfort to me," Mrs. McLeod said. "Of course we miss Ian terribly. There's no use in denying it."

"I'm sure you miss him. I know I do. He was such a fine fellow. I never met anyone I liked better."

"He was a nice boy, wasn't he. And I'm sure he'd have done well at his profession."

"I'm sure he would."

"I was so ambitious for him." Still looking very pale and ill, Mrs.

McLeod sighed deeply. "I've always been very ambitious for both my children. So anxious for them to get on."

She squared her thin shoulders with a determined air.

"Ah well, I still have Jeannie," she said.

Chapter 24

IN JUNE, 1870, when I was working on a piped water supply scheme in Somerset, I was sent for for a special interview with Mr. McNulty, at Head Office.

"Ah yes, Mr. Kelly." He looked at me across his desk, over the top of his glasses, and picked up a sheet of paper. "Now let me see, you were working on the Invercairn site with Mr. Butt, and then on the Weardale scheme with Mr. Fulton, and then on the Anderford site with Mr. Butt again, and now you're on the Denning-ton site with Mr. Playfair."

"Yes sir."

"And you contemplate leaving us at the end of the year. You're thinking of going to the United States."

"Yes sir."

"Well now, a certain position has arisen. . . . You know something about the Chelmerford scheme, I take it."

"Yes sir. A pumping station, filtering plant, and pipe line for Chelmerford. It's about half completed, isn't it, sir?"

"That is so. Mr. Nugent is the resident engineer in charge. However, we're taking Mr. Nugent and one of his assistant engineers away from his site and sending them to a new construction scheme in Canada. Mr. Butt will be taking over the Chelmerford site, and he's going to need a junior assistant—a salaried position. At present, owing to our many commitments, we seem to be rather understaffed with junior assistants with experience of water engineering." He paused, looking hard at me. "Well. D'you want the position?"

"Oh yes, sir. I certainly do."

"I imagined you would. Very well, I'll have a contract drawn up at once. A year at £3-10/- a week, with an option on our side to retain your services till the work is completed. The present date for completion is August thirty-first next year; I don't think it's likely to be delayed."

"Oh . . ." I said. "But I was thinking of going to America in the New Year."

"Will six months make any vital difference to you? You know this is a big chance we're giving you, Mr. Kelly—a very big chance. You'll be in a much stronger position landing in America with our testimonial, after working for us as a salaried employee, than you will if you arrive as an inexperienced pupil. Surely you appreciate that?"

"Yes. Yes sir, I appreciate that."

"Well then. What do you say?"

I wanted to say "No" but I knew that I should be a fool to do so. And after all, six months—what was six months. Reluctantly, I said, "Yes sir. I'd like to take the position."

"Good. The contract will be ready for you in the morning. You'd better take your annual holiday from tomorrow and report to Mr. Butt on the site on the fourth of July."

"Yes sir. Thank you, sir."

"Thank Mr. Butt; he asked for you." Mr. McNulty rose and held out his hand. "Allow me to congratulate you on your first appointment as an engineer. I think you'll be quite happy working under Mr. Butt."

"I know I shall, sir."

"Leave your London address in the office. And if you see Mr. Jackson, I expect he'll be able to dig up a set of tracings of the work you're going on. You might like to look over them during your holiday."

"Yes sir."

As was usual on my visits to London, I was staying with the McLeods, but on this occasion I had not wanted to. I would have rather gone back to my old landlady. However much one likes two people, it isn't pleasant to stay with them when they're continually quarreling.

As I entered the house and climbed the stairs towards their living room, I could hear them. Evidently a singing lesson was in progress. Mrs. McLeod's voice came to me.

"Jeannie, you're not trying. You're simply not trying. I know you can do it if you want to."

"I am trying. I've told you, I can't do it. My throat aches."

"Well, try again. Once more. Make up your mind this time that you really will do it. Now . . ."

"No, Mama. I'm not going to practice any more today. I shall only get worse and worse."

"Will you do as you're told, Jeannie. You must allow me to know . . ."

The sound of the door opening made her break off. Jeannie gave a sigh of relief, and came towards me.

"What happened at the office, Justin? What did they want you for?"

"They offered me a position. They're going to pay me for working for them. I'm on the staff now."

"Oh Justin, I am pleased." Laughing, Jeannie gave me a light kiss on the cheek. Mrs. McLeod said, "That is good news. They must think highly of you if they've offered you a position on the staff."

"Not really. The truth is, they couldn't find anybody else. Still, I think we ought to celebrate. What shall we do? Would you both like to come out to dinner, and to a theater?"

"I think Jeannie's too tired to go out this evening," Mrs. McLeod said. "She seems to be too tired to practice."

"It's my voice that's tired," Jeannie said. She looked at her mother, and added, "I think I shall give up singing, and stick to the piano. I don't believe I was ever meant to be a singer."

I saw Mrs. McLeod's thin face flush; her lips compressed for a moment. In a level, reasonable voice she said, "You know you don't mean that, Jeannie, so why say it? Your ambition has always been to be a singer." Jeannie, looking at the floor, did not answer. Mrs. McLeod glanced at me and said graciously, "Perhaps it would do us all good to go to a theater. Thank you, Justin, we'd like to come out with you."

The following morning Jeannie and I went to lunch with Lord Bracca. Betty Somers Cox and her husband were there. After luncheon the others all went to an exhibition of Flemish pictures at the Burlington Galleries, while I went to the McNulty offices to sign my contract and pick up the tracings of the Chelmerford scheme. What with talking to people, and looking quickly through the thick wad of tracings, the time was nearly six when I returned to Westbourne Grove. I had told Mrs. McLeod I might not be in for tea.

Jeannie had not returned either, and Mrs. McLeod was slightly annoyed about it.

"She should have been back at four for her lesson. She knows I keep that time for her when I could be taking a paying pupil. It's rather inconsiderate of her."

"I expect she's still with Bracca and the Somers Coxes. I shouldn't worry about her."

"I'm not worried about *her*. It's her career I'm thinking of. Jeannie can't afford to miss singing lessons."

I could see she was angry, and I didn't propose to argue with her. I took my tracings up to the top room, which once had been Ian's study, spread them out on a table, and began to look through them. I had been working for an hour when the door opened and Jeannie entered quickly, closing the door after her. She still had her outdoor clothes on, and she looked flushed and out of breath. I looked into her face, and rose, and said, "What is it, Jeannie? Is something wrong?"

"No . . . that is . . . I came straight up to you. I . . ." She paused and swallowed, and then added in a small, almost tearful voice, "I've been to see Garcia. That . . . that's only one thing I have to tell you."

"Oh." I knew this was very important; I had an uneasy feeling it might be disastrous. Manuel Garcia, son of a famous tenor, brother of the imcomparable Malibran, was the most famous teacher of singing in the world. Among his pupils had been such singers as Jenny Lind, Helen Nielson, George Santley.

"What did he say?" I asked.

"He . . . he asked me what criminal had been trying to give me singing lessons," she answered in a choking voice.

"Oh Lord!" I pulled out a chair. "Now sit down, Jeannie, and take it easy. There, that's better. Now tell me about it."

"What is there to tell? Everything's all wrong with my voice. For one thing, I'm not a natural coloratura; I'm a mezzo. All this time Mama has been trying to force my voice up, when she ought to have been training it down. That's why my throat aches, and my voice cracks, and I can't sing softly at all. My breathing's all wrong. There's something wrong with my throat; it's what they call clergyman's throat, and it comes from faulty voice production. If I ever want to sing I have to rest my voice completely for six months, and then start training all over again. Right from the beginning, with an entirely different idea of tone and muscular action. That was when he asked me what criminal had been trying to train my voice."

"But he didn't say you wouldn't be able to sing any more."

"No, he didn't say that. He advised me to rest my voice first, and then go to a good school or conservatoire for a year, and then come to see him again." She gave a hopeless little shrug of her shoulders. "I suppose I can't really blame Mama. She thought she knew what she was doing. Only unfortunately she didn't."

"Does she know yet?"

"I don't know if Rupert's told her. He's with her now. He took me to Garcia."

Her use of Bracca's christian name made me stare. She flushed and continued in a low voice, "That's something else I have to tell you. I'm going to marry him."

"What!"

"I'm going to marry Lord Bracca." She said it, and closed her lips tightly, looking at me doggedly as if to add, "And that's that."

"Jeannie. . . . Has he asked you?"

"Yes."

"Yes, I suppose he must have done. But Jeannie . . . you can't marry him. He's nearly fifty. You . . . you don't know what you're doing."

"He's given me all the warnings you're going to give me. And I know what I'm doing." She paused. "I . . . I've always liked him, ever since the day I broke the Chinese vase and he was so nice about it. And when we were all ill. He did everything for us. And he understands my singing—he knows how I feel about it. I think he understands me better than anybody else in the world. He always has."

"Don't marry him, Jeannie. Don't do it."

"Why not? Because he's older than I am? I don't mind him being older than I am. I know I can be happy with him. All I'm afraid of is that I shan't make him happy—that after a time he'll find me young and silly. He says he won't."

"Think about it, Jeannie. Don't make up your mind in a hurry."

"There's no time to think about it. We're going to be married in three or four days. And I don't need to make up my mind. It's made up. There won't be any big ceremony. We shall be married very quietly, and then we shall go away."

"To Paris?"

"Yes. What is it, Justin? Why are you looking so angry?"

"You're making a mistake, Tessie." I saw the look of astonishment come into her face, and realized that by some slip of the mind I had called her by the wrong name. "Don't do it, Jeannie," I added. "Bracca's not the right man for you."

"Why do you say that? It isn't fair, Justin. He's always been your friend." She came to me and took my arm. "Justin, don't be so unfriendly and harsh. Not with me, or with Rupert. Even if you do think we're wrong."

"I'm not unfriendly, Jeannie. But I wish I could persuade you not to do that."

"You can't. I've given my promise, and I mean to keep it. I expect Rupert is with Mama; we ought to go down. And don't look angry and disapproving, Justin. You won't, will you? You won't spoil everything, and make me unhappy?"

"I'll try not to look disapproving. And you know I hope you'll be happy."

"And I hope you will, when you go to America. There's a girl there, isn't there?"

"What! Who told you that? There isn't really." I laughed. "All right, Jeannie, let's go down and congratulate the bridegroom."

We went down. Bracca was standing by the sitting room fireplace, looking very calm, very Olympian, and slightly disdainful; he had an air of finding himself out of place in the fussy, shabby, middle-class room. One could imagine him raising his fingers to his mouth to hide a yawn. Mrs. McLeod was in a condition of twittering excitement. She gave a shrill, tittering laugh and came hurrying towards us.

"Jeannie. . . . Well, this is a shock! This is a surprise! I never imagined . . . not for a moment." She flung her arms round Jeannie and kissed her warmly. "You bad girl. So that's why you've been neglecting your singing lessons. Now I understand."

"Are you going to congratulate me, Justin?" Bracca asked. His voice was light and cool, almost mocking; his eyes were mocking. I knew that he knew exactly how I felt about the marriage and was amused by what I felt. I said, "Certainly I congratulate you," trying not to sound too stiff.

"I knew you'd be delighted." Bracca turned from me to Mrs. McLeod. "Wednesday afternoon, at two o'clock then," he went on, almost as if concluding a business interview. "And we shall leave for France immediately after the ceremony."

"But must it be Wednesday? There'll be no time to let anybody know, no time to buy any clothes," Mrs. McLeod pleaded.

"So long as Jeannie and I and the parson know, I think we shall manage," Bracca said smoothly. "And we shall find plenty of clothes in Paris." He turned smiling to Jeannie. "Would you like to see me to the door, my angel."

They left the room together and went down the stairs.

Mrs. McLeod sank into a chair looking overwhelmed and also elated.

"Imagine it, Justin. Jeannie will be Countess of Bracca. What do you think of that?"

Before I could answer, she went on, archly, "Of course, I shall have to give up my teaching. Except for one very special pupil. I shall go on giving Jeannie her singing lessons. I shall insist on that.

Even if she is going to be a Countess, she mustn't give up her singing."

I had nothing to say to that.

They were married very quietly in a church in St. George's Square, with only Mrs. McLeod, Mrs. Satterley, the Somers Coxes, and myself present. Jeannie looked happy, and composed, and very pretty; she gave her replies in a clear, steady voice.

But Bracca, to my surprise, was unmistakably nervous. His hands were unsteady, his smile painfully forced; his voice was a hoarse mumble. I had never seen him looking so old. "Rupert looks more like a man facing a firing squad than a man getting married," Mrs. Satterley whispered in my ear.

But they were married, and afterwards we drank champagne in Grosvenor Square, and then Bracca and his new Countess drove away to Victoria station to catch a train for Dover.

"And that's that," observed Somers Cox, as we turned back into the house. "Fancy old Rupert with the ball and chain round his ankle. It's the last thing I'd ever have expected. Y'know, at one time during the ceremony, I had an idea he was going to balk at the last fence."

"It's about time he settled down," said Betty.

We all separated, rather glumly. "Dine with me," Mrs. Satterley whispered in my ear as we were parting, and I nodded. I felt guilty about leaving Mrs. McLeod alone for the evening, but I also felt I could not bear an evening alone with Mrs. McLeod. She and I drove back to Westbourne Grove in one of Bracca's carriages.

"It was a very quiet wedding, wasn't it," she said in a slightly disappointed voice, as we drove away. "But I think Rupert was quite right not to have a huge affair, with a lot of drinking and jollification afterwards. He realizes that marriage is too serious an institution to be made the occasion for mere vulgar display."

"Yes. Yes, I'm sure he does."

In the evening, when I went to her house, Mrs. Satterley in a cynical voice said, "Well, Justin. And what did you think of all that?"

I shrugged. "I only hope Jeannie hasn't made a great mistake."

"Jeannie? If she's made a mistake, she'll have time to correct it later. But Rupert . . . If this gamble of his doesn't succeed . . . ?"

"Gamble?"

"Yes. He's plunging everything on Jeannie—everything he has left. It's not altogether uncommon, you know, for men of Rupert's type to marry when they approach middle age, and they usually pick somebody young and inexperienced. I might almost have guessed that something like this would happen. I did notice the way Rupert made a habit of turning up at my musical evenings whenever he knew she'd be there."

"Do you think he's in love with her?"

"I don't think he's ever genuinely loved anyone, except himself. But he likes being loved. What he must have, more than anything, is love and admiration, especially from women. And that may not be quite so easy for him as it has been. Perhaps you haven't noticed how he's been aging lately."

"I haven't seen much of him."

"He'll be an old man in five years, and he knows it. He's beginning to *feel* old. That toss he took in Ireland—even his riding isn't what it was. Considering the way he's lived, the wonder is that he's lasted as long as he has."

"It's done now," I said gloomily. "I hope it will turn out all right. Whatever one may think of Rupert, he's generous and understanding. He understands Jeannie much better than her mother does."

"Yes, he's generous and understanding. But vain, Justin, colossally vain. He always has to be the best shot, the best horseman, the best with women. He can't bear to fail at anything. And if he sees Jeannie's love change to contempt, or pity . . . and he sees things like that very clearly . . ." She broke off, shrugging her heavy shoulders. "I don't know what will happen," she said.

I was glad to get away from London and into the company of engineers. Work kept my mind occupied. But during the second week in July I had a letter from Jeannie. It was an unrevealing letter, friendly, but uncommittal.

She loved Paris. She had visited the Tuileries and various exhibitions. She had been to the opera and to a reception given by Princess Pauline Metternich, Bracca had bought her some new gowns from Worth, he wished to be remembered to me. She hoped I was happy in my new position, and she remained my loving Jeannie.

On July sixteenth, out of a clear sky, came the news that France had declared war on Germany. The English newspapers were inclined to condemn France for this drastic step.

"What do you think about it?" I asked Mr. Butt.

"Ah, these wars. There was the one between France and Austria, and between Austria and Prussia—it'll be over in a few weeks. It's not worth bothering your head about."

Early in August there came another letter from Jeannie. She wrote:

Rupert has offered his services to the French Army and because of his military experience and his perfect French has been given an appointment in the French Foreign Legion. His rank is Capitaine. Of course the French are delighted to have him, but Lord Lyon, our ambassador, is very angry. He says it will place the Government in a very awkward position if Rupert is captured by the Prussians. But Rupert was determined to go, and I could not dissuade him. Fortunately he will have to do some training before he is sent to the battle front, so his chances of seeing active service are slight. Nobody believes that the Prussians will be able to hold out against the magnificent French Army for more than a few days.

Yesterday the Emperor himself left for the battle front to take command of the army. There were huge crowds of people in the streets, all roaring *à Berlin, à Berlin.* I watched from the balcony of an apartment which we have taken in the Rue St. Maurice. I shall remain here while Rupert is away which will not, I hope, be for very long. He is joining his unit tomorrow. He wishes you were going with him.

I must finish now.

Your loving,

Jeannie.

This was written in Jeannie's neat handwriting, but beneath the signature was a hastily scribbled postscript. "P.S. Do you remember the walks and picnics we had with Joe and Rodney the first year you came to London. I often think of those days."

After that I heard nothing from Jeannie for six months, but in England the newspapers were full of stories of the French Armies reeling back from defeat after defeat and surrendering to the Germans in huge batches. Before mid-September the Emperor of the French was a prisoner, and Paris itself was besieged. There were stories, brought out of the city by balloon post, of incredible hardships, of people living on rats and dead horses, and of fierce quarreling among the defenders themselves.

At the end of January, the French Government surrendered and German troops entered Paris. Their occupation was brief. They withdrew to positions outside the city during the first week in March. Then a new horror fell on Paris. Communists seized the city and held it for two months, looting, burning, and shooting down priests and officers. Under the eyes of the disdainful Germans, Paris had to endure another siege before regular French forces could drive the Communists out and restore some kind of order.

Halfway through April I received a letter from Mrs. McLeod telling me that the Foreign Office had informed her that Bracca had been killed, and Jeannie was on her way to England. She could give me no details of what had happened. Three days later I received a letter from Jeannie from a hotel in London.

> Burton's Hotel,
> Albemarle Street,
> London.
> April 22, 1871.

Dearest Justin,

You will not be surprised to hear from me, because Mama has told me she has already written to you.

I arrived here yesterday with a French lady—a Madame Curel, whom I met during the siege in an Ambulance Post in Paris. After her husband was killed she came to stay with me in our apartment, and she was very kind during Rupert's last illness.

I am longing to see you and talk to you. I wish you could come to see me. Do you think you could? It is not so very far from Chelmerford to London, is it? If you can't come to see me, I will go to see you.

If you can come, and will tell me when, I will keep my time free for you. There are so many people bothering me about all kinds of things, and I wish they'd leave me alone. But I want to see you, Justin.

> Please write soon.
> Your loving,
> Jeannie.

Mr. Butt readily gave me permission to take a weekend leave of absence, and at eight-thirty on Friday evening I called at Burton's Hotel.

"Lady Bracca." It seemed odd to be referring to Jeannie as Lady Bracca. "My name is Kelly."

"Yes sir. Her ladyship is expecting you. Will you come this way, please."

I was shown up to a private sitting room on the second floor. Jeannie was alone, sitting by a coal fire, with one dim gaslight burning. When I entered she rose, and came to me quickly, and gave me her usual light kiss on the cheek. Her hands, I could not help noticing, were very thin.

"Here you are Justin, at last. It was nice of you to come all this way."

"Of course I came. Let me look at you, Jeannie."

"No, don't look at me. Leave that till tomorrow. I'm like a scarecrow. That's why I've left the light low—so that you shouldn't see me."

"I can see you," I said. "And you're not in the least like a scarecrow."

She looked very thin and fragile, and much older, but her face still had its pretty lines, and her eyes their candid, friendly expression.

"An old woman, then," she said. "I feel dreadfully old, Justin. A feeble old woman of twenty. But I'm getting better. Very much better."

"It must have been dreadful, Jeannie. Worse than Lucknow, I suppose?"

"Not as bad in some ways. In others it was worse. The people were so awful. So mean and spiteful to each other. Some of them seemed to hate each other worse than they hated the Germans. Some of the women—I often wondered if the story about women sitting knitting under the guillotine was true. Now I know it was."

"I'm terribly sorry about Rupert."

"Yes," she said slowly. "Poor Rupert. They shot him."

"Don't talk about it if you'd rather not."

"But I do want to talk, Justin. I must talk, and you're the only person I can talk to. Do you mind if I talk?"

"No, Jeannie. Tell me about it."

"It was bad. The siege, I mean. So long and dark. And cold. And there wasn't much food. It was all rationed. We used to eat all kinds of things—horse, and elephant."

"Elephant?"

"Yes. They killed all the animals in the zoo. And there was the firing. All our windows were broken. But that wasn't as bad as Lucknow, except for the last few days before the surrender. But we managed. I told you, Madame Curel came to live with me. I met her at the Ambulance Post. She used to be an opera singer; that's really what brought us together. She's nice, Justin. I think you'll like her. You'll meet her tomorrow."

"Was Rupert there?"

"No. He was with the garrison at Mont Valerien. I hardly saw him till after the surrender."

She paused, staring into the fire. Then she went on, "He came in one day just after the Germans had left. He was terribly tired. I gave him a little soup—it was all we had—and he lay down on the bed and slept for twelve hours.

"The rioting had started already; a lot of the National Guard were joining the Communists. There'd been fighting in the streets. But the English and Americans were sending some food supplies into Paris, and when Rupert woke up he went out to try to get some. He was in uniform. Two or three hundred yards down the street he met some of the National Guard who'd joined the Communists. They were drunk. One of them shot Rupert through the chest. Madame Curel had seen it happen from the window. We ran out and dragged him back to the apartment and got him into bed. I knew a doctor in an American ambulance unit, and I went and fetched him. He did what he could for Rupert.

"The next morning some more Communists came to the apartment. They looted it. Rupert was conscious, and he got out of bed and tried to stop them. One of them knocked him down with a rifle butt. They were going to kill him, but Madame Curel told them he was an Englishman who'd fought for France. That made them change their minds. But they took everything we had, even the few bits of food."

She told me all this dry-eyed, in a quiet level voice. And I felt like weeping. But she had reached a stage beyond tears.

"We got him back into bed," she continued. "And Madame Curel fetched Doctor Haven. There wasn't much he could do. Rupert never recovered consciousness again." She closed her eyes momentarily, as if terribly tired, and added in a tone of astonishment, "It was only a week ago."

"Oh, Jeannie." I could find nothing to say.

"Dr. Haven and a Mr. Colter from the Embassy helped us to leave Paris. The Prussians let us pass through their lines. Mr. Colter found a cart to carry Rupert's body. He's buried at Versailles."

"What are you going to do now, Jeannie? Have you any plans?"

"Yes. Yes, I have plans. I shall go on with my singing. What else can I do?"

"I don't know, Jeannie. Have a good rest before you do anything else. Then you might travel. A voyage would do you good."

"Travel? You mean just go from one place to another. No, I won't do that. But I shall leave London . . . as soon as I can. I

[253]

shall go to Milan. Madame Curel studied there. And . . . and Rupert told me to do that."

"Rupert?"

"Yes. He told me to go on with my singing. He . . . he knew he was going to die." She paused again, a long pause, and added, "Poor Rupert. He was so brave at the end."

"He always had plenty of courage."

"Yes. I need some." She smiled faintly. "Have you ever felt that the only thing you can do is to go somewhere you've never been before, and start everything again, from the beginning. That you've got to try to make a new person of yourself. Though I suppose you can become a different person without trying. I don't think I'm the same Jeannie McLeod I was a year ago."

"I expect you are, underneath. Will you take Madame Curel with you to Milan?"

"Yes. She's looking forward to meeting old friends there—people she knew twenty or thirty years ago. I expect we shall take a small apartment together."

"Have you any idea when you're going?"

"When they'll let me—the lawyers and people. They're all at me all the time about Rupert's will. He left everything to me, but a lot of the property's entailed and has to go to his cousin. I've told them they can have everything they want, but they say that's not business. I don't want very much; I hardly feel I was married to Rupert at all." She flushed suddenly, and added, "I mean we were married such a short time. We only had a week or two before he joined the French Army. I don't really deserve to inherit a lot of money from him."

"If he hadn't meant you to have it, he wouldn't have left it to you."

"Perhaps he wouldn't. That's what Mama says." She sighed. "I don't know. I don't know anything, Justin. I'm in a muddle. All I can think of, is to sing myself out of it, as Mama used to say. That's really why I want to go right away. To find out just who and what I am. Do you understand what I mean?"

"Yes. That's why I want to go to America. To be myself in a country where I belong. Though I like it quite well where I'm working now."

"There's a girl in America, isn't there, Justin. Somebody you met in Ireland."

"I don't know, Jeannie. I did meet a girl in Ireland, but it was years ago. She may be married now. Or she may have changed so much that I wouldn't recognize her."

"I expect you would. There are some people whose lives seem to be crossed—once they've met they're bound to go on meeting." She smiled. "I think you and I are like that. You're going to America, and I'm going to Italy, but I'm sure we'll meet again. It may not be for ten or twenty years, but we shall meet somewhere. Do you think that's silly?"

"I hope it's not. You're my oldest friend, Jeannie. Perhaps the only friend I have now."

"Yes. Since Rupert died," she agreed softly. "He was your best friend for a long time, wasn't he. And mine. We both thought there was nobody like him."

"We may have been right. I find it very difficult to realize I'll never see him again. It's as if a part of my own life was finished."

She nodded.

"I feel that. He was . . . dazzling while he was there. It was difficult to see anything else. Now we're both going on our different ways without him. In the end, I wonder whether we'll be any the better, or any the worse, for knowing him."

She sailed for Italy during the following week, and I didn't see her again till six years later, when I called on her in a dressing room in the Metropolitan Opera House. My own work with Mc-Nulty's finished in August, and I sailed for America in the middle of September.

Chapter 25

DRIVING AWAY from the railroad depot, my feelings were a mingling of high excitement and intense nervousness. The place was exciting. It had an atmosphere of great bustle, of things happening. The people on the sidewalks looked keener and brisker than the people of Chelmerford or London. Even the air was different. It was hot, and dry, and had a smoky tang. The gaudiest sunset I had ever seen was lying in a welter of red across the western sky. On either side of me enormous new buildings rubbed shoulders with small dilapidated houses, and even wooden shacks. A huge and particularly imposing new block took my attention, and I touched the colored cabby's arm.

"What's that place?"

"Dat's de Gran' Pacific Hotel, sah. De finest hotel in de world. More'n two thousand rooms."

Mackinaw House, when we reached it, was no Grand Pacific. It stood at the intersection of Lake and La Salle Streets, an unpretentious, three-story building with a small, semi-circular front porch. A colored porter took my cases into the hotel. I asked the cab driver what his charge was.

"What yo' please, sah," he told me, grinning widely. He recognized me for a mug. I gave him a dollar, which showed that I was one. I wasn't yet accustomed to American currency.

Entering the hotel, I found myself in a square hall where a few people, mostly men, were standing idly, talking. On my right was the door of a dining room, and beyond it was a sign pointing along a passage, on which was written: "Gentlemen's Smoking Room and Bottom Bar." On my left was a lounge or drawing room in which I could see people sitting, talking or reading. At the back of the hall was a wide staircase with a large potted palm at the bottom, and then a door, and next to the door a small reception counter with a girl sitting behind it. I went to the reception counter.

"My name is Kelly—Justin Kelly. I wrote from England and confirmed it with a wire from Boston. You have a reservation for me."

"Yes, Mr. Kelly, number 14." The girl behind the counter looked me up and down with some curiosity. "If you wouldn't mind waiting a moment, I think Mrs. Kelly would like to see you."

She vanished into an office at the back of the counter. I waited, my nervousness increasing. The door beside the reception counter opened, and a woman came into the hall.

She was tall and full-busted, a large, heavy-limbed woman, towering upwards like a cathedral. Her dress was a magnificent affair of shot purple, with a deep lace collar and decorated with coral ornaments. Her fair hair, obviously dyed, was piled high on her head in an elaborate coiffure; it seemed slightly out of keeping with her fine, sparkling dark brown eyes. Her cheeks were obviously touched with rouge.

But her manner was hesitating. She looked formidable, but I saw with surprise, that she was even more nervous than I was.

"Are you . . . pardon me . . . are you Mr. Justin Kelly? From Ireland. The son of Michael Kelly."

"I am. Are you my Aunt Zoe?"

I smiled as I spoke, and her answering smile was immediate.

"That's right. We-el." She drawled the last word, and looked me up and down, and her eyes crinkled with good humor, and she gave a loud laugh—it was a laugh, as Bracca had once told me, to set the glasses jingling. "And here you are," she went on. "Large as life, or even larger. Come right in, into our own parlor."

She led me through the doorway and along a passage to a room at the back of the office.

"Sit down now, and make yourself at home. I'll just leave you a minute while I fetch your Uncle James."

I sat down in a deep leather chair. On the walls were signed pictures of actors and actresses, jockeys, and prize-fighters. From the nearby smoking room came a hum of conversation and the clink of bottles and glasses. There was a smell of cigar smoke on the air.

"This is the kind of room I like," I said.

"You like it." She sounded pleased. "We like it too. But I must find your uncle. He'd have been at the depot to meet you if we'd known what time you were coming. Just you wait a minute; I'll be right back."

My uncle was exactly as I had imagined him from Bracca's description—tall, portly, red-faced, bald-headed, wearing a Prince Albert coat, with gold watchchain and a large seal hanging across his chest, and a red flower in his buttonhole. He entered hurriedly, walking with one leg slightly stiff.

"Well, be japers. Me own nephew—me brother Michael's son. How are you, me boy. Did you have a good trip over? Would you like a drink—but of course you'd like a drink. Can you drink Old Kentucky?" He was shaking hands vigorously with me all the time he was talking.

"I never tasted Old Kentucky, but I'm willing to try it."

"Now tell us about yourself," he went on, when we were sitting down, and the drinks were poured out. "What brings you here, and how long are you staying? We'll have to show you Chicago. The greatest city on earth."

"It looks like it to me from one of the hotels I passed on the way. The Grand Pacific."

"That's only one of them. There's the Palmer House, and the Tremont House, and the Bigelow—though that one's not open yet. And you'll need to see Freed and Leiter's Store on State Street—the greatest store in the country. And the Opera House; they just spent eighty thousand on the Opera House, getting it ready for the winter season. I tell you, Justin, this is the place. The first time I came to this town, twenty-five years ago, there were thirty thousand people here. Today the population is three hundred and thirty-four thousand—and growing all the time. But never mind all that; you'll see it for yourself. How long did you say you were staying?"

"I'm not quite sure. I have to find some work, and the firm I worked for in England has given me a letter of introduction to a company in St. Louis."

"St. Louis. That one-horse shanty town. Why, Chicago has it beaten all the way. You'll not want to go to St. Louis." He paused, looking suddenly surprised, and then added, "But . . . did you say you want work? Does that mean you'll be staying in the country? You're not in the English Army?"

"No, I'm not in any army. For the last four years I've been working at engineering."

"Engineering, is it. But what made you change your mind about going into the Army?"

"We don't know anything about you, Justin," my aunt said. "Except a little we heard about you from an old friend."

"Would that be Captain Fay?" I asked, trying to sound as if I didn't really care. "How is he?"

"He's dead, the poor man. He died—it must be eight or nine months ago. You'll remember Mollie, his daughter."

"Yes. I suppose she'll be married by now."

"Married? Now who would have told you that. Mollie's not

married. She works here with us, in the hotel, and helps with the hall. We have a hall in Franklin Street where they hold concerts and meetings and such like. That's where she is now. She'll be coming in presently."

"The Orpheus Hall, is it? Captain Fay told me about it."

"Ah, you know about the hall. If . . ." He broke off, turning his head as one of the small glass panels in the wall went "click" and slid to one side. A voice from the office said through the opening, "Mr. Spearman has come in, Mr. Kelly. You said you wanted to be told if he came in."

"So I did, so I did. I have a piece of news for him. Will you tell him I'll be with him in the half of a minute." He turned to me. "You'd like to go to your room. There'll be supper soon, when Mollie comes in." He smiled. "In the Tremont or the Palmer House, they'll give you evening dinner. In this hotel we serve supper from six till eight. It tastes the same."

My first-floor room was comfortable and cheerful, with mahogany furniture, paper with a rose pattern on it, and a large window, shaded by a blue curtain, which looked out, past an iron fire escape, into a small cobbled yard with stables in it. Hot water was waiting for me. I washed and unpacked a few clothes, and then judged that it was time to go downstairs.

A few paces outside my room was a central landing from which one flight of stairs led downwards and another upwards. That was where I met Mollie. As I reached the landing I saw her coming slowly down from the upper floor, her eyes looking downwards at the stairs in front of her, one hand sliding along the banisters. Deep in thought, she came on down, and I stood quite still, watching her. When she reached the landing, she took her hand from the banisters, and looked up, and saw me.

She stopped—it was more of a hesitation than an actual halt—and then flushed and came toward me. Her glance was on me intently, and I stared back at her eagerly and closely, trying to discover any way in which she might have changed. And she had changed. She was taller, her figure more rounded and womanly; she had an added air of dignity. Yet she was still the same long-limbed, dark-eyed, dark-haired girl I had known, and with our glances meeting I was reminded vividly of that last moment in Ireland when we had looked long and closely at each other, I on my horse, and she on the ground. To me it seemed we had stepped straight from that moment into this, and all the years between meant nothing at all.

"Mollie," I said.

She said politely, "Mr. Kelly, I believe," and her voice was cold, as if she were administering a rebuke to an impertinent stranger. But I was not crushed, because I knew with a feeling of elation and absolute certainty that she was experiencing exactly the same sensation I was—the sensation that we were resuming, almost without interruption, at the precise point where we had left off in the Wicklow Hills. I could recall precisely her warmth against the crook of my arm, and the scent of her hair in my nostrils.

"But you've given up your pigtails," I said.

She made a little motion with her lower lip as if dismissing the remark with contempt. It was another impertinence. In her too formal voice she said, "Did you have a good trip over?"

Copying her voice, I said, "Excellent, thank you. The *Scotia's* a comfortable ship."

"So I've been told." Her voice was firm enough but her gestures were undecided. She made a little movement, as if to walk away from me toward the stairs, and then checked it. There was something she wanted to say, but she didn't know how to say it.

"When did you leave Ireland?" she asked.

"Four years ago. You may remember we had a bit of a ride over the Wicklow Hills. I left Ireland in a hurry the same day."

She hadn't expected that answer, and she was disconcerted. She looked away from me, her features downcast. Then she said slowly, "You left the same day? Why did you have to do that?"

"I felt I needed a change of scene. The air of Ireland didn't seem to be agreeing with me very well."

She was silent for a moment. Still not looking at me, she asked, "What happened to your grandfather's man, Dooley?"

"He died. And nobody found out."

"Found out?" She glanced quickly at me and away again. She was very pale and her eyes looked big.

"That he was a Fenian agent. I guessed it four years ago. It was because of his illness that you had to guide the men through the hills."

"Yes, I had to. There was no one else. I had to do it," she murmured, almost to herself, and then she looked at me directly and asked, "What happened afterwards? Tell me the truth of it. How many were hanged?"

"Hanged! Nobody was hanged. What makes you think anybody was hanged?"

"But . . . didn't the police and soldiers go round the villages arresting men and women and afterwards hanging them without trial? The story I heard was that more than thirty were hanged."

"It's not true." I laughed. "Heavens, you can't go round villages arresting men and women and hanging them without trial, even in Ireland."

"So it wasn't true. My father didn't believe it. He thought it was a story put out for political purposes." She gave a deep sigh, and I knew that a great weight of grief had been lifted from her mind. I smiled at her and said, "You needn't worry, Mollie. You weren't the cause of anybody's death."

"I'm glad of that." She turned from me, as if closing the interview, and began to descend the stairs. I kept pace with her. I said, "Mollie."

"Yes."

"Do you remember the rides we used to have across the hills?"

"I remember them." Her voice was cold. After a moment she asked, "What brings you here, to Chicago?"

"To see my aunt and uncle. And you."

"Save that kind of talk for your Rose Corfields," she said.

We had reached the foot of the stairs. My aunt was waiting in the hall. She looked at us with a certain twinkling interest.

"So you already met," she said. "Of course, you're old acquaintances, aren't you."

Mollie said nothing. And there was nothing I could find to say either.

"Well, I think we'll go right in to supper," my aunt went on cheerfully. "Mr. Spearman's joining us." She glanced towards the girl behind the reception counter. "Tell Mr. Kelly, will you, Bella?" She turned back to me. "If I let you into that smoking room with James it'll be introductions all round, and five or six drinks and another twenty minutes before we can eat. Mollie and I want our food."

My uncle came along the passage from the smoking room accompanied by a tall, thin man in baggy tweed clothes. He had small friendly eyes which peered amusedly from behind steel-rimmed glasses.

"Ned, I want you to meet my nephew Justin. My brother Michael's son. Justin, this is Ned Spearman, of the *Examiner*, a very good friend of mine."

"Glad to know you, Mr. Kelly." We shook hands and then moved in a group into the almost empty dining room, where waiters were clearing tables.

"Supper's nearly over," explained my uncle. "That's one of the penalties of being the manager—you usually eat last."

"Well now, Mr. Kelly," Spearman asked me when we had sat down. "Your uncle tells me you make mighty fine engines—the best engines in England. What kind of engines would those be, and where d'you sell them?"

I laughed.

"I don't make engines. I'm a civil engineer; my job is constructing harbors, reservoirs, pipe lines, dams, pumping stations—in a very junior capacity."

"Pumping stations, is it?" exclaimed my uncle. "We have the finest pumping station in the world right here in Chicago. It pumps—what's the figure, Ned? You're the boy who knows all the statistics."

Spearman smiled.

"The average water consumption for Chicago is around 22,000,000 gallons a day, I believe. Just now, with the long drought, it may be even more. You'll have noticed how dry the air is, Mr. Kelly."

"Yes, I have noticed it. And there seems to be a slight tang of smoke in it."

"That comes from the prairie fires, burning miles away. We've had a record dry spell this summer—no rain at all for the best part of fifteen weeks. But what about yourself, Mr. Kelly. What can you tell me about yourself that I can put in my paper?"

"I don't think there's anything very much about me to interest newspaper readers. I'd like to hear something about Chicago."

"Well, it's the finest city in the world," Spearman said. "You'll have heard that already."

"Yes."

"And it's the most progressive city. It has the finest buildings, the most beautiful women, the most millionaires, the most enlightened citizens, the greatest number of churches—and incidentally the worst haunts of vice—of any city of its size in the Republic."

"That's the kind of city I've been looking for."

"You think I'm boasting," Spearman went on. "And you're dead right. Every citizen of Chicago boasts about his city. The surprising thing you're going to find is that most of the boasts are true. We're brash, vulgar, boastful—and going full steam ahead. We have the world by the tail, and we know it. Isn't that so, James?"

"That's right. Any time I walk a little way out of this building I can see seven- and eight-story hotels and office blocks where ten years ago—five years ago—there were only frame shacks. This is the land of opportunity, Justin me boy. You'll see."

I saw. For six days, sometimes with my aunt and uncle, but often alone, I wandered around, one of a vast crowd of people—Irish, Polish, German, Swedish, and native American—who had been drawn, as if by some enormous suction, into the huge ferment that was Chicago.

The city was uproarious. It was strident. It was like a great shout, challenging the heavens.

"Look!" it shouted proudly.

Every morning, from wooden shacks and tenements, the workmen poured out in their thousands to work on the great new office blocks, warehouses, stores, and hotels which had changed the whole face of Chicago inside a decade. In the residential districts the new millionaires were building themselves mansions with art galleries, and organs and cellars full of imported wines. Along the waterfront were the docks, crowded with shipping, and the great grain elevators, towering up to over a hundred feet, and capable of emptying a six-thousand ton grain barge inside an hour. The lumber yards held 300 million feet of lumber; the Leiter Store, employing hundreds of salesmen and girls, was built of white marble; the Union Stockyards, covering 345 acres, held over 120,000 pigs and cattle; the Sherman House Hotel had a mile of halls. Some of these things I was told, and some I saw for myself.

For almost a week I went around taking in the sights, and in the evenings I joined my uncle and his friends in the crowded smoking room of the hotel. On Friday evening Ned Spearman came in. He gave me a friendly nod and asked the usual question: "What do you think of Chicago?"

I laughed. "I haven't had the time yet to stop and think. I'm still trying to get my breath."

"Then you don't hate the town. You're not thinking of going back to Europe."

"Why would he want to go back?" my uncle asked. "He plans to find work here."

Spearman nodded again and said to me, "I don't suppose you ever heard of Colonel Houston?"

"I've heard of him. I was in the docks yesterday where they're building the big extension and the long breakwater. One of the engineers showed me over. I asked about the prospects of getting work there, and he said he thought they might be pretty good. He advised me to see Colonel Houston."

"That's right. He's in charge of the big extension scheme. And he has another project at Calumet, outside the city, where they're enlarging the harbor. I met him this morning and mentioned your name to him. He's looking for trained engineers, and he seems to know quite a lot about your old firm, McNulty's. If you'll go to his office between nine and ten on Monday morning, he'll see you."

"Monday at nine. You bet I'll be there. And thanks very much . . ."

"It's nothing," he interrupted. "But take my advice and make the most of your freedom this Saturday and Sunday. If Houston hires you, he'll put you to work right away."

"That'll suit me."

At midnight every night the bars were closed, the day's takings were locked in the parlor safe, and the front door of the hotel was shut for the night. On that Friday night of October 6, 1871, my uncle and I were the last two downstairs. When the money had been locked away, he took the bottle of Old Kentucky from the parlor cupboard.

"We'll have a small nightcap and drink to the success of the work you'll be starting."

"If I get a job."

"You'll get one." He poured the drinks and handed me a glass. A little shyly he added, "And what then? No doubt you'll be making plans. Will you be wanting a place of your own, or would you think of staying on with us here?"

I was embarrassed. I said, "I . . . I like being here. If you . . ."

"We want you to stay," my uncle interposed eagerly. "That is . . . Zoe and I . . . we like having you. And Mollie . . ." He paused, and then added brusquely, "What's wrong between the two of you? You like her, Justin. Zoe's sure you like her. And she's a good judge."

"I like her. She doesn't like me."

"That's a pity. A great pity. Why wouldn't she like you, I wonder?"

"I don't know. Unless it's because of something that happened in Ireland. You'll have heard about that from Captain Fay."

"I did hear something about it. There was an ambush that failed. Larry Fay told me about that."

"Then he told you quite a lot about me."

"He did. But he'd nothing against you. I can tell you that. Nothing at all. Far from it. He'd a good opinion of you."

"Has Mollie ever said anything about me?"

"Never a word. And that's a queer thing." My uncle looked at me slyly. "Because you were friends in Ireland, or so I've been told."

"Yes, we were. But we're not now. Every time I go into a room and she's alone there, she goes out with her nose in the air."

"With her nose in the air. Well, now . . ." My uncle shook his head solemnly, as if contemplating something sad and mysterious. "That's bad. That's a very bad thing, Justin. No girl who had any regard for a feller would leave him with her nose in the air."

My uncle emptied his glass, and smacked his lips, and leaned forward and refilled my glass and his.

"You know," he went on confidentially. "It's a queer thing about women. I remember—it was years before I met Zoe—I was on a tour with *The Colleen Bawn* company. And in the company there was a young woman by the name of Mabel Lestrange—that was what she called herself—who'd do the same thing to me. Any time she'd be passing me she'd be like an iceberg, with the tip of her nose pointing to the sky. So one day, when she was passing, I gave her a little pinch on the bottom. Only a little pinch, mind you. And she turned and gave me a great slap across the face."

My uncle paused, and a slow smile spread across his florid face.

"And after that," he went on blandly. "Why, after that everything was smooth and pleasant as silk between us till the end of the tour."

"I don't know what kind of a girl Mabel Lestrange was. But if you think . . ."

"No, no, Justin me boy. I think nothing," my uncle interrupted hastily. He waved a large hand as if disclaiming thought altogether. "And if Mollie doesn't like you—well, it's a small thing, after all. You'll soon find yourself a girl, and Mollie has plenty of admirers. Just leave her to go her own way, and she'll leave you to go yours, I've no doubt."

He put down the glass and rose, slightly unsteadily, from his chair.

"Time we were going to bed. It's getting late."

Next morning after breakfast I helped my uncle to check the stocks of drink in the bottom bar and smoking room. When that was done, he and my aunt went out marketing, and I entered the parlor. Mollie was sitting at my uncle's desk working on the hotel accounts. She glanced up as I entered and then bent back over her work.

"Mollie."

"Yes." She did not look up.

"Put that pen down and talk to me."

"I've no time to talk. I'm busy."

"Then stop being busy for a few minutes." I went to her and took the pen from between her fingers. She made no resistance. She merely sat back in her chair and let her hands fall in her lap. Her features were resolutely composed. I was an unwelcome interruption, and she was trying to bear me with patience.

"Can I have my pen back, please."

"In a minute. If you'll tell me why you won't talk to me."

"I don't think we have anything to talk about."

"I think we have. Let's talk about a couple named Mollie and Justin. One lived at Hazel Lodge and the other at Springhill. Do you remember?"

"I do. The girl was very young and very foolish. The boy . . ."

"Yes?"

She flushed. Standing looking down at her I could see the dark, shining curls of her hair and a little pulse beating in her neck above the collar of her white blouse. She wasn't as calm as she was pretending to be. I could have stretched out my hand and touched her, and I wanted to. But I didn't.

"What about the boy?"

"There's nothing to say. I told you in Ireland it would be better if you stayed with your friends and I with mine. I still think that way."

"Is it because of what happened that last night? Do you blame me for that?"

"I blame you for nothing," she said obstinately. "What happened in Ireland was a long time ago. It's best forgotten."

"But you do blame me for something," I protested. "And what happened in Ireland isn't forgotten. We were friends then; you must admit that. Those days when we used to ride over the hills together."

"And you think you have only to come walking into this place and raise a finger, and I'll come running to you? Is that it?" She stared at me, her dark eyes full of anger, and added, "You've a fine conceit of yourself, haven't you."

"No, I don't think that. But . . ." I paused, searching for words. "Look, Mollie, ever since our last ride together I've been hoping for the day when I'd see you again. And that's the truth. I wanted to come to America four years ago, but I wasn't able."

"You expect me to believe that?" She stared for a moment, scornful, and then added abruptly, "What happened to Rose Corfield?"

"I heard she'd gone to Malta. I don't know where she is now. I don't care."

"You should have gone to Malta. You came to the wrong place."

"I don't care a hang about Rose Corfield. I never did, really. I always liked you much better, though I only realized it that last night, when we parted. I've been realizing it ever since."

"You never cared for her?" Her voice was cold and mocking. "Then perhaps I should tell you I saw you that afternoon in the wood, when you fought with her brother." She shook her head decidedly. "I was a silly girl then, Justin—only a silly child with pigtails. I'm not a silly girl now."

"Are you certain of that, Mollie? Are you sure you're not being silly in a different way?"

"Sure enough to tell you one thing. This is your uncle's house and you've a right to be here. But if you stay here, I shall go." She held out her hand. "And now may I have my pen?"

"Mollie . . ."

"I'll not listen to you. I don't want to hear any more." She took a deep breath and her hands were clenched. "Can't you see that all I want is for you to leave me alone? Can't you understand that?"

"All right then," I said in a sudden temper. "I'll leave you alone." I handed the pen to her, and turned and left the room.

The day passed. That night, two actors who were staying in the hotel brought in a party of friends from the Dearborn Street Theater, and a great time was had by them and my aunt and uncle exchanging stories of past triumphs and failures, and reminiscences of dear old Jimmy this and dear old Billy that. At midnight, when the smoking room closed, my aunt and uncle accompanied a rather merry group to the front door. Mollie and I waited in the hall, not looking at each other.

We heard my uncle shout, "Justin! Mollie! Come here a minute. For God's sake, come and look at this."

There was a sharp urgency in his voice. Mollie and I hastened to the front door to join him and his friends. They were all staring towards the south, where a great patch of sky was vividly lit by an intense red glow.

"Did you ever see anything like that sky?" one of the men asked in an awed voice. "That must be one hell of a blaze." He coughed and added, "Begging your pardon, Mrs. Kelly."

"Don't mind me," my aunt said.

"It certainly looks as if something's burning," another man said dryly. "About a mile, or a mile and a half away, would you say. Somewhere on the other side of the river."

"That's about it. Jackson, or Clinton Street," another man agreed. "It could be the lumber yards."

"By God, I'm not going to miss this," my uncle said. "I love a good fire. Who's coming along with me?"

"I'm not," my aunt said firmly. "Nor Mollie. We're going to bed. If you're going out, James, give me the keys so that I can lock up the takings."

"I'll lock up the takings," Mollie said. "You go on up to bed."

"Are you coming, Justin?" my uncle asked. He was detaching a bunch of keys from a chain. He gave the keys to Mollie.

"I'm coming," I said.

We moved away in a group. When we reached Market Street, which ran its full length toward the river, we could see, leaping upward from the west bank of the river, an enormous furnace of red and yellow flames, with a great dark smoke pall over the top. The smoky smell in the atmosphere was very strong.

Market Street was crowded with a jostling, excited mob of people hurrying toward the fire. There were a good many drunks among them. More people were pouring in from side streets to join them. The whole street was full of people.

From somewhere behind me there came a wild sudden clamor of clanging and bawling, and I found myself being carried sideways by a great eddy of people. The crowd split like the Red Sea as a steam fire engine came cleaving a path through the middle of it. For a few seconds I found myself jammed immovably, a close prisoner in a dense press of people. Next to me a man was cursing agonizedly. In the confusion somebody had trodden hard on his foot.

The pressure lessened as the crowd surged back into the middle of the roadway. I had lost sight of my uncle, but near me I recognized an actor named Felton, who had been one of our party.

"What's happened to the others?" he asked me.

"I don't know. They can't be far away."

"Not much use looking for them in this," he said.

I let the crowd carry me along. Soon I found myself one of a packed throng at the eastern end of one of the bridges. It was not possible to go any farther; the police had cordoned off the road.

From where I stood I could see the broad red reflection of the river, with the tall masts of shipping sticking up blackly against a lurid backcloth of towering flames. Along half a mile of the waterfront on the opposite bank of the river, houses, sheds, lumber yards, coal dumps were all wrapped in a fierce incandescent glow from which a constant shower of sparks shot high into the sky, like fireworks. The sight was fascinating, and horrible, and awe-inspiring.

Hot air drifted to us across the river. The people watching round me on the bridge were mostly silent, except for coughing. My eyes began to smart, and I got a little smut or cinder in one of them, which was painful. A man next to me muttered, "It's like the end of the world," and a hollow voice near him said, "It's God's punishment on this city for the worship of the Golden Calf."

Refugees, carrying their belongings, were coming across the

bridge from the burning area and the police thrust the crowd back to make way for them. The heat grew fiercer, and breathing became painful; my throat began to feel as if it had been sandpapered. Round me the crowd was moving, the front ranks retreating, getting farther away from the fire. A man fainted, and ambulance men dragged him away.

After an hour or so I had had enough, and I began to worm my way slowly through the crowd, making for Market Street. I was a little worried by the thought that I had no door key with me, and somebody would have to be waiting up for me.

It must have taken me three-quarters of an hour to get back to the hotel, and during that time my eye was steadily becoming more painful. When I reached the hotel, I couldn't even keep it open. Mollie answered my ring at the front doorbell.

"Sorry I'm late. Is Uncle James home yet?" My voice was hoarse with smoke.

"Not yet." She stood aside to let me enter, and closed the door after me. A single gas jet was burning in the hall. I raised a hand to my face and rubbed my smarting eye.

"I could do with a drink," I said.

"I'll unlock the parlor cupboard."

We went into the parlor. Tears were running from my right eye, and I was dabbing at my face with a handkerchief. Mollie unlocked the parlor cupboard and took out a bottle, and then turned to look at me.

"What's the matter with your eye?"

"Nothing very much. I've got something in it. A small cinder, I expect."

"Don't rub it. You must bathe it at once. I'll bring some warm water."

She left the room. I poured myself a swig of bourbon, and drank it, and it made me feel better, so I poured another. Mollie came back with a basin of warm water and a piece of clean linen.

"Come here under the light, and let me look." Her voice was cold, her manner businesslike and practical. She was frowning a little.

I stood under the light and stooped slightly, while she gently prised apart the eyelids of my right eye. We were very close. I could see her bosom rising and falling, and the white hollow of her throat. She said, in a cold, steady voice, "There's a little black speck . . . stand quite still," and then a corner of the linen touched the inside of my eyelid, and she said in a faint voice, "I think it's out now."

I put my arms round her and drew her close to me. She gave a gasp, and began struggling violently. I felt her arms pushing at me with all her strength, and her body straining and twisting against mine. Neither of us spoke. I had a curious illusion that we were back in Wicklow, struggling for the revolver, and another feeling that if I let her go this time I should never recapture her. She would escape me for ever.

She was strong. Once she almost struggled clear from me, and we staggered against the table, slopping water from the basin, but I recaptured her, and drew her close again. There came a long, tense moment when I felt her calling desperately on every bit of strength she had. Then her resistance collapsed quite suddenly, and she came forward against my chest with no more struggle at all, her body limp and her head drooping on my shoulder. I raised her face gently and kissed her lips and she gave a little shuddering moan, but her lips were parted and her body was submissive. When I kissed her again she murmured "no" in a soft, sighing voice.

"Mollie, my darling," I whispered back.

There was a shrill jangling peal on a bell that startled me like a bucket of cold water thrown over me. My arms fell away from Mollie; we drew quickly apart. She stepped backwards, away from me, raising a hand as if to ward me off, and then turned and went quickly out of the parlor. I went after her a little way calling, "Mollie," but she took no notice. I heard her footsteps as she ran quickly up the stairs. The bell jangled again.

"Oh, damn," I said.

I went to the front door and opened it. My uncle and the two actors were there waiting to come in.

"Ah, you're back already," my uncle said. "Glory be, what a blaze. The damage will run into a million—easily a million, I'd say. Has Mollie gone to bed?"

"Yes. She's gone upstairs."

"I left my front door key with her, fool that I am. But you'll know that."

"Yes. Is the fire out?"

"Dying down a little—just a little. They're beginning to get the upper hand of it."

"I'm told every fireman and every engine in the town has been called out," one of the actors said. "And I don't wonder." He coughed, and put a hand to his throat, and added, "By God, what I need is a drink. I'm as hoarse as an old bull frog."

"That's a thing we can all do with," my uncle said. "A drink to take the dryness from our throats, and then our beds. Look at the time, beGod. 'Tis nearly four in the morning, and we've a heavy day in front of us."

We all went to bed, and I slept badly. In the morning I came down feeling stale and jaded, and found that my aunt and uncle and Mollie had already breakfasted. But halfway through the morning, when my uncle was busy in the bottom bar and my aunt in the kitchen, Mollie came to me in the parlor. She looked very tired. Her face was pale, and there were dark rings round her eyes.

"I've something to say to you. It's only this. If you're not out of this place by Wednesday, I will be."

"Mollie . . ."

"That's all I have to say." She turned abruptly, to go, but I reached out a hand and caught her arm.

"Leave me go." She spoke sharply. "There are people about now. It's not like last night. I can call for help."

"You're running away from me, are you?" She flushed, her dark eyes angry, and I added, "I'll make an agreement with you, if you dare."

"What do you mean by that? What kind of an agreement would I want to make with you?"

"Stay here for another month, and I'll stay a month. At the end of that time, if you haven't promised to marry me, I'll go away and never bother you again."

I saw the flush come quickly to her cheek; she snatched her arm away from me violently.

"I'll make no agreement with you at all. Do you think I could ever trust you?" Those were her parting words as she turned and went away from me.

All that day the talk in the smoking room was about the great fire.

"It started in Lull and Holmes planing mill, on Canal, and burned right across to Van Buren one way and as far as Adams Street the other. There's half a dozen lumber yards, three or four coalyards, the Express Company's freight depot and the best part of a hundred houses gone—maybe more. They reckon it's the worst blaze since '57."

"This licks the blaze of '57. Every steamer in Chicago was there. Those boys of the fire department had a rough time. I guess they'll be taking it easy today."

During the afternoon I walked to the scene of the fire. It was a scene of complete desolation. About twenty acres of buildings on the west bank of the river had been reduced to a wilderness of rubble and ashes, which were being blown about by a violent wind from the southwest. Hoses were still playing on a burning coal dump, which glowed alternately brightly and dully as the gusts of wind increased and decreased in power. A glow of heat still came from the burned area.

We were all tired that evening. At eleven my aunt sent Mollie to bed, first of all giving her two small tablets "to make you sleep, my dear. Swallow them down with a little warm milk, and in the morning you'll be as fresh as a daisy again."

The bars closed very promptly that night, and almost immediately afterwards the rest of us went to bed. By twenty minutes past twelve the hotel was in darkness except for the gas jets burning in the corridors.

My dreams were uneasy. In a half sleeping, half waking state, I seemed to hear distant clangings and shoutings which reminded me of the previous night's fire. Grumbling, I turned over, and thrust my head into the pillow, but the sounds went on, and became even louder. Eventually the sounds were not to be denied, and I sat up in bed, listening. I was just about to get out of bed when my uncle came hurriedly into the room.

"Ah, you're awake. There's another fire. Would you believe it, there's another fire. Last night, and now again tonight."

"Perhaps it's the same fire started up again. Is it in the same place?"

"It is not," my uncle said grimly. "Tonight it's on this side of the river. What I'm afraid of is the Orpheus Hall. I shall have to go down there."

"Just wait a minute, and I'll come with you."

I pulled some clothes on hastily. As we left my room the door of the next room opened and the actor, Felton, looked out at us.

"Hey, have you looked out of the window?" he asked. "Don't you ever have anything except fires in this town?"

"I've seen it. I'm on my way to the Hall," my uncle answered.

We hurried down the stairs and out into the street. There we stopped for a moment, literally gasping. Everything round us was lit by a bright, reddish glow. To the south of us, scarcely half a mile away, was a vast tossing sea of red flames reaching from the Lake as far as the river. A solid mile of fire, with the force of a full southwesterly gale behind it, was eating deep into the heart of Chicago. The noise the fire made was a continuous booming roar, and mingled with it we could hear the deep tones of the great Courthouse bell, tolling the alarm.

The street was full of frantic and distracted people, some trying to make their way toward the fire, and others, many of them half clad, struggling to get away from it. And I remember the rats, the thousands of rats that dodged and squirmed under our feet.

Shoving and edging through the crowds, my uncle and I managed to thrust our way south as far as Monroe Street. There we were obliged to stop, because the whole flow of the crowd was against us. Nobody was trying to get closer to the fire now; everybody was trying to get away from it.

The street was a wild chaos, with men, women, children, horses, donkeys, dogs all mixed together in a seething, roaring jumble. Many of the people running from the fire were trying to drag their possessions with them—tables, chairs, bedding, and trunks full of things hastily snatched together. A woman thrust her way past me clad only in her nightclothes. She had a fur coat over one arm, a couple of blankets over the other. An old man passed, dragging a trunk, and behind him was a child carrying a kerosene lamp in his right hand, and a picture under his left arm. Across the street a gang of toughs had broken into a liquor store, and was throwing bottles out.

There came a thunderous explosion as a gasworks blew up to the north of us; a great gush of flame spouted up into the sky. A rain of flaming debris was falling over a wide area. Great pieces of burning timber were being sucked into the blaze, whirled aloft by the tremendous updraught of hot air, and spewed out as if from a volcano to fall on hitherto unburned areas.

"Ah, my God," said my uncle in a shaky voice. "We'd better be getting back."

We turned and joined the main stream of people flowing northward. On our right, two or three blocks away, a wisp of smoke arose, and then a flame, and then, with dramatic suddenness a whole building burst into flames, and then the building next to it, and the one next to that. Over to our left another bright flame sprang up. The most appalling thing about the fires which were now breaking out everywhere was the suddenness of their onslaught. With everything bone dry after the long drought, and temperatures raised almost to ignition point by the fierce heat thrown ahead of the fire, a spark only had to touch a building to turn it, in a few minutes, into a flaming furnace. And it was not only the wooden shacks and frame buildings which were burning. Already the City Hall had gone, its great bell giving one last resounding boom as the roof collapsed; the Chamber of Commerce had gone, the Armory, the gasworks, and a mile ahead of the main blaze a huge balk of burning timber had fallen through the roof of the waterworks, setting them ablaze, and the great engines, which pumped 22,000,000 gallons of water to Chicago daily, ran down and stopped. In this critical moment, Chicago had no water.

In the great luxury hotels many of the visitors, sleeping in the comfort of their rooms, with window curtains drawn, knew nothing of the fire till it was almost at their front doors. Then there was panic and wild shrieking, as men and women, half clad, poured out into the streets to join the great fleeing multitude. The fire was irresistible. It took in its stride the great hotels, the Tremont House, the Palmer House, the Sherman, the Bigelow, the Grand Pacific, and thirty other principal hotels; it took all the huge blocks of office buildings, the pride of the business section; it took the Opera House, the theaters, the huge stores, packed with merchandise, the tall grain elevators fringing the dockside, the breweries, the railroad depots, the homes of the millionaires, the churches. In its fury it destroyed 17,500 buildings, a third of the whole city; it killed 250 men, women, and children, and injured many others; it made 100,000 people homeless. And as an aftereffect, it put fifty-seven insurance companies into bankruptcy.

But that is getting too far ahead.

When my uncle and I re-entered the Mackinaw House, we found most of the guests assembled in the hall. They looked sleepy, bewildered, and uncertain of what to do. As we came in, everyone turned to look at us, and my aunt came toward my uncle with an air of relief.

"Ah, here you are, James, and thank the Lord for that. Now you can tell us what's happening. Is the Orpheus Hall all right?"

"Happening!" my uncle gasped wheezily. He stood for a moment panting, sweat pouring down his face, leaning with one hand on the back of a chair, and the other hand pressed to his ribs. In a deep, heavy voice he went on, "You ask what is happening, with the whole town toppling into ruin about us like the flaming towers of Troy. We must get out of this place. We must get out of it at once, the whole lot of us. At once, do you hear me?"

It seemed, for a moment, that nobody believed him. The circle of faces stared at him blankly.

"Get out?" my aunt echoed in a dazed voice. "Do you mean that, James? We've got to . . . get out. But where shall we go?"

I had been glancing quickly round the hall looking for Mollie. She wasn't there, and I remembered that my aunt had given her a sleeping draught the previous evening. I ran to my aunt.

"Where's Mollie? Which room?"

"Number 29, on the top floor. But Justin . . ."

She broke off abruptly and we all jumped back as, with a great crash and clatter, a large burning log came through the roof and slap down the well of the stairs. A shower of plaster and brickwork followed it. I ran for the stairs and went up them three at a time, and the actor, Felton, came after me. He reached the first landing just behind me and shouted, "I'll see if there's anybody on this floor." I went on up the second flight of stairs.

The top floor was in darkness. I flung open the first door I came to, and shouted "Fire," and banged on the bed with my hand, but nobody was in it, and the same with the second and third doors in the corridor. There was a man still in the fourth room I came to, but he was already out of bed and alarmed, and I didn't waste any time with him. The fifth room was empty, and the sixth door I came to was Mollie's.

The room was in darkness, but I could just distinguish a sign of movement in the bed, and I stretched out a hand and grasped Mollie's shoulder; she was in the act of sitting up. She gave a startled cry, and shrank back, trying to brush my hand away. I grabbed the bedclothes, and pulled them from her, and shouted, "Mollie. Get up at once. The house is on fire."

"What?" she said. She was hardly awake.

"The house is on fire," I yelled. "Come on. Get up." I grabbed her by the wrist and started to pull her off the bed. "Quickly," I urged.

"How dare you. Let me go . . ."

I let her go, and stepped to the window, and pulled back the heavy curtain. Through the window a glare of red light came into the room. By it I could see Mollie sitting on the edge of the bed, her arms crossed protectively over her chest, her figure shrinking back, her eyes blinking in the sudden light.

"We've got to get out," I said. "Quickly."

She stood up, her nightdress hanging about her. Her eyes were wide open now, and looking at me with incredulity. She said, "Justin . . ." and then, as if understanding had dawned suddenly on her, she added, "Wait outside. I'll be as quick as I can."

"Hurry, for God's sake."

I stepped outside the room and waited, dancing with impatience. Thick smoke was pouring up the well of the stairs and seeping along the passage, and I saw a little flame dart up and waver delicately. I thrust the door of her room open and shouted, "Are you ready? Come along," and she answered, "Yes, I'm ready." She had on a skirt and blouse and coat, but her long hair was hanging in pigtails down her back.

"The stairs are hopeless. We'll have to use the fire escape. Is there one here?" I ran to the window, and there wasn't.

"We can get to it through number 27, the room next to this," she said.

Flames, roaring up the well of the stairs, were already spreading along the passage; the air was thick and hot. I took her hand and drew her after me into room number 27, and we went to the window. There was a small iron platform outside the window. By climbing over the sill one could step on to it.

"Out you go." I turned momentarily back into the room and snatched a blanket from the bed, and tucked it under my arm. Holding onto my hand, she climbed out of the window, and I followed her.

As we climbed down the narrow, spindly fire escape, we could feel the building vibrating with the energy of the fire rampaging round the rooms inside. The escape ended in the small yard where the stables were; a doorway led from the stable yard to the street. Through the open doorway I could see people passing in an unending procession.

"Where are your aunt and uncle?" Mollie asked.

"I think they're safe. We're the last out of the hotel."

"What are we going to do?"

"We can't stay here. Put this blanket over your head, and keep hold of my hand. We mustn't get separated."

She draped the blanket over her head like a shawl. Hand in hand we emerged from the stable yard and joined the crowd drifting by. And hand in hand we went on and on, two items in a great crowd heading north. Sometimes we passed along streets which the flames had not yet visited; at other times we passed along wide streets with buildings blazing on either side of us. We saw horrible things. At one point the whole crowd halted to watch four people on top of a high burning building. There were shouts for ladders, but before ladders could be brought the whole building collapsed. We saw two men jump from the top of another building. And still we went on, stumbling along with the stumbling, shuffling weary crowd. And still the fire burned, spreading deeper and deeper into the North Division of the city.

At about eleven in the morning we saw an open space in front of us. It was the old cemetery, at the south end of Lincoln Park. There, with relief, we sank to the ground, and all round us were other people, men still dragging along their remnants of belongings, women with children in their arms or clutching their skirts, staggering blindly forward till they could find some small clear space where they could sit down and rest themselves.

Before evening there were more than thirty thousand of us in the park and cemetery, black-faced, red-eyed, tired, hungry, and above all, thirsty. The cries of the children were pitiful, but nothing could be done to relieve their distress. The men lay about, talking in low voices, or sitting silent and gloomy, as the mood took them; the women were mostly too exhausted even to cry. And through the long hours the fire encircled us like a besieging army.

When nightfall came, clasped in each other's arms, Mollie and I slept in the shelter of a gravestone. Some hours later we woke in darkness, soaked through by rain which had started falling soon after midnight. Round us dim shapes of people were moving restlessly; we could hear the constant, subdued murmur of voices. And looking toward the city, we could see that the flames had shrunk and were going back from us. The fury had left the fire. It was dying down.

Mollie shivered in my arms.

"Ugh! I'm cold. I suppose that's better than being too hot. What do you think?"

"It makes a change. At least we're alive. There's a lot to be said in favor of that. And we're together. That's another very good thing."

"Is it?" She stirred in my arms. "I suppose you think you've won that bet you tried to make with me in the hotel."

"I hope I have. You'll marry me, Mollie. Say you'll marry me."

"I'll marry you. Though you nearly broke my heart back there in Ireland. You know that, don't you?"

"Mollie . . ."

"You don't have to say anything. You thought of me as a child, and my father warned me about being too serious about you. But I was in love with you all the same."

She clasped me to her fervently, and added, "Promise you'll never do anything like that to me again. Promise, Justin."

"That's a promise I can easily make. I'll never want anybody but you. You're my girl."

"Yes, I'm your girl. I know that well enough." She raised her wet face, and we kissed again; and we were cold and shivering, but we were happy.

In the morning the fire had died down enough for us to be able to leave the cemetery, and the relief trains, loaded with food and clothing and medical supplies, were rolling into Chicago from all over the country. During that day a hundred thousand people were fed and clothed, and temporary shelter found for them.

We had a meal at a soup kitchen and then went in search of my aunt and uncle. Most of the West Division, where the Spearmans lived, had escaped the fire, and Mollie suggested that that was where we should be most likely to find them. That was where we did find them. They had been in the Spearmans' house since five the previous afternoon.

Then there was a scene of laughter and tears, with Mollie and my aunt clinging to each other, and my uncle slapping me on the back, and Ned Spearman bringing out the drinks.

"I knew you were safe. I was sure of it. I said so, didn't I, James," my aunt declared, her tears belying her words.

"You did," agreed my uncle. "And you were absolutely correct. Which is, after all, the only thing that really matters."

The following night there was a three-cornered conversation between me and my uncle and Ned Spearman, after my aunt and Mollie had gone to bed.

"It's staggering," Spearman said. "The biggest fire in history." He made a wry grimace. "Trust Chicago to set up a new record, even when it has a fire."

"What happens now?" I asked.

"The city will be rebuilt," he answered confidently. He smiled at me. "You'd better go to see Colonel Houston. There'll be plenty of work for engineers."

"I shall go tomorrow. What about you, Uncle James. Have you any plans?"

My uncle shrugged and spread out his hands.

"The hall's gone and the hotel's gone. I only rented the hall, but I had a quarter share in the hotel. I guess I'll find something. I'm no worse off than thousands of others."

"How about rebuilding the hotel? There'll be the insurance."

"We were insured for $15,000—and the insurance company's bust. We'll be lucky if we collect $2,000, and that may take months. All I own now is a quarter of the site the hotel stood on."

"Could you buy the other three quarters?"

"What good would that do me, even if I had the money?"

"We might rebuild. I was thinking of a building of six floors, with a restaurant and bar on the ground floor, and self-contained apartments on the floors above. That would be ten apartments—one for Aunt Zoe and you, one for Mollie and me, and the rest—well, I guess there's going to be a big demand for apartments in Chicago for some years to come."

"It'd be a good idea all right, if we could put down about $25,000."

"I can put down $25,000. It's in England now, but there'll be no difficulty in getting it transferred to this country. The important thing is to get started quickly."

My uncle stared at me incredulously. Spearman stared too, and then laughed and said, "Well, well. You'd better look out, James, or you're liable to wake up one morning and find yourself with a millionaire in the family. I can see the first tender shoots beginning to sprout."

In the burned areas, the last flames flickered and died out. Before the ashes were cold, the citizens of Chicago, toiling like giants, were already starting to rebuild the city. I was one of the citizens.

India and Ireland, all the scenes of my boyhood, were now behind me. I was a man, twenty-one years old, beginning a new life in a new country. I was my own master. I had good health, I had a girl I loved, and I had a job which was worth doing.

What more, I asked myself, could life possibly have to offer?